Fragments of Gray

Fragments of Gray

GOLDEN BAY BEACH
Book Two

HOLLY CASTE

Fragments of Gray
Paperback Edition

Love N. Books Press
An Imprint of Wolfpack Publishing
1707 E. Diana Street
Tampa, FL 33610

www.lovenbookspress.com

Edited by My Brother's Editor

Fragments of Gray was originally self-published in 2023 by Holly Caste.

Paperback ISBN 979-8-89567-709-4
Ebook ISBN 979-8-89567-708-7
LCCN

For those who grew up too soon yet still believe in a happily ever after

Foreword

Dear Reader,

Hey! Thank you so much for picking up my book! Before you dive in, please check out the trigger warnings:

Explicit language, detailed sex scenes, grief/loss, physical violence, suicidal ideation, addiction/overdose, leaving toxic purity culture. Talk of grooming/sexual assault of a minor, gun violence.

Although Fragments of Gray is part of an interconnected series, the books need to be read in order. Anything Rae Touches must be read first. If you haven't read it yet, you can click here.

As with my other books, this story isn't for everyone. The characters are flawed and the journey is raw, but I promise there's a happily ever after!

Fragments of Gray

CHAPTER ONE

WINTER

I have every intention of dying alone,
with nothing and no one attached to my name.
Jaded, stunted, and calloused—I now see life for what it is.
The pain of the world consumed me.
Crushed me.
Until I became nothing but fragments of a person.

CHEWING ON MY PEN CAP, the taste of plastic coating my mouth, I reread the latest poetry that popped into my head.

It's stupid, writing my pain onto these pages for someone to read once I'm dead and buried, but at least it keeps me occupied while I wait for my time to come. I don't care when or how it happens, as long as it's after my parents are gone so they don't have to grieve for another child.

I've been floating in this bizarre limbo space since I was ten years old, with no drive or ambition to chase after a faraway dream. I've just been watching the time pass slowly, my vision fogged over from the trauma.

The world keeps spinning while pieces of me are stuck between memories of tragedy and disaster.

My soul has been at a standstill.

I scribble the words down in my brown, leather-bound notebook while I stretch out my legs in my car.

Writing has always been my outlet, even before I sank into my rabbit hole of isolation and suffering.

I write to remember.

I write to forget.

Prose, flashbacks, the scraps of my creativity come in. It's all laid out in my notebooks.

For years, I kept my thoughts and feelings locked up tight. There was a time when I wouldn't speak. The only words I let out were on paper. "Too much trauma too young," the shrink told my parents.

My mind flips back to a time I'd much rather erase from my memory—the day my sister, Cara, was murdered. But it's always at the forefront, reminding me why I hate the world so much. Why I hate society. Why I hate being forced into surviving, fighting, and carrying on.

Glancing at the time on my phone, I let out an aggravated sigh, knowing that I have several minutes to kill before my next task.

Getting antsy, I decide to turn to another page and write down a glimpse of the past that's been living in my head, hoping that by letting it out, it'll stop eating me alive.

I'm ten years old, sitting down at the kitchen table working on my latest superhero story while Mom makes herself coffee. With my pen to paper, I just started writing the part of the story where the superhero fights the evil villain when Mom interrupts, wanting me to find out what Cara and Rae—my other sister and Cara's twin, want for breakfast.

After huffing and puffing, annoyed to do this simple task, I eventually peeled myself away from my notebook and bang on their bedroom door, asking what they wanted to eat.

Cara wants yogurt and strawberries.

Rae wants nothing.

After relaying the message to Mom, I sit back down to write. Getting sucked into my story, I don't realize Cara and Rae are in the kitchen until Cara starts peeking over my shoulder. I never hide what I'm writing from her. She's always supportive and loves my work—or pretends to at least. I'm in fifth grade, and she and Rae are in ninth, so I doubt my stories are even borderline good. Still, Cara acts like they're phenomenal.

"Never stop writing, Grayson." That was the last thing Cara said to me, aside from a quick goodbye before she and Rae left for school.

I glanced over at Rae when Cara said that to see if she'd say anything similar. Rae's too busy fidgeting with her choker necklace.

With an immediate pinch in my heart, I stop writing, not ready to go down that road. Thought I was. Guess not. Giving up on any efforts to write more tonight, I toss the pen and notebook on the passenger seat.

My leg bounces up and down, pissed I even began unboxing those memories. If I could black out the last decade of my life, I would.

No one knows that during these long, tiring years of misery, there's been a storm brewing inside of me. A dark, ominous typhoon that's been growing deep within my soul.

I had no idea where to let my anger out until recently.

Picking up my phone, I shoot off a text.

Me:
here

Shutting my headlights off, I lean back against my car seat. There's one dim streetlight at the corner of The Mighty Glass Bar's parking lot. I made sure to park far away from it, just like I have every night this past week.

No one has walked outside yet, but in a few minutes, someone will. The fucking idiot hasn't caught on that I've been watching him from the other side of the lot for the past seven nights. That right there tells me he's a shitty drug dealer.

The image of both of my sisters suddenly pops into my head.

My relationship with Cara was one out of those picture-perfect family books. Everything was always at ease.

Our brother-sister bond was one that I had hoped to have with Rae as well. As a little kid, I thought Rae was cool as fuck, and even though we were always distant, I looked up to her.

Until I stopped.

The day Cara died was also the day any hope of me and Rae having anything resembling a significant sibling bond vanished.

Cara's death was the turning point for both me and Rae. She spiraled into drugs while I recoiled into myself, shutting down.

Ten years since Cara's been gone.

Ten years of agony. My world was completely shaken up, flipped upside down, and slammed onto the ground.

Nothing, and no one, ever felt safe again.

I once lived in an imaginary universe where heroes would swoop in and deliver justice, restoring everything back to its original state. Naively, I believed that villains would never cross my path—they were something made up or lived nowhere in sight, never to touch my life.

But now I know the truth.

My attention goes back to my phone, waiting for it to light up.

My breathing is calm, my heart strumming along as if I'm sitting on my couch reading a book. I might even say that I'm *bored*. I should probably feel some twinge of apprehension, fear even. But I don't, and I won't.

Terror lived deep within my bloodstream for many years. But then I got older.

And now it's turned into rage.

910-555-7498
ok

Turning my car off, I step outside, the brisk winter air stinging my face. With an extra jolt of cockiness in my step, I stroll through the dark parking lot, past banged-up cars, until I approach the dumpster behind the bar.

The shithead dealer sniffles as he rounds the building, checking his phone.

My heart rate picks up only a notch.

I've been studying this dealer for a week, watching him stumble out of the bar when someone pulls up to this lot in the middle of the night, noticing how he bullshits and laughs with the addicts. Once he gets his money, he ambles back inside until a little while later when he's back for another deal.

I paid attention to where he might keep a gun hidden on him, and I haven't noticed anything. A knife maybe, but he talks with both of his hands.

I'll be fine.

The moment he lifts his head and sees me, a fire fueled by wrath runs up and down my spine. Anger powering enough to snap every bone in his body pumps through my veins.

But I keep it all inside.

Tamed. Controlled. Restrained—until the time comes.

"Hey," I mumble, nodding my chin upward.

"What's up, man?" He slurs his words.

"How much?"

He opens his jacket to sift through the baggies in his inner pocket. Even though it's dark, I catch a knife case hooked onto his belt. "You want a gram?" he asks, bringing my attention back to his face.

Intensity builds around my joints.

"Yeah," I say calmly as I begin balling my fist, letting all my rage flood into my arm and down to my hand.

He goes to pull out a small baggie from his pocket. "It's gonna be—"

My fist connects with his nose before he finishes his sentence. A shocked look flashes on his face as blood trickles down.

"What the fuck?" He blinks, stunned.

Adrenaline explodes in my body and before he can regain his composure and reach for his knife, I drive my fist into him again.

Heat courses through me, and I sense myself smirking as the guy falls to the ground.

I keep going for good measure, hearing a crack in his ribs when I kick him.

"Stop!" he screams, and he continues to fish for his knife.

Crouching down onto the cement, I jam my arm up against his throat, cutting off his airway. His hands automatically fly up, abandoning the search for his weapon. He coughs as his feet push against the ground, trying to squirm away from me.

This right here is my outlet for my anger. I've been waiting to beat the shit out of this guy for a fucking week. All my pent-up aggression goes straight to his face when I punch him again.

I raid his jacket, stuffing whatever drugs and cash I can into my jean pockets. Then I reach down and take the knife from its case.

"Look, man, I don't want any trouble—" he pleads

with me, the sound of his voice grating against his semi-compressed throat.

"Then you shouldn't have sold this shit to my sister." Seething with fury, it takes every ounce of my control not to drive this blade into him right now as I think back to a few weeks ago finding Rae milliseconds away from death in her bedroom.

She overdosed because of this motherfucker right here.

And if we didn't already have Narcan in our house, she would be dead, and I'd be doing much worse to this dealer.

Lucky for him, she lived.

Beads of sweat coat my skin as the tendons in my hand flex, turning my fist white as I tightly grasp the weapon.

"I-I'm sorry, man—"

"Shut the fuck up." Before I let my emotions fully consume me, I swiftly hop to my feet. He doesn't expect it, and when the air is fully allowed into him, he violently draws it in. My foot flies into his abdomen one last time to make sure he doesn't have it in him to follow me back to my car. He groans in pain, rolling back and forth in a fetal position. "Get a new job. You suck at this one," I say, then start walking to my car.

The knife is still in my hand as precaution, but I don't foresee him getting up any time soon.

The burst of adrenaline still floods my body. My veins buzz as I try to steady my breathing.

Still feeling the rush, I sit back in my car. Driving off, I can feel the satisfaction settling into my bones.

Thing is, I was a kid when Cara was killed. But I was an adult when Rae overdosed. I might not have any control over what happened in the past, but I sure as hell am going to have control over what happens in the present.

Hell will freeze over before someone I care about gets hurt again.

CHAPTER TWO

Emma

SPRING

THE SOUND of seagulls squawking outside wakes me up. I quite literally lift my head out of my book and readjust myself on my bed.

I must've fallen asleep while reading again.

If it were one of my romance novels, I could easily pull an all-nighter getting wrapped up in a steamy love story, but my overpriced textbook for statistics class is a lot less riveting—so much so, that I got coaxed into taking a late evening nap rather than learning about variables.

The warm sea breeze from my open window tickles my nostrils and the salty air has me alert enough to push off my mattress. My bare feet touch my dusty-pink rug, then onto my hardwood floor as I pad across my room until I reach the window. Now that it's mid-April in North Carolina, I can finally leave it open to let the air float through.

As I gaze out at the ocean, a sense of tranquility

swims through my bloodstream. My home life might not have always been peaceful, but at least where it's located is soothing.

There are two sides to Golden Bay Beach: the south side where tourists thrive off of the shops, attractions, and Adventureland amusement park, and the north side where well-off families keep their luxurious houses hidden between sand dunes and tall beach grass.

It's quaint and quiet on this side of town.

"Emma," Dad's voice crackles through the intercom that's built into my wall. "I expect dinner at six thirty."

Well, at least sometimes it's quiet here.

Before trudging downstairs to our kitchen, I take one last look out the window. Where our home is planted is beautiful. Nothing but the endless ocean in front of me, the outline of the pier at Adventureland in the distance to my right, and the lighthouse off to my left. We're the last house on the north side, the only ones that live in the small inlet.

Our home is close to the water but raised on stilts. If we were up any higher, we'd probably reach the heavens.

"Emma?" His voice comes through the speaker once more, this time causing me to jolt from the volume.

Peeling myself away from the scenery, I scurry toward the intercom.

"Sure thing, Dad. What would you like?" I ask.

"Shrimp scampi."

"Okay. I'll start it in a minute."

Grabbing my statistics textbook and highlighters off my bed, I neatly place them on my desk, next to my Bible that Dad got me shortly after my thirteenth birthday. I was told to leave it out, so it's been sitting on the corner of my desk for years. The same birthday he also adorned me with a purity ring, which sits like a weight on my finger.

Dropping my highlighters into my ceramic pen holder, I fan them out so they look nice. Everything in my room is in perfect order—neat, organized, and aesthetically pleasing to the eye.

This hasn't always been my room, but when I started college, I somehow convinced Dad to let me move into the spare guest bedroom. It's bigger than my childhood bedroom and has its own en suite. Not to mention it's on the opposite side of our house, away from Dad's bedroom and office. This is the only space in my home where I feel like I can truly be myself.

My eyes drift off my desk and onto the massive bookshelf mounted on my wall. It houses classic novels, historical fiction, and some fantasy. Even though romance is my favorite, I don't have any physical copies of those kinds of books—they stay on my Kindle, hidden under my pillow.

My most recent romance book is about a girl locked in a castle, and her love interest defeats her captors in order to save her. It is a little cliché, plus I'm not big on the whole "damsel in distress" thing.

I've never depended on a man to come in to save the day.

I'm well aware of the confines of my castle.

And I plan on saving myself.

Drifting out of my room, I walk down the long hallway and down our double staircase. A grand chandelier hangs in our foyer, each crystal elegantly illuminating the space.

Heading to our massive kitchen, I go straight to our

fridge to get the ingredients for dinner. This is nothing out of the ordinary. As long as I'm home, I cook the meals. The only time I'm excused from preparing our food is when I'm at school, work, or the rare occasion I'm out with a friend—which doesn't happen often.

The pungent scent of garlic fills the room as I mince it into tiny pieces, the knife hitting the chopping board in quick movements.

"Smells wonderful." Dad enters with a wide smile. He's still in his button-up, but his tie is loosened, which means he's done working for the day.

"Thank you."

"But next time I say a specific time, I'd like to be served by then. Not still waiting for you to finish."

My spine gets tense. Smashing my lips together, I hold in what I actually wish I could respond with and instead settle on, "It should be done in a few minutes," letting the ingredients sizzle in the skillet. "How was work?"

"Stressful." He sits down, running his hand over his salt-and-pepper hair. "I had to make a house call to Mr. Daddario. His wife isn't doing well."

Keeping my focus on cooking, I feel a slight tug at my heartstrings. "That must be really hard for him."

"Loss isn't easy for anyone. You and I both know that."

Sadness settles in my stomach.

I don't know if I ever grieved Mom properly, considering I never had her to begin with. She died from cancer before I turned one year old, gone before I had the chance to even know who she was or truly know a mother's embrace.

Not a day goes by that I don't wish she was here

with me. I think about how different life could have looked if I had her in my corner. Would she have grown sick of Dad's holier-than-thou presence, too? Would she have yearned to break free, and the two of us could've lived a mother-daughter life?

Once the dishes are prepared, I set a plate down in front of him and the other at my chair, then grab sparkling water for the both of us.

We both bow our heads as he prays over the food before we eat, then he goes back to speaking about work.

He's a pastor at a church far off the beaten path, in the countryside town called Bristol.

Correction—he's the pastor at *his* church.

The residents of Bristol took such a strong liking to his sermons years ago, they actually came together to build him a church.

My father, Pastor William Carnell, has a following so big they'll probably petition to rename their town after him once he passes. He's a powerful man who countless parishioners respect and honor. Many frequently ask him to make house calls, such as Mr. Daddario, so he can offer counseling and tell them which prayers will be most helpful in their situation. People come to Kingdom Church requesting to speak with him as if he has all of life's answers. He's treated as a celebrity, and people willingly donate to his church every chance they get so he can continue to keep his services going.

The irony of Dad using his faith, which is based on humbleness, to gain a larger status and deeper pockets.

"Anyway," Dad says, interrupting my thoughts. I

blink a few times, realizing I zoned out while he was speaking about the Daddarios. "How was your day?"

I take a bite of my dinner, letting the oil mix with the shrimp and linguine. "It was good," I respond. "Went to work, then studied for one of my business classes."

He frowns before taking a sip of his drink.

A wave of unease rolls through me, but I shove it away. He's not keen on me going to college for a business degree, to the point of him refusing to pay for it, even though he can afford it tenfold. The idea of me going to school was always an argument, but it wasn't until a month before I officially started that he dropped the bomb that he'd be cutting me off if I went. It was his final attempt to stop me, but three years later, I'm still going—even though I had the rug pulled out from under me.

Panicking, I had to scramble to find a job, which is how I ended up working at the front desk at SeaScape Condos, which is on the south side of Golden Bay Beach.

Dad's made it very clear he would rather me live my life doing household duties for him, which I sometimes think is the sole reason he hasn't kicked me out since starting college.

He'd be perfectly content with me staying here until the end of time, waiting on him hand and foot, and volunteering the rest of my free time at Kingdom Church.

Which is exactly why I'm going to school for business. It's a lucrative field and low risk when starting out a career. I'll save as much as I can working at SeaScape, and as soon as I graduate with my bachelor's next year,

I'll have enough to pay rent while searching for an entry-level job. While somehow juggling paying off my school loans.

It's been my plan for years.

The way I'm going to save myself from my castle.

"What time do you go to work tomorrow?" he asks.

"Four."

"Good, I could use your help at the church beforehand."

I wipe my mouth with a napkin, then clutch it in my hands under the table. "I'm sorry, I already have plans in the afternoon."

"You don't have class."

"I know." I wring the napkin.

"So, you're free."

My knuckles turn white, but I keep my voice level. "No. I'm not."

"What are you doing then?"

"My friend Rae asked me to help her with something."

Dad scowls. "Who's Rae?"

"She moved into SeaScape not too long ago, and I'm helping her adjust to living there."

While it took some time for Rae to warm up to the idea of holding more than a thirty-second conversation with me, when we finally did start hanging out, we clicked. We're very opposite from each other, and she's the most closed-off person I've ever met, but she's so effortlessly cool. She lives her life authentically, something I always dreamed of being able to do.

"How old is she?"

"Twenty-four."

"What do her parents do?"

"I don't know. She lives on her own." God willing, that'll be me in a year's time.

"Then what does *she* do?" his tone grows frustrated.

"She's an artist."

Dad scoffs. "What's her background like?"

"She's a lovely person, Dad."

I know Rae's backstory is filled with pain and heartache. I noticed the small circle scarring on her arms, near her elbow creases. They're faded, and no one would be able to see there are track marks unless they look hard. But I noticed them, and she also confirmed it. So yes, she's a lovely person and a recovering heroin addict. The two parts of her can coexist—although I won't tell Dad the latter.

Looking across the table at Dad, I soften my hazel eyes. "She asked for my help, Dad. I'm trying to do the right thing and be kind to others—just like you always taught me."

He stares me down for a beat, debating with himself. "Fine," he says, then goes back to eating dinner.

"I fucking hate shoe shopping," Rae groans, even though going shoe shopping was her idea to begin with.

Giggling, I place another shoebox next to her. Rae always has a way with words, whereas I think I slipped up and swore twice in my life. "Try these," I instruct, my red hair swishing back and forth in a ponytail as I search the store for more options.

She continues to complain about trying on another pair, but I eventually coax her into it.

Hanging out with Rae is freeing. Truthfully, any time I walk out of my house I get a sense of freedom, but especially when I'm on this side of town. My job at SeaScape is on the boardwalk, a quick stroll away from Adventureland. There are restaurants and stores galore, and this time of year is when there starts to be an uptick in tourists visiting the beach.

Dad never ventures down to this part of Golden Bay, so I feel more comfortable having fun and enjoying myself.

"You win. These are better," Rae says about the shoes.

Smiling, I watch as she begrudgingly pays. The cashier tries to make small talk with Rae, but she's not having it. But that's who she is, she doesn't aim to please others which is why I like being around her so much. I hope some of her self-assurance rubs off on me.

One look at Rae, and Dad would hate her and probably forbid me to see her again. She's covered head-to-toe in tattoos, smokes nonstop, and curses more than any person I've ever met.

When we step out of the store, the sun shines so brightly, I need to squint. There are a few people scattered about, popping in and out of shops. The sea breeze gently moves past us, and I let out a deep breath of joy.

Linking my arm with Rae, I drag her into a nearby boutique which I know is totally not her style. But there's still a few hours until I have to work, and there's no way I'm going back home—so, off to Hayden's Boutique we go!

Lavender-scented candles make the entire place smell delightful. There's lots of cream and beige clothing, but I rush to the racks with splashes of color on them.

"This shit is so expensive," Rae whispers as she checks out a price tag on one of the shirts.

"I know. Too bad I'll never be able to buy anything from here because I'm in love with everything," I respond, riffling through the clothes, pretending I'll use my checks from work to splurge on an overpriced romper. "Oh, this would look *so* good on you!" I pull a black shimmery cocktail dress off the rack.

"And where exactly would I be wearing that?"

"I'm sure Miles could think of a good place to take you," I tease.

Miles Kingston moved to Golden Bay a few years back but had been the missing puzzle piece in this town. He's the local repairman, always willing to go above and beyond to help others—not to mention he's extremely good-looking. Rae recently started dating him, and while the two are night and day from each other, I have a feeling he's the reason why Rae is softening up toward everyone.

"He's going to meet my family later today," Rae informs me.

My mouth hangs open. "What! Oh my gosh! How did things move so quickly?" My excitement for her flutters through my stomach.

She shrugs. "I'm not entirely sure if I'm being honest. Things are just starting to click into place."

Caught up in my own fantasy of meeting a wonderful man and having Dad approve, I let out a sigh. "That sounds lovely. I wish that would happen to me one day. I'm not sure with who, though." The thought of my recent ex-crush crosses my mind, and a sour taste fills my mouth. "Thankfully, I'm over Travis. Any feelings I had for him vanished into thin air—I even start to cringe when I look at him."

Very true words. I once was infatuated by Travis in my business class, but he ignored me when he realized I wanted more than just a hook-up. And he's treated me like dirt ever since, flashing girls in front of me while not saying a peep when he looks my way.

"Miles seems so romantic," I continue. "Is he?"

Rae clears her throat and focuses on shifting through the clothes. "Yeah. He'd probably be even more romantic if I gave him the chance, but...that's not really my thing."

There goes my mind again, wandering into some romance novel where the guy intuitively knows exactly what the girl wants and needs. "God, I'd love a romantic man," I say more to myself than to Rae.

"Sounds like you should wear that dress." She points to the one I picked out for her. "And then we can go out and find you a good guy."

I give a halfhearted smile. "I don't really go out much. Just occasionally to hang out with friends between work and school, but even that's a battle."

Rae's features pull in tight. "A battle with who?"

My focus goes back to the rack in front of me, mindlessly glancing at the shirts and dresses. "My dad. He's really strict."

"But you're twenty—you're a whole-ass adult."

"Not while I'm living under his roof, I'm not. Which is why I'm saving every penny I can to go toward a place to live the second I graduate."

"Damn. I thought I had strict parents."

Strict doesn't even begin to cover it

When Dad found out about my past sexual encounters, that was it for me. No boys, no dates—nothing. He even turned down a churchgoer's request to have their grandson accompany me to the annual church fundraiser.

It wasn't until recent years that he allowed me to go to lunch or get my nails done with friends from school. And that's only because he finally realized he can't keep tabs on me when I'm in college, going back and forth between classes.

It's been a delicate balance of staying in my lane and pushing my luck. Which is why I have to play my cards right.

Only one more year of obliging, then I'll be on my way.

I'll be set free.

CHAPTER THREE

Grayson

MY BEDROOM IS DARK, the curtains closed tight, not allowing any sunlight to enter. I had planned on sleeping in, but Mom clearly has other plans.

"Grayson!" she exclaims. I pop one eye open to see her standing in my doorframe with her hands on her hips. "How are you still sleeping? We're supposed to be leaving to go see your sister in fifteen minutes!"

I grumble something that resembles words, even though I'm not sure what they are, then flip over onto my other side.

"Were you out late last night?" Mom asks, then adds with a gasp, "You weren't out getting into trouble again, were you?"

"For the love of God," I mumble into my pillow.

My parents busted me over the winter when I kicked the shit out of Rae's dealer. It was kind of impossible not to see that my hand was bruised, bloodied, and swollen. They read me the riot act, but I didn't care.

I had to do *something*. These dealers are getting away with literal murder, ruining families and torturing those who are hurting. I did the world a favor by kicking his ass. And as long as my heart still has blood pumping through it, I'll fight to make sure that Rae is never in that situation again and that my parents never go through the pain of almost burying her.

The memory of finding her lifeless body with a needle sticking out of her arm is tattooed onto my brain for the rest of my life. The sound of Mom's shrill scream, Dad calling the ambulance. All of it is sewn onto the fibers of my soul.

Never again.

"Grayson, are you getting into fights again?"

Did I get into a handful of fights after the incident with the dealer? Yes. I've found it to be a very effective way to release my anger, and I quite enjoy the adrenaline rush. Was last night one of those nights? No. I just like to fucking sleep.

"John!" Mom shouts into the hallway to Dad. I let out a frustrated sigh, already anticipating the conversation that's about to follow.

"He's not up yet?" Dad's voice joins in.

I kick off my blankets. All hope of sleeping in is over at this point.

"I'm awake," I mutter, rubbing a fist over my eye.

Mom moves into my room, stepping over a pile of books and a bag of chips to open my curtains. She's the kindest person on the planet, but the second the sun shoots into my room, blinding me, I internally curse her.

"Maybe it's time for you to start looking into going to school. It would be good for you to get on a regular schedule."

"I agree with Mom," Dad chimes in. "Or I can get you a real job in the office. I think it's time you started thinking of your future. No more odd jobs here and there, it's time to get serious."

I've had jobs over the years, but being a cashier or a stock boy didn't stick.

"Do you want to at least take a class or two at community college?" Mom asks.

Slowly suffocating from them bombarding me with questions as soon as I wake up, I shake my head, glancing up at her. We've had the college talk numerous times, yet she still has a distraught look in her eyes, a mixture of concern and hopelessness. "But you're so smart. You can do anything, Grayson."

She's right. I probably could do anything if I wanted to. I'm a quick learner and pick up new information in an instant. But with no sense of purpose, it all feels useless.

"What about trade school?" Dad crosses to stand next to Mom, the two of them pleading with me to do something with my life other than isolating and digging myself into a hole. "You can be an electrician, or mechanic, or carpenter," he goes on to list potential careers.

The stupid organ in my rib cage gets heavier the longer I stare at them.

The air around me is stripped away as they hover over me. Their pleading faces make it tough to continue this argument we've had time and time again. They look like they're a breath away from crumbling into pieces, this conversation being their last chance of staying intact.

Even though my shoulders round as they slump, I nod.

Mom gasps as Dad says, "Really? You'll consider going to trade school?"

"Yeah."

"Well, all right." Dad beams. "Let's talk about it on the car ride to see Rae."

Great, from one failed offspring to the next.

After Mom and Dad are done babbling about different trade schools for me to look into, they move on to another topic that thankfully has nothing to do with me. It's a three-hour car ride to get to Rae's new condo in Golden Bay Beach, and the majority of it has been taken up by false hopes of dreams for my future.

Stretching out my legs in the back seat, I glance to my side at my notebook I brought with me to help pass the time. Reaching for it, I also grab the pen and use my teeth to pry off the cap and begin to jot down my current thoughts.

There should be a law against being forced to spend time with your sibling. Especially when they hate you, and you've barely spoken to them for the last half of your life.

Let's be honest, I've barely spoken to anyone the last ten years. Not just Rae.

After Cara died, I shut down. Not little by little, but all at once. Paralyzed by anxiety and fear. I stopped talking. For all everyone knew, there was nothing going on inside my head when they were speaking to me. But in reality, there was an explosion of sensory overload and extreme emotion going off in my brain.

I went to a special high school for kids who had emotional needs. Not that I minded—there's no fucking way I'd want to go to my sister's high school. Where I went, I had teachers and specialists work with me to get me to a point where I can hold conversations with people again.

Although, I'm quite selective about who I'm speaking to and what comes out of my mouth.

Might be a control issue. Might be the fact that I don't want to waste my breath on nonsense.

Before I was able to speak, the school found my sweet spot: writing. I'd communicate through little notes here and there. They eventually had me read them aloud and get comfortable speaking sentences. But even when I wasn't writing for school or to convey what I wanted, I would still write my fiction stories. Only, as the weight of *reality started to sink in; my stories didn't take place in a fantasy universe.*

Villains lived among us with no hero in sight.

While I was struggling to talk, Rae nosedived into drugs.

I tried—I swear I tried to help her. But every time I went to her she was either blazed out of her mind or I couldn't push out the words that she probably needed to hear.

I was useless as a brother.

Even when I started making friends and talking to Mom and Dad again, I still couldn't hold a conversation with Rae.

"We're here!" Mom singsongs as Dad parks the car in a lot next to the boardwalk.

Golden Bay Beach is somewhere we vacationed when I was really little. I remember the amusement park and obviously the beach, but not much else.

We walk along the pavement of the boardwalk as Mom navigates, telling us Rae picked out a nearby restaurant. There's a slight breeze, warm enough to remind us that winter is long gone and all that came with it.

Rae went to rehab for three months after her overdose, and our parents moved her into a condo here to "help her out with starting her new life."

I haven't seen her since she was being lifted onto a gurney and taken into an ambulance.

A twinge of nerves hits my stomach, but I ignore it. I don't even know what it's there for.

When we finally hit the restaurant that's overlooking the ocean, we scan the room looking for my sister. It's not until we notice there's outdoor seating that we spot her.

She sure as hell looks better than the last time I saw her. There's some meat on her bones and color in her face. I watch as her eyes light up as she speaks to someone. That's when I realize there's a guy sitting next to her.

Fumes blast in my body the same time my jaw clenches, and my fists ball up.

Oh fuck no. I swear to God if this is some asshole junkie, I'll rip his head off with my bare hands.

Mom and Dad rush up to Rae and embrace her while saying their hellos. I give her a nod of my chin.

"Hey, Grayson," Rae says, giving me a timid smile.

"Who's this?" Mom asks about the guy next to her.

"Oh, everyone, this is Miles. He's my...boyfriend."

Boyfriend? Me and Rae aren't close at all, but I know for a fact that she's never had a boyfriend because that's something she'd occasionally bitch about at home. Fucking fantastic. She goes to rehab, moves here, and probably got with the first guy that had a stash of something on him.

There's more pressure in my jaw, my teeth grinding together.

"It's nice to meet all of you," Miles says. Mom hugs him, overjoyed that Rae is apparently in a committed relationship. Miles gives Dad a handshake then extends one to me.

I glance down at his hand, untrusting of it. I opt for another tilt of my chin.

We eventually all sit down at the table, and both Mom and Dad go straight into asking Miles questions, getting to know him.

They bullshit for what feels like forever, so I start zoning out on the menu. I tap my finger against the laminated sheet of paper until my ears perk up when I hear Rae mention that Miles is the town's repairman, anticipating what's going to come out of Dad's mouth.

"Maybe you can teach Grayson here a few things," Dad suggests to Miles as he pats me on the back. "He's going to be starting trade school."

Christ. I half-assed agreed to the idea three hours ago, and now Dad's trying to get me an apprenticeship with Rae's "boyfriend."

"You are?" Rae asks, her eyebrows shooting up in surprise.

I shift my attention back to my menu and slowly nod. I'm not getting into this conversation right now and especially not with her.

The topic shifts off of me as soon as the waiter comes to take our drink order.

As dinner moves on, my attention bounces from Rae and Miles off to random thoughts floating in my head.

Once we're finished eating, Rae invites us back to her condo. We walk in a group along the boardwalk and up to SeaScape Condos. I hang in the back, not wanting to put in the effort of talking to anyone. My gaze is fixated on the pavement while Dad asks Rae questions about her new life here.

When we finally reach her building, we walk into a nautical-themed lobby with pictures of the ocean and fake anchors on the wall.

I internally groan, wanting to hurry this night up so I can go the fuck home.

"Emma," Rae begins speaking to someone at the front desk, introducing her to our parents.

The second I lift my line of sight to see who Rae's speaking to, a rush of pleasure bursts out of my chest, spilling down my body.

She's gorgeous.

Seconds stand still, and the room tilts on its axis the longer I stare at her. My breath gets caught in my throat as sparks continue to scatter up and down my limbs.

I've seen a lot of beautiful girls before, but none made my insides go haywire.

She's stunning, as if she just walked out of a timeless classic novel.

There's an air of delicate wholesomeness surrounding her as her full lips lift upward into a radiant smile.

My heart beats faster as I admire her red hair, half of it pulled back while the other half cascades down her shoulders in gentle waves.

"—and that's my little brother, Grayson, back there," Rae says, poking her head behind Dad so she can see me.

"Hey." The sound of my voice reverberates in the room. The first word I've spoken all night, and it's to Emma.

I know everyone's staring at me right now, but the

only pair of eyes I care about are the hazel ones looking right back at me.

"H-Hi," Emma stammers, coiling a strand of her hair around her index finger.

I watch the movement of her hand and can't help but take the opportunity to check the rest of her out. My body heats up as I note the dusting of freckles scattered across her collarbones. I drop my gaze down the rest of her, taking my time to study her curves.

An explosion goes off inside of me, my stomach jumping up and down.

"Christ," Rae mutters. "All right, let's move it upstairs, people." She shuffles us along to the elevator.

Still in the back, I steal another glance at Emma while the others walk ahead of me.

There's a light pink tint shading her cheeks as she continues to coyly grin.

Just seeing her smile makes me smile, too, the corners of my mouth lifting.

"Grayson, let's go!" Rae snaps as the elevator dings right before the doors open.

My focus goes back to my family as we make our way to Rae's condo. And that's when my head gets screwed back on.

What the actual fuck was that?

I pride myself on having tremendous control, and within a matter of seconds, my body went wild, and I spoke on impulse all because of a pretty girl.

That can't happen again.

Forcing myself into the moment and to stop thinking about Emma, I bring my attention to Rae's space. It's a decent size, with an open-floor plan kitchen and living room. Of course, Rae decided to paint murals on the walls in her living room.

She's an artist. Her choice of weaponry is a paintbrush, whereas mine is a pen. Or at least it used to be. Aside from jotting down random things that come to my mind, I haven't written an actual story in several years.

Just another part of me that drifted away.

"This is fascinating!" Mom says about the gruesome image that's plastered on her wall. Everyone goes up to admire it, taking in the painting of a broken skull with blood and bugs pouring out of it. But I hang back by the front door, itching to leave.

They go on to look at her other artwork, then Rae goes to the far end of the living room to show them the balcony. They all step out except for Miles, who goes into the kitchen to grab a drink.

It's just me and him.

Now's the opportunity to see what this shithead is all about and to see if I need to stake him out to add him to the list of assholes I can take my anger out on and use as a punching bag.

I stalk over to him. Miles does a double take when he notices me, almost as if he forgot I was lurking in the side view. "Can I get you anything?" he asks, opening up the fridge.

I don't answer.

As he goes to get his water, I crowd his space. He spins back around, startled.

We stand face-to-face as I stare him down.

"What are you on?" I snap.

His brows draw in. "What?"

"Drugs. What type of drugs do you use?"

He shakes his head. "I'm not on anything—"

"Bullshit." I spit out the word. I've heard enough lies from addicts to last a lifetime.

"Grayson, I promise I'm not using anything. In fact, I'm in recovery. Three years sober."

My eyes narrow, assessing him. I can't tell if he's telling the truth or not, but God, do I hope he is. If Rae has to have a boyfriend, then having one who's also in recovery could be the best option for her.

Still, I can't tell if he's talking out of his ass or not.

"I swear to God, if I find out you're lying, I will hunt you down and fuck you up." The unearthed anger deep within my soul boils my blood the more I speak. "I already have one dead sister, and Rae would've been dead too if I found her a minute later. If you're one of those asshole lowlifes who's gonna drag Rae back into that shit, mark my words—I *will* find you."

Miles nods in agreement and gives me a smile, completely unfazed by my threat. "I appreciate where you're coming from. On my honor, I have every intention of keeping myself and Rae sober." He pats me on the shoulder. "You're a good brother, Grayson. You should come hang around more often."

I blink, not understanding how my declaring to off him if he derails Rae somehow got me bonus brother points and an offer to hang out with them. Not that Rae would actually *want* to spend time with me.

"Well, we don't want to take up all your time tonight," Mom says as she, Dad, and Rae come back inside from the balcony.

I step back toward the door and watch everyone as they say their goodbyes. Rae looks over at me, and I give her another head nod before dipping out the door and waiting for Mom and Dad to get to the elevator.

I ignore the confusion from my interaction with Miles and bury any hopes from his suggestion to hang out with them in the future.

Who knows the next time I'll even be here, considering I have no relationship with my sister. This could very well be my first and last time.

And with that final thought of never coming here again, I glance over my shoulder when I get to the lobby, locking eyes with Emma.

My body spins out of control once more as I slowly move away from her.

Yeah. Definitely never coming back here again.

CHAPTER FOUR

Emma

THE CHOIR'S high note resonates in Kingdom Church as they finish singing their song. The sound of the organ echoes off the walls. I don't have to look over to see who's playing it because I already know it's Kane, Dad's dutiful churchgoer who's been playing the instrument at Sunday service for years. Every week, we sit at opposite ends of the church, never glancing at each other but knowing we exist.

The church has a steeple ceiling where rectangle skylights let the sun pour in right over Dad's pulpit. The oak wood gives off an inviting and homey feel, although I've never felt either of those things while sitting here.

A room filled with people, yet I still feel alone.

"Beautiful singing," Dad says, head turned to the choir on his right. He focuses back on the rest of us sitting in the pews. "Let's give them a round of applause for those incredible voices."

Everyone claps, including me, as if we've never heard them sing before.

When the applause dies down, Dad starts his sermon. "I'd like to discuss a keyword that appeared in today's scripture: morality." He takes the microphone out of its holder and begins pacing in an attempt to connect with more people.

I've never been to another type of church before, but I imagine they're not all like this. Dad picks the songs and which passages he wants to read from the Bible, then he gives a homily, speaking as if he's God himself.

If someone sins, they must go through Dad in order to be forgiven. And sometimes, he won't forgive. In his eyes, forgiveness is a privilege and not a right, no matter how much someone repents.

I would know more than anyone.

I spin the thin gold ring around my finger, only half paying attention to what Dad's saying but making my facial expressions seem engaged since my spot is in the front row.

"When it comes to morals," Dad continues, everyone's fully entranced by his speech, "it's black and white. Virtuous versus evil. There is no gray area."

My stomach does somersaults the second he says *gray*.

"Many of us try to find loopholes and excuses when we don't uphold a moral life, but deep down, we know. We know there is only one true way of being: unmarred, righteous, *good*." His eyes land on me. It's a quick glance but enough for me to feel a slap of shame across my cheek. "I say 'we' because I've slipped up, too. Only once or twice, though," he jokes, his entire face lighting up when everyone laughs.

I force a chuckle, then actively make sure I don't listen to the rest of what he says.

Instead, I let my thoughts drift to something else. The one place they've seemed to go nonstop the past week or so. Grayson.

I never thought my body would feel a ripple of shockwaves like it did when I made eye contact with him. Everything about him was alluring, his tall stature, dark, messy hair, and mysterious irises that seemed to reflect the color of his name, only with a hint of blue. Almost as if, at one point in his life his eyes held a vibrant hue, but over time, they dulled and darkened from ashes.

I've had crushes before, but never have I felt so consumed by someone just from one simple word. His "hey" has been playing on repeat in my head as if it's my favorite song.

I even went as far as asking Rae if he's single—something I'd never been so forward to do. When she told me he was, I nearly burst out of my skin with excitement.

She passed along my number to him yesterday, and I've been glued to my phone, waiting for it to light up with a message from him ever since.

Well, except for now, of course. My phone is off and put away in my purse sitting by my side in the pew.

"Let's all pray together for the deliverance of our souls. Acknowledging when we haven't lived a moral life and instead chose a path of sin," Dad says.

Giving Mrs. Sterling a small smile, we clasp hands, and the rest of the churchgoers follow our lead, everyone linking palms.

Dad leads us in prayer, one of his favorites he's

created over the years. We all bow our heads before him and mouth the words.

Once the service is over, Dad stands by the open wooden doors to say goodbye to the parishioners as they exit. There's already a small group congregating inside, eager to speak to him once he finishes his farewells. I'd bet anything Kane is part of the small cluster, but I don't check to confirm. Just like every Sunday, I keep my head held high and try my best to forget he's still breathing.

As Dad shakes hands and cracks jokes, I do a quick scan of the church, noting if anything needs to be straightened up. Once things are in order, I move toward the doors to join Dad.

Passing by his group of fans, a piece of paper falls from someone's hands and drifts down in front of me.

"I got it!" I say, reaching to pick it up. The moment I realize it's sheet music, I wish I hadn't been so willing to help. My stomach knots as I hand it over to Kane.

He's ten years older than me with hair as black as night. All the single women in the church fawn over him. He's a charmer, no doubt, but the look of amusement in his eyes sends a chill of unease down my spine.

"Thank you." He smirks as if pleased I was the one to come to his aid.

I give a curt nod before swiftly walking around him, going to my place next to Dad. He's still schmoozing with parishioners, and I idly stand by his side, saying goodbye as people leisurely exit.

"Wonderful sermon today," Mr. Parson says to Dad. He then glances over at me. "And Emma, you look just as lovely as every week."

"Thank you, Mr. Parson," I say, adjusting the

peach-colored straps of my dress so I'm not over-exposed.

"She's becoming quite the young lady with each passing day," Dad chimes in.

"You're doing a wonderful job with her."

"Why thank you, Mr. Parson."

My shoulders tense as I bite my tongue, forcing myself to smile through their conversation.

I'm not a child nor a pet, I'm a woman. A woman who had to fend for herself and navigate healing from my past on my own. If anyone is responsible for how lovely I turned out, it's myself.

I keep fake grinning until my cheeks hurt, then Mr. Parson finally leaves. The group inside grows as if Dad is some type of celebrity that they have VIP passes to.

"Do you need me to do anything before I go?" I ask Dad.

"I don't think so." He waves to the group. "Looks like I have a lot of people to meet with. I'll be back home later tonight, after dinner." He turns his attention back to me, a glimpse of sternness crosses his features, reserved for only me and no one else in the congregation. "Be good." Those two words hang in the air, not as a request but as a demand.

"I always am, Dad." I give him a one-armed embrace, and he kisses the top of my head—an action that's familiar to us but is done more for show than genuine affection. "I'll see you later," I say right before we part ways.

As I walk out of Kingdom Church and into the sun, I feel the same sensation of relief that I do every Sunday. My muscles loosen, there's a pep in my step and fresh air in my lungs.

This is how it is every week morning service, then Dad hangs back to be with his groupies for the rest of the day. Since he gets so wrapped up with them, I'm free to leave.

Driving out of the gravel parking lot, I let the windows down and let the breeze fly through my hair. I travel between the trees, down the dirt paths until I finally hit a paved road. There's no other building in sight, just my dad's. We're out in the countryside with nothing and no one nearby. Which is why I think people like coming to Kingdom Church so much. It gives them a sense of community when there isn't really one in this area. I think the closest convenience store is thirty minutes away—which isn't that convenient. All of the houses are scattered. Sometimes I catch a glimpse of one tucked way off the road, but other than that, there's nowhere for people to come together other than church. People will spend their entire day there—and I'm thankful that they do because I get to do whatever I want in the meantime.

The road eventually leads to the highway, which eventually leads me toward home. Only today I have plans with Rae, so I'm headed to her place instead.

After the long drive, I'm finally back in my comforting beach town.

"It's open," Rae says from the other side of her door when I knock on it.

When I enter, Rae has an unlit cigarette hanging from her lips. Her balcony door is ajar, and she's ready to step outside to smoke. I can hear the sound of chatter and laughter coming from the boardwalk.

"Hi!" I say, happiness beaming through me.

"You look fancier than normal," she says before motioning her head for me to come outside with her.

"I just left Sunday service at my dad's church."

We each take a seat on her Adirondack chairs and admire the ocean in front of us. Rae lets out a plume of smoke but tries to aim it away from me. "Your dad has a church?"

"Yeah, I don't really advertise that part of my life." I laugh. "I would much rather talk about other things, such as—"

"My brother?" She playfully takes a jab, smirking.

"No." My cheeks get hot. "Maybe."

"Did he text you yet?"

I shake my head in response, and she lets out a frustrated sigh. "Sorry," she says. "I have no idea what his track record is like with girls. He could be a total douchebag for all I know, so it might actually be a good thing he didn't reach out."

"You two never talk about that kind of stuff?"

Rae scoffs. "We don't talk at all. Texting him for you to see if he was single was the most conversation we've had in years."

"I'm sorry, I didn't mean to put you in an uncomfortable spot."

"You didn't at all. I wouldn't have done it if I didn't want to."

Another reason why I admire Rae. If only I could've been living my whole life only doing what I wanted and not what was expected of me.

"I'm surprised he even answered me," she continues. "I'm pretty sure he hates me."

"I doubt he hates you."

"No. He does, and I don't blame him. I was awful during my full-blown heroin days."

My heart breaks for her and Grayson. Miles, too. I know their story. She and Miles are survivors of a school shooting, which is how she lost her twin sister, Cara. I don't even want to imagine what their family might've gone through. I can understand why Rae turned to drugs to cope. And I can only assume the horribly traumatic event impacted Grayson as well.

"You're going to have to forgive yourself for that eventually."

Another cloud of smoke escapes her. "Is that what you learned in church today?" she teases.

"No. Forgiving myself is something I learned on my own."

"And what type of sin have you committed that you need to forgive yourself for?"

"The usual. Beating up people in a dark alley and stealing their money," I joke.

She snorts. "I knew I liked you for a reason."

CHAPTER FIVE

Grayson

I SWORE to myself I'd stop fighting.

I was on a decent streak until tonight.

Mom suggested I get out of the house, so I went to the gym—the only place I've been venturing out to recently. My workout was over. Everything was fine until I overheard a conversation in the locker room. A guy with sweatbands was bragging about how he had laced someone's joint.

If someone were to ask me what he laced it with or when this happened, I wouldn't be able to answer them because the second I heard the word *laced* followed by his obnoxious cackle, immense rage took over.

I waited to strike. Tried real fucking hard not to do anything. I even considered writing my anger out instead of using my fists. But my notebook is at home, and this piece of shit is right in front of me.

He left the gym alone, so I followed him to his car and snuck up on him.

With one swing, sweatband guy's nose snaps against my knuckles. He's down on the ground, trying to hit back, but I've got the upper hand. With a kick to the ribs, he whimpers in pain.

My pulse whirls in my ears, more adrenaline pumping through me. I've got a lifetime of wrath to unleash, but only a few seconds to do my final task.

Taking advantage now that he's down for the count, I quickly reach for his gym bag, scouring through his belongings.

"Don't touch my shit!" the guy grits out but ends up wheezing. Holding on to his abdomen, he tries to kick me, but I jump back.

Sweat pours down my body.

My fingers finally connect with what I knew I'd find. Little baggies and a wad of cash.

With that, I silently left sweatband guy to fend for himself, dropping his gym bag on top of him before speed walking to my car.

I drive off, my pockets stuffed with cash and bags filled with God knows what. There are drop boxes at pharmacies where people can anonymously dispose of prescription drugs, which is where I'm headed to now. Of course, the ones in my pockets aren't prescription, but either way, they're off the streets.

I did this last time with the drugs I had found on Rae's dealer. It wasn't my plan to do this a second time, and I don't intend on making it a habit, but it's slightly more satisfying knowing I'm fighting a dealer rather than just a random asshole.

Pulling up to a twenty-four-hour pharmacy, I make sure to park my car out of the view of the overhead cameras and then toss on my hoodie.

I'm quick to get rid of everything on me—minus the cash, then head back to my car for my drive home.

My heart rate begins to steady as I come down from my adrenaline high.

When I finally pull into my driveway, all the lights are off in my house. Quietly I enter, heading to the fridge to ice my throbbing hand. I'm already annoyed, knowing the conversation I'm bound to have with Mom and Dad once they spot my knuckles. It's not like I'm going around fighting every person I come across, but I'm sure they don't see it that way.

Carefully pulling out the kitchen chair so it doesn't squeak, I sit down and rest my hand on the table with a wad of paper towels and ice plopped on top of it.

With my free hand, I take my phone out, mindlessly scrolling. But before I get too carried away, my attention is pulled to the text thread from Rae. She messaged me the other day, out of the blue, and when I found out why, my heart nearly flung out of my chest.

Emma wants to know if I'm single.

She likes me.

Rae gave me her number, the ball is in my court. But I can't bring myself to go through with it for two reasons—one of them being fear. Not scared to message Emma but scared of how else she'll make me feel. If I nearly had a heart attack just from locking eyes with her, what else could possibly happen when we say more than hello to each other?

The other reason I decided not to message Emma is because of Rae's last text to me.

My thumb moves to click open the thread.

Rae
Don't get with Emma unless you're going to treat her right. I swear she's the purest fucking human on the planet. She deserves someone good

My stomach drops at the same time I let my phone fall on the table. I glance over to my sore hand, splattered with dried blood.

She deserves someone good.

That's definitely not me.

CHAPTER SIX

Grayson

SUMMER

WEEKS HAVE GONE by with the same nothingness that has become my life.

As I'm about to devour a bowl full of Froot Loops, Mom and Dad both take a seat at the kitchen table with a hardened look of determination in their eyes. My spoon hovers in the air, milk dripping as I freeze in place, awaiting a conversation.

"Grayson." Mom's tone is serious.

I blink.

"We need to talk."

I blink once more, but this time it's followed by me shoving sugary cereal into my mouth. As I crunch down, I hope to tune out whatever is going to come out of my parents' mouths, but no such luck.

"We know you got into another fight a few nights ago," Dad states.

Yeah, I did, so sue me. I hadn't gotten into any fights after the guy at the gym, until this past one. And truthfully, I couldn't even pinpoint what started it. I think I just wanted to hit something that resembled a face.

I remain silent, knowing my plan of secluding in my room and trying to hide my hand wouldn't fully work.

"This is becoming an issue."

Rolling my eyes, I drop my spoon. "It's only happened a handful of times."

"And that's more than enough," Mom says, her features pulled in tight. "You've taken a major step backward since Rae's overdose."

Every muscle in my body goes rigid.

My focus immediately goes from Mom to the colorful circles in my bowl, drowning in milk and turning to mush.

"Do you want to start going back to Dr. Reed?" Mom asks, referring to my old psychiatrist.

"No."

"I think it'd be good if you start talking to someone. You've been isolating again."

My heart rate picks up as the room begins to shrink.

I wouldn't call what I've been doing *isolating*. I drifted away from people because people only cause pain—why the fuck would I want to subject myself to that? I've been going to the gym, and now that my twenty-first has come and gone, I occasionally hang out at bars. Sure, I'm always alone, but I'm not living in a cave in my room every second of every day.

Mom continues, "Are you writing at least? We know that always helps you."

"Not like I used to," I mumble. That creative part of me has malformed into a wilting flower. I water it from time to time, trying to bring it back to life, but in the end, it's useless.

Everything I've ever done or tried to do in life has been useless.

"We're worried about you, Grayson," Mom's voice softens, and my gaze shoots up to look at her.

My stomach sinks when I notice her chin quivering.

Shit. Pile on the extra guilt while I watch Mom force back tears.

"If you don't want to see Dr. Reed, maybe a trip to Golden Bay might change things for you," she suggests.

My forehead crinkles. "Why?"

"To spend some time with Rae and mend your relationship."

I shake my head in protest. Rae wants nothing to do with me—she's made that very clear. And besides, I don't know how spending forced time with my sister is going to fix this "major step backward."

"You need to do *something*, Grayson," Dad interjects, his tone stern. "You could go to Golden Bay and spend some time with your sister while learning skills for trade school. It's the middle of June. You'll need to start enrolling in a program by the end of the summer."

I stare at him, unresponsive, my face not giving away any emotion.

Is right now the opportune time to bring up this trade school bullshit? I said yes to this to get my parents off my back, but they haven't brought it up in over a month. I thought we were all past this.

Dad starts up again. "We spoke to Rae yesterday—"

"What!"

"Not about how you're struggling, but about you possibly spending the summer there to shadow Miles."

"Is this what this conversation is really about? Me getting a career?"

"No. It's about you making changes and working on different aspects of yourself—including a career. Your mother and I have talked, and we both agree that you need to start taking your future more seriously."

Future? I don't even want a future.

I'm just passing the time until my end comes.

"I don't even know if I want to go to trade school for the same shit he does—why did you even ask her?" The words tumble out of my mouth quickly.

"Well, this can be a great way for you to narrow down what you want to do. If you don't like the type of work Miles does, then you can try something else out."

"No."

"Grayson, we think you need a change of pace," Mom says.

"No," I repeat.

My leg bounces up and down, powerful enough to make the table tremble along with it.

"This could be a great chance for you and Rae to reconnect. She seems to be doing wonderfully. She told me she even went bowling with some people from NA." Mom chuckles to herself. "I can't picture her bowling."

"I'm not going."

"Grayson—"

"I'm not hanging out with Rae and her boyfriend for the entire summer."

Dad's jaw sets as he levels with me. "This isn't up for discussion."

"You're not giving me a choice?"

"Grayson, please." Mom reaches across the table and places her hand on top of mine. "We want to see you flourish, and that's not happening for you here. We're just asking you to try something new for a little while, see which new doors open up for you. It'll only be for the summer, and then you'll come back home."

I bite the inside of my cheek, frustration building inside of me, but the words I wish to get out evaporate. Not that they'd understand even if I spoke to them. They want their kids to have a normal life, I get it. But nothing about the past several years has been normal, so all hope for a regular life has been lost. But the two of them held our family together the best they could. They've suffered enough. I don't want to add to their pain.

Which is why, when I look across the table at them, my muscles get heavy, and my shoulders drop.

"You never know, it could be the start of something great. Will you at least try it out?" Mom half-asks, half-begs.

I nod.

Guess I'm headed to Golden Bay.

CHAPTER SEVEN

Emma

A SUDDEN WAVE of heat washes over my body, my legs tangling between my bed sheets, as I read the latest romance novel on my Kindle.

"Don't stop," Yvonne whispers against my lips.

"I wasn't planning on it." I loosen my grip on her hair and slowly slide my hand to her throat. Her pulse beats against my fingertips, and the moment my other hand slides up her dress, the rhythm gets faster.

I can sense my cheeks becoming flushed. Before I read any further, I highlight the excerpt, knowing that I'll want to go back and reread it, pretending to live out the moment.

I annotate everything I read, but the books that live on my Kindle are marked up the most. From the tender acts that make my heart swell to the downright dirty scenes that are brought to life on the pages—it all gets highlighted.

I love romance books for a multitude of reasons, but one of them is the sense of freedom I feel while reading. I get to escape to all these different worlds where women are celebrated and honored. Their needs are met on every level—physical, emotional, spiritual—and it's all done in the name of love. It doesn't matter if the main character is a virgin or doing the deed in the bathroom of some dirty bar for the thousandth time. It doesn't matter if she's never stepped foot outside of her castle or is running away from her sordid past. She's loved for who she is.

I would love to escape my home and live out my wildest dreams with someone who loved me for me.

I'm holding onto hope that one day, it'll happen.

Continuing to read, my body temperature rises.

"You're already so wet for me." I trace over her panties, feeling her dampness. My cock aches for her—

My phone rings, causing me to immediately snap out of the scene. Dropping my Kindle, I search for my phone that's lost somewhere in my comforter.

When I see Rae's name popping up, a flurry of concern runs through me. She's only ever texted me, never called.

"Rae?" I answer.

"Hey, sorry to bother you," she replies.

"You're not bothering me at all. Is everything okay?"

"Yeah, everything's fine. I just want to give you a heads up. Grayson's going to be staying with me for the summer."

Butterflies fill my stomach. "Oh, okay."

"He never reached out to you, did he?"

"No, but that's all right—"

Rae huffs. "Sorry he's a dick."

"He's not. It's fine he never messaged me." Admittedly, I'm still super disappointed.

"He's hanging around so Miles can teach him some shit before he starts trade school."

"That sounds like a good opportunity for him."

"You're too nice for your own good, Emma. It's okay to say my brother's an asshole."

I chuckle. "He's not. If he doesn't like me, there's nothing I can do about that. I'm glad he's coming to stay with you and Miles. Maybe you guys will start talking again."

She scoffs. "Yeah, okay." There's a sound of the flick of a lighter, and I hear her blow out a puff of air. "He won't be here past the summer, promise."

We say our goodbyes, and I go back to my Kindle. Only this time, my body isn't heating up from the words on the pages. I'm melting over the fact that I'm going to see Grayson again. He might not have any feelings for me, but my feelings for him sure didn't calm down.

It doesn't help that over the past couple of months, every time I read a romance book, it's been *him* that I've been picturing.

Nevertheless, I'm sure I can play it cool when I see him.

I don't have another choice.

CHAPTER EIGHT

Grayson

SWEAT FORMS AT MY HAIRLINE, and not from the summer heat. My heart pounds entering SeaScape Condos, knowing that I might see Emma. I'll have to come up with some lame excuse as to why I never texted her or act like a dickhead who doesn't give a shit about her or any other girl.

Opening the doors, the blast of the cold air pouring out of the air conditioner chills the moisture on my forehead. A rush of relief goes through me when I notice that a man is working the front desk and not Emma.

Hiking my duffel bag up on my shoulder, I give him a curt nod as I make my way to the elevator and up to Rae's home.

When I knock on the door, Rae answers. "Hey."

"Hi."

With zero rapport built between us, we just stare at each other for a beat until the door opens wider, and Miles appears.

"What's up, Grayson!" He grins. "Come on in."

How the hell my sister ended up with someone so different from her is beyond me.

"You can crash on the couch." Rae points to it. "I don't really have any empty drawers for you to put your shit in."

"It's fine," I mumble, letting my duffel bag smack down on the floor before I sit on the couch.

"Your dad said you want to shadow me for a bit and see what I do for work," Miles states.

I shrug, not wanting to explain to Miles that I'm basically being forced here against my will so my parents don't think I'll shrivel up in my bedroom for the rest of eternity.

"When do you want to get started?" he asks.

"Doesn't matter."

"I have some work to do at Rae's art studio tomorrow, want to join?"

My attention shoots over to my sister. "You have an art studio?"

She twists around her choker necklace, a nervous habit of hers that I learned years ago. "Yeah," she replies. "It's newly acquired. Just a one-year lease so I'm gonna try it out and see what happens."

Weird. My sister has never been the go-getter type.

"So, what'd you say?" Miles asks. "Want to come to work with me tomorrow?"

"Whatever."

Uninterested in having a conversation with either of them—or being anywhere near here in general—I unzip my bag, take out my notebook, then head for the balcony.

Only it's not quieter out here because it's fucking summer and the beach is packed. I swear there are more people than sand when I look out over the boardwalk. Nevertheless, I'd rather be out here.

Cracking open my notebook, I continue to log whatever's coming to mind.

The fragments of my broken spirit blew away with the night fog

no remnants of them to be found

I'm not who I once was

that boy is long gone.

Seclusion and loneliness are my only companions.

My parents call it isolation

I call it self-preservation.

With more attachment comes more pain.

The balcony doors open. "You want food?" Rae asks.

"No." I keep my focus on my notebook.

She leaves, closing the door again. I let out an aggravated sigh, pissed that we have to pretend to do the fake sibling-bonding shit while I'm here.

It's only for the summer, I remind myself.

I can skate by on a few meaningless conversations with Rae, watch Miles do whatever he does at work, and spend the rest of my time alone.

It's only for the summer.

CHAPTER NINE

Grayson

"THE AIR CONDITIONER IS LEAKING," Miles informs me as we enter Rae's art studio. There's a mural of the sun in the middle of the night sky on the back wall, while the other walls have paintings and mosaics hanging up for sale. "Have you ever fixed one before?"

I shake my head.

He leads us toward the back, his toolbox in hand, and stops to show me the basic wiring. As he rambles on about connectors and circuits, I blankly stare at him, not even pretending to be interested in what he's saying.

"Hand me the multimeter."

I glance in the toolbox and rummage through it. I have a very basic knowledge of handyman tools. I *could* learn it if I wanted to. But I couldn't care less.

After a few seconds of me still not giving him anything, Miles glances over his shoulder. He studies me, and a knowing look grows on his face.

"You don't want to be doing this, do you?" he asks.

"No."

"Then why are you here?"

I shrug. "So my parents don't think I'm directionless."

He goes over to his toolbox and instantly picks out what he needs. "Sometimes being directionless leads you to exactly where you need to be."

"Yeah, well, I don't think Golden Bay is my destination."

He smirks and continues working on the air conditioner. "Neither did your sister, but she's doing pretty well for herself."

"If you say so."

Surveying the room, I scan her latest artwork. Sketches of broken hearts, abstract fluid paintings, sea glass mosaics of the beach. It's pretty impressive. But her talent is nothing new to me.

"Tell you what," Miles says. "I won't torture you by having you come on jobs with me every day if you promise to hang out with Rae while you're here."

"I don't know which sounds worse."

Miles chuckles. "I have four other jobs to do after this. The choice is yours."

I blow out a puff of air, already knowing what I'm going to decide.

I left Miles once he fixed the air conditioner and headed back to Rae's condo.

As soon as I open the door, my stomach drops at the sound of a giggle that I know is not my sister's.

"He did *not* hit on you with that awful line!" Rae says in disbelief, standing in the kitchen.

"It was years ago, but yep, that was his idea of romantic." The sound of Emma's voice comes from the living room.

When I step inside, I spot her sitting on the couch where I'll be sleeping for the next several weeks. My heart springs out of place, dangerously close to bouncing right out of my body.

Rae swings her attention to me. "You guys are done already?"

"Miles only needed me for one job."

"Hey, Grayson," Emma says from across the room, a delicate smile landing on her lips. The sun from the balcony door shines from behind her, lighting her up even more than the first time I saw her.

"Hi." I go to the fridge, turning my back to both of them, and busy myself with getting a drink and something to eat, even though I'm not hungry.

There's more talking between them, but it's clear the energy has shifted, and neither of them are laughing any more.

They speak in hushed tones, and I don't have it in me to turn around and see what they're chattering about because I know it has to do with me.

After what seems like several hours of me occupying myself by making a sandwich, Emma speaks a little bit louder. "All right, I gotta head downstairs and start my shift," she states.

"See you later," Rae replies.

"Bye, Grayson."

Shoving a bite of ham and bread in my mouth, I glance over my shoulder and give Emma a wave before she walks out the door. As she turns away, I'm quick to memorize the way her hips sway in the pastel skirt she has on.

Once she's gone, my heart rate calms down a bit, and I finally spin around.

"Listen, I know you're not interested in her—which is fine," Rae starts. "But at the very least, you could talk to her. Or say words that are more than just one syllable."

"Yeah."

"That's one syllable."

"You said when I'm speaking to Emma. Not you."

"Don't be a smart-ass."

Shrugging, I take another bite of my sandwich before finishing it off.

"I have to go to work, and then I'm going to an NA meeting after. Need anything before I leave?"

"No."

Rae glares at me.

"No, thank you?" I question if that's enough syllables for her liking.

Spinning on her heels, she goes into her room to get ready before she goes out. With the rest of my day free and nothing for me to do, I sit down on the couch and turn the TV on.

I get a whiff of flowers coming from the seat next to me. The lingering scent of Emma makes my veins light up with something unfamiliar. I don't know anything about flowers, so I can't pinpoint what the exact scent is, but all I know is that I want more of it draped across my entire body.

My mind conjures up an image of Emma, laying on this couch in her little skirt and nothing else, and me devouring every part of her, so that by the time I'm done with her, *I'm* the one who smells like flowers.

Nope. Don't go there, Grayson.

Hooking up leads to attachment.

Attachment leads to pain.

It's very simple math, there's an ending to everything, whether it be sudden or a slow fade, there's always going to be an end. Fewer people in my life equals fewer endings I have to endure.

I'm protecting myself. I don't see anything wrong with that. Which is why I push the thought of a half-naked Emma out of my brain.

There's no way I'm going down that road.

Hours tick on, and I've occupied myself by writing, watching TV and scrolling through my phone. Nothing I wouldn't do if I wasn't back at home, but for some reason my parents thought it was imperative to waste my time on Rae's couch rather than in my bed.

Out of pure boredom—and a little bit of curiosity—I do a little digging to see if Emma has an Instagram. After several attempts, I find her.

The strum of my pulse speeds up as I glance through the few pictures she has posted. Even though she's in regular clothes, I can't get it out of my head how graceful and dignified she comes across. Like her soul belongs in a time period where elegance was something highly regarded.

There's something about her energy, even as it

permeates from my phone screen, that tells me she's too kind and gentle for this hardened world.

A light tap on the door brings me back to the present, and I quickly swipe out of Instagram, acting as if I didn't get lost in a couple of photos of a gorgeous redhead.

Forcing myself up off the couch, I go to the door, and when I open it, I spot Emma pinching the bridge of her nose as she walks away from Rae's condo and toward the elevator.

"You all right?" Three syllables. Progress.

She spins around, looking almost surprised to see me. "Is Rae home?"

I shake my head in response.

"Oh, okay." She tiptoes backward, nearing the elevator once more. "No worries, I'll find her later—"

"I'll tell her you stopped by."

Emma pauses as if stunned I spoke an entire sentence. It's not that I can't. It's just that I've gotten comfortable staying silent.

"You don't need to," Emma says. "I just stopped by because of my car. I wasn't sure if I had missed Rae coming up here during my shift because I was so busy dealing with residents' complaints." Her cheeks turn rosy as she continues to talk with her hands. "My shifts usually aren't that busy, just saying hello when people walk in and answering phone calls, but today was heavy on the complaints." She clears her throat. "So, um, yeah, I was just coming up here to see if she happened to be here because my car's not starting."

My lips twitch. "And you were going to ask my sister for help?"

She shrugs and before she carries on with the rest of

her thoughts, I reach for my keys. Stepping into the hallway, I lock Rae's door with the spare key she gave me.

Without a word, both of us head for the elevator. Stepping inside the metal contraption, it suddenly feels extremely small. The scent of flowers seeps into my pores as we stand in silence.

I glance at her as she smooths over her hair. The movement of her arm gives me a clear shot down her shirt.

My mind wanders, getting lost in the fantasy of taking her in this elevator.

The movie reel of me hiking up her skirt and pressing her up against the cold wall plays on a loop until I realize that I should probably be speaking to her instead of staring off into space being a perv.

I go to open up my mouth, but the second I do, the elevator dings, and the door opens.

"My car's this way," Emma states, leading us to the back lot.

I might have limited handyman knowledge, but I know the basics of mechanics. Or at least I hope I have enough background to know what's wrong with her car.

With each step I take, a sense of determination builds within me, not wanting to let Emma down.

Going against everything I've been swearing I wouldn't do. Here I am—*wanting* to help her.

CHAPTER TEN

Emma

THE SUMMER SUN beams down on us as Grayson silently tinkers with my engine and other car parts. Biting on my cuticles, I try not to check him out as he gets his hands greasy.

Who am I kidding—I can't stop looking at this man.

Every part of him makes my heart flip-flop. The veins straining in his forearms, the ends of his dark hair kissing right below his neckline, the way his mysterious eyes laser-focus on what he's doing.

After several minutes, he delicately puts the hood down. "You need a new alternator."

"So...I need to get it towed to a mechanic?"

He nods.

"Great."

I don't know how much an alternator and a tow costs, but I'm sure it's more than what I just made during my shift. My shoulders hike up, annoyed that I'll have to dip into my small savings.

Opening up my phone, I start looking for mechanics nearby. The last thing I want to do is call my dad for help, so I won't. It's not like he could get here anytime soon even if I wanted him to. He's holding a prayer group at his church, so he won't be available for God knows how long.

Frustration builds in my fingers with every tap, but I make an effort to remind myself that people have it worse in the world.

This is just a slight inconvenience. It's no big deal.

Pausing, I close my eyes and take in a deep breath, then blow it out, recalibrating myself.

"I can give you a ride back to your house," Grayson's voice cuts through my thoughts. "They'll probably keep your car overnight since it's already late in the day."

Glancing up at him, my stomach flutters. "Thank you. I'd appreciate that."

Once my car gets towed away, we drive off to my home. Grayson stayed with me the entire time while I waited for the tow truck to come, but he barely made a peep.

Grayson's quietness followed him into his car. The only noise is the low hum of the cool air coming through the vents. I thought the few exchanges we had would break the ice between us, but obviously it didn't.

I guess he's uncomfortable knowing that I like him.

And here I am, looking like a damsel in distress running to him for assistance.

I make a mental note to learn about cars. I'll have some free time now that school's on break for the summer, so I can brush up on how to properly maintain and fix a car.

The ten-minute ride feels like an eternity, as we travel away from the tourist spots and into the secluded area of Golden Bay.

Not a sound is made from the driver's side.

Just an excruciating long stretch of awkward silence.

And now it's been so long that *I'm* uncomfortable talking.

But I need to in order to get home. "Make a right," I say, breaking the quiet.

Grayson follows my direction, turning down the narrow road. As he continues to drive, I notice his eyes widen at the only house in view.

"That's—" he clears his throat. "That's your house?"

"Yep."

Grayson slows down, rolling up to my massive home. It towers over us, held up by the numerous stilts. There's a wraparound porch on both levels of the house, connected by a set of stairs in the front and another set in the back by my bedroom. The lower-level porch has a long staircase going out to the front of the house, hitting the driveway, and a separate staircase in the back leading to the beach.

"Wow," he whispers to himself, looking at the gigantic building I call home.

He has yet to shift into park, and I doubt he's going to, so I take that as my cue to get out. I don't think either of us can take another moment of us sitting together not speaking.

"Thank you for the ride," I say, placing my hand on the door handle. But before leaving, I get a sudden urge to clear the air between us. "And for the record, I'm not one of those girls who will read into this."

Grayson shifts his focus to me, his head tilting to the side, unsure of what I meant.

Feeling slightly embarrassed I need to spell it out for him, my face heats up.

"I know you're not into me, and that you're just giving me a ride as a friend." Nerves jump around my chest. "Maybe not even a friend—acquaintance?" Now that my mouth has started moving, I can't stop it. "Rae's brother—that's what you are. You were being nice to me as Rae's brother, and I will completely respect that boundary." I pause for a hot second to see if he'll respond, but all he does is blink. "Okay, I'm going to go now so I can stop talking."

I open the car door, but before I can even place a foot onto the ground, a sudden flush of warmth hits my body as Grayson places his hand around my wrist. Bolts of electricity run up my arm as if I just got struck by lightning.

My gaze flies to his long fingers wrapping around the smallest part of my arm. My pulse goes wild as I gradually peel my line of sight away from his hand and up to his eyes.

They're exquisite.

The color of them reminds me of how the summer sky looks when a storm is about to roll in. Electrifying, powerful, thrilling.

Everything that I want.

Everything that I *need*.

"Is that what you think?" Grayson asks, interrupting my thoughts about him. "That I don't like you?"

"I...well, yeah."

"Why?"

"Well for starters, you've barely said a word to me this entire car ride." I shut the door, even though I should probably be getting out.

He shakes his head, releasing my wrist. Looking away from me, he says, "I get caught in my head a lot."

There's a mixture of frustration and sadness that paints his face. My heart is doing all sorts of gymnastics, yearning to know more about him. "Oh."

"I became comfortable not speaking much, so sometimes I stay quiet. But you seem like you'd be a really great friend."

Friend. Got it.

"I didn't mean to act like an asshole," he states. "Sorry."

"You don't need to be sorry, Gray."

He snaps his head back in my direction, a glimmer of amusement lighting up his once melancholy features. "Gray?"

"...yeah?"

"No one's ever called me Gray. Just Grayson."

"Sorry—"

"No, I like it, Red." He smirks as his gaze follows the waves of my hair. I'm pretty sure my cheeks are turning the exact same shade.

"Real creative."

"It's about as creative as your nickname for me."

"Your *name* is *Gray*."

"Your *hair* is *red*."

"Well I'm not some feisty firecracker, so don't expect me to fit the redhead stereotype," I tell him, making sure that I lower any fantasy expectations he might have.

"I don't expect you to be anything but yourself, Emma." The sound of Gray's voice becomes low, striking a chord somewhere deep within me.

I don't know how, but just that one sentence made it harder to breathe. The air thickens as I notice the way he studies me, his focus drifting from my eyes to my lips, down the length of my body and then back up again.

My head spins, a burst of excitement flowing through my bloodstream.

This feeling shouldn't be here since he just implied that he only wants to be friends. But the more I try to fight off the rush of adrenaline, the stronger it grows.

"Do you want to hang out?" I gesture at my house. Another fun rush hits me, making me feel lighter.

A boyish smile appears. "Yeah."

He goes to put his car in park, but I stop him. "You can't park here," I say. God forbid Dad gets home early and spots Gray's car outside of the house. "There's a dead end a little further down. It's not really a parking lot, but it can fit a few cars." I point ahead of us, and he begins driving. "Fishermen come down here at all different times throughout the year. I guess the inlet is a good place to cast. I'm just assuming—I don't fish. I never had an interest in fishing, the whole thing seems kind of boring to me. Oh—I didn't mean to offend you if you enjoy fishing. It's just not for me. But if fishing's your thing, that's cool—"

"Emma."

"Yeah?"

"I don't give a fuck about fishing." He parks. "And I'm pretty sure you just set the world record for the amount of times someone said 'fish' in thirty seconds."

I giggle, realizing my nerves have taken over. "Sometimes I forget when to shut up. At least I can make up for all the times you get caught in your head and don't talk."

He smiles at the comment, and I can tell by the little lift in his cheeks that he doesn't do it often.

We get out of the car, and I lead us toward a tall sand dune. Feeling the sand sneak its way between my heel and my shoe, I make the decision to take off my wedges before I land face first on the ground.

In a flamingo-like style, I lift one leg up to unbuckle the strap around my ankle. Becoming wobbly balancing on one leg, I feel Gray's hand on my elbow, steadying me.

He doesn't say anything. He's just there, making sure I don't topple.

With him still holding me, I slip off my other shoe until they're both in my hand.

"Thank you," I say, and he gives me a nod.

We move up the sand dune, and I try to modestly climb over it, making sure to keep my skirt in check.

When we get over the hill, the ocean greets us. It's calm, with barely a wave in sight. I watch as Gray looks out to sea as we move toward my house.

"Do you want anything to eat or drink?" I ask as we get closer.

He shakes his head. "I'm good."

"My dad doesn't hang out by the beach, so I'm the only one who uses this staircase," I start to explain as we travel up to the lower-level porch. Walking along the length of my house, I lead him up the connecting stairs to the second level. "And I'm the only one who comes in this way."

Unlocking the door to our upper mudroom, we enter the space wiping our feet and dusting off the sand on our ankles.

If he doesn't want anything to eat or drink, I might as well take him to the only place in this house that feels like mine.

"Damn," Gray says over my shoulder when we step out into the hallway. He takes in the large estate, crystal chandelier, and pristine furnishings.

I shrug. "It's all right."

"*All right*? Your home looks like it belongs in a movie."

"It doesn't really feel like home to me. Only my bedroom does," I explain as we walk down the lengthy hallway. "It wasn't always my bedroom. It was one of the guest rooms until a couple years ago. But now that it's mine—and being all the way in the corner of the house away from everything else—it feels more like home."

Opening the door, we arrived at my mini-sanctuary.

Gray enters, his feet moving cautiously inside. His eyes wander around my room, soaking everything in. When he hits my rug, he's careful not to let his sandy shoes linger on it for too long.

Out of habit, I shut the door behind him.

I watch as he zeros in on my bookshelf, eyeing all the books. His fingers gingerly hover over the spines, looking at my collection.

"You read," he states.

"Yeah, it's a giant hobby of mine."

He smirks, taking a book off my shelf. "*War and Peace*?"

"I like a lot of genres, some of the classics included."

"Me too," he says, flipping through the pages.

"So, you read as well?"

There's this strange sense of trust I feel being around him. Maybe because he's Rae's brother.

"You have to be a reader in order to be a decent writer."

I let out an excited gasp. "You write?"

He pauses, a perplexed look briefly crosses his face as if he's surprised those words came out of his mouth, but he's quick to shake it off. "I used to. Not anymore." Shutting my book, he puts it back.

There's a twinge in my heart, noting the damaged expression he wears, letting me know it's a sensitive subject.

His gaze drops down to my desk, his eyes falling on my Bible. "Religious?"

Opening my mouth, nothing comes out. Confused by my own lack of response, my head tilts to the side. "It's complicated," I settle on saying.

He nods as he continues to quietly examine all the stories on my shelves.

"If you could live in any book, which book would it be?" I ask with extra pep in my words, hoping to get him talking more.

"That's a tough one."

"Yeah, it's tough for me, too." Chuckling, I move to sit on my bed. Kneeling on my mattress, I continue, "Okay, this is easier; which genre would you like to live in?"

Gray glances away from my bookshelf and over to me. "I..." He pauses, his gaze floating over my body. He lingers a little too long on my skirt, and I feel the warmth of his attention land on my thighs. His Adam's apple bobs as he swallows, forcing himself back to answering my question. "Mystery would be cool. Or some type of action."

"Oh, that's a good one! You could fight off all the bad guys."

He scoffs. "Yeah, something like that." He studies me for a brief moment, then asks, "Which genre would you choose?"

"Romance."

One of his brows arches, intrigued. "Your favorite?"

I nod. "I'm a bit of a hopeless romantic." My insides start to stir as he deliberately ambles over. "What about you?"

Gray gets closer, his voice dropping in pitch when he admits, "I'm just hopeless."

His words are laced with a bitter sadness, but it does nothing to deter me. In fact, it makes me want him even more.

"Which...um, which type of character would you be?" I ask, becoming very aware of his proximity.

"Which type would I be or would I *like* to be?"

"Which type would *you* be?"

He inches closer, no longer hovering at the foot of my bed but drawing nearer so we're face-to-face. His electrifying presence zaps my heart as it erratically strums, beating out of rhythm.

"That's an easy one," he says. I have to tilt my chin up to make eye contact, and as soon as I do, heat washes over me. "I'd be the broken hero."

"Why?" My voice comes out as a whisper.

"I'm a tortured soul. Just an angry person, mad at the world."

His face lingers closer to mine, close enough to kiss.

My chest pounds as I force myself to not glance at his lips that are now perfectly aligned with mine.

"Are you angry now?" I ask, curious because his words don't match the energy that's blossoming between us.

Gracefully, he takes two fingers and brushes a thick strand of hair away from my face, then drags them down my neck, sweeping my hair off my shoulder. Goose bumps scatter across my skin. "This is the first time in a while I haven't felt angry, Red."

Butterflies fill my body. I wet my lips in anticipation, knowing it's coming. It *has* to be coming. Gray's gaze follows the flick of my tongue, and his warm breath hits my face.

My veins buzz with hope as he edges closer.

"Emma?" Dad's voice cuts through the intercom.

Gasping, my stomach plummets to the bottom of the house, and I catapult off the bed, running to the intercom. "Yeah, Dad?" my voice squeaks as my entire body trembles.

Fear creeps up my spine, and I say a silent prayer that he doesn't know Grayson is here.

"Dinner at six thirty," Dad responds.

"Okay, sounds good."

Panic flooding me, I pivot on my heels and barrel toward Grayson. "You have to get out of here," I whisper.

"What?" He takes steps backward, stunned by the sudden shift.

"I'm sorry—he can't know you're here." My clammy palms meet Gray's chest as I push him toward my window. "I can't have you walk out of my room—you have to go out the window—I'm so sorry."

He keeps walking backward. "Are you okay?"

"I'm fine—you need to go—now!"

With that, he's opening up the glass pane and starts stretching his leg out over the opening.

"Wait!" I stop him. "What if he's in his room? He's going to see you!"

"I'll cover for you," Gray assures me.

"How?"

"I'll act like I'm trying to rob the place."

My eyes widen. "You can't do that—you'll end up in jail!"

He shrugs. "Much rather me get in trouble than you."

"No. I can't let you do that." I begin to pace, my hands shaking fast, nausea churning in my belly. "Okay, just give me a second to think about what we should do. Maybe I can—"

"See you later, Red."

Grayson jumps out before I'm able to finish my thought. I rush to watch him, wanting to get his attention but knowing I can't make a sound out the window. He effortlessly hops from the steps to the lower-level porch, then races down the long staircase and onto the beach.

Once I can no longer see him trailing along the sand, relief flows through me, and I take a deep breath, relaxing my shoulders.

That could've gone so badly.

CHAPTER ELEVEN

Emma

LATER IN THE EVENING, after I made Dad dinner and cleaned the kitchen and bathrooms, I'm finally able to unwind. Dad doesn't know Gray was here because he didn't bring it up—and I know for certain he immediately would if he found out. Seeing that he's now sound asleep and didn't mention it before bed, I know I'm in the clear. I'm able to breathe easier knowing we flew under the radar.

However, my head is still spinning from my afternoon with Gray. So, in an effort not to get my thoughts caught up in him, I choose to get sucked into another couple's life.

Freshly showered and in a camisole and rolled-up, striped shorts, I snuggle under my covers, getting lost in another fictional world.

Three wisteria-scented candles flicker on my nightstand, creating more of a relaxing vibe.

My gaze goes back and forth between my Kindle and my bookshelf, where *War and Peace* sits. I fight the urge to pick it up and feel the same places Gray's fingertips touched.

That's creepy, Emma. Not cute.

Snapping out of my Grayson-daze, I go back to my latest romance story. Where I left off has me already clenching my legs, as an ache that can't be soothed builds.

Easton's fingers circle my clit before he enters me. "That's it, baby," he says, gruffly. His movement grows harsh as he pounds into me. "Your pussy belongs to me now."

Heat rises across my chest, and the more I read the tighter I press my legs together. As I continue to read about this unhinged couple wildly making love on a balcony, my body temperature continues to rise.

Just as I'm about to get to the climax of the scene, there's a tap at my window.

Pausing, I glance over at it to make sure I'm not just hearing things.

My curtains are closed over. I can't see anything even if I wanted to, but I don't hear the tap again so I go back to reading.

"Emma?" A whisper comes from the other side of the window. "Emma, let me in." There's another round of tapping.

The second I realize it's Gray, excitement skitters up and down my spine. Rushing over to the window, I open the curtain, and sure enough, he's standing on the other side with a little smirk on his face.

I'm quick to unlock it and help him climb inside.

"What are you doing here?" I ask.

He pushes his dark hair out of his face and rights his footing. "You left this in my car." He holds up a pen.

The cap has teeth marks on it, not to mention it's not a ballpoint.

It's not mine at all.

My eyes narrow, trying to assess him and this situation. "Um. Thanks?" Slowly, I take it from him.

We stand in awkward silence, toe-to-toe, as I hold a pen that's not mine.

"All right, fine," he says, letting out a loud sigh. "I came here to see if you're okay."

"Of course I am, why wouldn't I be?"

"What's up with your dad?" he cuts to the chase.

"Nothing."

"Does he hit you?"

"What!" My eyes nearly burst out of their sockets.

Once again he runs a hand through his hair, only this time he's tugging at the roots. "You didn't answer the question."

"No, he doesn't hit me! Why on earth would you think that?"

"I've never seen someone so spooked by their dad coming home." Gray's gaze presses into mine. "You swear he doesn't hurt you?"

"Look at me, Gray." I step back, outstretching my arms. "Not a mark on my body." I do a little twirl so he can see that there are no bruises or scrapes.

When my eyes land back on him, his eyes aren't locked on mine but rather taking their time to memorize every inch of my skin. My nipples harden under my shirt, which is when I realize I'm not wearing a bra—and so does Gray.

He forces his attention back to my face, killing any lustful flames that flickered across his features.

"Why are you scared of him?" he asks in a soft voice.

"My dad's just strict about me and the opposite sex. I swear, he's not hurting me."

He nods, then after a beat he says, "Sorry for bothering you."

"You didn't. I was just reading." I gesture to my Kindle on my mattress.

"What were you reading?"

"A romance book."

His attention goes from to my bed, then over to my candles, then back to my body. His eyes widen as if a lightbulb just went off. "Shit—sorry if I was interrupting—"

"What?" Then it clicks for me, too. "Oh god, no, that's not—I wasn't..." My cheeks heat up.

Gray lets out a small chuckle. "I'll let you get back to your book." He takes a step back. "I don't want you to freak out about your dad hearing me."

"Oh, I'm not worried about him now, that man can sleep through anything. I went through a phase where I purposefully left the door to the movie theater open as a test to see if he'd wake up. He didn't."

"You have a movie theater?"

"Just a small one," I state. "And besides, my dad's room is downstairs, all the way at the end of the hall."

"What times does he usually go to sleep?"

"Around ten, sometimes earlier."

"So, any time after ten would be a good time to come over?"

I chuckle. "Are you planning on making a habit out of sneaking in through my window?"

"I'm stuck in Golden Bay for the summer. Might as well make it interesting."

My head spins, going from him barely talking, to him wanting to be friends, and now to him standing here being oddly protective over me.

"I'll see you later. Enjoy your book," he says, already placing a foot out of my window.

"Good night, Gray."

"Night, Red."

CHAPTER TWELVE

Grayson

THE SOLES of my shoes crash down in the sand, and I start walking toward my car. Glancing around Emma's house, I scan to see if any lights are on just to make sure her dad isn't awake, and she's not about to get in trouble. I shouldn't have come here to check on her, but I couldn't get the image of her fearful face out of my head. I've never seen someone that scared of their parents before; she was shaking, on the verge of tears, and kinda looked like she was about to puke.

There's a nagging feeling inside me, telling me that there's something off with her dad. He might not hit her, but something is definitely up.

I don't know how or when Emma made it onto my short list of people I feel the need to protect, but I couldn't make it through the night without knowing she'd be safe.

I head to my car, in the spot where Emma showed me to park earlier in the day, and give one last look at her house as I drive past.

I grew up pretty nice, thanks to my parents, but

nothing like living in a mansion on the beach. That's a different kind of money.

Forcing myself to stop thinking about her, I focus on the road.

Stupid of me to go to her house again.

Stupid of me to promise another night of me climbing through her window.

But despite those things—I *refuse* to get attached.

Tingles scatter throughout me, thinking about how sexy she looked in her skimpy pajamas. Blood starts to rush to my cock as I begin to imagine her in her bed, getting herself off to whatever she was reading.

I bite down on my lip, wishing I could watch her touch herself and hear her moans.

Shaking my head before getting too lost in my fantasy, I try to push the thought of Emma out of my mind. But no matter how much I think about other shit, I keep going back to how I felt standing in her room.

It was nice.

No. Better than nice.

It was exciting. The scent of flowers whirling all around me, learning more about her and her hobbies, the fluttering sensation in my stomach, taking the time to look at her, getting to *talk* to someone.

It was fucking amazing. And there's a strong yearning building in my core, wanting to get that feeling any chance I can get.

Don't go there, Grayson.

Increasing the volume of the radio, the guitars blare through my car speakers, and I flip my concentration onto the song in hopes the noise will drown out any thoughts of Emma.

My hands grip the steering wheel as I drive around,

not wanting to go back to Rae's and have her ask me where I went.

So, avoiding my thoughts and my sister, I drive around and end up at a hole-in-the-wall bar called Captain Bill's, several miles away from the boardwalk.

As I park, I check out my surroundings.

There are a few people outside bullshitting while they smoke, none of them paying any attention to me.

The moment I step inside, my nose wrinkles from the scent of stale beer, cigars and dirty fisherman. There are only a handful of people hanging out; some sit at the high-top tables, others play darts off to the side. Four people sit at the bar, getting drunk and chatting with the local bartender.

Sitting down at the bar, I twirl a flimsy coaster between my fingers. It takes several minutes before the bartender notices me, but I don't care because I have nowhere to be and nothing to do.

"What can I get you?" he asks without bothering to check my ID.

"A beer. I'm not picky," I state.

With that, he pops open the top of a glass bottle from a local brewery and hands me my drink. I take a pull, not enjoying the hoppy taste as it hits my tongue.

I've had beer here and there but don't like it enough to consume it regularly.

As fucked up as it might be, I sometimes *wish* it would be shit like this that destroys me. But it won't be. It'll be my own mind, body, and soul that turns me into ashes.

A man from the other side of the bar comes and sits next to me. He's got greasy, thinning hair with bloodshot eyes, nearing the age of fifty.

"How's it goin'?" He slurs his words, then his lips stretch into an off-putting smile.

My spine stiffens as warning bells go off in my head. I give him a tip of my chin, then go back to drinking. I focus my attention on the wooden plank wall ahead of me, hoping he'll get the hint that I'm not one for small talk.

"Hanging out by yourself tonight?" he keeps speaking.

"Trying to."

He signals the bartender for another drink, and in a flash, a glass of beer appears for him, and the bartender goes back to his conversation at the other end.

After an obnoxious sip of his drink, annoyance constricts my muscles. I slam my half-empty bottle down, ending this night early, and take out my wallet to pay for my drink.

"Want me to hook you up with something?" the man asks.

Snapping my head to look at him, I notice his eyes are fixated on the dollar bills in my hand. "What?"

"What are you looking to buy?" His face lights up at the prospect of making money.

Every part of my body tenses.

My annoyance abruptly switches to anger.

There's no fucking way he's trying to sell me drugs right now.

"You didn't say what you were looking for in your text." He continues to blend his words together. He's too far gone to realize that whoever texted him earlier isn't me.

And he's about to wish he never opened his goddamn mouth.

Even though my bones begin to clamor, I play it off cool. "What'd you have on you?" I ask.

"Got some roofies, if you feel like getting lucky tonight." His grin contorts into something wicked.

Sheer hatred instantly blinds me.

Rage fills my bloodstream, white hot anger pumping through my heart.

That choice of drug never even crossed my fucking brain.

A whole new layer of revenge bursts through me as my mind begins to paint a horrible picture of what some people might've gone through. Bile immediately shoots up my esophagus, and it burns as I swallow it down.

I have to force myself to stop creating images in my head because it's quickly turning into people I know, and if I find out anyone in my life has gone through anything like that, I swear I will slit a motherfucker's throat.

Wrath wraps around every fiber in my muscles, tensing my entire body.

I didn't come here with the intention of letting out some of my anger, but clearly fate had other plans.

I keep myself in check, giving the douchebag a smirk, I carefully scope out the room.

Bartender is talking with people at the far end.

Wasted idiots playing darts far away from me.

There are probably still people smoking out front, but I can run fast enough before they catch on.

"How many do you have?" I ask, a fake smile playing on my lips.

"Seven."

"A whole week of fun." I open my wallet once more, and he laughs at my comment, so I force out a chuckle. "How much?" I ask, flashing some of the bills I've stolen from other dealers. His eyes grow wide, taking the bait.

"For that much action, there's gonna be an upcharge." He keeps on rolling with laughter, and he digs into his pocket and takes out a small baggie.

Being the stupid shithead that he is, he places it on the bar top.

"Three hundred," he states.

"Sounds reasonable to me."

As I pretend to go in for the cash, his gaze drops along with my hand. In the split second I have him distracted, my fist punches upward, upper-cutting his chin and instantly breaking the skin of my knuckles. He flies backward, hitting the back of his head on a stool as he crashes down on the sticky floor.

"Hey!" the bartender yells.

Swiping the baggie, I dodge someone swinging at me as I dart out the door.

"Get him!" someone shouts to the smokers as I run past.

My heart races along with my feet as people start to chase after me.

Getting into my car as quickly as possible, I hightail it out of the lot, hearing screaming and cursing in the distance.

Anger continues to course through my veins even though I can no longer see the bar. My molars grind into each other, fucking fuming that humans like this have the privilege of existing when I'm one sister down and one sister almost dead.

It's not fucking fair.

Nothing about this cruel, evil world is fair.

Adrenaline is still pumping through me when I pull up to SeaScape. In the dark of the night, I go toward a nearby trash can placed outside the building. Holding onto the baggie, I press into it, letting my remaining energy crush all the pills into dust.

Dumping the powder into the garbage, I wiggle the can around so there's not a lump sitting on the top. It's now sprinkled between Sam's Dinette to-go cups, candy wrappers, tissues, and a Target bag.

Staring at the trash, I slowly inhale, forcing myself to calm down my breathing.

My hands are balled into fists, wrath still powering through me.

It's not fair that people like him get to freely move about their lives all the while causing innocent people to suffer.

I have enough rage in me to find several more people to kick the shit out of, but instead of seeking someone out, I decide to channel my anger toward something else.

Tonight, I'll write.

CHAPTER THIRTEEN

THE SCENT of acrylic paint fills my nose, waking me up. That, plus the throbbing pain across my knuckles.

"What happened?" Rae's unamused voice floats from somewhere in the living room, but I ignore her. Keeping my eyelids screwed shut, I pull the hood of my sweatshirt up over my head and yank the blankets that are wrapped around my ankles up to my chest, trying to go back to sleep.

"I know you're awake," she states.

Hopefully not for much longer.

I flip over, my face pressed up against the back of the couch as I curl my knees.

There are several minutes of silence, except for every so often when Rae taps her paintbrush against something.

I slowly drift back to sleep, enjoying the nothingness that encompasses me.

No feelings, no thoughts.

Just...nothing.

"Hello?" Rae obnoxiously calls out.

My eyes pop open. "What?" I bite out at the same time I turn to look at her. She's planted on the floor, painting something on a canvas.

"What happened to your hand?"

"Something fell on it."

"Another person's face?"

"Maybe."

Rae tosses her brush to the side. "Grayson, you can't go around fighting people. I'm responsible for you while you're here."

I scoff in disbelief. *Now* she wants to pull some big sister rank, when our entire childhood she couldn't have cared less about me? I sit upright, ready to have it out with her. "You're not responsible for me. I'm a fucking adult," I snap.

"What are Mom and Dad going to say?"

"I don't know—probably something along the lines of 'thank God he only got into a fight and didn't turn out to be a junkie.'"

Rae stares me down, the ice in her eyes piercing through me. "That was low."

"Still probably not as low as you went to score some dope."

Regret.

Instant fucking regret repeatedly stabs my chest for uttering those words.

She rises to her feet, leaving her canvas on the floor. "You barely speak to me for years, and *those* are the words you choose?"

No. Those aren't the words I really wanted to say. But I don't know how to be vulnerable, and neither does she, so that's what flew out of my mouth.

My head hangs in shame. Swallowing down my pride, I try to muster up an apology. I don't have it in me to look at her when I lowly say, "Rae, I'm—"

"Don't." There's a sound of keys jangling. "I deserved it."

No, you didn't.

Say the goddamn words, Grayson.

Be a good fucking person, and let the words move from your brain to your mouth.

For the love of God—say something.

But nothing comes out. The words freeze in my head.

I hate this feeling. I have so much to say but turn mute.

And before I can let out a sound, Rae's out the door.

I slam the heel of my palm against my head, over and over again, wanting to hurt myself into making this stupid thing in my skull work properly.

My eyes prick with a deep pain that I keep hidden, buried underneath the years of rage.

Going into my duffel bag, next to the couch, I dig out my notebook and begin writing. Because if I'm gonna sit here like a bitch and be upset, it might as well amount to something.

The mind is a terrible thing to waste,
but it's also a terrible place to reside if
you've got mine.
Self-loathing unravels through the
trenches of body,

each release intensifying the war within me.

Hating my brain.

Hating living like this.

Hating the war I never asked to fight in.

A sharp pain throbs between my temples. Life would be a lot easier if I was void of all emotions. God, I wish I didn't feel so heavily. It's my greatest curse.

Just once, I'd like to know what life would be like with a little lightness.

Would the dark cruxes of my soul be capable of finding a way out, guided by the flicker of a flame?

What would that light feel like,

taste like,

be like.

If only I could steal it.

Capture it in my hands, letting it burn my skin raw.

If only for a moment of light.

Looking at the page in front of me, I scoff. I probably wouldn't even know how to enjoy the light, no matter how hard I would try to seize it. Add it to the list of shit I suck at—talking, vulnerability, enjoying life even if happiness were to smack me across the face.

Do other people live like this? Do they live a life of loneliness and pain because they don't know how to open up to others? Or am I the only messed-up one?

My mind flashes to the last time I tried opening up.

I'm thirteen, sitting at my kitchen table, mouthing words, trying to practice what they taught me in speech therapy.

Rae comes into the room, getting a glass of water. I notice as she takes pills out of her pocket, swallowing them.

A pit in my stomach grows until I feel sick. A sour taste coating my tongue.

I've been watching my sister slip away. She hasn't been herself in years, but every time I catch her taking those pills I know it's getting worse.

Fear expands in my heart, pumping into my veins as she drifts into her bedroom.

I can't lose my sister. I can't lose anyone ever again.

Hysteria begins to grow.

My hands tremble as I build up the courage to talk to her. It feels like an eternity passes before I finally stand. The sound of my pulse thudding in my ears with each step I take. My eyes burn, tears welling behind them.

Opening up Rae's bedroom door, I find her on Cara's ghostly side of the room, lying on her mattress. Our parents have been begging Rae to change the room around but Rae refuses, wanting to keep Cara's side a memorial.

I stare at Rae. Her eyes glossed over as if someone else took over her body. The shell of her curled up in a ball, emotionless and cold.

My lips move over and over again as I struggle to make a sound. They dry up as I keep opening and shutting them like a fish out of water.

"Rae," I finally whisper, my voice scraping the back of my throat.

She looks at me blankly, but maybe if she knows someone wants her to stop, she will. Maybe if she heard it from me, she'd change. If only I could say the words.

"P-Please." Before I could say anything else, tears

burst out, a deep sob cracking from my chest. She continues to stare at me as if she were a zombie. I hold on to the doorframe, unable to stop crying, trying to catch my breath. "Please." I know I can get more words out, I just need to fight off the tears.

"Please stop."

I slam my notebook shut.

I didn't intend on taking a trip down memory lane, yet here we are.

The hours move on. My thoughts weave in and out of the past and present, only to leave me with a wasted day and a shit ton of unprocessed emotions crushing down my spine.

By the time night falls, Rae still isn't back home. No clue if she went to work or spent the day at NA or went to wherever the hell Miles lives.

Taking my phone out of my pocket to send her a text, I get distracted when I notice it's ten p.m. on the dot.

A spark of life gets awakened inside me, and I know exactly what I'm doing next.

CHAPTER FOURTEEN

SCANNING Emma's home as I walk along the beach, the only light I see is hers. I stealthily climb up her porch, then tiptoe my way up to the second level.

When I get to the glass pane, I tap my knuckles on my non-fucked up hand against it.

"Emma," I whisper. "It's me. Open up."

I don't even know what I'm doing here. But my veins are humming with a new feeling.

The curtains are pushed to the side, and when I glance at Emma in her teeny tiny PJs, my cock immediately twitches in my gym shorts.

With a smile on her face, she unlocks her window and lets me in. The sweet summer smell of her signature floral scent fills my lungs as soon as I step inside. Suddenly, the heaviness of my past gets lifted off my chest.

Nervousness pricks my fingertips, but more than anything, a new feeling of excitement whirls around me.

"Should I start expecting you every night?" Emma playfully places her hands on her hips.

I shrug. "Can't make any promises, but probably most nights." I still don't know why I'm here.

The sense of exhilaration mixed with anxiety has me fidgeting. Pushing my hair out of my face, Emma gasps.

"Oh my gosh! Grayson, what happened to your hand?" She carefully takes it to examine it, and little zaps go off in my heart from how smooth her skin feels against mine.

"Something fell on it." I clear my throat, adding, "When I was working with Miles."

I hate that I just lied to her, but I can't have her knowing that I occasionally get into fights. I have a feeling a gentle soul who has the Bible out on her desk and has yet to drop a curse word wouldn't be keen on me beating the shit out of people.

"It looks awful! We have to take care of it."

"It's fine."

"No. My hand is fine, your hand looks like it started going through a meat grinder."

I snort. "It doesn't look that bad."

"It doesn't look that good."

She breaks contact and starts walking to another part of her room. I watch as she goes into what looks like a bathroom.

"You have your own bathroom?" I ask.

"Yep, just another perk of this room," she says, her voice traveling into her bedroom. As she shuffles through things, I glance around to see if she's having a repeat experience of last night.

Her candles aren't lit, and there's no sign of a book on her bed.

Maybe she was anticipating my visit and didn't want to get caught getting herself off.

Emma comes out of the bathroom, holding several different items.

"You got an entire store back there that I don't know about?" I tease.

She smirks. "I like to have my own supply of the necessities. If they're already in my room, then I don't have to step out and search for them in the house."

"Why don't you like stepping out of your room?" My eyes press into hers, letting her know I'm picking up on something that's being unsaid.

Emma drops the supplies on her bed. "My dad asks a lot of questions and has a lot to say. Sometimes I don't have the energy to entertain a conversation with him. You must know how annoying that can be. You don't like speaking much, right?"

I nod. She's got a point.

"Sit down." She pats her bed, and my stomach goes crazy as if I'm on some epic rollercoaster.

As I sit down on the comfortable memory foam, she stands next to me, checking out my bruised hand. It's scabbed over, and there's probably no point in whatever remedy she's trying to do, but I don't stop her.

With a warm washcloth, she carefully washes my skin. When she traces over my middle finger, I flinch.

Her eyes flash up to look at me. Heat pours throughout my body as I become mesmerized by the amber and gold that swirl around her hazel irises.

"See?" She gestures at my hand. "Not fine."

I smirk, and she continues to wash me up. My pulse speeds up, breathing becoming labored, as I watch her delicately dab rubbing alcohol on the few scrapes I have.

Emma's focused on healing my wounds, and a part of me wishes she could salvage the ones that are living in my soul as well.

Taking an ointment, she places a small amount on the cuts, then places a Band-Aid on top.

"There you go," she says, her voice coming out breathy.

She should let go, but she doesn't.

Desire swims throughout my body as I begin to tangle our fingers together. Taking my sweet time to feel how soft she feels against my damaged hand, I notice her breath stutter.

Sparks go off inside my body, with no sign of stopping.

This must be how addicts feel when they first find the magical drug that gives them that amazing high because I'd do fucking anything to chase this exact feeling for the rest of my life.

My chest rapidly moves up and down as I reach for her other hand to pull her in between my legs. But before I can position her closer, something catches my attention.

"What's this?" I ask, referring to the gold band on her ring finger.

She draws her hand away and starts to hide it by running her fingers through the waves of her red hair. A rosy pink color blossoms under the freckles on her cheeks.

"That's...that's my purity ring."

I nod, not exactly surprised, although I always thought those things were more a myth than a practice.

"How strict are those purity rules when it comes to kissing?" My gaze lands on her mouth.

"*My* rules aren't strict at all," she says with rebellion laced around her words.

"Good."

Smirking, I move in to tenderly cup her cheek. Her lashes flutter as her tongue darts out to wet her lips. My heart hammers away, beating riotously against my ribcage.

In one swift movement, my lips land on hers, and my insides light on fire, ignited by everything that's Emma.

Heat radiates out of me, completely melting against her touch as she weaves her fingertips in the ends of my hair.

She works her tongue into my mouth as my hands explore her curves, needing to feel every part of her.

And in this second, I know I need more of it. The tiny flicker of light I crave is in my very arms, tangled around my tongue.

My entire being becomes hypnotized by her–her taste, the little moans she's letting out, the feel of her hips as I tightly squeeze them.

I position her between my legs, and she pushes into me, blood rushing to my cock.

"Gray," she whispers against my tingling lips. The delicate sound knitting its way into the seams of my broken heart, illuminating the dark and depressing crevices.

My fingers sneak under her shirt, and she allows me to let them dance along her ribcage, just south of where

I'm itching to be. Goose bumps form under the wake of my touch.

She takes her time to explore me. Her hands snake around my neck, down my chest, and stop at my stomach.

Wishing she'd drop her hand, my pulse continues to escalate imagining all the filthy things we could do to each other.

Which is why I begin to slow our kisses down. As much as I want to give in to the thoughts in my head, I don't want to make her uncomfortable.

Our foreheads press together, and we breathe in each other's air.

I run my fingers down her arms and interlace our hands together.

"Wow," Emma sighs out.

"Yeah," I respond in disbelief that one kiss could feel this brain altering.

Gradually peeling back, she looks at me with confusion swirling in her stunning hazel eyes. "How come you never reached out to me back when Rae told you that I had feelings for you?"

"It's not that the feelings aren't mutual," I admit. "It's because I can't give you what you want. And you deserve someone who can." Nervousness twists around my veins at the thought of letting this brief moment be it for us. Selfishly, I want to hold on to her a little bit longer. "I can't promise you anything, Emma. I can't guarantee forever. I can't even be your boyfriend. But I can give you a fun summer."

Fun. I'm not even sure if I know the concept. I don't know if I've ever experienced it aside from right now.

"Contained fun." I glance down at her purity ring,

making it known I won't break her boundary. "What do you say, Red?"

She grins. "I could really go for some fun." Leaning in, she brushes her lips on mine. "And more of this," she says into my mouth.

Bolts of excitement take over my body.

Even though mere hours ago I wrote down how much I suck at enjoying life, maybe this is my opportunity to try—giving me a taste of something I'd never had before.

Something new, carefree, and bright.

Something a lot like light.

CHAPTER FIFTEEN
Emma

"GOOD MORNING, EMMA," the sound of Dad's voice sputters through the intercom.

Startled, I jump right out of bed, rubbing my eyes so they could adjust to being open. It's early, the sun just beginning to rise up over the ocean.

Dashing over to the intercom, I respond, pushing my finger against the button to speak. "Good morning, Dad."

Anxiety begins to spark inside me, wondering if he found out about Gray, and that's why he's waking me before my alarm.

I bring my fingers up to touch my lips, they still tingle from my kisses with Gray.

He didn't stay late, just long enough to steal a few more pecks, but god was it an incredible night.

"Can you come into my office?" Dad asks.

Automatically, my heart sinks into my stomach making me nauseous. I quickly reach for my robe and slippers and hurry down the hallway.

When I get to the far end, I glance at my old, childhood bedroom.

I shudder, knots forming in my gut. There's a swirling sound in my ears from my heart racing, as I hurry on down the stairs and to Dad's office.

Wrapping my arms around my torso to keep myself calm, my spine grows ridged as I stand in the doorway. Dad sits at his ornate wooden desk, focused on his computer. Behind him is a large shelving unit with books, gifts from his parishioners and a framed picture of Mom.

It's the only one I've ever seen. Every time I spot the picture I feel a connection between us. Perhaps it's because we share the same hair and smile. I've heard very little about her, but was told she was known for being altruistic, and she liked donating to charities.

I doubt Dad has ever donated a cent to anyone in need.

My goal is to follow in Mom's footsteps and end up nothing like how Dad performs in the world.

"Everything okay?" I ask, trying to hide the trembling fear in my vocal cords.

Dad looks up over his glasses at me. He's already in a button-up, working diligently.

"Sorry to wake you so early. I didn't realize the time. I've been doing some budgeting before heading out for house calls. The Gardiners gave us a sizable donation."

The knots in my belly swell up when I hear the name. The Gardiners are Kane's parents. They were the ones who put Kingdom Church into motion, making Dad's head bigger than it ever needed to be.

"It's all right, I was getting up soon anyway." I yawn, ignoring the feeling in my stomach.

"Sit down." Dad gestures to the leather chair opposite from his desk. "I'll be leaving before breakfast and want to discuss something with you." I do as he says, sitting across from him. Letting out a sigh, he takes off his glasses before continuing. "I understand it's been a particularly hot summer so far, but I need you to dress appropriately at Sunday service."

I freeze.

"Excuse me?" I ask, because I'm pretty sure I misheard him.

"Make sure you dress appropriately for my church," Dad's voice flips to an air of annoyance.

Taking a beat to process what he said, I stare at him, confused. "I do."

"No. You don't."

"I *always* dress modestly."

"Then tell me why Mr. Parson was gawking at your lack of fabric across your chest."

My mouth hangs open, revolted that we're even discussing this. It has been a solid year since he's reprimanded me for my attire, and that's only because his hurtful words broke me down to the point where I finally gave in—not that I was wearing anything revealing to begin with.

I flip back to this past Sunday, wondering if I had missed a scandalous reaction from Mr. Parson, but he gave his usual speech to Dad, telling him how wonderful I am but nothing more.

"The straps on your dresses are becoming increasingly thin," Dad continues, "What would your mother think about you going to church dressing like that?"

A shot of guilt hits my chest. I loathe when he uses Mom as leverage. A woman whom I've only had a ghostly relationship with is played like a pawn, getting me to do what he wishes.

Despite the sorrow building behind my eyes, I tilt my chin up. "I believe she'd say the same thing I plan on telling my daughter one day."

"Which is?"

"That a woman is not responsible for a man's action."

"It is if the woman's tempting him, Emma. Only evil comes from temptation." He presses his hands onto his desk. "When women tempt men, they get tricked into behaving sinfully—even the best of men."

His eyes bore into mine, not needing to say another word as his look of disgust pours from out of him and on to me. He glances down at the ring on my finger as a reminder that he's sworn me to modesty.

My body contorts with shame and wrath, wishing the damn circular metal would combust into flames, incinerating this entire house.

A silent scream of rebellion echoes inside of me, yearning to be set free.

Like the good daughter I am, I don't fire back another round of self-defense because it's pointless. I will forever be the one in the wrong.

Still, something in me snaps. Even though I keep my thoughts inside, I'm done playing by his rules.

Standing up, I turn to leave.

"I'm only doing this for your protection, Emma," Dad states before I can make it out the door.

I scoff. "Right." Glancing over my shoulder, I spit out one final thought before exiting, "Thank the Gardiners for their lovely quarterly donation for me."

CHAPTER SIXTEEN

Grayson

SOMETHING SMACKS down on the ground right by my face, waking me up.

"Rise and shine, Grayson, we've got a whole day of work ahead of us." Miles stands above me with his arms crossed.

As my vision comes into focus, I realize the noise I heard was his toolbox crashing down next to the couch.

"I thought we said I'd only work with you on a few jobs," my voice scratches in my throat.

"That's before I found out you were a dick to Rae yesterday."

"So, this is payback?"

"Sure fucking is." He grins. "You got ten minutes before we leave. Get your ass up and ready."

Can't say I blame him. I'd make me do bitch work all day, too.

Sluggishly, I get my day started. I probably would've slept better if I didn't spend the night tossing and turning thinking about a gorgeous girl with amber flames lighting her eyes.

I've never had a real girlfriend.

I had Kelly, a girl at my emotional needs high school. By the time we crossed paths, I was able to speak, but even with her it was far and few between. She never gave me the desperate need to fill the void in my heart like Emma does.

Kissing Kelly was nothing compared to Emma's lips on mine.

Kelly kept wanting to take things to the next level, but I knew with sex came emotions. And the last thing I wanted was to form an attachment, especially with someone I had only basic-level feelings for. My horny teenager-self was livid that I called things off before I could round all the bases.

So yeah, I'm a twenty-one-year-old virgin who has become well acquainted with my right hand and filthy porn. But my fear of loss has always outweighed my desire to get laid.

Attachment equals pain—I will stand by that until my dying day.

At least with Emma there's no chance of a real attachment. We both know we're only doing this for the summer, then I'll be on my way back home.

How much connection can truly be formed in such a short amount of time? Certainly not that deep of a physical one since that ring on her finger sets the limits for us.

We'll just hang out for a little bit, then it'll be over.

No big deal.

No attachment.

Once I was finished doing bitch work for Miles all morning, he suggested we grab lunch at a diner on the boardwalk.

When we enter, bells chime over the door as we make our way into the restaurant with newspaper clippings and vintage signs hanging on the walls. Miles slides into a sea-foam-colored booth as if it's his usual spot.

I sit across from him, drumming my fingers on the table.

"I come here all the time. The owner, Sam, is a good friend of mine," he explains.

I nod, not interested in making small talk.

An older man with gray hair and wrinkles comes over to us. "Hey there, Miles, how are you doing today?"

"I'm great! I've got Rae's brother in town helping me out with some jobs." He gives me a shit-eating grin, knowing that he just made me do stupid crap for the entire morning.

"Rae's brother!" The man lights up. "It's a pleasure to meet you. I'm Sam."

"Grayson."

When there's a beat of silence, Sam chuckles. "I can see you and your sister are both the chatty type."

I stare at him, unamused.

"Well, I'll give you a moment to look over the menu," he says. "Can I get you both some coffee?"

"Sure thing," Miles answers for the both of us. "Thanks, Sam."

Sam trails away, and it's just me and Miles again. "So, I know you're pissed at the world—which, trust me, I get, but maybe you should try making the most of your time while you're here," Miles states

"Meaning...?"

"Meaning, strike up conversations with people." He gestures to Sam. "Learn from people, go have fun and make out with a hot tourist, go for a swim in the ocean, try being nice to your sister." He adds in the final part at the last second, causing me to scoff.

"Yeah. I'll see what I can do."

Once we order our lunch, and it's placed in front of us, Sam hovers over our table, and he and Miles do most of the talking. I zone in and out of their conversation, most of the time thinking about Emma and nothing else.

After eating at the diner, Miles goes to Rae's studio to spend time with her, while I head back to take a much-needed shower.

Entering the lobby, a fluttering stirs in my chest as I spot Emma. She's preoccupied, speaking with another resident, so as I stroll by, I give her a wink.

She gets tongue-tied for a beat, then focuses back on the person in front of her.

On my way to the shower, my thoughts begin to spin into lustful ones, wanting Emma in a way that'll feel so good, yet so dangerous, to my heart.

Twisting the knob for the water, my muscles start to relax as I step into the lukewarm shower. Cleaning off the remainder of the day, my mind teeters on the edge of wanting to take this moment to indulge in my fantasies about Emma.

So, I do.

Wrapping my hand around my hard length, I imagine what it'd feel like to be inside her. To feel the warmth of her pussy as I slide in and out. To hear her moan out my name. To get to kiss every single freckle that graces her exquisite body.

Groaning, my hand moves faster.

My mind flips from position to position, unable to settle on one. I greedily want to take her from every angle.

Screwing my eyelids shut, water drips down my face and onto my body as I continue to envision her riding me. Beautiful and hypnotic as I imagine what she looks like when she comes.

"Emma," I mutter between my lips as tension builds. The speed of my hand increases, knowing I'm getting closer.

My legs tense up.

"Emma," I say again, only this time a bit louder as my head rolls back.

"Are you okay?"

The sound of her nearby voice is like a bomb going off, ripping me out of my fantasy.

Out of pure panic—and stupidity—I swing open the shower curtain open to see if I *actually* heard her voice.

The moment I do, I spot a stunned Emma, face turning a deep shade of scarlet, standing outside the bathroom door—because I apparently fucking forgot to fully close it, too preoccupied by my horny thoughts about her. She glances down at my hand around my cock, and her hands go flying up to shield her eyes.

"Oh my god–I'm so sorry!" She darts down the hall.

"Wait!" My heart pounds as I reach for a towel and quickly wrap it around my waist as I chase after her.

"I came up here to see you on my break," she speed-talks, rambling. "I knocked on the door, but then it pushed open because it wasn't locked, and then I heard my name coming from the bathroom–I heard the shower running but the door was open, and I thought you were hurt or something." She finally pauses, turning around to look at me, as I drip water all over the floor. Her eyes flash down to where I'm fisting my towel, then back up. "I'm sorry."

"It's okay."

"I didn't mean to intrude–"

"Emma, I swear it's fine," I try to assure her.

She continues to stare at me, not retreating or moving to leave.

Instead, the longer she studies me, a look of curiosity and enticement crosses her features.

There's a shift in the energy. She's no longer needing to run away from me, but rather, she takes a step closer.

"You, um..." She loops a strand of hair around her ear. "You were thinking about me? Or another Emma–because if it's Emma Watson or Emma Stone, I totally get it. They're gorgeous."

I smirk. "You're the only Emma I was picturing."

She takes a beat, the air around us thickening as she swallows. After hesitating for several seconds, her full lips part to ask me, "What were you picturing?"

My gaze rakes along the length of her body, thinking of all the places I'd love to kiss and mark up.

"An image that a girl with a purity ring shouldn't think of."

One of her eyebrows arches, as if she's just been offered a dare.

With an air of confidence, she defiantly twists her ring off and moves to place it on the kitchen island. The sound of the metal dropping onto the granite echoes throughout the room.

It then becomes silent. Except for the beating in my chest.

"Don't do that," I rasp.

"Don't assume I haven't pictured those exact thoughts running through your head."

She steps in, the warmth of her body sparking a flame in mine. My head dizzies, surprised by her sudden reaction. My Adam's apple bobs as the scent of flowers invades my space.

The amber flecks in her eyes morph into lustful flames as she brushes her fingertips over my bruised knuckles holding my towel in place. My cock pushes up against the plush material, aching for relief.

"Did you finish?" Emma whispers.

"No."

She places her hand next to mine, at the point where the ends of the towel meet. All of my brain cells evaporate when she says, "I want to help you finish."

My body buzzes with anticipation as I let her undo my towel and watch it fall to the floor, puddling at my feet.

Her small hand wraps around my length, and heat instantly coils around every single one of my muscles.

I nearly fucking faint when I watch her drop to her knees.

She looks up at me through her thick lashes and smirks before sticking out her tongue and swiping over the precum that's dripping out of me. I shudder, the sensation almost too good to bear as she does it again.

And a third time.

She's fucking *teasing* me. And it's the hottest thing I've ever experienced.

Automatically, I groan as she begins to take me into her mouth. One of my hands holds her hair back, while my other is pressed up against the wall, steadying myself.

She licks and sucks, and when she goes to cup my balls, I almost lose it.

My legs stiffen and sparks of heat go off in my core.

"Fuck," I mutter curse words as I try with all my might to fight off my orgasm.

Emma picks up her pace, and my hand in her hair grasps her wavy strands tighter. Droplets of water roll down my stomach and land on her mouth and fingers. My muscles begin to contract as I continue to be enamored by her, watching her take as much as she can between her lips as she kneels in her summer dress in the middle of the hallway.

She glances up, piercing me with a burning desire in her eyes.

And then she allows me to take control, using my fist in her hair to set the pace. With each sharp movement I make, she moans around my cock, sending me into a frenzy.

She full on fucks me with her mouth.

I begin to moan along with her, hypnotized by the sight in front of me and the sensations running through me.

Emma holds onto my thighs, pushing me even deeper into her mouth until I hit the back of her throat. She sucks me harder, and I'm gone.

An explosion of pleasure bursts out of my veins cascading down my body. Warm cum shoots into her mouth before I can pull out. She holds me tighter, almost forcing me to stay put—to empty myself into her.

My muscles go rigid as I moan.

Sweat and remaining shower water continue to slide off of me and onto her.

She keeps sucking, even though I've finished, and my body shakes, my eyes screwed shut as I bask in the euphoria.

As I feel Emma gradually pull away, I focus back on her. She rises, running her fingers through her hair.

Both of us catch our breath, staring at one another.

My heart skips a beat, high off of Emma. Her swollen lips, her wrinkled dress, her rosy cheeks.

"What was that?"—the stupidest fucking thing to ever come out of my mouth.

She pants, running her tongue over her bottom lip. "Just having a little fun." The corners of her lips mischievously tip upward.

Without a second thought, I pull her in for a kiss, my hand hugging the back of her neck. Her small fingers brush over my jaw, while I stand here bare-ass naked, full on melting into this woman.

Warmth spreads across my body once more, but before I can get too tangled up in the moment, Emma steps back.

"I have to go back to work." She lets out a small giggle, walking over to the kitchen island.

As I watch her slip her purity ring back on, a

mixture of guilt and satisfaction curls around my bones. Both of which warn me that I'm getting too close to her.

But then as she floats away, giving a little wave before shutting the door, my heart lurches forward wanting to take possession of her. Hold her, kiss her and make her body mine, while she does the same to me.

A loud sigh falls from my lips, deflating me.

Shit.

I'm so fucked.

CHAPTER SEVENTEEN
Emma

MY CANDLES ARE LIT, the scent of wisteria enchanting my bedroom. I've made sure to wear one of my nightgowns instead of my other pajamas as I wait for Gray.

I surprised the both of us this afternoon and don't regret it for a second.

Deep inside my chest, something new was unleashed.

The first choice I've made for my body—and it feels *incredible* to take a leap and follow my desires.

It might've been out of character for me, but that's exactly what I've been my whole life—a character. A person who has been manipulated by guilt and fear, obeying Dad's orders. I act, speak, and dress the way he wants me to. The mold of a perfect daughter. A character in someone else's story.

I've never truly been myself—I don't even know who that person is.

But I know I want to find out who I am.

I want to push my limits, experience new things. Be freaking brave for once.

My heart pounds in anticipation as I check the clock for what seems like the hundredth time. It's nearing eleven, but my hopes are still high that I'll hear the light knock on my window.

As I wait for the sound, I run a brush through my hair, making sure it looks nice.

Time keeps ticking, and my excitement starts to dwindle bit by bit. I rearrange my bookshelves, make my bed for the second time, refold my clothes, and still no Grayson.

I even popped my head out the window to see if he's roaming on the beach, hesitating to climb up the porch—but still nothing.

The corners of my mouth tilt downward into a frown as my body slumps. Crawling into bed, I shift under my comforter hoping I can force myself to fall asleep instead of staying up thinking of him.

Just as my head hits the pillow, my phone vibrates.

984-555-7713
I don't think I should come over tonight

Me
Gray?

984-555-7713
How many other guys do you have sneaking into your room at night?

Me
It's a long list

Sensing my frown flipping upside down, I save his number into my phone. It's about time I got it.

Me
Why aren't you coming over?

Gray
I'm not sure if I should

Me
Because...

There's a slight pause, then he texts consecutively.

Gray
Today was amazing

Gray
Beyond amazing.

Gray
But I don't want to be the reason you compromise anything.

Glancing to my left hand, I roll my eyes at the ring that might as well be a ball and chain at this point.

Me
I'm just wearing the ring to appease my dad. I don't hold the same beliefs as him. I wouldn't be compromising anything.

Another pause. Then finally—

Gray
You swear?

Me
Yes.

Three dots pop up on the screen as he types, deletes, then retypes.

Gray
Get changed, I'll be there in ten mins

Me
Changed?

Gray
I'm not sneaking in tonight. You're sneaking out.

Exhilaration bursts through my veins. In a flash, I'm out of my bed, searching through my closet for something to wear.

My heart wildly bangs in my chest as I slip into one of my summer dresses. Stepping into my sandals, I can't help but smile in sheer excitement.

I have no clue what we're doing or where we're going—but I don't care.

For the first time ever, freedom awaits me right outside my bedroom window.

Before I know it, there's a tap against the glass. Dashing across my room, I yank the curtains open. Gray is on the other side, his face lit up with a similar sense of liberation.

Pushing my window open, he holds out his hand for me to take. "You ready?" he asks.

"I hope so." My trembling hands grip onto him as I swing my legs over, standing on the porch.

The night sky greets me, and the humidity instantly clings to me like another layer of skin.

A mixture of nervousness and joy swirl around my insides as we carefully tiptoe down toward the beach.

Once we hit the sand, Grayson takes my hand in his once more, the both of us checking out the rest of my house to see if any other lights are on as we scurry past.

Our pace picks up with each step, my cheeks rising so much they hurt. His hold on me tightens as we move quicker, jogging toward his car.

A round of giggles escapes me, the both of us darting to the car and jumping inside.

Within seconds, we're driving off until I can no longer see my house behind us.

The car windows are fully open, the sticky summer air forcefully flowing through my hair as Gray's speed picks up.

"Where are we going?" I ask, a permanent smile on my face.

"No fucking idea." He chuckles, and so do I. "Where do you want to go?"

"Anywhere! I don't care!"

The streetlights briefly flash over his face, lighting him up then putting him back in darkness. "Where do you normally go when you sneak out?" he asks.

"I've never snuck out before."

"Why not? You said your dad sleeps like a rock."

"Guess I never had someone worth breaking the rules for."

Gray glances over at me with a glimmer of pride. "What other rules do you feel like breaking tonight, Red?"

"We'll see where the night takes us."

I turn my attention back to the road as he reaches across to thread his fingers through mine. Our clasped hands rest on my half-exposed thigh, the heat of his body burning straight through me.

The air continues to whip through my locks as the laws I live by at home temporarily lift. A feeling of escapism pulsates through me as we continue to drive with no destination in mind.

"Oh! Let's go there!" I point to the lit-up fast-food sign that's drawing closer.

"You want McDonald's?"

"Yes! Greasy, salty food is the perfect almost-midnight snack!"

He grins, pulling into the drive-thru. The car slows down, and both of us order an unhealthy amount of food and gigantic sodas to top it off.

When we finally get our bag, my hand dives in to grab a bunch of french fries. Grayson laughs as he parks under a lamppost in the empty lot.

We settle into the moment as the calmness of the night relaxes us.

"So, what did you used to do when you snuck out?" I ask, noshing on my food while he does the same.

"I didn't," he replies.

"No one worth breaking the rules for?"

"No one worth enjoying life for."

His fingers freeze, hovering over his drink, and I watch him instantly get lost in his head. A display of grief and regret washes over him. He doesn't speak, but I know there are thoughts barreling through him. I witness them appear on his face, although I don't know everything he's thinking.

"Tell me what words are coming to your head," I say.

Gray snaps his focus back into the present. "What?"

"You told me you get caught in your head a lot. Maybe it'll help if you let out some of your thoughts." I shift closer to him, and he swallows. "You don't need to tell me everything that you're thinking, maybe just let out a few words."

My attention goes straight to his lips as they part. A buzzing sensation zips down my spine, but I make sure to focus on him as he says, "I never had the chance to be young."

His shoulders dropped as if admitting that sentence offered him immense relief.

"Me neither," I divulge. "I was always envious watching other kids my age going out and partying."

He nods.

"I've always been an outsider, looking in." My voice gets quieter as I say the words more to myself than to him.

"Yeah," he breaks the beat of silence. "Me too."

My focus goes back to him, only knowing bits and pieces of his story, but knowing we still feel similarly.

"Tell me something, Red," he rasps. "What do you keep hidden behind that smile you wear for everyone?"

My features draw in. "I'm not sure I know what you mean."

He nods. "Okay."

Our gaze locks, and slowly, piece by piece, I feel like I'm being stripped bare. "I like finding joy in the little things," I tell him, letting him know that being here with him is genuine happiness. I'm not faking my smiles.

Neither of us got to experience a carefree childhood, so I'll take advantage of the feeling any chance I get. Especially with him.

"I know you're not in Golden Bay for long," I say, the reality stings when I acknowledge it. "But do you want to be young with me for the short time you're here?"

Even though it's dimly lit, I can see the softness in his eyes. His chest rises and falls at a faster pace, and I sense that he's struggling to give in to my offer.

"I think I want that more than anything," the pitch in his voice deepening as he confesses his thoughts.

Butterflies invade my stomach, instantly lightening my mood back up.

With the sense of adventure sweeping over me, I get a spark of inspiration. Cranking up the radio to whatever song is playing, I shout over it. "Let's go!" I unbuckle my seat belt.

"Go where?"

"We're being young and stupid!" I call out over my shoulder as I hop out of the car.

Gray is quick to follow my lead, unsure of what we're doing, but up for whatever I conjured up in my head.

An upbeat alternative song loudly flows through the speakers, polluting the quiet environment. Rounding the car, I reach for his hand and twirl around him, jumping around to the music.

He chuckles but continues to let me sway around him until he begins to loosen up.

His arms wrap around my waist. Both of our

laughter builds as we dance to a random song in a McDonald's parking lot under a streetlight, not caring if anyone sees.

An air of light-heartedness wraps around our spirit, letting the world revolve around us in this moment as if we were in a movie.

Gray spins me around, and I unravel then coil back up into his chest feeling his heart pound beneath his shirt.

Breaking contact for a slight second, he leaps up onto the hood of his car and extends his hand to me.

"We might mess up your car," I say, even though I'm placing my palm in his.

"Get up here," he replies, hoisting me up.

A little squeal escapes me as I'm placed on top of his car. We continue mindlessly dancing without a care in the world.

Freedom flowing through us.

Hearts opening up to each other and this moment.

Suddenly, an annoying squawk of a seagull interrupts our locked gazes as it circles overhead.

"Hang on." Gray jumps down and reaches into his car window. Holding a wrinkled fast-food bag, he climbs back up. Taking my hand once more, he rushes us up the windshield, our shoes squeaking against the glass as we make our way to the roof of the car.

"This would be a cool view if we had anything nice to look at," I say, chuckling at the lackluster surroundings.

Gray sits down, his feet dangling over the edge of the passenger side, and I cozy up next to him.

"My parents used to let us do this when we were kids," he explains, grabbing a few fries out of the bag.

"Before everything went to shit," he adds. "I guess this was their way of occupying us when we were bored."

With that, he launches the fries into the lot, feeding the ravenous bird. It swoops down, grabbing the food and already pleading for more.

"All of you?" I ask, wanting to know if his sisters would join him. Although, I'm not sure if he's aware I know about Cara.

He grabs another handful, passing some to me, and I toss a few with him.

"Yeah. It was nothing special, just a weird memory that stuck with me."

We keep throwing the fries as the music plays, not a worry surrounding us as we get caught in the magic of summer nights.

More seagulls flock around us, fighting over crumbs. We scramble to throw them more, and suddenly the group of birds triple in size. They hover over us, forcing gusts of air from their frantically flapping wings as they screech, getting even closer.

"Oh shit!" Gray says as we duck down, laughing. "I must've forgotten how out of hand this gets." He jumps down onto the pavement, scaring off a few.

Without a second thought, he reaches up tightly clutching my hips as he moves me down to join him. He opens my car door, and I plop myself back in the seat so we can escape the birds.

Once he rounds the car and gets in, we're on the road again.

Hand in hand.

Wind in our hair.

Grins on our faces.

"Any preference on where we go next?" he asks

over the music. "I promise I won't fuck it up by almost getting us killed by angry seagulls."

"Nope, no preference." As long as this joy follows us the rest of the night, I don't care where we go. "Take me anywhere. Take me to all the fast-food parking lots to dance in!"

He chuckles, then brings my hand up to his lips, placing a tender kiss on my knuckles.

So small, so minor—yet my body is acting like he just claimed me in the back seat of his car the way it's shooting off sparks.

We keep driving with no concept of time or space. Just careless adventure.

Gray makes a few turns, leading us to a boat yard with dozens of various-sized boats docked, floating in the water.

"What are we doing?" I ask as he turns his car off.

He shrugs. "Going for a walk by the docks."

Open for whatever, we step out of his car, linking back up as we stroll along the edge of the water. The familiar stench of low tide drifts under my nose, but it doesn't bother me.

It's peaceful here, not another person in sight.

"My dad had a charter boat for a few years," I inform him.

"Not anymore?"

I shake my head. "He would always complain about how it was a money pit, so he sold it."

"What about your mom? You haven't mentioned her."

"Oh, she passed from cancer when I was a baby."

Gray glances over at me, not saying a word but emanating his empathy through his stormy eyes.

"It's okay, I'm used to it. I don't know what it's like to have a mom in my life." My thoughts begin to jumble, and my mouth moves quickly. "Although, there were plenty of times I *wished* I had one. I think things would've played out a lot differently, if I did—or who knows, maybe everything would stay the same."

"What type of things?"

My mind flashes to the past, and a gross, repulsive sensation crawls all over my skin.

Our gazes connect, and for a split second, I have the urge to spill my guts all over the wooden planks. But I curb the temptation, continuing to keep my secrets locked up.

"Just like, everyday stuff." I'm quick to think on my feet. "You know, periods, how to do my eyeliner, going shopping together."

He slowly nods as if he doesn't completely believe me.

I clear my throat. "But either my dad helped me, or I figured it out on my own, so I'm all good!"

As if he can sense that I'm not interested in discussing the topic anymore, he's swift to change the energy.

"Let's go over here." He leads us to a large, two-decker boat. We walk down the creaky, narrow dock, and I clutch onto his arm as we wobble back and forth. My fingers wrap around his muscular biceps as I struggle to keep a straight line.

We travel along the length of the boat until we're near the end. Once we stop, we become sturdier, and I loosen my grip on him.

"What are we doing?" I ask in a whisper, even though no one's around.

Without answering, he tosses one leg over to stand on the boat then extends his hand to me.

"Grayson! We can't steal a boat!"

He laughs. "We're not committing grand theft boating. We're just gonna hang out."

Once again, I place my hand in his. "Great, so we'll just get in trouble for trespassing instead."

He carefully guides me onto the boat. It rocks back and forth, and my body crashes into his as his arms link around my waist.

"Blow job, sneaking out, and trespassing in under twenty-four hours. How does it feel to be a rule-breaker, Emma?"

Glancing up at him, I arch into his body, his hands leisurely run up and down my back. "It's better than I ever imagined."

He grins slightly before giving me a small peck. There's a cool sensation on my lips the second he pulls back, and I'm instantly left craving for more.

But the whole night is ahead of us.

We begin to explore the sizable boat. Grayson hops up onto the second level and sits in front of the nautical-looking steering wheel, while I kneel on the plastic cushion at the bow, overlooking the ocean. There are several boaters out in the distance, their small lights popping up in various places throughout the landscape.

"Having fun?" Gray asks.

Checking over my shoulder, I start laughing when I notice him putting on a captain's hat. "More than fun. I feel like I'm allowed to finally enjoy myself." I shift back to look at the open sea, closing my eyes as the salt air swirls around me. "To live is the rarest thing in the world. Most people exist, that is all."

"Oscar Wilde."

My attention snaps back to him, surprised. "You know that quote?"

"I told you I read."

"True. But I didn't think that meant essays from dead playwrights."

He shrugs. "I get bored a lot and read different genres. Although don't quiz me on any of your romance novels."

"Guess you'll have to expand your repertoire a little more."

He spins the wooden wheel, making a clamoring sound. "Why's romance your favorite genre?"

"It's sort of like a form of safety," I answer, watching his brows wrinkle in confusion.

"Safety?" His head tilts to the side, interested in knowing more.

For whatever reason, my heart starts to pump faster, and I can sense my cheeks becoming flushed.

I play with the ends of my hair as I explain. "In romance novels, the characters can go through all these horrible, real-life events, but no matter what, they'll always pull through. There's always going to be a happily ever after."

He nods. "That's how you know it's fiction."

"You don't want a happily ever after?"

"I would love a happily ever after. I just don't believe in them. Even with love—the only thing that's going to be left in the end is pain."

Curiosity rushes to my tongue, wanting to ask him more, but I already know I won't get any more words on the topic as I watch him stare off, a solemn look pulling at his features as he becomes lost in thought.

Rising, I tiptoe my way up to where he is, the boat slightly rocking as I drift toward him.

Grayson's attention returns to me as soon as I'm by his side. He adjusts himself in the captain's seat and gestures for me to sit on his lap.

Draping my legs over his, my stomach flutters as my body temperature rises.

"Not all stories have to end in pain, you know," I whisper.

"I'll pretend to believe that. Only for the summer."

Only for the summer. The clock is ticking, and I want to make the most of every second I get with him.

"Do they ever go on adventures in your romance novels?" he asks.

"Sometimes."

Taking off the captain's hat, he places it on me. "Well, you're in charge now. Where are we headed, Red?"

"Hmm..." I shift with my back leaning against him, looking out at the ocean. "We could travel down the shoreline." I put my hand on the wheel, rotating it, acting as if I'm sailing us away.

As I'm imagining all the places we could travel and all the things we could see, Gray's mouth hovers over my shoulder, the warmth of his breath hitting my skin.

"I like that idea." He presses a tender kiss onto my skin.

I swallow, my nerve endings buzzing with desire.

"Or we could travel up north. All the way up to Canada."

"Nah. I like the idea of going south." His fingertips play with the hem of my dress.

He kisses me once more, only this time it's closer to

my neck. Goose bumps erupt under the gentle caress of his lips.

His fingers dip under my dress, still tracing along the length of my thigh as if he's testing the waters.

My breath stutters when he inches closer to my panties.

Heat spirals around my core. My body melts against his, yearning to give into his every touch.

He continues to place open-mouth kisses along my shoulder.

Letting out a sigh as I tilt my head back, the strap of my dress slips down my arm, exposing more of myself to him.

The small flick of his tongue makes me want to rip my clothes off so he can use his mouth in other places along my body.

Gray's other hand wraps around my torso, securely locking me in place as I rest against his pounding chest.

With each shaky breath we take, Gray moves his hand closer and closer to where we both want it to be. Glancing down, his wrist has completely disappeared underneath the cotton fabric.

Taking his long finger, he runs it along the lace of my panties, hitting my clit.

My body instantly trembles in his hold the moment he touches me. Adding more pressure, I shudder once more, only this time my stomach contorts into anxious knots.

I want this—I want *him* so badly.

But even though it feels divine, there's a horrible pit in my gut.

I didn't have a problem giving, but clearly I have an issue receiving.

Bringing up my past, even though it was only for a split second, has somehow weaved its way into my night, cloaking me with shame. I'm usually skillful at compartmentalizing, but I can't right now.

My muscles stiffen.

I hold my breath.

A film of disgust shrouds my body.

"Which boat is it?" a man's voice comes out of nowhere.

The both of us automatically freeze. My feelings of shameful lust switch to hysteria as I spring off of Gray.

"Lady of the Sea," another man calls out.

Grayson takes my hand, yanking me down so that we're hiding behind the captain's chair.

We watch as two men hold their phones out to use their flashlights, reading the names of the boats they pass.

Bile shoots to my throat. "Grayson—I can't get in trouble!" I whisper-yell. "My dad's going to kill me. Oh my god—Gray—"

"I'd never let anything bad happen to you," he says, his tone resonating with fierce protectiveness.

Once again, a fire ignites inside me.

My head spins with a flood of polarizing emotions—but my hands still shake in fear as nausea takes hold of me.

"Did you happen to catch the name of this boat?" Gray asks me while he keeps eyeing the two men.

"No."

He pauses, studying our surroundings. The sound of my frantic breathing is the only thing I can hear as I watch him figure out how to get us out of this.

Squeezing my hand, Gray says, "We're going to

very carefully walk down to the lower level. When we get to the dock, walk slowly so it doesn't wobble too much. Try not to make a sound. Then we're going to get the fuck out of here."

I nod even though I only caught half of what he said. The thumping sound of my pulse makes it difficult to hear anything else.

With a gentle tug, he guides us down the steps, onto the first level of the boat.

"I think it's down a little further," one of the men says.

Cautiously, Grayson gets us both off the boat and onto the dock. It rocks, and I begin to lose my footing. My grip on his hand tightens as we tiptoe away. The sound of the wooden planks creak underneath our feet, my muscles seizing up with fear every time it makes the sound.

One loud squeak has the men sharply turning in our direction, their flashlights shining on us.

"Let's go!" Grayson yanks me forward, the dock violently swaying, making me trip over my feet.

Clutching onto me to help keep me stable, Grayson rushes us toward the parking lot.

The men shout something out to us, but the sudden thrill of almost getting in trouble has me laughing over their yells.

Air tugs at something on top of my head, and my hand flies up to catch it as we run toward Grayson's car. The moment my palm is placed on top of my head, I realize it's the captain's hat.

"I took the hat!" My eyes widen with guilt as I look up at Gray, his dark hair pushing against the wind as we barrel forward.

"Add stealing to your list." He shoots me a wink, and I swear if I wasn't in the middle of running, I'd melt into a puddle.

Our hands break contact as we reach his car, and we both get in.

In between our laughter, we catch our breath as we peel out of the parking lot and get back on the road.

"I can't believe I stole his hat—I should return it," I say, my voice working against the air that's blowing in from the windows.

"Don't. Keep it as a memento. That way you'll always remember tonight."

I don't think I'll ever forget tonight.

My very first taste of being young and free.

Taking the hat off, I study it in the dark light of the night. It's white with a navy-blue brim and golden threading. It'll match nothing in my room, and I obviously can't wear it.

But I think I'll do what Gray suggests and keep it.

That way, I can always have this feeling within reach.

CHAPTER EIGHTEEN

Grayson

I PUSH up Emma's unlocked bedroom window so she can crawl inside. I'm not far behind, entering her room so I can give her a good night kiss.

Her grin is wide as she immediately goes to her bookshelf, rearranging the space so she can place the captain's hat on it.

"You free tomorrow?" I ask, not wanting to end our night together, but knowing it's coming to a close. I'd love to spend the night, but judging by the way her body became rigid the second I began touching her, I'm assuming she's the farthest thing from being okay with us sharing the same bed tonight.

"I work tomorrow, but I can see you after my shift." Emma takes a beat to admire the hat on her shelf, then spins to face me, her fiery-colored hair windblown for our car ride. "Same for Saturday, but I'll be free on Sunday after I attend my dad's church service. He stays there until after dinner, so I have the entire day to myself."

I cock my head to the side. "Your dad's a preacher?"

"He's a pastor."

"Huh." My gaze dips down to the Bible on her desk.

"At his own church."

"...his own church?"

"Yeah, he's pretty much the holiest man to ever touch the earth aside from Christ himself—or at least that's what people in Bristol think since they built him Kingdom Church."

My brows shoot up. "They *built* it for him."

"Yep. A place for them to worship God *and* my father."

"Sounds a little cult-y."

She chuckles, waving off my comment. "It's not, I swear. People find their faith in different places. Those people happen to find it in what my dad says."

Taking a stride closer, I interlace our fingers. "But you don't," I state as fact because I have a strong suspicion I'm correct.

"No," she whispers, the word barely leaving her lips.

"Where do you find your faith?"

Her amber eyes bounce back and forth to look at mine, as if she's unsure where to focus. Unsure if she wants to speak a piece of her truth.

"In summer nights," she admits.

The corners of my mouth lift upward. If the rest of the summer feels anything like it did today, I, too, might find a string of belief to hold on to.

Bending down, I place my lips on hers, and she immediately wraps her arms around me. Sparks fly around us as we give in to each other's embrace. The gentle kiss melting the armor that's been shielding my heart.

As she carefully pulls back, I have to stop myself from lurching forward.

"Tonight was the best night of my life, Gray," she says, her breath hitting my lips once more.

"Mine, too, Red."

After another kiss good night, we break contact, and I begin trailing toward her window. "See you tomorrow," I say, hanging one foot over the ledge. "Night, Red."

"Good night, Gray."

And just like that, I'm out of her room, off the porch, and strolling across the sand. There's a lightness in my chest, an unknown part of me being set free.

The feeling follows me all the way back to Rae's condo. When I walk inside, the lights are off, and her door is closed, signaling that she's asleep for the night.

I crash down on her couch, my eyes getting heavy, but my mind begins to whirl, and I know I won't be able to sleep until I let my thoughts out.

Digging through my duffel, somewhere under my pile of clothes, I reach for my notebook and pen.

Stolen kisses and property
all for a moment of freedom,
a night not to lament in my self-imposed torment.
I found the flame,
touched it,

tasted it.

And now I yearn for more of it.

I'd welcome burn if she's the one holding the match.

CHAPTER NINETEEN

Emma

THE BOARDWALK IS PACKED with tourists as I stroll down the pathway to get to Rae's art studio after my work shift. I told her I'd stop by to say hello and see if she needs help with anything, seeing that she recently opened up the business.

"Wow!" I beam, walking into her space, mesmerized by all the art that's hanging up.

"Hey," Rae says, glancing over her shoulder as she works on the finishing touches of a mural. I thought she was already done with it, but I guess not.

"This is breathtaking," I state, admiring the bright golden sun painted onto the wall.

"Thanks." She dips her brush into white paint, adding more stars.

After staring at her work, I blink myself back into reality. "Do you want me to help with anything?"

"I don't think so, but you're more than welcome to hang out and chill."

"I'll do some sweeping so at least I can say I helped

with something." With that, I grab her broom and start moving along the floor as we catch each other up.

"You know how Miles and I did an interview for a documentary a few weeks ago?" she asks.

I nod, knowing exactly what she's talking about. It was right before Gray arrived, she and Miles were asked to be a part of a documentary by a streaming service called IntraFilms. She hasn't brought it up at all, so I'm surprised she's freely giving up any information now.

"How did that go?"

Rae left out a defeated sigh, her shoulders dropping. "It was excruciating to do, but felt important, like I was honoring Cara."

A prickle forms at the corner of my eyes as I offer her a soft smile.

My heart endlessly goes out to them, including Gray. I can only assume that pieces of the traumatic event collapsed onto Grayson's shoulders as well.

"Anyway," Rae continues, "The guy, Jake, from IntraFilms said he should be finished editing it soon and wants to let me view it early. He said he can set it up here if I want, and it got me thinking...now hear me out because this might sound weird–"

"I'm all ears."

"I was thinking about inviting the people in Golden Bay who've helped me, to come watch it–all the people at the diner, my friends from NA, and you–obviously. Plus, my family and Miles, of course. It sounds strange out loud, I don't know..."

"No, it makes sense. You want your community to help you through this next part of your journey."

"Yeah." Rae puts her brush down and takes a step

back to examine her latest addition. "All types of art can help people heal."

I go to stand next to her as she gets quiet. My gaze becomes fixated on her mural, the whips of yellow beams radiating into the darkness.

"Can I tell you a secret?" she asks.

"Of course."

"I didn't think I'd love having this art studio as much as I do, and now that it's open, I'm nervous about it being successful. I want to do well, it's another way to honor my sister."

I shift to look at Rae, who's lost staring at the wall. My chest cracks open for her and Grayson. The loss of their sister has weighed so heavily on both of their lives, I wish I could erase that pain from them.

I wish I had the power to erase the pain from everyone's life, including my own.

I can't help but wonder how differently I might've turned out if I didn't go through my own painful history, and I'm sure Rae and Grayson wonder about their own lives, too.

"I'm certain Cara would be proud of you," I say softly.

Rae turns to face me. "Would you come watch the documentary if I decide to have a viewing here?"

"Are you kidding me? Of course, I'll be here!" I don't know when it happened, but Rae and I have soared straight into best friend status.

Smiling, she goes back to her mural, and I go back to sweeping.

The air around us gets lighter as Rae swiftly changes the subject to a *Friends* episode Miles made her watch last night.

We continue to chat about mindless things, and as I hit the back corner, I spot thin, lacy fabric that definitely resembles a thong.

"Um." I chuckle, hesitating to touch it with the broom. "Do you have another secret you want to tell me about?"

Rae spins to see what I'm talking about. "Oh shit." She tugs at her jean shorts to double check that she's not going crazy. "Yep. Totally forgot to put them on after me and Miles fucked."

I burst into laughter. "Oh my god!"

"If you came in here a half hour earlier, you would've been mortified. Or maybe turned on. I don't know what gets you going," she says, completely serious.

"Mortified."

She shrugs and goes over to her discarded thong, picking it up, and shoving it in her back pocket as if it's nothing.

My head spins with the desire to be that free with my sexuality.

She's shared stories about her and Miles's wild rendezvous, and it sounds like something out of one of my smutty novels.

How I yearn to have that boldness, if even for a couple of weeks.

"This might be a weird question." I clear my throat, and Rae pauses, her focus entirely on me. "And if it's too personal, you can tell me to shut up."

"You don't need to preface with that but continue."

"How do you know what you like?" I ask, and her brows pinch together, unsure of what I mean. "When it comes to sex," I add.

"Oh," she says, unfazed. "I guess it's a combo of knowing what I *don't* like and experimenting with other things to see what turns me on." Her features suddenly brighten. "Are you seeing someone?"

"I..." Did Grayson not tell her he's been coming to my house at night? That was what I meant by the weird question. Does he not want her to know? "I'm not sure," I state because that's the truth.

"Take it from me, if you're unsure, *and* you're not coming—he's not worth it."

"We haven't gotten to that point yet. I just...might want to." I mutter the end of the sentence and glance at the broom in my hand, feeling awkward that her brother is the person of interest.

"Honestly, Miles is the only guy I've had mind-blowing sex with, and it's only because he makes me feel safe enough to. It's all about trust. If you're wanting to explore new shit, you and the person need to be open, and you have to trust that they'll stop if you're not liking it."

My stomach rolls at her last statement, but I ignore the simmering nausea and try to focus on Grayson.

"Makes sense," I say, already knowing that in the little time I've spent with him, I do trust Gray enough for that.

"So, you gonna tell me about the guy?"

I smile. "Once I figure things out with him, I will."

"I'll be waiting."

Dad's fast asleep as I sit in my room, anxiously picking at my cuticles, waiting for Gray. My talk with Rae was the confirmation I needed to move things forward with him. I might've panicked for a hot second last night on the boat, but I'm more clear-headed tonight.

And making sure my thoughts stay in the present.

The scent of flowers sweeps over my room, coming from my candles. I only have my lamps on, so the entire room is dimly lit.

Adjusting the dipping neckline of my nightgown, the color catches my attention. It's the same navy-blue from the captain's hat. *Guess I was wrong about it not matching anything*.

Gliding over to my bookshelf, I carefully take the hat and place it on my head. I spin to face my full-length mirror, noting how I look.

The hat presses down the waves in my hair, draping the strands over my chest. There's a slit in the night-gown on my left thigh. I'm sure if I added a pair of pumps this outfit would sell as a Halloween costume.

Confidence runs through my bloodstream the longer I stare at myself. Because, yeah, I look sexy. And I like it.

My heart pounds faster with a mixture of excitement and nervousness.

I force myself to remain focused on the here and now. Focused on Grayson. If I let my thoughts wander to the past, even if for a split second, all of this will be ruined.

Compartmentalize.

I can't let the lingering shadows in my mind wreck this for me.

I refuse to have another thing stolen from me.

Exhaling a shaky breath, I try to allow my new self-assurance to wash over me. Praying it fully encompasses me, taking over all of my insecurities.

Through the reflection in the mirror, I spot Gray pushing up my unlocked window. His shoes carefully hit down on my floor, and when he's finally fully inside, he stills.

Completely transfixed on me.

Our eyes lock through the mirror.

"Whoa."

CHAPTER TWENTY

HOLY FUCK.

My mouth waters the longer I stare at Emma, my gaze raking over her from head to toe. Blood rushes to my cock, heat swirling around my insides as Emma stands in front of me in a silk nightgown, thin enough to instantly rip off.

She spins around to face me, taking off the captain's hat. "The blues matched, so I tried it on," she explains.

"I like it," I rasp, inching closer.

"Yeah?"

I nod. "I never envisioned a sexy captain before, but it's working for me."

She chuckles, her cheeks getting rosy as they lift. I intertwine our fingers together, feeling her soft skin under my calloused thumb as it grazes over her. My pulse strums loudly, and I do everything I can to tame my accelerated breathing before bending down to place my lips on hers.

Her kiss is slow and tender as her plush lips caress

mine. Light soars through me the more I feel the graze of her tongue.

Judging by her outfit and the scene she's got set up in her room, I can tell what her plans are. And it takes every ounce of self-control not to selfishly indulge in the curves of her body, which is why I slightly pull away.

Her lips are already swollen, similar to how they looked when she went down on me. "Want to break another rule with me?" she asks, her words laced with sultriness.

You have no fucking idea how badly I want to break the rules with you.

"Depends what it is," I respond even though I know exactly which rule, and I know I'll have to turn her down. Because at the end of the day, she's not ready. It was evident last night on the boat. I don't expect that to suddenly change.

"Sleepover." She tugs me toward her bed, and my feet follow.

"What about your dad?"

"I figured that part out—you can sneak out when we're downstairs eating breakfast, there's no way he'll see you crawling out the back window when the kitchen is in the front of the house."

Her eyes twinkle with excitement, but apprehension pinches my insides.

"Maybe another night," I suggest.

She pauses, dropping my hand as her body deflates in disappointment. "Why not now?"

"I don't want you to think I'm expecting anything from you."

I inadvertently glance at her ring, and her features automatically twist with anger.

"Seriously!?" she snaps. "I already told you I'm only wearing this stupid thing to shut my dad up!" She rips off the ring and slams it down on her mattress. "Am I going to have to do this every time just to prove to you that I can be sexual?"

"You don't have to prove anything to me, Emma."

"Clearly I do. Why don't you believe me?"

Her gaze presses into mine expecting a response.

I become silent, arranging the thoughts in my head before they come out of my mouth, as she anxiously waits for me to answer her question.

My chest tightens, struggling to figure out if this is even worth talking about.

But she stands in front of me, so beautiful, so perfect, that I force the words out.

"You froze, Emma."

"What?"

"When I was touching you on the boat." I carefully step closer. "You froze–which is fine. You're not ready, and that's okay."

"No. I am ready." She glances up at me with her hazel eyes, the swirling amber flecks appearing conflicted. "I just..."

There's a long pause, as if *she's* the one who has issues getting her thoughts out.

"...froze?" I help her finish the sentence.

"Yeah."

"That's okay. I'm not expecting anything here, Emma. Maybe you thought I was after what happened when you caught me in the shower–"

"No, I wanted to do that, too." There's pressure in her words, vehemently assuring me.

"We can take things slow." Threading my hand

through her hair, I draw her in, preparing myself to share a glint of vulnerability. "I'm a virgin, too."

Her eyes widen, then slowly morph into amber pools as they become glassy. Her mouth parts, and she barely manages to say, "I'm not a virgin."

I pause, my mind doing a backpedal, growing confused. "Oh. I'm sorry, I assumed..." I glance over to the gold band lying on her bed.

A look of devastation, as if she's about to crack open with sorrow any second, paints across her features.

"No, seriously, Emma, it's fine. I don't care about any of that," I try to comfort her in her past decisions so she doesn't feel the need to have some type of religious guilt hanging overhead.

I watch it happen in slow motion as she crumbles. The well-positioned, smiling mask that she wears, slipping off her face, exposing what lies beneath.

"Not by choice."

The sentence is barely audible as it slips from her lips.

All of the air leaves my lungs.

The blood in my veins iced over.

"What?"

I must've misheard her.

I *had* to have misheard her because I refuse to believe that someone as gentle and innocent had those cards dealt to her.

The tears brim, shading over the swirl of hazel and amber. My stomach plummets, knowing what I heard was in fact true.

"Emma." A broken whisper escapes me as I clutch her into my chest.

The roaring beating of my heart pounds against her

face, and I hold on to her with all of my might, never wanting to let her slip through my fingers.

My insides shred to pieces as wrath, despair, hopelessness, and unyielding protection tear me to nothing but fragments.

All the emotions are slicing up my organs like they have in the past. Only this time, it's not just for me or my family.

It's for *her*.

A sob wretches from the back of her throat, as if this secret has been gnawing away at her soul. Her body shakes in my arms, and I hold her tighter and tighter, wishing I could absorb all her agony.

"Emma," I repeat, my voice cracking as I force myself to push my own feelings out of the way so I can solely focus on supporting her. "I don't know what to say or do right now to help you," I admit. "Please tell me what I can do. Do you want to talk about it? Because I'm here—I'm fucking here, and I'm not leaving."

She shakes her head, pulling out of my embrace. "No—I want to forget that he exists—I just want to think about you," she says, wiping the tearstains from her face. "I'm sorry I froze."

Dipping down to catch her gaze, I state, "You *never* have to be sorry for that."

Emma chokes back another cry. "You were the only person who has touched me aside from him. I don't even touch myself—I feel revolting, like my body isn't even mine. Every part of my body is just an accessory."

My bones get crushed just from witnessing this sliver of her past.

"I need to forget about him." Her voice grows with

panic. "I don't want to feel like he owns every part of my body—" She reaches for my belt buckle as the speed of her words pick up. "I need to feel you—I need you to make me yours and not his—please, I promise I won't freeze this time."

Her frantic energy has my head spinning.

"Whoa, wait." I try to stop her hands, but they have a mind of their own, fumbling with my zipper.

"You asked me what you could do—this is it, Grayson. I don't want to feel him anymore. I want to feel *you*. Please!"

I firmly hold her hands in place so that she stops moving. We stare at one another, the tip of her nose rosy as tears continue to trickle down her freckled skin.

The utter wreckage that pierces me through my chest as I study her is enough to take me out.

She's broken.

Someone purposely broke her.

Someone stole her light. The blazing fire that I know once lived inside her has been reduced down to a flame.

And I swear with everything in me, that I'll be the one to find all her pieces and put them back together.

I'll be the one who turns her flicker into a raging inferno.

"I'll make you mine, Red," I promise. "But I want you to be yours first."

Her brows dip in confusion. She remains silent as she stares at me, completely destroyed. Her breathing is labored as she struggles to contain her cries. Streaks of mascara mark her porcelain skin.

I have no words to give her. Not even ones that stay

stuck in my brain. Nothing is coming to me except for the desire to hold her.

So, I do.

CHAPTER TWENTY-ONE

Emma

EVERYTHING IS RUINED.

That wasn't supposed to happen.

I tried so hard to keep my head from sinking back into the past.

But the moment Gray assumed I was a virgin, I instantly went back there.

Back to when I was younger.

Feeling him on top of me.

His hands.

His mouth.

Over and over again.

Claiming my body.

Stealing it from me.

I never told anyone else what happened aside from Dad.

I'm waiting for Grayson to be repulsed by me and leave, but he doesn't.

Maybe if he knew the whole story he would, but I don't have it in me to let those words out tonight.

Admitting to him that I was raped was enough to completely drain me, leaving me void.

Grayson continues to embrace me. We somehow end up lying down on my bed, as I curl up into him. His fingertips run down the length of my arm then back up, soothing me.

"I'm sorry," I whisper into his chest, and his hand stills. Before he can respond, I continue speaking. "I didn't mean for that to spill out. We're supposed to be having fun—I *want* to have fun."

"There will be plenty of time for fun." Gray brings his thumb up to capture a stray tear on my cheek. "You never need to apologize for showing me the real you. I'll take all the darkness along with the light."

I gaze up at his hypnotic eyes, silently thanking him. I think he gets it because his face softens as he starts to lazily run his fingers over my skin once more.

We stay wrapped in each other's arms for a while, peacefully sinking into the embrace with every breath we take. This is new for both of us, yet here we are fusing together as if we've done this millions of times before.

"Does this mean you're sleeping over?" I break the quiet with my hopeful question.

"I'm gonna be real honest with you, Emma," he says. "The thought of not having you in my arms to protect is making me nauseous. So yeah, I'm staying over."

I softly chuckle. "I don't need a protector, Grayson."

"What do you need?"

"Just you. As you are."

He's silent, the blues in his irises spinning as I watch him get tangled in his thoughts.

There's a fight going on inside him as he struggles not to shut down, but when I push up slightly to meet his gaze, his attention falls back on me. He relaxes, nodding. Agreeing to be himself—unguarded and authentic.

I smile in acknowledgment, agreeing to do the same.

"I'm still going to want to protect you, though," he adds.

"I appreciate that. But I've been fighting my own battles for a very long time. My strength and resiliency are one of the few things I pride myself in."

"I envy your resiliency, Emma."

"What?" My face scrunches up, baffled. "You *are* resilient, Grayson."

"No." He shakes his head. "Not even close to the way you are."

"What do you mean?"

He twirls a strand of my hair around his index finger. "I don't know any of your story, but the fact that you can still carry on with kindness in your heart and have faith and are compassionate to others—those are things I never had."

"You're capable of all those things, Gray."

"You see the bad in the world and want to make it a better place. I see the bad in the world and want people to pay for what they've done."

A sucker punch packed with his pain hits me square in the gut. I can feel it—all his sorrow and anger.

"I still see you as kind," I whisper. "And gentle." I give him a peck on the lips. "And caring."

I know he sees himself as nothing more than a broken, angry man—he told me so the first time he was in my room. But I know the other side of him because it's here with me now.

It's amazing how brightly a person can shine when put in a different environment.

He pulls me in closer so I can nuzzle into his chest once more. His strong arms wrap around my torso, and he kisses the top of my head.

"I'm gonna hold you like this all night long," he states.

"Please do." I clutch onto his shirt, a smile gracing my lips as my eyes flutter closed. "This is totally worth breaking the rules for."

CHAPTER TWENTY-TWO

Grayson

EMMA'S PLAN WORKED, and I made it out of her house without being noticed.

My head and my heart are still reeling from last night, only today I'm letting my anger take the forefront. With each step I take, the more I become consumed with fury.

But before I can even begin to process anything, I'm pushing open the door to Rae's condo. She's walking out of her bedroom rubbing her fist over one eye when she spots me.

Her brows crinkle together, noting my same clothes from yesterday. "Are you just getting in?"

I shrug, not wanting to talk about it. I know if I say I was with Emma, there'll be questions, and I don't want to answer them. What Emma shared with me was extremely personal. I kept my emotions in check last night, but right now I have enough wrath beating out of my heart to hunt down her rapist and make him pay.

So instead of opening up to Rae, I head for my duffel bag.

"Were you out all fucking night?" Rae trails behind me.

I stay quiet as my mind goes into a whirlwind. Needing to settle all the thoughts in my head, I search for my notebook.

"Where did you go?"

Continuing to riffle through my shit, I don't respond.

"Answer me, dickhead!"

My head snaps in her direction. "Yes, I was out all night. No, I'm not telling you where I was." I go back to my bag and snatch my notebook up. "My answer was more than one syllable, happy?"

"No, I'm not happy. You should've fucking told me you were leaving—what if something happened to you?"

I scoff. "Shit has already happened. To all of us."

My comment confuses her enough to get her to shut up, and I go out to the balcony so I can be alone.

The beach is already packed. Staring at the endless flood of strangers, my blood begins to boil, wondering if any of them is the one who assaulted Emma.

Emma is just another person whose life got destroyed by an everyday villain. A monster hiding in plain sight.

Evil lives among us.
Every street corner,
Every neighborhood,
Standing in broad daylight.
It's a smile from a passerby,
a familiar backpack in a school hallway,

a cheers from a beer bottle.

It steals the same air we breathe under the guise of familiarity.

My pen taps against the paper.

The center of my chest snaps open as a new prose pops into my head.

I wish none of us had the markings of trauma scarred onto our souls.

How differently life could have unfolded if our ankles didn't have chains wrapped around them, linking us to the past.

Every step we've taken a direct result of the damage that haunts us.

But knowing that Emma has her own shackles, burdening her radiant spirit, makes me want to combat every affliction in order to set her free.

With bloodied knuckles and wounded muscles, I'd sacrifice the last little bit of fight I have in me just to know her mind doesn't dwell in misery.

I might not be able to save Emma from her past, but I can protect her in the present. That's really all I can ever offer anyone.

Not sweet words, kind gestures, lavish things.

But I *can* promise that I will do everything I can to protect someone I care about. Whether that be kicking a person's ass in a dark parking lot as retribution for the pain they caused or holding someone close as they share their dark secrets.

That's all I can give Emma during my time here.

The reminder of my short stint in Golden Bay strangely has my heart twisting. I'm quick to shake it off, ignoring the sensation.

There's something about her that makes me gravitate toward her energy. A deep, magnetic pull that I'm not sure I want to sever.

I know she's eager to break as many rules as possible, but I have a feeling I already broke the only one I have for myself.

I'm attached.

Which means I know that at some point, there's going to be pain.

I ended up napping on Rae's couch because I didn't get much sleep at Emma's last night. My phone vibrates against my thigh, just as I'm opening up my eyes.

> **Red**
> I'm going to grab a smoothie on my break, want to join?

Do I want to walk around in the sweltering heat, pushing through the crowd of tourists on the boardwalk? Absolutely not.

Am I going to anyway? Obviously.

In the blink of an eye, I'm outside melting under the sun, strolling alongside Emma. Her hair is in a high ponytail, the wavy ends brushing the nape of her neck and even more freckles on her skin seem to have popped up.

When I'm with her, I'm different. I feel lighter despite the weight of the world. I enjoy her company and *want* to talk to her. I don't know if I can articulate every thought that comes into my head or every emotion that crashes over me, but the point is that I try.

I try for her.

"So, about last night." She casually brings up the topic from yesterday as if she were telling me her favorite type of smoothie. Mango pineapple, by the way. "I don't feel comfortable sharing the details yet."

"You don't have to tell me anything, Emma," I assure her.

"I tried telling someone once, and it didn't go well." She lets out a halfhearted chuckle.

"Who?"

"My dad. I also went to a counselor at my college, but I never got the words out. She somehow surmised why I was there, and my time with her became more of a seminar about assault and how to cope. She gave me books to read and different guided journals to write in, which sounds silly, but it helped."

"It's not silly at all. If it helped you, then it's meaningful."

She nods. "I like educating myself as much as possible. Gives me a sense of control and acts as a reminder that it wasn't my fault."

I hate that an ounce of her feels like it's her fault.

My mind spirals, wondering who the fuck could've

done this to her. An anchor drops in my gut. It could've been one of those assholes from Captain Bill's. It could've been the dealer. It could've been anyone.

My eyes dart around the sea of strangers.

How many of them have done unthinkable things? How many of them have harmed another, completely altering the course of a person's life?

"But the whole reason I'm bringing it up," Emma interrupts my thoughts. "Is because I don't want it to stop us from doing anything."

"Emma...I don't know if we should—"

"No!" She stops short, and my steps stutter, nearly tripping over a kid eating an ice cream cone. When I turn to face her, her cheeks are flaming, eyes pressing into mine. "He has taken every single part of me—he doesn't get this, too. I want to be free for once! Free of him, free from the thoughts in my head, free in my body. No one gets to make the choice of what I'm ready for—not you or anyone else. Only me."

She stands tall, shoulders rolled back. There's an unshakable confidence in her words, as if she'd been working for years to release them.

The corners of my mouth tug upward at the tiny glimpse of the fire Emma is capable of owning.

"You're right," I reply.

"I know I am." Her chin lifts, but then she adds, "and I'm sorry for snapping at you."

"It didn't bother me one bit."

Her gaze flutters to my lips then back to my face. "You promised me fun while you're here."

"I did."

"I want that—I want wild, untamed fun. I want to

feel young." She pauses as she musters up the courage to say the next sentence. "I don't know if I'll freeze again, but if I do, can you help me work through my thoughts?"

"Of course."

I can't unravel the web in my own mind, but I'll put everything on pause to help her with hers.

"Thank you." A bright smile appears on her face, her energy obviously shifting back to her lighthearted nature, and we continue walking. "But I meant what I said, I'm expecting you to keep your promise of fun. I'm planning on letting loose this summer."

"I think the whole point of letting loose is to not have a plan," I tease.

"Well, then screw the plan!" She freely throws her arms up. "Planless, wild Emma's in town!"

"How wild we talking?"

She twists to look up at me, a mischievous look dancing across her features. "As wild as my brain will let me get."

A spark of an idea flashes, and my insides light up with excitement. I just need to figure out a few details before I can set it in motion.

"How late are you working?" I inquire.

She points to the smoothie place, and we gravitate to the shop while she replies. "Eight, but then I have to go food shopping so I can make my dad breakfast in the morning. He's on his own for dinner tonight."

I open the door for her, the gust of cool air clinging to the beads of sweat on my body. The place is small, with a few high-top tables and not much else.

Emma orders her mango pineapple smoothie while I order mixed berries and make sure to pay for both.

Over the grinding sound of ice and fruit, we continue talking.

"How often does he make you cook for him?" I ask, curious about their whole situation.

"Whenever I'm home."

"Jeez. You should save up to move out, then you can do whatever the fuck you want."

Our drinks get placed on the counter, and we carry them to a high-top table. The delicious taste hits my tongue as Emma speaks.

"That's my whole plan—work while I'm in school, then move out shortly after getting my degree. Of course, it would be nice not to be in debt the second I get my diploma, but what am I gonna do?"

My features twist. I'm well aware of where she lives. Her dad has more money than God. "He made you take out school loans?"

"Oh, I left that part out! Yeah, he cut me off the day I turned eighteen. I have a place to live, and I get to eat the food that I cook, but everything else is on my own. So, thanks for the smoothie," she says, lifting up her drink. "The five dollars I saved will either go toward future rent or my loan next year." She giggles at her own joke, but I'm not laughing.

Unable to comprehend why Mr. Has-his-own-church-and-lives-in-a-mansion-on-the-beach would completely cut off his daughter.

"Why?" I ask.

She rolls her eyes. "He got pissed that I wanted to go to college and not work for his church." She takes a sip of her drink. "It was for the best, though. It made me more self-sufficient and independent. And I really do enjoy working at SeaScape, plus it led me to you."

Emma smiles with a twinkle in her eyes. I grin back, although there's an unsettling feeling in my gut. I've never met her dad, but I don't have to in order to know that I already hate him.

"Anyway," she continues. "My dad will be asleep by ten, so you can come over then."

My brain goes back to the idea I had earlier. "I'll see what I can do." I give her a wink, and a blush creeps onto her skin.

She takes another sip to cool down.

If she follows through with the plan in my head, she'll need a lot more than a smoothie to calm her down for the night.

CHAPTER TWENTY-THREE

Emma

ENTERING my room after food shopping and fixing myself dinner, I take my phone out of my purse to let Grayson know Dad's asleep. As I wait for a reply, I go to take a nightgown out of my drawer, making sure it's a different color from the one Gray saw me in last night. Skimming my fingers over cream-colored silk, I start to take it out when something on my desk catches my eye.

It's a small, brown gift bag.

Hurrying over to my desk, I'm quick to realize there's a little handwritten note attached.

> *I told you I'll make you mine, but I want you to be yours first.*
>
> *Enjoy your first taste of wild fun, Red*
>
> *-Gray*

Dipping my hand into the bag, I pull out a plain black box. Opening it up, my eyes widen when I see a hot-pink U-shaped vibrator.

"Oh my god," I say to myself, reaching for my phone.

Me
you broke into my house!

Gray
I did

Gray
but I also left a gift

My lips press together to stifle my grin as my heart thuds against my bones. I stare at the toy as millions of contradicting emotions pump through my bloodstream. The yearning desire to touch myself, fear that I won't be able to because I'll find myself too disgusting, shame from all the years of being taught *not* to indulge in any act of self-love, and, of course, the uncontrollable side of me that is begging to be set free.

All of these thoughts and feelings bounce around in my head back and forth as I endlessly pace my room for at least a half hour.

I meant every word I said to Gray on the boardwalk earlier. I want this. I want him. I want to release all inhibitions and enjoy myself.

I just need a little help crossing the first bridge.

With that, I call Grayson, seeing that he agreed to being with me as I work through my thoughts.

"Hey, Red," Gray answers the phone with a cheeky sound to his voice.

"Grayson! You got me a vibrator!?"

He chuckles. "How do you like it?"

Glancing at the U-shaped toy on my bed, I reply, "I haven't tried it."

"Why not?"

"I..." My words get scrambled as I try to figure out how best to explain this indescribable feeling. "I want to. I'm just so detached from myself that I'm...nervous."

Nervous isn't the word.

I don't think there is a word for the hunger to be touched by myself and someone else, yet feeling so shameful and disgraceful if it were to happen.

So, for now, I'll stick with nervous.

"You've never done this before, right?" Gray asks.

"Never," I softly reply.

"Do you want me to coach you through it?"

"I'd much rather you were here and took care of it for me."

Another chuckle rolls through him. "I promise I'll make that happen. But tonight, it's about you becoming reacquainted with your body." Jitters dance around in my belly as he continues to speak. "I saw you looking at yourself in the mirror last night. You felt hot in your skimpy nightgown, didn't you?"

"A little."

"Good. I want you to feel that confidence every second of every day. Not a single part of you is an accessory, Emma. Your body belongs to you and only you."

My heart rate kicks up as an unsteady breath leaves my lips.

Hearing him say those words are my saving grace. What I've needed to hear for years.

My body is mine.

And Gray is going to help me take it back.

"Okay," I state.

"Stand in front of your mirror," he instructs, the

resonance of his voice deepening, sending lightning bolts down my spine.

Tiptoeing away from my bed, I do as he says, looking at my reflection in my full-length mirror. "I'm here," I inform him.

"Tell me what you're wearing."

"I'm still in the same dress you saw me in earlier."

"Zipper's in the back?"

I shake my head, even though he can't see me. "No, the side."

"I want you to very slowly pull the zipper all the way down." As I start to do as he instructed, he continues, "I want you to feel the cool air as it hits your skin little by little."

Tugging gently, my dress gets set free at a gradual pace. Goose bumps form as I expose myself.

I hit the stopper. "It's unzipped."

"Good," he croons. "Now, step out of it."

At a similar speed, I slide one arm out of the strap, then switch my phone to the other hand to slink my other arm out. When the dress falls to the floor, it puddles around my feet.

"It's off." My breathing becomes labored.

"Tell me what you see.'"

My gaze falls onto my half-naked reflection. "I'm in my bra and panties."

"I'm gonna need you to be a little more descriptive here, Red. You've read plenty of books. Tell me what you look like."

I bite down on my bottom lip to hold back a smirk. Continuing to soak in my appearance, I finally respond. "My bra is tan but it has white lace around the edges. My thong is the same, tan with white lace trim."

"Of course you match," he teases.

"I like to coordinate. Let me know which colors you prefer, and I'll be sure to wear the set," I joke back.

"What's the wildest color you own?"

"Um..." I do a mental recall of all my underwear. "Lavender."

"That's not wild, Emma."

I laugh. "That's all I own!"

"Guess I'll have to go shopping again after tonight's phone call."

Excitement shoots through me. "You're going to buy me lingerie?"

"I'll buy you anything you feel sexy in." Gray clears his throat. "Look at yourself and tell me if you feel sexy right now."

My cheeks get flushed. "I..."

"Look at the way your bra molds to you." Gray walks me through it, and my eyes land where he tells me. "Look at your bare stomach. Your thighs. Turn yourself so you can look at how the tan and white thong shows off your perfect ass."

I do a little twist, acknowledging every part of me.

"You like what you see, Red?"

I nervously swallow. "I'm not supposed to," I admit, my voice softly moving through the phone.

"What do you mean?"

"I was taught not to," I explain, a lump forming in my throat. "I was taught not to be prideful. To walk a path of humility—and that specifically meant with my body. I was taught that—" Tears suddenly surface, but I clamp my eyes shut to hold them in. My chin wobbles as I finish confessing to Grayson, "I was taught that my body was sinful and could lead others to do vile things."

"Emma—"

"I know none of that is right," I say before he can get more out. "I know that's not how I'm supposed to feel or think. And I don't believe any of that, but it's still there, in the back of my head, and sometimes it gets too exhausting to war with those thoughts."

"Well tonight you have me, and I'm fighting those battles with you." There's a slight pause, then he adds, "As long as you still want to."

Nodding, I open my eyes up immediately focusing back on my reflection. "I do. I *really* do."

"Okay. So tell me, Red, despite all those thoughts and whatever bullshit you heard in the past, do you like what you see in the mirror?"

My gaze drifts all over my body, admiring parts of myself that I've never had the chance to. The size of my breasts, the curve of my hips, the slender frame of my calves.

"I do," I state.

"Do you feel sexy?" His tone drops in pitch once again, making heat coil around my veins.

A smile tugs at my lips. "I do."

"As you should." My pulse moves quicker as I listen to him say, "Now take everything off."

Fingers trembling with anticipation, I unclasp my bra letting it fall beside me, then step out of my panties.

"Everything's off," I state, unable to stop looking at myself.

"Grab the vibrator and sit on the floor in front of the mirror."

With my heart racing, I follow his instructions. My phone in one hand and the hot-pink vibrator in the other, I adjust myself, sitting down.

"Get comfortable, you're gonna be there for a little bit," Gray says, adding, "but make sure you can see your whole body."

I scoot back, enough that I see my entire naked self sitting on my rug. "I'm not sure I like this angle." I chuckle.

"I promise you will in a moment. Open your legs, Emma."

The tone of his voice coaxes me to spread myself wide, my gaze traveling down my body to a place that's never felt like mine. My breath falls from my mouth a bit faster, and I think he can tell because he keeps speaking.

"What are you looking at?"

"Me. All of me."

"You see your gorgeous pussy?"

My body automatically heats up as I force myself to push through the clouds of embarrassment and step into a realm of confidence.

"Yeah," I respond, continuing to stare at myself, becoming mesmerized by my own body.

"Your pussy belongs to you, Emma. No one else."

"What if I want it to belong to you, too?"

Any other time in my life I would've felt too ashamed to say that aloud. But not right now. Not while he has me stripped bare so I can learn how to love myself and fight against everything that has told me differently in the past.

I'm exhausted from hiding myself. Exhausted from hiding my body and my desires.

I want to live authentically.

"Fuck," Gray breathes out on the other side of the phone.

"Where are you?" I ask.

"In my car."

"Are you touching yourself?"

"No. I want to focus on you." A swirl of lust cascades down to my core. "Ready for the next step?"

"Yes."

"Don't turn the vibrator on yet but take it and run it along your slit."

My voice trembles a bit when I say, "Okay." Taking the toy, I carefully placed it where he told me to, moving it up and down.

Connecting to myself like this is foreign, but sparks zoom through me as I use the vibrator to touch myself. Years of burning desire to become reunited with myself have been building up to this very moment.

My entire body shudders when I bring the toy up to my clit. "Oh my god," I whisper.

"Tell me what you're doing," Gray rasps.

"I-I'm circling my clit." My eyes roll backward at the sensation.

"Feel good?"

"Feels amazing."

"Are you watching yourself in the mirror?"

I flutter my eyes back open to focus on the image of my body in front of me. "Yes."

"Do you see your pussy getting wet?"

"Yes." The word strains at the back of my throat as I watch myself get off.

"Good. Keep going," he instructs, his tone signaling that he's having difficulty keeping his composure, too. "Look at how beautiful you are when you touch yourself, Emma. Watch your entire body as you keep circling your clit."

My face is rosy, chest rapidly rising and falling, stomach contracting—all as I stare at myself with my hand between my legs. The wavy strands of my hair fall away from me, tickling the space between my shoulder blades as I start to surrender to the sensations.

A moan escapes me.

Gray instantly lets out his own moan at the sound of mine. "How wet are you?"

"Really wet."

"Turn the vibrator on, and slowly slide it inside." His command causes me to hesitate, and he somehow senses it. "Are you okay, Emma?"

"Yeah. I want to, I'm just..."

Nothing else comes out of my mouth because my brain can't think of how to explain it.

"It's only you, Emma. You're in complete control," he reminds me. "Who are you looking at in the mirror?"

"Me."

"Who's been rubbing your clit this whole time?"

"I have."

"Who's making you moan?"

"I am."

"You're safe. You're completely alone with your body."

"Plus you on the phone." I smile.

"Yeah, next time we do this, we're doing a video chat."

"We can right now if you want—"

"No. This is about you being with yourself." His breath stutters. "Now, if you're comfortable, take your time and slide the toy in."

Taking in a long inhale, I work through the growing tension that surrounds my heart. My nervous fingers press the button, an immediate buzzing sound filling the space.

Keeping my attention on my reflection, I watch as I carefully move through my wetness, pushing the wider end of the vibrator inside me.

Instantly gasping, my entire body pulsates as the humming noise gets quieter, but my passion gets wilder.

I hear Grayson's low chuckle from the other end of the phone. "How does it feel, Red?"

"So. Good."

"Play around with it, see what you like."

I do just that, moving it in and out of me at a fast pace, the sound of my arousal evident. Biting down on my lip, I fight back the loud moans that are raring to be set free. My hips naturally move in sync with my hand, helping me get closer to the edge.

"I bet you look so fucking sexy right now on the floor, getting yourself off."

"I do," I say, unashamed because staring at how I look right before I'm about to make myself finish is really hot. And I'm not going to stop myself from admitting that.

"I can hear how wet you are. You like fucking yourself, Emma?"

Heat bursts out of my chest, both radiating up my neck and down to my stomach. "I do," I repeat, only this time it comes out as a moan.

"You like making your pussy feel good?"

"Yes." Placing the narrow end of the U-shaped vibrator onto my clit, I nearly explode out of my skin. "Oh my—Grayson!"

"Fuck." His voice gets caught in his throat as he listens to me.

I watch as my legs shake, my face flushed from the fire that's lit in my core. The vibrator touches my skin at lightning speed, my pulse moving just as fast.

Panting short little cries of pleasure into the phone, Gray groans in response.

Screwing my eyes shut as flames lick my veins, I clamp my mouth shut as I stifle screams of lust. Ecstasy floods every single part of me. A beautiful, euphoric feeling blasting inside of me.

My heart nearly flies out of my ribcage as I twist and tremble, letting flashes of desire shoot through me one last time.

Collapsing on my rug, I struggle to catch my breath as the toy still buzzes in my hand.

After what seems like a long beat of me pulling in and exhaling air, Grayson finally speaks. "How was making yourself come for the first time?" He sounds like he can barely get the question out.

My tongue wets my lips so I can respond. "Incredible."

"The night is young, Red. I'll talk to you tomorrow."

"You don't want a turn?"

"Another time. Like I said, tonight is about you."

I glance at the hot-pink toy between my fingers, grateful that Grayson helped me through my start to reclaiming my body.

This is only the beginning, and I'm nowhere near finished.

CHAPTER TWENTY-FOUR

Emma

Gray
I have something waiting for you when you get home from church

Me
Another gift?

Gray
Yep. Me

I'VE BEEN THINKING about that last text the entirety of Sunday service. Knowing that Grayson's waiting for me at my house makes me more impatient to get home than usual.

As the church choir sings, Dad walks down the aisle with me in tow. We stand at the exit, saying farewell to the parishioners as they slowly file out.

I've made sure to wear my cardigan over my thick-strapped dress so I don't have to hear Dad basically call me a whore once we're back home.

"Thank you again for your generous donation," Dad

says to Mr. and Mrs. Gardiner as they shake his hand. Kane proudly stands next to them with his sheet music tucked under his arm.

"You're very welcome, Pastor," Mr. Gardiner states.

"We're hoping that it's enough to fund the larger estate at this year's retreat," Mrs. Gardiner chimes in while fixing the pearls around her neck.

My eyes go wide. I've completely forgotten about Dad's annual retreat—the *only* church commitment that I don't have to attend because I'm not allowed. He sees it as a punishment, whereas I view it as a week of pure bliss.

Normally, I'd spend the week sunbathing on the beach, but this year, I'll have Grayson to keep me occupied.

Hurriedly shaking their hands, I try to move this process along without any more side talk. Even though I'm sleepy from staying up last night exploring my new toy, I'm too excited to give in to the heaviness behind my eyes knowing that I'll be with Grayson soon.

I never thought I'd be so welcoming to the idea of someone breaking into my house.

"We'll see you next Sunday," Mrs. Gardiner says, giving me a smile.

Kane is next in line to say goodbye to Dad. "Great sermon as always."

"I should say the same to you about your musical talent." Dad chuckles. "Have a blessed week, Kane."

"You as well."

He bypasses me, and we ignore each other like we do every week.

It's strange how I can be numb around him, but when my mind starts to wander, all hell breaks loose.

I'm not letting that happen today, though. So, I force my mind to think about the one person that'll get me through the rest of these handshakes.

Once the last parishioner exits, Dad glances inside the church. "Seems like there's already a small gathering," he says about the cluster of people waiting to speak with him.

"Better get to them soon, they look eager to talk to you," I state.

"I'll be home after dinner. Be good." Intimidation builds behind his eyes as he sears those last two words into my skull.

"I always am, Dad."

Too good.

"See you later, sweetheart." He switches back to the warm personality that everyone knows him as and wraps his arms around me, giving me an embrace.

I hug him back as we do our weekly routine. We know our lines and our stage directions.

And as soon as we break apart, we're on to separate things; he goes to the lingering churchgoers, and I try not to appear to be rushing to my car.

Windows rolled down, freedom flowing through my lungs, I raced home. Through the unpaved roads, onto the highway, and back to my comforting beach town.

The long drive goes by in the blink of an eye, and soon I'm parking in my driveway.

My feet dart up the long staircase that eventually leads to my front door. Sparks go off inside me, knowing that Grayson is on the other side.

My cheeks already hurt from smiling, fantasizing about the endless possibilities of what today might hold for me. But when I swing open my front door, my house is quiet.

Craning my neck in either direction, looking from the foyer to the kitchen and then over to the living room, there's no sign of anyone being in here.

"Gray?" I call out as I scurry up the stairs. When I reach my hallway, I repeat myself, getting closer to my bedroom. "Grayson, are you still here?"

There's no response, and my grin fades in disappointment.

Slowing down my steps, I eventually get to my room.

Padding inside, I wrangle myself free from my cardigan and step out of my wedges. Pivoting to go to my en suite, I nearly have a heart attack when I notice Grayson perched on my bed.

"Jeez!" My hand flies to my chest. "You scared me half to death—why didn't you say anything!"

Amusement dances across his features. "Sorry. I was caught up reading something."

"Is that what you've been doing this whole time?" I ask, taking my rose gold stud earrings out of my ears. "I expected you to be roaming my house."

"I was waiting for you to give me the grand tour. This is the only place I feel somewhat comfortable. I didn't know if your dad had a butler hanging out downstairs."

Chuckling, I put my jewelry away then move over toward him. "We don't have a butler."

"Well, I decided to stay in here anyway." His eyes light up. "My time spent in your room was pretty productive."

"Oh?"

Gray nods, reaching for my hand. His rough thumb grazes over my skin, our eyes locked as he begins to speak. "First, I spent a solid twenty minutes envisioning what you looked like last night." His Adam's apple bobs. "I pictured you on your rug, staring at the mirror as you fucked yourself."

Warmth blossoms across my chest.

"Then, when I went to sit down on your bed, I found something else to occupy my time."

My face twists. "What?"

Grayson stretches across my comforter and holds something up. The moment I realize what it is, I gasp.

"You read my Kindle!?"

A sly smile pulls at his lips. "I read your Kindle."

My jaw hangs open. A combination of embarrassment and enthrallment pumping through my veins.

"Technically, I only read the parts that were annotated." His grin grows wider. "Sweet little Emma has a bit of a kinky side."

"Grayson!" I squeak.

"I see you're really into..." He glances at my Kindle as if he's checking his notes. "Hand necklaces?"

"Oh my god!"

He hops off my bed, standing over me. The heat of his body rippling across mine. "But I also noticed you like the softer moments," he says, his pitch dropping. "Like getting kissed right here." Tenderly sweeping my hair out of the way, he brings his lips to where my neck and shoulder connect, lightly brushing along my skin.

I shudder at the contact, desire fueling me.

I swear my whole body is turning scarlet as it heats up, any shame quickly turning to ashes.

Grayson carefully pulls away to look at me but

brings his fingertips over my collarbones lightly tracing over them as I talk.

"I can't believe you read my romance books."

"I'd be stupid not to—the playbook is right there. A cheat sheet to everything you like."

Butterflies encompass my stomach. "Oh my god. You didn't just read my Kindle—you *studied* it."

The smirk he gives me is so sexy, I'm milliseconds away from claiming it as mine.

"I'm intelligent. I just always lacked the motivation to put effort into anything," he explains as his fingers leisurely dip lower, caressing my neckline. "But this topic? I'll have no problem taking my time to master what my Red wants."

My head dizzies as lust explodes through every particle of my body.

"I don't know if I'll like any of it, or if I just like what's written on the pages," I admit.

"Then, we'll explore."

"We'll explore," I repeat in agreement.

His warm breath skates across my skin as he leans forward, placing another kiss against my neck. Traveling upward, his lips skim over me, and his tongue marks the spot right below my ear.

Clutching onto his shirt, my breathing turns ragged as it gets harder to stand straight.

"We can try whatever you want," Gray whispers. "I'll touch you the way you want to be touched." He kisses me once more. "I'll say all the things you like." Kiss. "And if for whatever reason you don't enjoy it, you tell me immediately, and I'll stop."

With that, he breaks contact, and his focus goes directly to my eyes. I'm unable to look away, the stormy color in his that usually clouds the blue with melancholia, is now brewing with desire and passion.

"Does that work for you?" he asks.

I nod, thankful that he's letting me steer this ship.

"I have no problem doing exactly what you want," he makes clear. "And saying exactly what you want to hear." Liquid fire flows through my veins as he continues. "You want me to tell you how incredible your pussy feels? You want to hear me say how fucking wet and needy you are for me?"

Already sensing a dampness in my panties, I nod. "You really did pay attention to everything I highlighted," I say in a breathy whisper, more to myself than him, still in semi-shock.

"I did. I also noticed that you skipped over every time they said *good girl*."

"Yeah."

"Not into that?"

Shaking my head, my insides tremble with the longing desire to burst free. On the verge of combusting from the combination of years of repression and how sexy Grayson looks standing in front of me—I drop every defense I've ever had and liberate myself.

"I don't want to be anyone's good girl. I'm done being good. I want to be bad."

CHAPTER TWENTY-FIVE

EMMA'S LIPS crash into mine in a hungry frenzy, and I match her every move.

Desperate.

Deprived.

Ravenous.

Her dress bunches in my hands, acting as my only form of self-control, as I grip onto her hips. Our tongues tangle together at the same time our breath mixes. Her lips are soft compared to the force she's kissing me with.

Unsure which one of us is taking the lead, we somehow landed with me sitting on her mattress and her straddling me.

Emma tugs on my hair the same time she grinds against me, rolling over my cock. Groaning into her mouth, my grip on her gets tighter, begging myself to have some willpower.

She keeps doing it, over and over again.

The best form of torture as her breasts get dangerously close to my face.

I kiss along her jaw and neck, and she tips her head back in enjoyment.

"You want to be my bad girl, Red?"

When she rocks her hips again, I press her down further, adding more friction. She lets out a breathy moan when she responds, "Yes."

Her eyes flutter closed as we move her body together, both of us needing to relieve the growing tension. The color under her freckles turns rosy as her lips part, letting out another gentle moan.

Mesmerized by her beauty, my thoughts float away as I become enamored by her sensuality.

It's enough to make me forget every reason behind my one rule I uphold for myself.

Completely wrapped up in all things Emma, I'm anxious to see more of her. Learn her body. Cherish all that she is.

And although my cock is ready to burst through my gym shorts and claim her, I'm overwhelmingly aware that she has a chapter in her story that she doesn't want to talk about, yet it's scribed into her mind. So, I'm taking this as slowly as humanly possible.

Which is exactly what I do as I inch my hand up the back of her dress, aiming for her zipper. Carefully, I give it a tug, watching her reaction to see if she freezes.

A smirk plays on her lips, so I continue pulling on the zipper, letting it leisurely splay open, inch by inch.

Her lashes blink open, and she locks gazes with me. Pausing her movements, she takes a deep breath before sliding her arms out of the straps from her dress, letting the fabric drop, landing at her hips.

My attention drops to her white bra, heat spiraling down my spine and going directly in between my legs.

Inching forward, I bring my mouth to taste her supple skin as my hand trails up her back to unhook the clasp. Without any hesitation on her part, she hurriedly peels off her bra, letting it fall to the floor.

In a lust-hungry daze, I envelop her nipple with my lips, sucking and licking as desire fills me to the brim. Emma sighs in pleasure, arching her back so I can get more of her in my mouth.

With little to no self-restraint left, I flip us around in one swift movement, causing her to gasp in surprise when I quickly get her to land on her mattress.

Hovering over her near-naked body, it's my first time I've seen her like this. I dispose of her dress. My heavy breath shakes as I take my time drinking her in, memorizing every part of her.

Emma's wavy hair is wildly tussled on her pillow as she looks at me with wide eyes, waiting for me to do something.

My fingertips brush over her collarbones, admiring every single freckle that adorns her flesh. Carefully, I dip my head down, bringing my lips to join my hands, attempting to kiss each and every mark.

My cock lies heavy against her, eager for her touch. And as much as I want to devour her, the desire to give her exactly what she wants surpasses any selfish urge.

"You want gentle and delicate—I'll go as slow as you need," my words skate across her soft skin as my lips drag over her. "You want rough and wild—I'll treat you as fucking dirty as you want."

"I want all of it. And everything in between," she whispers as she tugs at my shirt, urging me to take it off.

Breaking apart for mere seconds, I rush to yank my shirt off, my heart pounding with anticipation.

Before I can get back to my original position, Emma reaches out and begins sliding her hands around my chest and torso. Her nails gently graze my skin leaving goose bumps in their wake.

Her touch is electrifying, lighting up every cell in my body.

My gaze floats over her, landing on her white lace panties—which matches her bra—to where her legs are parted as I kneel inside the space between them.

I run my hand over the only fabric that's left on her body, and her breath hitches.

"Did you have fun by yourself last night?"

Emma nods. "But I would've had more fun if you were with me."

Fingertips still dancing around the lace, tracing the intricate design of flowers, I bring my attention back to her face. "Show me what I missed out on. Let me see how gorgeous you look when you fuck yourself."

The amber color in her eyes flares, ignited with lust, as she reaches toward her nightstand. My heart thunderously pounds in my ribcage as I watch her take out the hot-pink vibrator. She untangles herself from me for a brief moment to slowly pull off the scrap of lace. The single barrier that kept me from seeing all of her is now gone.

Heat courses through my veins as Emma settles back into her spot, legs open and wide as they fall on either side of me.

My thirst for her intensifies as my eyes drop down to her glistening pussy on display for me.

"Fuck," I breathe out, unsure if I'll be able to keep my composure while I watch her. My cock already aches, straining against my boxers, and she hasn't even started yet.

"Luckily I put it on the charger last night after I wore it out," Emma states, turning on the toy. A low hum creates a soft noise in her room.

One of my brows quirks. "You wore it out?"

A sexy smile stretches across her face. "Maybe."

"Damn, Red. Who would've thought you'd turn into such a dirty girl overnight?"

"I didn't turn into her overnight." She slides the toy over her slit. "This part of me has always been trapped inside. But you're helping me set her free."

Same, Emma.

I had sworn off any type of connection like this in fear of attachment. But similarly to what she just said, she's helping me set free any apprehension. In fact, she's fully replaced that feeling with a heady yearning to be consumed by all things Emma.

Committed to immersing myself in Emma's wants and needs, not only will I make sure to live up to the annotated parts in her books—I'm going to supersede them.

I know the script. Memorized every blue highlighted line.

Now it's time for me to learn *her*.

Emma pushes the vibrator inside her, letting out a gasp.

Her body moves in sync; hand up against her pussy, hips pushing to meet it, the arch of her back lifting off the mattress.

It's fucking beautiful watching her. Unsure of where to look—or even where to start, my gaze pinballs around every part of her. Her hooded eyes follow me as

I admire her flushed face, then over to her peaked nipples, down to her stomach that draws in tight with every sharp inhale, and finally to where her hand remains at a steady pace as she gets closer to making herself come.

"Goddamn, Emma." I shove my hand into my boxers, gripping on to my length in a desperate attempt to get some sort of relief. "Look at you, fucking yourself for me." She moans louder, and her legs start to squeeze around me. "Such a bad girl."

Emma cries out, the tension in her body intensifying. Her head pushes against her pillow, eyes screwed shut.

I smirk in pride, realizing that she likes to be spurred on. And fuck, do I love being the one to coax her closer to the edge.

My free hand kneads her inner thigh as she begins to shake. Precum drips out of me the longer I focus on the vibrator effortlessly sliding in and out of her wetness.

"I want to touch you so bad," I blurt out, unable to refrain myself.

Emma's lashes flutter open, her gaze first going to my fist in my boxers then up to meet my eyes.

"Take over," she says, pausing her movements.

"You sure it's okay?"

"Yeah. Just keep talking to me." She opens her mouth as if to say more, then decides against it. But I get it.

Keep talking to her in case her mind goes somewhere else.

Now that I know what type of dirty talk she's into, I'll gladly deliver what she wants.

A boost of cockiness ripples through me. Not only am I helping to awaken her, but it's happening for me as well. Together, we *both* get to live out our filthy fantasies. The way she hands her body over to me is something I won't take lightly, and if she's yearning for me to hit all the marks, I'm going to do just fucking that.

In a silent exchange, I take the vibrating toy from her. But before I use it, I place it next to us and decide to let my wandering hands enjoy her.

With our eyes locked, I push one of my fingers into her soaked pussy. Immediately, both of us moan at the feel of each other.

"You're fucking drenched," I say, gently circling my thumb over her clit. Emma's legs automatically go back to trembling. Carefully, I let a second finger enter her, causing her to loudly moan. "You like how my fingers feel inside you, Red?"

Bucking her hips up to meet me, she furiously nods her head in response.

"I'm gonna need you to use your words, pretty girl."

"Grayson," she cries out, the sound going straight to my dick. Heat spirals around my insides as I witness my name fall from her plush lips once more.

Bending down, I draw Emma's nipple into my mouth. My tongue moves with the same rhythm as my thumb, and her sounds get louder. Her chest heaves, body writhing underneath me as her arms wrap around me.

Dragging my mouth up to her neck, I press a kiss right under her ear, and she shivers.

"Tell me how much my bad girl likes being finger fucked by me."

Her back arches off the bed, pressing up against me.

Her sounds are no longer controlled, each moan giving her a sense of liberation.

"You make my pussy feel amazing, Grayson." Her words come out as a whine. Not an ounce of shame for saying her thoughts aloud appears on her, she's fully wrapped up in this moment.

And so am I.

"That's it, Red." I kiss her neck. "It's me making you feel this good." A kiss on her collarbone. "Remember that the next time you fuck yourself." Kiss on her nipple.

Her walls tense up around my fingers as I make my way back to kneeling between her legs.

Bringing the vibrator back to play, I press it up against her clit while curling my two fingers inside her.

Emma screams, her entire being trembling in ecstasy.

My body floods with fiery lust as I make her come.

Her wetness coats me and the toy as she squirms, moaning out my name. Passion scorches my bloodstream as I become transfixed on the epitome of beauty and sexiness that radiates from Emma.

As she comes down from her high, I keep the toy steady, sending shockwaves through her.

"Oh my god." She slaps her hand to her heart, struggling to catch her breath. Her legs jolt every few seconds, still riding out the last of it.

"You did so good, Red," I rasp. The words nearly get caught in my throat, I'm wound so tight, anything might make me combust at this point.

I slowly withdraw the vibrator and my hand, admiring her dripping wet pussy.

Emma pushes up onto her elbows. "That was the

most amazing orgasm," she breathes out, causing me to smirk.

Still focusing on how wet she is, I lick my lips, suddenly famished. Warmth prickles under every inch of my skin, begging me to let her relieve the ache in my boxers. But my tongue craves to know what she tastes like, and my pride yearns to make her come again.

I'm lacking in lots of practice, but I've seen and read enough to know what I'm doing.

My pulse races, no longer wanting but rather, *needing* to have my mouth all over her pussy.

"Come here," Emma says, letting me know it's my turn to get off.

Instead of looking at her, my eyes bounce over to her Kindle that's next to her pillow. Self-assurance washes over me. "No. I feel like reading."

CHAPTER TWENTY-SIX

Emma

"READING?" I ask, still panting. My legs are wide open as he kneels between them, but I feel no need to cover up.

In fact, with the way Gray's looking at me right now, I'd gladly lie like this for the rest of the day.

"Yeah." He reaches across my body, grabbing my Kindle. "Why don't you read to me one of your favorite scenes?"

My stomach flutters. "What?"

"Let's play a little game." Gray turns on my Kindle, scrolling through my library. "I'll do to you whatever it is you're reading, but the second you stop, so do I."

Fireworks go off inside me, shooting down between my thighs. A mischievous expression dances around the hypnotizing color of his eyes in a silent dare.

A dare to be his bad girl.

"I'm game," I state, not willing to let this moment slip away from me. Every single one of my inhibitions no longer exists. Not in this bed with him. "But—" I add a slight condition, watching a smirk play on his lips. "You need to pick the scene."

"Me?"

"If you did a decent job at studying, you should remember some noteworthy parts."

He chuckles. "Emma's a different girl in the bedroom—bad *and* sassy." Scrolling through the books I have downloaded, he's quick to find a steamy scene that's almost entirely highlighted. "Here you go."

He hands it to me, and I do a quick scan of the motorcycle romance he chose. "Bikers turn you on?" I tease.

"No." He hovers over my body. "The hot redhead in the story does." A grin spreads across my face. "Start reading, Red," he commands, making my skin prickle as he dips down to draw my nipple into his mouth.

My words shake with my breath as I begin to speak. "*He lightly flicks his tongue over my nipple, while his traveling hands caress every curve.*" Grayson delicately skates his hand over my frame while his tongue flutters. "*Snaking one hand up my body, he captures my throat, carefully applying pressure on either side.*"

Gray does exactly as I say, his hand wrapping around my neck.

In an instant, my eyes shut close, relishing in my surrender to him. The feel of his calloused palm against my tender skin. Enjoying our give and take of the power play. Feeling unrestrained by allowing him to touch every part of me.

Suddenly, he releases me, and my eyes spring open.

"Keep reading." He smirks.

Nodding, I bring my focus back to my Kindle. Only now, all the sentences are starting to blend together. My eyes jump ahead to a random highlighted part, and I continue.

"*Dragging his mouth down my stomach—*" Gray repeats the action, leaving open-mouth kisses on my abdomen. "*When he hits my hips, he tenderly bites down—*"

I cry out, bucking myself up closer to Grayson. A chuckle rumbles in his chest, and he stops when I do.

"Shit. Okay." I fumble to find the spot where I was just reading, not caring that I swore because I have a feeling curses will be tumbling out of my mouth left and right if Grayson keeps up his teasing. "*He kisses along my thigh, spreading my legs apart, nestling between them—directly in line with my pussy.*" My heart hammers away, my eyes darting between the words on the page and Grayson reenacting them.

"*H-His finger spread me wide, p-putting me on full display.*" I moan, feeling Grayson's fingers open me up for him. I wiggle underneath his touch, pleading for some relief.

"Emma..." he warns.

My chest rapidly rises and falls as I continue, "*He blows cool air from my opening, up to my clit.*"

Instantly, my back flies off the bed.

Forcing myself back to my Kindle so he doesn't stop, "*His tongue darts out, following the same path as the cool air.*" Another moan flies from my mouth. "*L-Lapping up my desire, he envelops my clit with his mouth—*" My legs start to tremble. "*Licking and s-s—*"

I can't keep my eyes open anymore. My pulse races through my bloodstream, heart about to burst out of my chest. The feel of Gray's tongue against my most sensitive part has my entire body shaking as I sync up my movements to his.

This is exactly what I've been wanting. To let every ounce of repression leave my body the moment Gray touches me. To not let the past shame my present. To allow me to explore this side of myself.

"Someone's a little distracted," he says, hovering his mouth over my pussy, his lips glistening from my arousal as he proudly grins.

"Keep going," I pant.

"Keep reading."

A frustrated groan comes from the back of my throat even though I love every moment of this. I wiggle closer to his face and continue, "*Licking and sucking*—" Gray's mouth is back on me, and my hips buck up. "*Teetering me on the edge, v-violently pleasuring me until my insides twist and I-I can no*—" My free hand flies into his dark hair. "*Longer*—" I shudder, twisting and turning under his tongue. "*Take it*!"

Screeching, my legs wrap around Grayson. My toes curl as lust explodes through my veins. I watch as he rocks his hips against my mattress, needing some type of relief as well.

"I'm—so—close," I cry out in choppy breaths. Struggling to continue, my vision gets blurry as I attempt to focus on the words in front of me. "*He*—" I gasp as Gray's tongue slides over me. "*He licks*—"

Gray takes the Kindle and tosses it next to us. "New game."

"New game," I repeat.

"I'm gonna keep going, and you're gonna tell me everything you enjoy so I know exactly what you like when I fuck you with my tongue."

The second I nod, Grayson goes back down on me. Flattening his tongue, he swipes over me nice and slow, causing me to shudder. His eyes fixate on me when I moan.

"That feels so good." Reveling in the sensation, my eyes close. He continues to pleasure me with long strokes, and I melt into my mattress.

Bringing my hands up to meet my breasts, I pinch my nipples, appreciating my body and all the incredible feelings it's capable of bringing me.

"Fuck. Keep doing that, Red," Gray moans against me. His words vibrate over my clit, and he decides to change up his pace, moving quicker.

I gasp. "Gray!"

Closing his mouth over, he starts harshly sucking.

Screaming, my hands fly to his hair, yanking. "Don't stop!"

I violently shake. My eyelids screw shut, writhing and squirming–the pleasure too much to take.

"Fuck!" I yell.

A blast of lust sparks every nerve ending, making me hot with desire. With toes curled, my insides ignite with flames.

Every inch of my body is on fire as my orgasm bursts through me.

My sprinting heart rate makes it hard to breathe.

Panting, desperate for air, I open my eyes to see Grayson pulling away from me. In a hurry he pulls his boxers down, his length heavy in his hand as he pumps himself over my body. His lips and chin are wet, turning me on once more even though I'm still coming back down to earth.

"You're so fucking hot, Emma," Gray groans out the words as he releases himself all over me.

His head tilts back, muscles hard and tense as his cum shoots onto my stomach and chest, coating me.

My skin is covered, feeling warm and sticky, and I love it.

And I completely love the way I just made him unravel.

If this is what my Sundays look like for the rest of the summer, I can certainly get used to it.

CHAPTER TWENTY-SEVEN

EVEN THOUGH EMMA has a huge house, I've only ever seen her bedroom aside from the first time I was here when I snuck into the mudroom and down the hallway. So standing in her kitchen, having free range to walk around, feels a little strange right now.

Nevertheless, I sip on my soda, watching Emma flitter around wearing only my T-shirt.

I never thought seeing her wearing my shirt would feel so gratifying, but goddamn does she look good in it.

"I don't have many snacks," Emma states, opening up her pantry. "But I did happen to pick up some Rice Krispies Treats when I went food shopping the other day."

She tosses me one before I have the chance to say yes. But instead of eating, I hold on to it, still captivated by her. Still hung up on what happened in her bedroom. Still relishing in the taste of her on my tongue.

Is it weird that I wish I had my notebook on me so I

can write down all of my thoughts about how beautiful Emma is?

"Do you not want it?" Emma gestures to the Rice Krispies Treat in my hand. "I can see if I have anything else."

I shake my head.

"Is...is everything okay?" she asks, tiptoeing closer.

"Yeah, of course."

"It's happening again, isn't it?"

"What is?"

"You're getting caught in your head," she states.

My stomach flip flops, realizing that she's starting to know how to read me. "I'm just processing everything."

"Processing what?" She has a slight frown, concerned.

I swallow, prepping myself to be vulnerable with her once again. "Whenever I'm with you, I feel different."

"Different how?"

I flip through a mental vocabulary list in my mind, searching for the perfect word to describe how I feel when I'm around Emma. But I can't pinpoint what it is, so I settle on a far more elementary word than what I'd like it to be.

"Happy," I state. "I'm not used to feeling happy."

"I'm glad I can make you feel that way." Her voice softens. She tenderly places her hand on my bare chest, right over my heart. "You carry so much pain in here." Her fingers tap against my skin.

I nod, an uncomfortable sensation simmering inside me as I stand here more exposed than I've ever been.

"How do you not let your pain consume you, Emma?" I ask, genuinely wanting to know her answer.

She halfheartedly shrugs. "I guess I've always held on to the hope that things will get better."

Hope. I could use some of that.

I place my hand over hers. "You're the gentlest soul I've ever known."

Her cheeks get rosy as the corners of her mouth tip upward. Admiration shines in her amber eyes as if I'd just given her the biggest compliment of her life.

The thumping in my chest gains speed as I continue to fixate on her.

"Tell me something about yourself," I blurt.

"Like what?"

"Anything. Everything." It's come to my attention that I know how she tastes, what she sounds like when she moans, some of her heartbreaking past—but I don't know the basics. "Your favorite color."

"Rose gold."

"Favorite book?"

"*Pride and Prejudice.*"

I smirk at her response. "Tell me more."

And for the rest of my time there, she does.

We sit on her couch, talking and laughing. I learn that her favorite food is french fries, despite the intricate meals she cooks. I learn that she loves Taylor Swift, caramel macchiatos, and paddle boarding.

The entire day flies by as we continue to discover new things about each other. My stomach growls, and I know it's near dinnertime, and I'll have to put our day on hold when her dad comes back home.

We walk toward the front door—because I'm actually able to leave that way instead of climbing out of her window—and say goodbye, lingering a little too long in the doorway kissing.

Before long, I'm back at Rae's sitting in my usual seat on her balcony as the sun sets. My pen drifts over the paper, only this time what I'm writing down has a different energy to it.

The air is intoxicating,
the saltiness from the sea encasing me in a summer haze,
drowning me in the heat of her desire.
The flames of passion never tasted so tempting,
scorching me from the inside out.
I'd burn for this until I'm nothing but ash

I continue to write, pressing my lips together as I focus, and I swear I can still taste the sweetness of Emma's pussy lingering on them.

"Hey." Rae steps out onto the balcony.

I glance up at her and give her a tilt of my chin. She's one of the last people I'd like to see as I revel in this afternoon's events.

Forcing myself to ignore her presence as she lights up a cigarette, I bring my attention back to my notebook.

"Mom called me," Rae states. I stay silent so she continues, "She wants to know how you're doing."

"What'd you tell her?" I ask, not bothering to look her way.

"I didn't get into details if that's what you're worried about."

I scoff. "What details?"

"I don't know, Grayson, maybe the fact that you spend all your time scribbling in your fucking notebook instead of talking to anyone," she snaps. "Or maybe how you came home late one night with a fucked-up hand which I'm assuming means you got into a fight. And speaking of late nights—I also didn't tell her how you've been slipping out after ten and disappearing to God knows where, doing God knows what."

Oh. Those details.

"So, don't worry about it," she keeps going. "I covered for you but said you're probably looking forward to going back home when the summer ends."

My stomach drops at the mention of me leaving. I'm nowhere near ready to leave, and the sole reason is a gorgeous redhead who's the first person in a damn decade to bring a smile to my face.

I've barely done any of the things I was told to do since coming to Golden Bay.

No bonding with my sister.

No learning new skills from Miles.

Glancing up at Rae, her arms are crossed, daggers aimed right for me coming out of her eyes.

"Thanks?" I take a guess on what type of response she's looking for.

She rolls her eyes, exasperated.

Guess she wanted a different response.

"Miles has a job for you tomorrow morning. Be ready at nine." With that, she puts out her cigarette in the ashtray and exits, letting me be by myself once more.

The sun sinks into the ocean, and the stars start to peek through the sky. But instead of enjoying the serene view, I turn back to my notebook.

However, this time around, my writing goes back to my familiar state of mind—pain.

CHAPTER TWENTY-EIGHT

Emma

THE NEXT DAY, I decide to stop by Rae's condo before my shift starts. Grayson is helping Miles on a job, so we're having some girl time.

I sip on my fruit smoothie while handing Rae a black coffee I picked up for her.

"Thanks," she says, moving things around in her living room. "Sorry this place is a disaster, I'm working on a new project for my art studio and subsequently my supplies are everywhere." She condenses her belongings into a pile as I make my way to her couch. "Of course, it doesn't help that my brother leaves his shit lying around." She tosses a T-shirt near his duffel.

"How's it going with him?" I ask, hoping that the two of them have been able to spend some quality time together.

"Fucking pointless. He doesn't want anything to do with me, he hates me."

"You've said that before, but I really don't think it's true."

"He barely holds a conversation with me. He

spends all his time writing in that fucking notebook." She points to a brown, leather book sticking out of his bag.

My chest brews with curiosity, wondering what he's written. My fingers itch to grab it, yearning to know the layers of his mind.

I can't keep my eyes off it, glancing between the tempting book and Rae as she continues to speak. "Anyway, enough about my brother." She places her paints in a big basket. "Whatever happened to that guy you were telling me about? Did you guys fuck yet?"

I choke on my smoothie, going into a full-blown coughing fit as my throat and nostrils burn.

"Are you okay?"

"Yeah. I'm fine." I tap on my chest.

"The sex is that good you forget how to drink when asked about it?" she teases.

My cheeks get hot. "We're not up to that yet. But everything else is surpassing my expectations." I bite back a grin and go back to my drink.

"Have you done some fun *exploring*?"

"A little. But I'd be open to more." I chew on my straw, attempting to stifle my smirk. After what went down in my bedroom yesterday, I'd be open to *a lot* more.

"Who would've thought you'd be so scandalous," she jokes, picking up her basket of art supplies and shoving the remaining items into it. "I'm just gonna put this shit away in my room, and then you can tell me some dirty details." My stomach tumbles with awkwardness, wanting to confide in my best friend but certainly not when it's about her brother.

As she walks around the couch, she trips on

Grayson's duffel. "Shit," she mutters when she notices some of the contents of his bag spilled out.

"I'll get it."

"Thanks. I'll be right back."

Rae walks down the hall, and I carefully pick up Gray's shirts, neatly folding them and placing them in his bag. When the last shirt is folded, my heart lurches when I notice his notebook on the floor, flipped open to a random page.

My pulse strums faster as my fingertips reach for it.

Just put it back, Emma.

I lift the book, feeling the smooth leather against my palm.

Don't look. Don't look. Don't look.

But my eyes have a mind of their own, jumping to glance at what is written. The sound of my heart beating fills my eardrums, knowing that I shouldn't be reading this. I should just close the notebook and put it away. But I don't.

My life has been measured in affliction and sorrow,
each tribulation strangling me.
The more it happens, the tighter the invisible noose
around my neck,
not letting me speak
not letting me breathe.
Overcome by agony.

My hand goes to my chest as his poem strikes me. His words have me hooked, and despite the growing apprehension that I shouldn't flip to another page, I do anyway.

I become enthralled by every sentence he's written.

Some pages are fully formed poems, others have lines scribbled here and there.

He has ideas, inspiration, and pain overflowing off every single sheet of paper.

Her delicate fingers glide in between the spaces of mine
as if filling a void.
We promise each other a season of thrill.
Capturing our youth before it slips away,
most of it already stolen from us.

The powerful beating of my heart pushes against my hand.

Grayson wrote this about us.

He wrote a poem about *me*.

My insides get tingly, wondering if he's written more about our time together. I can still hear Rae rummaging through things in her room, but I know I'm walking on thin ice. So on a split-second impulse, I pick one more random page to read.

Only, this isn't about me.

And it's not a poem.

It's a memory.

Twelve hours before Rae's overdose:

I race inside my house, darting into the kitchen where Mom and Dad are cooking dinner. They're smiling as they talk while chopping vegetables. But as soon as I run into the room, their faces drop.

"Rae's using again," I blurt out, catching my breath as my hands nervously shake.

"What happened?" Mom goes pale.

"I was driving past The Mighty Glass and I saw her in the parking lot buying—"

The front door opens and I instantly shut up. Rae tiptoes into the kitchen, spotting the three of us frozen, staring at her.

"What?" she asks, knowing that something's up.

"Where were you?" Dad demands.

"Out with a friend."

Mom lets out a heavy breath. "Rae, I think we need to revisit the conversation of you going to rehab."

Rae's face twists into something awful, her hardening gaze zeroing in on me causing my heart to freefall into my stomach. "What did you tell them?"

I shake my head.

"What did you tell them!" Rae storms closer.

"Nothing!" I shout.

"You're a fucking liar!" She lunges toward me but Dad's quick to intercept. The two of them wrestle as Rae calls out over his shoulder, "I hate you, Grayson!"

Panic pounds through my chest.

"Call the facility," Dad tells Mom, still struggling to move Rae away from me and calm her down. Mom nods, immediately reaching for her phone.

"I'm not going to a goddamn rehab!" She breaks free from Dad's hold. "You should've kept your motherfucking mouth shut, Grayson!"

"I'm trying to help you—" I cry out.

"Help me by staying out of my life!" She stomps down the hallway, toward her and Cara's room.

I can hear Mom already on the phone asking the facility if they have an open bed. Dad says something to me about how Rae doesn't mean it and it's her addiction talking.

But my panic mutates into anger, my jaw clenching.

Instead of staying put, I follow Rae.

Right before she reaches her door, I make sure to spit out, "Cara would hate who you turned out to be."

She snaps, spinning around and before I'm able to process what's happening, her fist is slamming into my cheek.

"Fuck you. As far as I'm concerned, as of today, both *of my siblings are dead."*

I let out a muffled gasp, that last sentence stinging me to my core. A pit in my stomach grows, my soul aching for the both of them.

I get why both Grayson and Rae assume the other doesn't like them.

I understand why Grayson asked me how to not be consumed by my pain. It's all he's known for the second half of his life. It's shown on every page I've seen so far, including the poem about me. His adolescence was robbed by something he had no control over, just like mine.

My heart swells, thinking back to what he said last night—how he's happy around me, and he's not used to that emotion.

I want to make him feel that way always.

The sound of footsteps nearing has me slamming Grayson's book shut and shoving it in his bag. My legs tremble from nerves as I pop up just in time for Rae to get back in the room.

The reality of what I just did begins to seep in, instant remorse plaguing me for breaking his trust.

"What time do you have to go downstairs and start your shift?" she asks.

"Um, soon." I go to check my phone, and as if on cue, it vibrates with a text.

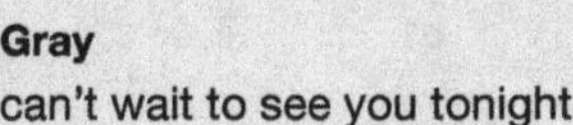

Guilt swims in my stomach, causing it to cramp. I can't in clear conscience see him again without letting him know that I pried into his personal thoughts.

Me
me, too

CHAPTER TWENTY-NINE

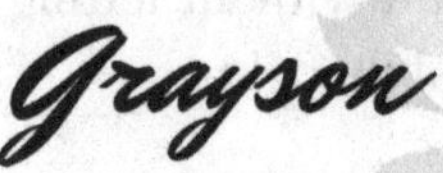

WHEN I SNEAK through Emma's window, I spot her pacing back and forth nervously chewing on her cuticles. Her brows are drawn inward, and the expression in her eyes tells me something's not okay.

"What's wrong?" I ask, my shoulders already inching toward my neck.

"I did something I shouldn't have, and you have every right to be mad at me," Emma rushes out her words.

My shoulders soften a bit, because I know whatever she did it won't be enough to make me *that* mad.

"Sit." She gestures to her mattress, and I do as she says, unease coiling through me. She walks back and forth the length of her room a few more times before she finally turns to face me. "I read your notebook."

My stomach drops.

"You what?"

"Only a little bit of it—which doesn't make it right, I know, but it was just lying there—"

"Lying where?" Concern heightens the stress of my voice.

"Let me backtrack." Emma takes a breath to compose herself. "Rae was cleaning up the living room, she tripped over your bag, and stuff fell out. I put your things back in and stumbled upon your book."

I blink, processing what she just said.

The beating of my heart intensifies.

My throat closes in, wondering what she's read and what she thinks of me now.

"How much did you read?" My question scrapes against my insides.

"Not a lot. Two poems and a small thing about Rae." Emma goes back to biting her nail beds.

My mind spins, wondering which poems and what she read about Rae. If Emma saw any significant memory of Rae, I'm sure there'd be questions. Probably one of my pages bitching about having to spend time with her.

But the poems...they're extremely exposing. I might as well stand in front of her with my bleeding heart in my hands.

"It was an invasion of privacy," Emma continues. "I shouldn't have done it."

"Why did you?" I stare at her quizzically. Not angry with her, but rather confused by her actions.

"I guess I wanted to know you better." She takes a cautious step toward me, but then glances at me to see if I'll hesitate having her closer. "I've seen the few times you get caught in your head, and I wanted to know what your thoughts are like."

"And now that you do, what do you think?" The

strumming against my ribcage picks up in a flush of nervousness.

"Your writing..." Emma pauses, wetting her lips with the slightest peek of her tongue. My pulse swirls, anxiously anticipating her response—while the other half of me wants to jet out of here before she can continue. "It's heartbreaking and breathtaking all at once." The delicate sound of her voice travels over to me, the same time she gets close enough to touch. I tilt my chin up to look at her, admiring how the waves of her hair softly frame her face and slender neck. "It's beautiful, Grayson."

I swallow around the emotion building in my throat. "Thank you."

"You told me you didn't write anymore."

"I don't. Not anything of substance. Like you said, it's just random thoughts in my head."

"No. It's more than that," she whispers, her small hand cupping my cheek. "You have a story living inside you."

I stare into her amber eyes, letting them awaken an unfamiliar place burrowed deep within my chest. She knows very little of my life, yet knows I'm carrying the burden of untold stories of my past.

She can read me.

I don't know if that terrifies me or beckons me even closer.

Judging by the way my hand holds hers, dragging it over to my mouth, giving it a tender kiss—I think I have my answer. Whether I like it or not.

"And what about the stories living inside you?" I rasp.

There's a tinge of pink dusting her cheeks as she begins to feel as vulnerable as I do.

We both recognize that there's more to who we are than what rests on the surface. I know she's also weighed down by the shattered pieces from her history.

"I think the more I keep them to myself, the more it hurts to hold."

Emma's fingers wrap around mine as her eyes turn glassy. Her mouth parts then shuts as if she's unsure if she should say any more.

She does it a few more times, but even though she's apprehensive, there's a need for release building behind each breath.

"I want to hear all your stories, Emma. Let me hold some of your pain."

If I could, I'd take every second of anguish from her and scar my own heart with her wounds, proudly letting it injure me instead.

"In one of your poems, you wrote something along the lines of youth being stolen," she states, her voice getting quieter. I nod, waiting for her to continue. "That's my story. Everything was stolen from me."

My stomach shoots to the floor as I remain quiet, giving her the space if she wants to share more.

"From my first kiss to my first time—he took them all."

"Who's *he*?" I ask, trying to suppress the anger flowing into my bloodstream.

She blinks several times in an attempt to push the tears back in. Letting out a loud exhale, she joins me on her bed, her legs tucked by her side.

"He'd moved to North Carolina with his family when

he was twenty. I was ten. His family attended the church my dad used to preach at, and since they're extremely wealthy—my dad took a liking to them." Her line of sight drifts away from me, moving downward to stare at the comforter. "Truthfully, I did, too. We became close with them; we'd play golf at their country club, go on religious retreats, and everything in between. They were the ones who funded the construction of Kingdom Church."

She peeks up at me as if to ask if she should keep going, and I nod, even though I know the rest of this story is going to have me tearing this state apart searching for her assaulter.

"It got to the point where every Sunday, instead of hanging around at Dad's church bored, he'd drive me back home and hang out with me. It was like that for years; he'd buy me my favorite Snapple and let me pick out whatever candy, then we'd make our way back here, where we'd play beach volleyball and watch movies."

"When did things change?" I ask as gently as possible even though my insides are contorting into an agonizing knot.

"One day he just looked different to me. I was thirteen when I became more aware of him—and I *hate* what I'm about to say—but he became handsome in my eyes." Emma scrunches her face with disgust, pinching the bridge of her nose. "He'd make small comments about what I looked like in my bathing suit when we'd be on the beach, and it would give me butterflies. Girls in school were talking about getting boyfriends, and I wanted one so badly. I wanted the stuff in the movies and books—a true love who'd risk everything to be with me." She drops her hand. "I was so fucking naive."

Intertwining our fingers, I make sure to never take my gaze off her. "You were thirteen, Emma."

Tears roll down her face, hitting her lips. Her shoulders begin to shake as more sorrow builds inside her. The seams of my heart burst open the more I witness her break down.

"When he asked if I liked anyone, I played shy, but I think he knew because he then asked if I'd ever been kissed. And thinking about it now, I feel so filthy because I *wanted* him to kiss me, Grayson." A sob crackles from the back of her throat, the sound of shame etched into my bones. "And when he did, I felt over the moon. He said I was prettier than any other girl he'd kissed. I hate how much I loved hearing those words."

I bring my thumb up to wipe her tears in a desperate attempt to catch some of her agony.

Emma leans into my touch, her lashes gracefully closing.

A blanket of silence falls between us as we breathe together.

My body rattles with unfathomable emotions, but I keep them locked up tight so as not to scare her.

When she feels ready to continue, her eyes open, and she focuses back on me.

"I was told that everything between us had to be kept a secret—even when he'd take me shopping, letting me buy whatever I wanted. The gifts were more expensive—not snacks anymore but clothes and jewelry. He'd always give me a wink and say 'our little secret,'" she explains. "It felt special, at first..."

She draws in a deep inhale, the air stuttering as it fills her. My muscles sink, predicting her story.

"Then, one day we went past just kissing, and

I *knew* it was wrong." She winces, her hand covering her stomach as she curls up in pain. "I can still sense the excruciating churning in my gut when I think back to how his hands felt on me. He'd tell me he was giving me 'lessons.' It was like that every week."

Nausea shoots up my throat.

An agonizing expression colors her once cheerful eyes. "I swear I tried to stop it, Gray—I tried everything. I tried staying at church longer, I tried giving back the presents he gave me, I tried offering him other things, I—"

"I believe you, Emma."

Her shoulders drop in relief—which kills me even more to know that she wasn't sure I'd believe her.

"Every Sunday became a dreadful day where he pushed the limit more and more until he took everything from me."

My whole being aches as I listen. I don't know how to respond, and even if I did, I'd stay quiet to let her finish speaking.

"It continued for almost two months in my childhood bedroom," she states. "And the only reason it stopped was because my dad caught us in the act. He wasn't feeling well and left church early and came home to find us."

My eyes bulge. "Did he rip the guy's head off? Because if he hasn't yet, I fucking will," my thoughts pour out on impulse.

Emma pauses, studying me. Her features draw in, a look of disappointment crossing her face as if she's trying to let me down gently.

"He blamed me," she whispers.

My breath gets stuck in my lungs. A blaze of rage

lights in the very depths of my soul, and my arms begin to shake from holding so tightly onto my composure.

"What do you mean he blamed you?"

"It was more valuable to keep the wealthiest donor to the church than a good relationship with his daughter, so he blamed me for it. No matter how many times I tried to explain, he put the responsibility on me. What I was wearing, how I acted, what I said—if I had been more respectable, then none of that would've happened. It was all my fault, and for a long time, I believed the lies he was spewing."

My jaw clenches so hard, I might break my teeth. Rage thrashes around my body, loathing the evil people in Emma's life.

Emma spins around the gold band on her finger. "He made me take an oath in front of the entire church —including my rapist, vowing my celibacy, and remaining a virgin until marriage."

My fists ball up, fumes pulsing through my veins. I stare at the purity ring, wishing I could destroy it with my bare hands.

"No one found out what happened, not even his parents. Dad forbade me to spend any time with him, which I was obviously thankful for. His parents went on without a clue. And when I stood up at the podium and accepted this jail sentence"—she holds up her hand —"I thought my dad would forgive me and love me again."

Tears form at the corner of her eyes once more.

"But he never did," Emma states. "I tried so hard to get his love back—he's my only living parent. He's all I got. So, I was the perfect daughter, cooking, cleaning, no going out, no questioning his authority, abiding by every rule. I was so *good*." Her chin quivers. "He called me dirty and disposable. That no man would ever want me after I'd been touched."

"Listen to me, Emma." I inch closer, carefully cupping my palms to her face. "You are none of those things. You are the most exquisite person I know, and if I could, I'd rewrite all the horrible stories you had to live through."

She softly smiles through the stream of despair dripping down to her lips. "I really wish you could've been my first," she whispers. "I'm sorry."

"I don't care about being your first. I only care about being your last."

I freeze, stunning myself with my own words.

But I don't want to take the time to make sense of what I meant by that right now. All I want is to be here for Emma.

I hate that she's suffered from the world's cruelty. She doesn't deserve any of this.

The seams of my heart rip open one by one.

If I think about this too long, it'll consume me, my wrath taking over. And I can't have that, at least not at this moment. This is about her. I don't know how she's functioning with all the horrid experiences she's lived through, grief, assault, being repeatedly stabbed in the back by her father.

It's too fucking much.

I hold her in my arms, right where she belongs, for the rest of the night. And after a long while of being in each other's embrace, we finally fall asleep.

CHAPTER THIRTY

I'VE BEEN TOSSING and turning all night, despite Emma's memory foam bed. My mind won't shut off since she shared her past with me earlier.

After what feels like only two minutes of sleep, I flip over once again, only this time there's a light coming from her bathroom. I prop myself up, realizing Emma's not next to me.

When she steps out, there's a sleepy smile on her face.

"Sorry, I didn't mean to wake you," she whispers.

"You didn't, I've been sleeping like shit all night."

She crawls back into bed, settling under the covers. Her smooth legs brush up against me, making my belly flutter.

"Is everything all right?" she asks.

No. Nothing is all right. This world is sick and twisted, and I'm fucking fed up with bad things happening to good people. Murder, addiction, rape—the list goes on and on, endlessly twirling around my brain with the gut-wrenching possibilities that innocent people have to endure. And for what?

"Yeah," I answer.

"I'm not buying that response." One of her fingertips lightly caresses my cheekbone. "I can tell by that look in your eye that something's on your mind." Her voice comes out hushed.

"I've just been thinking about you." I brush the strands of her hair away from her face.

"How convenient. I've been up thinking about you."

Emma presses her lips to mine, the both of us smiling as we kiss. My arms loop around her, tugging her closer so I can feel the warmth of her body.

Her hands slide down the length of me, her tongue tangling with mine in a desperate attempt to get closer to me.

While we both might've been awake thinking about one another, we clearly were thinking about different topics.

"You know," she rasps as her hand continues to travel downward. "I have the perfect remedy to help you out of your head *and* help you sleep better."

I chuckle, my body sizzling from her soft touch.

My body aches to do what she's asking for, but not before I know this is the right time for her after everything she disclosed to me earlier in the evening.

"Are you sure?" I ask.

"Yes. I've spent far too long letting my past rule my present and far too long being good." She grazes her hand over my gym shorts, waking me up. "I want you. That is, as long as you still want me."

"Of course, I do." My fingers run over the small of

her back. "There's not a second that goes by where I don't long for you."

"Then have me." She pushes up against me, heat flooding the lower half of me.

This is how Emma's taking her power back, reclaiming the parts of herself that were robbed and manipulated. I'm going to let her own every part of her body and mind by liberating her sexuality.

"Make me yours, Gray." Her gentle, yet sultry, voice hits my lips. "Take me. In the most possessive way you want."

Blood rushes to my cock hearing her longing.

I know what she wants, what she likes and wants to explore.

So, we'll explore together.

Bringing my lips to her collarbone, I delicately kiss her skin. Dragging my lips up her neck, she shudders. Tilting her head back on a breathy release, she sighs out my name while I suck on her earlobe.

Her fingers brush against my skin, and I can feel her purity ring. The reminder infuses anger into my desire. I place my mouth next to the shell of her ear and drop my pitch as I allow her to fully embrace herself while I do the same. "Get rid of that motherfucking ring, and show me how much of a bad girl you are."

A flame flickers in Emma's eyes as she sits up, kneeling. With our gazes locked, she twists off her purity ring and places it on her nightstand.

I wet my lips in anticipation as I watch her slowly drag down the straps of her nightgown until her arms are free. Wave after wave of heat tumbles through my body, hypnotized by the way the silk fabric caresses her hips before dropping on the bed.

Completely bare, my eyes rake boldly over every inch of her.

"How do you want me?" Emma's voice is thick with need.

I shake my head. "How do *you* want it?"

Her manicured fingernails delicately dance over my chest, and even though my heart jolts out of place, anxiously wanting to anoint her body with mine, I remain collected.

"I want to ride you." Her sultry whisper electrifies me, sending bolts of lust through my spine.

"You've been thinking about my cock?" I bring the pad of my thumb to her bottom lip as she nods. "Tell me. Use this pretty mouth of yours to tell me what dirty thoughts you've been having."

Emma smiles against my finger. "I've been imagining what it'd feel like to come with you inside me."

"Oh yeah?" I ask, her tongue swiping over my thumb. "And you've been picturing riding me when it happens?"

She nods.

"Have you gotten yourself off while thinking about it?" My gaze drifts over to where I know she keeps her vibrator.

"I have."

"Such a bad girl."

With a flare of desire, she draws my thumb into her mouth, sucking it while her lashes flutter closed. More blood shoots down to my lower half, my cock aching.

She leisurely takes my thumb away from her plush lips, and with an overwhelming need for the both of us to get closer, our bodies collide.

My pulse leaps as she climbs on top of me. We

struggle to get my clothes off, not wanting our mouths to leave one another's for too long. Our heavy breaths fill each other up as our kisses grow more urgent.

Unrestrained.

Untamed.

She hovers over me in a hungry frenzy. My head dizzies from the spell I'm immediately put under when I'm around her.

Everything feels expansive.

Everything feels *better*.

Her hand finally reaches my length, and I'm groaning into her mouth at the sensation of her soft palm wrapping around me.

"Fuck," I rasp as my muscles strain.

My hand slides between our bodies, exploring every peak and valley, and finally settling between her thighs. The moment I coat my fingers in her wetness, she sighs out a breath of relief.

"You have no idea how much I want you," she says.

I chuckle to myself, knowing that it's nowhere near the amount of how much I need her.

"I'm yours."

Carefully pressing herself up, she sits upright just a fraction away from where I want her to be. Her chest rises and falls rapidly as mine does the same. Her wavy, red locks fall from her shoulders giving me the perfect view.

She stares at me, an eager look flashing across her face.

That's when it clicks for me that she's waiting for me to take over. Waiting for a command.

"Lift your hips for me, Red." I darken my tone as I squeeze her supple skin.

With a smirk painting her face, she does as I say, the heat of her pussy kissing the tip of my cock.

I give her the go-ahead by nodding and adjust myself to align with her opening.

With our eyes trained on one another, studying each other's features, Emma slowly sinks down onto me.

In an instant, divine ecstasy zips through my body. My heart furiously pounds against my bones as Emma's pussy envelops me.

"Holy fucking shit," I spit out as I clench on to her even tighter.

I've never felt another woman like this, but I'm immediately sure that I never want to know what anyone else feels like after having Emma. I only want her.

Warmth floods me, spiraling at the base of my spine. A lustful glaze drifts over me as I get high off of Emma. Every sensation of her body gracing me with ripple effects of pleasure.

Her wetness.

Her warmth.

Emma's mouth hangs open as I stretch her, the intense look of pleasure scorching my insides the more I gaze at her.

"Grayson—" she gasps. "You're so big."

"You're so tight." The corded muscles in my neck tense.

She looks and feels unbelievable—it's almost too much to bear.

Her nails dig into my torso as she braces herself. "Oh god, this is incredible," she whines as she begins to roll her hips over mine.

My breathing is labored, short pants flowing from my lips. I fight with my own sense of haste, wanting to experience the euphoria at the end of the finish line but to take my sweet ass time getting there.

I will never get enough of this.

And I will never get enough of Emma—all of her, not just the way her tight pussy squeezes around me, although at this moment, it's a significant plus.

Her eyes screw shut as the sensations build.

"Eyes on me, Emma."

She moans at my command and does what I ask of her with a smile on her face. I can see the shift in her expression, a glimmer of rebellion sparkles around her as her wild side awakens.

I reach my hand up, wrapping it around her slender throat. Her thunderous pulse dances under my fingertips.

"Fuck me, Red." My other hand travels to where our bodies meet, and I begin circling her clit. "Show me how bad you are, and make yourself come on my cock."

Biting down on her plush bottom lip, she fucks me faster.

A downpour of fiery sensations cascades through my bloodstream as I watch Emma's body control mine.

I apply more pressure to my fingertips around her neck and feel her pussy flutter. My other fingers continue to work her clit, the slickness dripping all over the both of us.

Her breasts bounce and her stomach contracts the quicker she moves.

When I bring my hips up to meet hers, her eyes enlarge as she clamps her mouth shut to stifle the incoming squeal.

Tingles shoot through me, and I know I'm getting close.

"Shit," I say through gritted teeth.

Without stopping my movements, I take my gaze off her for a beat staring up at the ceiling. The struggle builds in every single one of my cells as I fight off my orgasm.

Think about something else for a brief second.

I try to let my mind wander away from how exceptionally sexy Emma is and onto random things.

Food. Working out. Punching people in the face.

"Oh, Gray," Emma moans.

Nope. Nothing's going to take my mind off of her.

The sound of our bodies working together fills up her room. Glancing back at her, my body goes into a frenzy.

Her hair is messily flipped to one side, a sheen of sweat glistens on her flushed skin. Her body begins to shudder as she rides me into oblivion.

The way Emma grinds onto me feels like pure heaven. And I'm seconds away from dying the happiest man.

My drenched fingers move erratically.

My grasp on her throat is more dominating.

It's unadulterated, blazing passion between us.

I can't last any longer. I know I can't. I'm about to lose my restraint, and Emma knows it.

"Make me yours," she cries out, wanting me to finish inside her.

The fucking irony of that statement.

She's not mine—I'm hers.

Her legs start to shake, and my thighs stiffen. But

I'm not ready to call it quits just yet. With my heart about to explode, I let out one final command.

"Be my bad girl, and beg for my cum."

"Fuck," Emma moans, trembling. "Please—please come inside me, Gray. I want you to have every part of me—"

Before she can finish another word, a rip of pleasure ruptures through me, and I'm painting the inside of her with my desire.

My vision goes white as Emma grips onto me, reaching her climax. Her pussy spasms around me, savoring every last drop I have.

Each of my muscles strain as I shudder. Air flows in and out of my lungs at a rapid pace, and I'm surprised I can even remember how to breathe.

The sound of Emma finishing is the sweetest song I've ever heard.

Slowly, the tension dissolves and is replaced by a blissful sensation. When I focus my attention back on Emma, the lazy smile that appears on her lips is the exact way that I feel.

Intoxicated.

Satisfied.

But already craving more.

CHAPTER THIRTY-ONE

Emma

MY DAYS BECOME CONSUMED by a boy with storm-colored eyes who appears broody on the outside but is so tender-hearted on the inside. And my nights have turned into a sexual awakening for the both of us as we get twisted in my bedsheets.

It feels like a huge weight has been lifted off my chest after telling him about my past. I was worried he'd see me differently—I even had the minuscule voice in the back of my head telling me he'd agree with Dad, even though the rational part of me knew that would never be true. Still, it's a relief to know that I can confide in Grayson and share my stories with him.

The week seems to fly by, and it's already Friday, and instead of Gray sneaking in, we decided to sneak out.

Sand kicks up under my feet, little pellets tapping at my calves as Grayson takes my hand, guiding me to his car.

My smile is wide, laughter bubbling in my throat as we dart away from my house. The ocean is extra quiet tonight with calm tides softly rippling against the land, so I do my best to tame my giggles just in case they echo into the night.

He drives us to the south side of Golden Bay, parking behind Adventureland.

"You don't strike me as the amusement park type." I poke fun at him while we stroll down the crowded boardwalk. The scent of hot dogs and soft pretzels whirls under my nostrils as we pass by a food stand.

"Isn't this the biggest attraction in this town? Might as well show me what it's all about."

"I'd be more than happy to!" I thread my fingers in between his.

"I used to come here with my family when I was little," he says, his focus fixed on the rides. The colorful lights gleam across his face. "It was so long ago, I barely remember it. Although, I'm pretty sure I begged my sister to go on the carousel with me."

My ears perk up, noticing he said *sister*. Singular. As if the acknowledgment of Cara would be too painful, blanketing our night of fun. At this point, I'm pretty sure he's not aware that I know who Cara is... was.

He conveniently left her out to save himself, which I understand completely.

"Oh my god!" A cluster of drunk girls stumble out of a nearby bar, one of them falling flat on their face.

Hysterics ensue, myself and Grayson included, as a girl in a twenty-first birthday sash is helped up. Her tiara is sliding off her knotted hair, eyeliner smudged under her eyes, and she smells as if liquor is seeping straight out of her pores, but she has a giant grin on her face as she laughs.

The group ambles over to the next bar, tripping over themselves as they giggle and scream inside jokes.

As I watch them carry on, I can't help but feel a sense of sadness spinning around my chest.

"Did you celebrate at any of these bars for your twenty-first?" Grayson asks, drawing my attention back to him.

I snort. "My twenty-first included a potluck dinner with members of my dad's church and a glass of red wine. What about you?"

"Didn't do shit."

My attention drifts back to the group. A sense of nostalgia for something I've never had settled heavy in my core.

"Let's make up for our awful birthdays," Gray says as if he had felt the same thing I did. Before I can respond, my hand gets tugged as he leads the way, walking us toward the bar.

My lips pull at either side, grinning ear to ear as we make our way inside. It smells of alcohol and sweat, and I can barely hear myself think over the thumping bass and people shouting.

There's a single barstool open, and Grayson quickly guides me to sit down before anyone else can.

Standing directly behind me, his hands find my waist in a gentle hold. Bringing his lips to my ear, he says, "Let's see how wild my girl can be with a couple of drinks in her."

My heart soars when he calls me his. "I'm just as curious as you are."

Even though I won't get wasted because I still have to make it back home, I'm still wondering what I'd be like with one or two drinks in me.

"What can I get you?" the bartender asks me, loudly speaking over the music.

"Something fruity and sweet."

"And for you?" she asks Grayson.

"The opposite."

We flash her our IDs, and she nods, making our drinks in the blink of an eye. Within seconds, two different drinks appear in tall glasses in front of us.

"Here's to our twenty-first," Gray says, lifting up his drink to clink mine.

"It's your twenty-first birthday!?" a sloppily drunk woman shouts into my ear, making it ring.

"Yep. The both of us are celebrating," Grayson replies.

"Oh my god! Let's do shots!" she exclaims, then gathers round her group of friends. "We're doing shots with them." She points to us. "It's their twenty-first!"

There's a sudden roar of excitement, and I glance up at Grayson with a rush of exhilaration. "Guess we're doing shots."

The bartender gets waved down, and the woman orders all of us tequila. Before I can drink my fruity cocktail, I'm holding a shot glass with clear liquid that has a scent strong enough to burn the inside of my nose.

"Happy fucking birthday, you two!" she shouts.

Grayson chuckles next to me, and all of us clink our glasses together, then tip back the alcohol letting it scorch our insides.

Coughing, I sip on my original drink to get some relief.

"That shit's strong!" Gray states, doing the same with his drink.

"Let's do another!" the woman exclaims.

I turn my line of sight to look up at Grayson, who's looking directly back at me. "Wanna do one more?" I ask.

"It's our birthday, might as well." He winks.

With that, another shot glass of tequila gets thrown our way. We down it, coughing like we did just before and quickly inhale our original drinks.

The alcohol bursts through my veins, warming me up and loosening my muscles.

Lightness flows through me, and I think it does the same to Grayson because his fingertips run over the space between my shoulder blades, touching both the cotton fabric of my dress and the exposed part of my skin.

I know I shouldn't have much more to drink, but the thought of celebrating my fake twenty-first with Grayson makes me forget about everything else.

And I'm one hundred percent fine with that.

Grayson bursts into laughter as we trip and stumble our way out of our third bar. The boardwalk is spinning, the lights from all the rides blur together. I can barely think straight—but god, is it *fun*!

Giggles keep escaping my lips. I don't know how many times we've told people about our birthdays and how many shots we've gotten in return—I've lost track of everything.

"Did I tell you how hot you look in this dress?" Gray slurs.

My cheeks lift higher. "Only about a hundred times."

Okay, I lied. I didn't lose track of *everything*. But aside from Gray's compliments, everything else has gone out the window.

Strolling along, gently knocking into each other as we struggle to walk in a straight line, he pulls me away from the bars and the noise, and over to a row of benches. He crashes down on one, coming to a sloppy seated position as he holds his hand to his head.

"Fuck. Everything's spinning."

Collapsing onto his lap, I chuckle, knowing exactly what he means because I'm pretty sure there are five of him right now.

"How'd you like your twenty-first?" he asks, trying to focus his gaze on my face.

"I'd say this is my favorite one."

"Same." His lips curl upward, and the expression in his bloodshot eyes turns soft and dreamy, making my heart sing. "You make it hurt less," he says in a low voice as if I were part of the conversation in his mind.

My head tilts. "Make what hurt less?"

"Life."

My fingers find the neckline of his shirt, toying with the fabric. "You make my life hurt less, too," I whisper.

The words float into the air and out to sea. Words that I've never thought would tell anyone. Words that are sealed with a deeper meaning behind them. And Grayson now knows that.

He tugs me closer, planting his lips on mine. The potent taste of tequila mixed with whatever bitter alcohol he had dances along my tongue, getting me drunk off of him.

I shift my position, knees on either side of his legs, straddling him. My hands get lost in his thick, dark hair while his roam my body.

Everything melts away.

The people.

The places.

The sounds.

It's just me and him. The only two in existence as our bodies press up against one another.

The bulge in his jeans is hitting just the right spot. My wasted, unfiltered thoughts begin to peek through as I slightly break contact, my lips hovering over his. "What were you thinking about when you were jerking off to me?" I ask, recalling the time I caught him in the shower.

"Which time?"

"You've done it more than once?"

He laughs as if the question is ridiculous. "Have I jerked off to the thought of your tight pussy taking my cock on more than one occasion? Of fucking course, Emma."

My body flushes and I shift my hips over him, his jeans running over my clit once more. I shudder at the sensation.

Grayson leisurely trails his hands up my thighs, skimming over the hem of my dress, as he continues speaking. "I've wanted you since the first day I laid eyes on you. I just didn't want to admit it to myself."

"What do you want to do to me?" The seductive tone in my voice causes him to smirk.

"Is my bad girl coming out to play again?"

A blaze of fire surges through me.

Whenever he calls me that, I awaken.

With Gray, I'm free to step out of the confines that I've been pressured into and get to explore another side of me.

Biting down on my bottom lip, I nod in response.

Once he has the green light, his fingers dip under my dress, eagerly pushing my panties aside.

"Fuck, you're already soaked." His voice is deep as he runs his fingertips over my slit.

Stifling a moan, I bring my lips to meet his neck, sucking on his skin to keep myself from making noise.

"Talking about me getting off to you turns you on this much?" Gray asks.

I nod. "And when you call me your bad girl," I whisper the words against the shell of his ear.

He pushes two fingers inside me, and I gasp, clutching onto him. My head is dizzy from the alluring blend of alcohol and Grayson that's coursing through my veins.

"Ride my fingers, Red."

Drunk with lust, I slowly rock my hips. My eyes roll backward as he meets movements, the heel of his palm rubbing my clit.

Tingles fly around my insides, my muscles growing tense.

Just then, a loud group of inebriated people passes by, heading to another bar. Although I'm still moving, I'm immediately aware that we're not alone or in a private place by any means.

But I don't stop.

Blame it on the shots.

Blame it on the way Grayson's curling his fingers inside me.

Or blame it on my first real taste of what it's like to not be pressured into being *good*.

Whatever the reason, I keep going, my wetness coating Gray's hand.

"People might be watching us." My breath hits his neck as I notice different groups of people move along the boardwalk.

"Not might. They *are*, Emma," he states. "People are going to get so turned on from watching you come all over my fingers."

"Gray." I squeeze his arms, moaning into the crook of his neck.

"Show me how bad you are, Red. Let me make you come in public."

It's as if he hand delivered the key to my repressed reckless side, unlocking that part of my soul and letting it break out.

With his sexy dare taunting me, lingering in the thickened air between us, I move my hips over him at a faster pace. Heat drips down my body, landing between my thighs as I continue.

Burying my head into Gray, my heavy breaths hit against his skin. His chest moves quicker each time I push forward. Latching his free hand around my waist, he helps guide my movements, racing me toward my climax.

Lust whooshes through my spine, and I let out a small cry as I yearn for more friction.

"There's my girl." Gray twists his fingers inside me, and I suck in a sharp breath. "Let everyone who walks by see how sexy you are."

My nails dig into his biceps as every single part of

me becomes rigid. A rush of exhilaration and ecstasy builds in my core, lighting up my body.

"Grayson—" I moan against him, trying to strangle the sound.

"Fuck," he grits, trying to compose himself as his fingers work harder, fluttering at a rushed pace.

I hear more people walk by, and I know they can see us—we're so incredibly obvious. But I don't care. The more I unravel with Gray, the hotter this experience is for me.

Heaving, I lift my head up to look at Grayson. Our eyes lock, a naughty expression emanating through those cloudy blue irises. Ignoring the sounds of hammered people dipping in and out of bars, I press my lips against Gray's in a needy kiss, my hands gripping his face.

He meets me with an equal amount of passion, swiping his tongue around mine, swallowing my sounds of desire.

As we keep working together, treacherously close to setting me off, my breathing starts to stutter. Short puffs of air fall from my lips. Gray moves his mouth, kissing my jaw and moving down to my neck—making me lose my sense of control and loudly moan as he tugs on my sensitive skin.

He slithers the hand that's around my waist, up to the back of my neck, holding me in place.

"Come for me," his rich voice whispers into my hair. "Out in public. Where anyone could be watching you." He plants a peck below my ear. "Be my bad girl, and make them watch you come for me."

His thumb circles my clit, and in one swift movement, he buries my head back into his shoulder as I shriek against him.

Liquid fire scorches my veins as my orgasm flies through me. Shuddering and writhing against Grayson, he keeps pumping his fingers inside me until they're drenched with my desire for him.

Panting, my body jolts, begging to hold on to this high a little bit longer.

After several seconds pass, I go limp in his arms feeling his heartbeat racing against my own frenzied chest.

Delicately pushing myself up, my head is woozy as I look at Gray. There's a smirk on his lips, and he slowly drags his fingers out of me, trailing my wetness along my thigh, then up to his mouth, sucking them clean.

Still heavily intoxicated from him and the alcohol, I blurt out, "That was so much fun!"

Then burst into a fit of giggles.

CHAPTER THIRTY-TWO

Grayson

I CAN'T HELP but laugh along with Emma as she lets herself go, her wavy hair twirling in the sea breeze as she tilts her head back and giggles some more just after getting off in public.

My cock is *aching* in my pants, and the fact that Emma's still straddling me and her cum is lingering on me, is not helping my current situation.

But my needs take a back seat as I watch her light up with bliss, truly enjoying this night of release. The way her cheeks lift and her smile sparkles makes my stomach tumble, and I know that I need to give her more nights like this.

Nights where we're not tortured by the past.

The more I admire her, the more my vision blurs together. Winding down from our high, the alcohol settles deeper into my bloodstream, hitting me even harder.

My eyelids get heavy, as does the rest of my body.

"Let's do another shot!" Emma jumps off of me and tugs my hand, forcing me to peel myself off the bench.

We misstep, crashing into one another and burst into another round of laughter as we make our way to a bar.

We throw back some more shots, losing count. As I do another one, it tastes like water going down. When I glance over at Emma, I notice how flushed her face is, and she's struggling to stand upright. She blinks a few times, trying to keep her eyes open, but when she lets out a cute little yawn, that's when I know our night is ending.

It's also when realization hits me in my gut.

I fucking drove her here, which now means I have to figure out how to get her back home because I'm too shitfaced to walk straight, let alone drive.

Digging my phone out of my pocket to get an Uber, I let out a frustrated groan when I'm met with a black screen. Just as I'm about to ask Emma if her phone is charged, she leans her body weight onto me.

"I'm having so much fun," she mumbles, half asleep, her cheek squishing into my chest.

Wrapping my arm around her, I chuckle. "Let's figure out how to get you back home."

Exiting the bar, our steps are languid and messy. My head spins as we amble our way along the boardwalk. Even though the buildings are blending together, I can still make out SeaScape not too far off.

"We're gonna get my sister to drive us," I state as the idea strikes.

Emma gives me a thumbs up, then her movements slow down even more until she comes to a complete stop. With her shoulders rounded she lets out a deep sigh.

"What's wrong?" I ask.

"I'm so tired," she whines. "Can we just stand here for a minute? Or like, somehow make the building come closer to us?"

Laughing, I stare at SeaScape with her, wishing one of us had telekinesis powers.

When neither of us are able to make it move, I take it upon myself to keep us going. Scooping Emma up, she squeals as one of my arms wraps around her back while the other is under her knees.

My body sways a bit, and it takes several seconds for me to find my footing before I keep walking.

Emma curls into my chest, and I can sense her smiling against me as she holds on to my shirt.

"I always think it's so romantic when a guy carries a girl like this," she says, the sound of her voice becoming airy.

"Romantic, huh?" I pry for more information. "What else do you find romantic?"

"Hmm..." She clutches me tighter. "Picnics, gardens, kissing in the rain, love letters—those sorts of things."

Even though my brain has gone to trash, I make sure to memorize some of what she's saying.

Picnics, gardens, rain, letters.

Picnics, gardens, rain, letters.

If I repeat it enough times, maybe it'll stick.

Those four words float around my insides, making my heart feel lighter despite being weighed down by booze.

When we finally reach SeaScape, Emma seems to get a second wind as we step out of the elevator and into the hallway. She sways back and forth as I knock on Rae's door.

I give it a couple of seconds before knocking again.

"Rae's probably asleep," I tell Emma. "Which means she's gonna be even more of a bitch because I woke her up. So just hang behind me, and let me deal with her."

"I'm sure she'll be fine," she says, chuckling, but moves behind me anyway.

I continue tapping my knuckles against the door until it swings open. I reach out for the doorframe to stop from flying forward.

Rae's jaw is set tight, and her eyes are fuming with anger. "What. The. Fuck."

"Hi!" Emma squeaks, popping up from behind me.

Laughter bubbles inside me, and I press my lips together to try to keep it in, but the more I fight it, the larger it becomes as my shoulders shake.

Rae's head tilts when she spots me and Emma together. And for whatever reason, the look on her face is fucking hilarious, and my laughter explodes, the sound bouncing off the walls in the hallway as I hold onto my stomach.

Emma follows suit, and the both of us are in hysterics, drunkenly laughing at nothing.

"What's going on?" Miles appears beside Rae.

"I'd like to know that as well," Rae states, crossing her arms.

I try to compose myself, taking a few deep breaths until I'm able to speak again. "We need a ride home. Well, Emma needs a ride home, but I'm staying with her."

Rae's features twist from the confusing information, and she eyes us suspiciously until things click for her. "Are you *drunk*?"

"They're shitfaced," Miles states. "Come on in, guys." He opens the door wider, and Emma and I stagger inside.

"You've got to be fucking kidding me, Grayson," Rae snaps, her voice becoming louder. "We're *addicts*! He's a recovering alcoholic!" She points to Miles.

"It's all good. If anything, seeing people like this reminds me of how much I don't want to drink," Miles says.

Rae scowls at him, pissed that he messed up her chance to reprimand me.

"See? It's all good."

A loud crunch comes from the kitchen, and we all turn our attention to Emma, who's shoving a handful of chips into her mouth. She pauses, looking as if she's just been caught red-handed. "Sorry," she mumbles.

A dazed smile hits my lips as I admire how perfect she is, even as a wasted mess. "You're so cute," I blurt.

Rae whips her head back to look at me. "*Cute*?" She looks back and forth between us, and a sudden look of disgust crosses her face. "Oh my god—is this the guy you were talking about?!" she asks Emma.

Emma nods.

"Ew!" Rae puts her hands over her face to shield herself from looking at me.

"You were talking about me?"

"A little," Emma admits.

Excitement jumps around my belly. "What'd you say?"

"Stuff that I don't want to know about my brother," Rae interjects.

Still staring at Emma, my eyes widen, slightly horrified by what information might have slipped out.

"Don't worry, I didn't tell her about the vibrator," Emma says, completely forgetting we're not alone.

"Oh my god!" Rae screeches while Miles tries his best to hide his laughter under a cough.

"Oops, sorry, Rae." Emma blushes when she realizes what she said.

"I thought you were cool with us being together. You're the one who gave me her number," I say to Rae.

"I was until I just realized what that entails!" She gasps and more puzzle pieces connect. "Is that where you've been sneaking off to at night?"

I nod.

"Was Emma with you the night you got into a fight?"

"You got into a fight?" Emma asks.

My face drops, and I'm pretty sure Miles catches my look because he's quick to speak, diverting the conversation. "Why don't you get dressed so we can drive Emma home, and I'll take care of them in the meantime," he says to Rae.

Glancing at what she's wearing, bile rises to my throat when I notice she's only in Miles's shirt. "Oh sure, you can waltz around here with no pants on, but I'm the disgusting one for wanting to hook up with my gorgeous girlfriend."

"Girlfriend?" Emma's dainty voice floats over to me. Her striking eyes are filled with a vast amount of hope. And although this isn't some romantic scene I'm sure she's played out in her head, this will have to do.

"Girlfriend." I smile. "As long as you're willing to have me as your boyfriend."

A giddy expression dances across her features as she scurries over to me, still holding a bag of chips.

Getting on her tippy-toes, her salty lips press against mine in a wistful kiss as we smile against each other.

As she pulls away, the air in the room changes. Rae's posture softens when she takes in Emma's happiness. And I think she realizes it is in me, too.

Sighing, Rae steps away, heading toward her room so she can put some fucking pants on.

"You guys want some water?" Miles asks, already going to the fridge.

"Yes, please." Emma hiccups.

He smirks, putting two waters on the kitchen island. When I reach out to grab it, I miss and try again, spilling some before it hits my lips.

The both of us down the water as it quenches our thirst while Miles wipes up the little puddle I accidentally left.

"First time being this drunk?" he asks.

I'm not sure who he's asking, but I respond anyway, "Yep."

His brows raise in surprise when he looks at me. "Oh. You, too?"

Guess he was asking Emma.

"We wanted to make up for the twenty-first birthdays we never had," Emma explains.

Miles chuckles. "A little bit of late bloomers, but I hope you guys had fun. Just don't get too carried away."

"Trust me, the sensation of the room spinning is not something I'd like to replicate on a daily basis," I assure Miles that I won't end up like him or my sister.

Rae comes back, fully clothed. "Isn't your dad super strict, Emma?"

"Yep! But I don't give a shit anymore!"

"I'll sneak her in, don't worry," I tell Rae.

"And if you get caught?"

"I haven't yet." I mosey over to my belongings, looking for my car keys. "Have you seen where I put my keys?"

"Probably in your pocket, along with the key to my condo." She glares at me, still annoyed I woke her up.

Tapping my pants, I feel the metal pressing into the palm of my hand. "Yep. You're right," I say, taking them out.

Rae automatically swipes my car keys from me. "Let's go."

My tongue flicks over Emma's neck right before I suck on her sensitive skin.

She chuckles, then whispers, "Grayson, not here. Wait until we're in my room."

"Fuck my life," Rae's voice comes from the driver's seat.

I forgot she was even here. And that we're in my car.

"Where am I turning, Emma?" Rae asks, trying to get our attention away from each other for a brief moment.

Emma nestles into me in the back seat. "The next block."

Miles's headlights come from behind us as he drives his car so he can take Rae back to her condo after she drops us off.

Once Rae goes where Emma tells her, and she

notices the only house on the block, her jaw drops. "*This* is your home?"

"Yeah."

"Why the fuck do we hang out in my condo and not here?"

"Her dad's a dick, remember?" I chime in. "You can't park in front, go down a little further until you hit the dead end," I instruct.

Once my car is parked in the sandy, faux parking lot, we all get out.

I take one step forward, trip over something and am nearly met with a mouthful of gritty dirt.

"Christ," Rae mutters as she and Emma help me steady myself.

Another car door shuts, and I don't even have to turn around to know it's Miles coming to assist. "Let me walk you guys back to Emma's house," he says, magically appearing by our side.

"It's okay, we're fine," Emma says, swaying. Her body weight makes her lose her balance, and Rae holds on to her.

"Come on, you lush," Rae playfully says to Emma. "Lead the way."

The four of us somehow successfully make it over the sand dune after a few attempts and several laughter breaks.

My feet drag as we move away from the shoreline and toward the house.

"Jeez, your home is gigantic, Emma," Miles whispers as we get closer.

"It's even nicer inside," I keep slurring. "I saw it for the first time a couple of days ago."

"What do you mean, I thought you said you've been hanging out here for the past few weeks," Rae says.

"I have. But I've only been in Emma's bedroom." I smirk, and Miles turns to me, his lips twitching.

Rae ignores the comment, but there's a knowing look that passes between me and Miles. Even though he's being fucking annoying and trying to steady me as we walk, the exchange of glances makes me find him less bothersome for a brief second.

"So how are you two going to make it inside without waking her dad up?" he asks.

"Easy. Climb those stairs, and sneak through her window." I point to the double porches and staircases on the back of her house.

Rae snorts. "You're gonna make it up all those stairs in one piece without making a sound?"

"Oh, I know!" Emma lights up, not trying to keep her voice down. "Rae, if my dad wakes up you can run around to the front and knock on the door and distract him by asking him to pray for you!"

"What?"

"It's not weird, people have stopped by in the past. And he'll believe it if you say you need extra prayers." Emma gasps. "Not because you *look* like you do. I mean everyone needs extra prayers sometimes. I pray for all of you."

"Even me?" I ask, my head tipping to the side in surprise.

Her hand goes over her heart. "Of course, I do."

"That's adorable."

"Oh my god, I hate drunk people," Rae groans.

Miles chuckles as we approach the first staircase. He and Rae navigate us up the steps. My vision crosses, and even though we're so close to Emma's bedroom, the night sky is making it extra challenging for me to see.

We somehow make it up the second staircase and right in front of Emma's window without a hitch. I lift it up for her, and she sloppily sneaks inside.

Just as I'm about to join her in her room, Miles whispers, "Call us if you need anything."

I nod and hook one leg over the windowsill.

"Grayson, *do not* get her in trouble," Rae warns me with an icy glare.

"Relax. I haven't gotten into any trouble from any of the shit I've done yet."

"Like what?"

I put my index finger to my mouth. "If I tell you I might get in trouble."

She rolls her eyes. "See you tomorrow."

I slip inside Emma's room, leaving Rae and Miles to stealthily make it back to the parking lot. My gaze floats over to Emma who's already curled up on her bed, giving me a tired smile.

A grin hits my lips, and I make my way in next to her, wrapping my arm around her frame. My body relaxes into the mattress, and my eyelids grow heavy.

Emma lets out a yawn before resting her head on my chest. "Best fake birthday ever."

CHAPTER THIRTY-THREE

Emma

"EMMA?" Dad's voice coming through the intercom jolts me awake.

I shove Gray's arm off my waist, spring out of bed, and race to the other side of the room. My head throbs in pain, and my heartbeat stutters with anxiety.

"Morning, Dad," I respond, then quickly check the time to make sure it is in fact morning, and I didn't sleep until noon. Although, a part of me wishes I did so I could sleep through this nasty hangover that I'm sure to feel more of once the adrenaline of hearing Dad's voice wears off.

"I'd like to see you in my office when you have a moment."

"Be right there."

Gray lifts his head off the pillow, hair hanging in his one popped-open eye. "Tell him to fuck off," his sleepy voice croaks.

Anxiety prickles under my skin as I wrap myself in my robe and slide each of my feet into my fuzzy slippers.

"I'll be back in a few minutes," I whisper.

"Should I sneak out now?"

Shaking my head, I answer, "When he eats breakfast, like usual." That way I can steal a little more time with Grayson.

Before I travel downstairs, I do a quick wash of my face and rinse my teeth so I'm not a dead giveaway that last night I was a drunken mess.

Looking somewhat acceptable, I hurry down the steps to the other side of our house and enter Dad's office. His gaze is trained on his computer while he jots down something on his notepad.

Ignoring the nervous thud of my heart, I draw his attention away from whatever he's doing. "Good morning."

He does a double-take when he spots me by the doorway. "You're just getting up?"

"Um, yeah, I slept in a little."

"I need breakfast in twenty minutes." His tone rises with panic. "Emma, I have so much work to do this weekend before Monday."

"What's Monday?"

"What's Monday?" Dad repeats. His pen drops like a brick on his desk, and he rips his glasses off his face. The space between his brows deepens as he stares at me, not in anger but out of concern. "Emma, are you all right?"

I pinch the skin on my arm, hoping it'll wake me up. "I'm sorry, I have a little headache." My brain finally catches up to speed, and I realize what's going on. "Monday is your retreat."

The week-long retreat where I get to be by myself

for seven days and not under Dad's thumb or at his beck and call.

The awareness of the situation brings me back to life, and now I'm standing fully alert.

I'd usually tan on the beach and order Domino's to the house during retreat week. But this year, it's entirely different.

I have Gray.

Who's currently in my bedroom after we both got beyond wasted last night. And who has been sleeping in my bed the past several nights after he fucks me to the point I'm passing out immediately afterward.

I have no idea who this new version of Emma is, but I'm totally in love with her.

An air of self-assurance swirls around me, my veins lighting up with a fierce independence.

"Yes, I leave for my retreat in two days," Dad says, interrupting my thoughts. "I have to make several house calls today, so I'm going to need you to handle logistics for the retreat and confirm our reservations." He extends his arm, handing me a piece of paper.

When I step closer, I take it from him and glance down at the information. Six hours away in a five-star resort called Peace in the Pines. He usually changes where the retreat is so that people can have a unique experience each time, but this is by far the most bougie place he's ever picked. And I can't help but curl my fingers in anger around the sheet of paper. Renting this place out for a week is at least the cost of one college semester.

"This place is expensive," I state.

"The Gardiners contributed to a good portion of it, remember?" He shifts back to looking at his computer.

"And the other portion? Where's that money coming from?"

Dad freezes and slowly turns his gaze back to me. "Excuse me?"

"It's a very nice resort. I was just curious if the rest of the payment is coming from other contributors or you."

"It's a combination of both."

"Both," I mutter to myself, staring down at the paper.

"Since when are you so concerned with my finances?"

Since you abruptly cut me off with no savings to my name and refused to help me with a dime for my college education because you're angry I chose a career path over being your maid for the rest of my life—all while sitting on endless loads of cash.

Biting my tongue, I shrug. "Just curious."

He nods, yet I can still sense that he's trying to assess me. An uncomfortable burning hits the center of my chest, and I begin to tiptoe away so I don't have to continue talking with him.

"Eggs Benedict for breakfast," he calls out.

My shoulders stiffen in the doorway. "Okay."

Before going into the kitchen, I decide to head back to my bedroom so I can see Grayson for a few minutes before he sneaks away.

When I open my door, he's stepping out of my bathroom looking more put together than how he first woke up.

"Everything okay?" he whispers.

"Yeah, my dad just needs me to make sure everything is all set for his retreat." I go to make my bed, and Grayson helps me, neatly arranging my comforter.

"You're going on a retreat?"

"Nope." I smirk. "I'm staying home. My dad will be gone for an entire week."

Grayson's eyes sparkle with excitement, his cheeks raising. "No fucking way!" he whisper-yells.

I cover my mouth to muffle my laughter at his reaction and nod my head. "Me and you get the whole house to ourselves starting Monday!"

His jaw remains open in disbelief, and I watch as the various scenarios of what our week could look like cross his face. Chuckling to myself, I fluff my pillows as he stands there staring at me.

"How the hell did you get out of going to the retreat?"

"I haven't been allowed to go in years. I get a week-long break from him every summer. I usually do nothing exciting, but this year I have you!" I manage to keep my voice soft even though delight is dripping around every word.

"Your dad practically monitors the air you breathe, yet he's fine with you being alone for an entire week?" Grayson's face twists. "Why doesn't he allow you to go?"

Spinning on my heels, I head for my closet and mindlessly pick out a summer dress to wear. It's light blue with tiny white polka dots, and the neckline is square so Dad shouldn't have anything to say about it.

"Because Kane goes, and we'd be sleeping in rooms that are in close proximity." I slip into my dress with my back turned to Grayson, trying to blow off the details of this conversation. "It's much more beneficial for my dad to have the Gardiner family there than his own daughter."

"I feel like I'm missing something here—who's Kane?"

Glancing over my shoulder, I spot Grayson with his features pulled in tight, perplexed. He has dark circles under his eyes, and his arms land heavily by his side as if they're weighing him down. He must be feeling the after-effects of last night, otherwise he'd be able to put the pieces together.

When a long beat of silence stretches between us, I decide to break it by giving him the answer. "He's the guy I was telling you about. From my past," I whisper. Knots in my stomach form, loathing that Kane has marked me to the point that *he* is my past.

"Wait." Grayson shakes his head as if he's misheard me. "He still attends your father's church?"

Nodding, I watch as tension ripples across every muscle in his body.

"What the f—!"

I lunge forward, slamming my hand onto his mouth. "Shhh! It's daytime, and my dad's awake, remember?"

His eyes burst out of their sockets, steam pouring out of his ears. He tries to speak some more, but I squeeze my hand tighter to remind him to stay quiet.

"I'm aware it's fucked up," I say in a hushed tone. "We can talk about it more tonight, but for now, I have to get downstairs, make my dad breakfast, and help him get prepared for his retreat so he can be out of my life for seven days, and you and I can be together in peace. Got it?"

Grayson's stunned expression settles into something calmer, yet unnervingly intimidating. I can see sparks of anger brewing in the storm clouds that are painted in his irises. A hurricane of sorts looms in the background, and the tension that had appeared in his muscles has now escalated, his shoulders inching up his neck.

A large exhale tickles my hand as he tames himself even further. And suddenly, the anger is masked.

Grayson nods, agreeing to be quiet so we can carry on with our day.

Carefully, I pry my hand away from his face. I study him as his gaze falls off of me. No longer a look of rage, but rather, sorrow has him frowning. He retreats into himself, and I know he's getting lost in his head.

I want to know what's on his mind, but the clock is ticking, and I need to get into the kitchen.

"I'll see you tonight." I brush my lips against his, and he holds me for a brief moment before letting me go.

He nods once more, giving me a smile that doesn't reach his eyes.

As much as I'm longing to stay and talk with him, I make my way downstairs. I'll answer whatever questions Gray has later tonight.

CHAPTER THIRTY-FOUR

"YOU LOOK LIKE SHIT," Rae says, spotting me lounging on her couch when she enters her condo.

My hand is wrapped around a Gatorade, nursing my hangover. With a pounding pain in my skull, I glare at her.

She places a grocery bag down on her kitchen island. "Guess I didn't look much better during my glory days." *No, you looked worse.* "But I'm glad to see your face is still intact, and your limbs are attached to your body. I'm assuming Emma's dad didn't find out."

I shake my head while watching her put food away. When quiet falls between the adjoining rooms, Rae clicks her tongue.

"So, what, you need to be drunk in order to talk to me? Because you sure were a chatterbox last night," she snaps.

"I have a headache," I mumble.

Going back to putting the groceries away, she purposefully makes loud noises, slamming the cabinets shut and plopping things down. I roll my eyes at the dramatics and adjust the placement of my head.

When she's finished, she stomps her way toward the couch. "I'm just going to level with you. I don't know what your history is like with other girls, but if you're playing Emma, I will hurt you."

I scoff. "I don't have a history with girls. I'm not a fucking player, Rae."

"Well, I don't know anything about you, Grayson!"

"And whose fault is that?"

Her jaw sets. There's an intensity around her icy eyes, and I wait for her to dish something back to me, but she doesn't. Instead, she keeps going with the original topic. "As I was saying," she states. "If I find out you're just using Emma, I swear on Cara, I will fuck you up."

"I'm not using her—and can you not swear on our dead sister?"

"That's how serious I am. Emma is the sweetest person I've known. Not to mention, she and Miles are the best people to enter my life in ten years, and I'm not going to lose her because of my douchebag brother. So, if you're her boyfriend, you better be an amazing one."

The thought of being a decent boyfriend—hell, more than a decent boyfriend—has my heart faltering. Deep in my bones, I know I can't give Emma all that she deserves. But I know at the very least, I won't inflict any pain on her.

Dropping some of my defenses, my gaze lands on Rae's. "I'm going to treat her right," I say with utmost sincerity.

Rae tilts her chin in understanding, but I can still feel the pressure shooting out of her.

She goes out onto the balcony to smoke, and while she hangs out there, I close my eyes hoping if I squeeze in a nap, I'll wake up feeling hangover-free.

It seems like only thirty seconds have passed when Rae reenters, still having a conversation with me.

"Emma texted me saying that her dad's going away for a week starting on Monday." Rae starts speaking about the information I recently found out. I blink a few times before focusing on her. "She invited me and Miles over during that time—and I'm assuming you, too. Is it cool with you if the four of us hang out?"

"Yeah. That's fine."

She goes to her phone and starts texting, then walks away from me.

Slightly more alert, a round of excitement twirls around my insides. My mind is in a bunch of different places, but right now it's zeroed in on the fact that me and Emma get to be alone in her house for seven days straight.

We just have to get through tomorrow. Sunday.

My thoughts automatically shift gears when I realize the day of the week. Emma has been devoutly going to her dad's church every Sunday since it's been built, tomorrow will be no different. Only, this week I'm going to find out who else attends.

Emma licks the salt off her fingertips. "Thanks for taking me to get fries," she says before diving into the bag to grab her last handful.

When I told Emma I wanted to take her out tonight

and that she'd get to pick the place, I didn't think she'd opt for similar scenery to our first outing. But, she wanted some McDonald's and to sit by the docks. So here we are, perched on the hood of my car listening to the gentle splash of the water coming up to meet the anchored boats.

Thankfully, the both of us are feeling better from this morning's hangover.

We decided not to find a boat to hang out on this time, but we still watch them occasionally rock side to side if a big enough wave rolls through.

Emma even brought the captain's hat we stole and is currently wearing it. The white and navy colored fabric tame her hair every time the sea breeze brushes past.

"Of course," I state, taking a sip of my soda, although I would've liked to step up my boyfriend game and do something a little more special. But I have several ideas up my sleeve which I plan on using during Emma's week of freedom.

"Are you ever going to address the elephant in the room...well, technically, the parking lot? Because you've been skirting around asking me questions about Kane all night, and I know you want to."

Rubbing the back of my neck, I debate which question I want to ask her first. And wonder how long I'll be able to contain my anger once I receive the answers. My mind is still reeling from the bomb she dropped this morning about him still attending her dad's church. I'm struggling to process it all, so I decide to start with the basics.

"You were ten when he moved here and thirteen when he..." I can't even get the goddamn words out.

Emma nods, waiting for me to continue. "Which would've made him twenty-fucking-three."

"Yeah," she replies timidly.

"And even though your father witnessed a grown man taking advantage of you, he blamed you *and* didn't kick him out of his church?" Fury simmers beneath my bones, enough for me to feel a slight tremor in my arms.

"That pretty much sums it up."

"What the fuck!" I spew my words out into the air, polluting the tranquil environment.

"My thoughts exactly." Emma twists the vile metal that's suffocating her delicate finger around.

The blood coursing through my veins gets louder in my ears, but I know I have to keep it together, so I stuff the turmoil down further into the cruxes of my being. "How-how do you manage seeing him every single fucking week?"

"It sounds messed up, but I've gotten accustomed to him being there." Emma continues to fidget with her purity ring, keeping her eyes off me. "Don't get me wrong, I still feel awful whenever I see him, but I'm used to feeling that way. I'm not allowed to speak to him per my father's rules—which is one rule I'm thankful for. And we just go on pretending that all is fine. It's been years of compartmentalizing and pretending."

I furiously shake my head.

This is wrong. All of it. Every word that comes out of her mouth makes my anger grow tenfold.

With every fiber of my body, my hatred for Kane intensifies. Not to mention her father, who is supposed to be someone who protects her from predators, not someone who plays mind games and makes her believe she's the one a fault all so he can keep getting money from the predator's fucking family.

"You said Kane's family doesn't know, right?"

"Yep. My dad told them some story, I'm not sure what, but I know it wasn't the truth."

Anger claws up my spine. "And everyone just acts as if everything's normal?"

"For the most part, yeah. Thankfully we stopped doing any family outings together. Aside from that, it's a normal Sunday."

"Except for the fact that it's not. Especially for you."

She nods, chewing the inside of her cheek as if to hold back any emotion that might be surfacing. "I just got used to the pain."

"You shouldn't fucking have to!" I slam my fist into the hood of the car, the sound echoing in the parking lot. Emma jumps in place, and I'm immediately remorseful and pissed at myself for not keeping my anger in check. "I'm sorry—I didn't mean to scare you." Add that to the list of shit I hate about myself. "It just makes me fucking furious for a multitude of reasons." My head spins with everything that's causing my internal chaos until it finally lands on something to pinpoint. "You shouldn't be afraid to go to church. Just like people shouldn't be afraid to dress a certain way, or kids shouldn't be afraid to go to school—"

I cut myself off, biting my tongue on that last sentence. My brain couldn't help but go back there—it always does. But I don't want to bring up my memories about Cara, I've never even told Emma about her or how she died.

Besides, this conversation is about Emma, not about my baggage.

"You're right," she states, her voice becoming firmer. I let out a small breath of relief that I didn't scare her away by my minor outburst. "I agree with everything you're saying, and I get livid about it, too."

"Yeah?"

"I hate that these terrible things are a reality for so many people." She freely talks with her hands, staring out to sea. "I hate that kids are still being groomed—that's what happened to me. I have never said it out loud before but here it goes: Kane fucking groomed me." Her face tightens with repulsion. "I spent so long researching and learning about it. I realized he hit all the fucking marks—building trust, buying me things, pushing boundaries little by little, being secretive. It was all right there, and I—"

Emma stops herself, and I can tell just by where she was headed that she was about to put some blame on her shoulders.

Instead, she takes a deep inhale, and I watch as she settles her emotions. She turns to look at me, vulnerability pouring out of her. "I was a child," she whispers, finishing her sentence.

Those four words slice my insides, shattering my heart.

Without realizing, my arm wraps around her, tugging her into my chest.

I don't know how she manages this day in and day out.

And yet, here she is, the brightest light I've ever seen, gracefully handling it all alone.

For an endless amount of time, Emma stays tucked

in my embrace. We relax on top of my car breathing in the salt air and listening to the soft current.

The night grows darker, and by the time we're sneaking up her back porch toward her bedroom window, it begins to drizzle. Small, cool droplets of water scatter across our bodies giving us a nice break from the summer heat.

"Looks like we made it back just in time," I whisper, glancing upward at the hovering rain cloud.

Emma shrugs. "I like summer storms. There's something alluring about the intensity." With that, she climbs back into her bedroom.

As I follow her, I'm struck with the drunken memory of what Emma finds romantic—kissing in the rain being one of the items on her list. As much as I'd love to hoist her back outside and make that fantasy a reality for her, she's already yawning and getting into her nightgown.

I'm sure there are other ways I can fulfill her romantic wish list.

As I lay my head down on the pillow next to her, my thoughts jump back and forth between protection and romance, until I finally fall asleep.

CHAPTER THIRTY-FIVE

Emma

DAD'S SERMON seems extra long this morning. Or perhaps I'm just at the end of my rope when it comes to tolerating what he has to say.

Speaking with Gray last night and seeing his reaction to how I was mistreated, validated just how fucked up this entire situation is. While his strike of anger startled me, it also made me feel seen. He's hurt because others have hurt me.

I normalized everything and kept it to myself because I was ashamed.

But now, it's as if another layer of myself is shedding as I step out of the mold I was forced to conform to.

The sound of the organ ricochets off the hollow walls, and normally I wouldn't glance over to Kane playing, but this time I do.

He's focused on the sheet music, his fingers powering down on the keys. As the music builds, so does my nausea.

Kane has gotten to sit up near the pulpit for years,

the parishioners praising him for his talent. He gets to carry on with his life, brushing everything under the rug while I get left with the ruins.

Waves of torment crash into me. Over and over again as I listen to the rich timbre of the pipes. As it gets louder, my heart beats faster. The waves smash harder.

Since I was thirteen, I have had to put up with this.

Both Kane and Dad placed the blame on me and went on as if nothing happened.

Tears prickle behind my eyes, and I glance up, trying to blink them away. My gaze lands on the cross hanging high on the wall. Dad doesn't live his life as a holy man and never has. It's always been about notoriety and money for him.

But there's an intuitive pull deep within my broken heart telling me that Mom was nothing like him. She was the epitome of benevolence, and it's her spirit that I hope to embody.

As the organ stops and Dad starts up again, I find myself internally speaking to Mom, hoping that wherever her soul is, she can hear my thoughts.

I need an out, Mom.

Please send me a miracle—anything.

Please guide me where I'm supposed to go because I know this isn't it for me.

The welling behind my eyes continues, starting to sting as I hold it in.

"Let's all pray together," Dad's voice booms, interrupting my thoughts.

As usual, everyone rises, reaching their arms out to link hands. Brushing my hair over my shoulder before clasping Mrs. Sterling's hand, something in the back of the church catches my attention.

Or rather, some*one*.

Oh my god. Grayson's at my father's church.

Gray stands all the way in the back, smirking when we lock eyes.

My stomach drops and rises as I become excited and terrified at the same time. He snuck out this morning as I prepared breakfast like usual, but I assumed he'd go back to Rae's and not show up at Kingdom Church out of the blue.

Heat rushes to my cheeks.

Dad goes through his prayer, and as I bow my head with the rest of the congregation, I try to steal a glance behind me. And when I do, I can't help but snicker to myself at Grayson playing the part and following along with everyone else.

"Have a blessed Sunday," Dad wraps up. "I look forward to seeing the majority of you here tomorrow morning, bright and early for our pilgrimage to this year's spectacular retreat."

Everyone claps, eager to assemble here tomorrow and travel together, blindly following Dad's lead to some fancy resort under the ruse of a spiritual sanctuary.

As Dad walks down the aisle, I trail behind him, my heart pounding as I pass Grayson. His eyes are fixated on me, and the smug, yet sexy, smirk hasn't left his perfect face.

Unsure of where to look, I glance between him and the back of Dad's head.

I bite back my own smile as I waltz past him and stand next to Dad at the exit. We go on to shake everyone's hands, and people are mainly saying how excited they are for the retreat.

My weight shifts from foot to foot as I hurry them along, trying to peek behind them to find Gray.

"We're all set for tomorrow, Pastor!" Mrs. Gardiner exclaims.

"At least someone is," Dad jokes and everyone laughs.

"Any last-minute arrangements that I can assist with?" Mr. Gardiner asks.

"No, no. I have Emma here to help me with some loose ends."

"You do?" I twist my head up to look at Dad, unaware of these plans.

He pauses for a beat, thrown off by my response. There's a slight flash of annoyance that crosses his features, but he masks it before anyone notices. "I must've forgotten to fill you in." He forces a chuckle. "I just need your help with making some phone calls, then you can get on with the rest of your Sunday."

"You'll be missed this week," Mrs. Gardiner interjects, giving me a sympathetic, yet also judgmental, look as she brings her hand to her heart.

I give her a tight-lipped smile with a curt nod of my head.

As the line continues to build behind them, they start to drift away but not before stopping at my side. "Be good while your father's away," she whispers to me.

My jaw drops open at the audacity of this woman.

I have no idea what lies my father told Kane's family, but either way his mother should learn to keep her mouth shut.

The words burn at the tip of my tongue, urgency flooding my lungs as I wish to scream out everything that her son has done to me. But before I can squeak out a sound, my attention is getting pulled to the voice coming next to me.

"Wonderful sermon today, Pastor," Gray says, shaking Dad's hand.

My head spins, now completely focused on the two of them meeting. With nerves jumping around my stomach, I watch their entire interaction.

"I particularly loved the part about obeying those who provide for you," he adds.

Dad smiles, but his eyelids narrow as he assesses Grayson. "Thank you. I don't believe I've ever seen you at my church before."

"That's because you haven't. I just moved here recently." He shifts his gaze to me, and my entire body lights up. "I'm Grayson." He extends his hand toward me.

Fighting back a grin, ignoring the whirlwind that's released in my veins, I shake his hand. The familiar calloused palm brushing up against mine. "Emma," I state.

"Pleasure to meet you." He looks over to Dad once more. "Thank you again. Have a fantastic week."

When he goes to leave, his gaze lands on me one last time. There's a fierce sensation of protection radiating from him.

More people move through the line, and as I say a halfhearted goodbye to them, I keep my attention trained on Grayson walking to his car.

When the line finally dies down, and Dad's fan club chats in the pews as they wait for him, he leans toward me. With an icy chill in his voice, he says, "Do not go anywhere near that young man."

Whipping my focus to Dad, my hair lashing across

his shoulder by the sudden movement, my brows dip. "Why?" I challenge.

"He's no good. I can tell." Dad straightens his posture and gently places his hand on my back with a smile as if he's suddenly aware that people have been watching him. "And I know my sweetheart is nothing short of moral."

With that, he leaves me to go talk to the others, expecting me to follow. Instead, I take my phone out of my purse.

Me
that sure was a surprise

Gray
I'm full of surprises, Red

Me
you got a few more up your sleeve?

Gray
what kind of surprise would it be if I told you?

"Emma, could you tidy up the pews?" Dad calls over to me.

"Sure."

As I do what he asks, making sure if one of the parishioners left anything behind, my phone buzzes once more.

Gray
when are you leaving?

Me
I need to help my dad with a few things. It might be awhile

Gray
I'll sit in the lot and wait

I smile at the screen.

Me
I'm fine, Gray. I've been doing this for years. Go back to Golden Bay, and I'll let you know when I'm leaving here

Gray
I don't want to leave you alone

Me
My dad will get suspicious if you hang out waiting for me. I promise I'll be fine

Waiting for his reply, I stare at my phone walking toward the front of the church. Not paying any attention to where I'm going, I slam right into someone.

"I'm sorry—!" My gaze travels upward as I spot Kane's dark eyes piercing into mine. There's an immediate lump in my throat, and I swallow around it as I attempt to shuffle past him.

"I heard what your dad said to you," he whispers.

My eyes dart around in the room in panic.

Is Kane actually trying to have a conversation with me right now?

Dad is too busy with the others to notice, but either way I don't want to waste my breath on Kane so I ignore his statement.

"He's right," Kane continues in a hushed voice.

My gaze hardens. "What are you talking about?" I snap.

"That new guy who was here, he's trouble. I can tell."

I can't help the bitchy laugh that climbs out of my throat. *Kane* is the one with a moral compass telling me that another man is trouble? That's got to be the most ironic comment I've heard in my entire life.

"I know what you were thinking when you looked at him. It was written all over your face."

An explosive blast of fury fills my chest, shooting up my neck and making my cheeks hot. "You know nothing about me," I bite out through gritted teeth as quietly as possible without causing a scene.

"You know that's not true," he states, unaffected by my reaction, as he gives me an arrogant smirk. "I'm just giving you a warning."

With that, he carries on and goes to talk with some of the choir singers who are loudly speaking about performing on some fancy stage at the resort.

My eyes burn a hole in the back of Kane's head as I watch him walk away. Abhorrence rips its way into every fiber of my body, seizing up my muscles the longer I fixate on him and his words.

The growing awareness that someone is noticing me has me pulling my attention away from Kane. My gaze moves over to Dad who's eyeing me curiously.

Schooling my features, I roll my shoulders back and paste on a fake smile.

I just have to put up with helping out around here for a little bit, and then I can go back home to Gray for the afternoon.

CHAPTER THIRTY-SIX

Emma

AS I ENTER MY HOME, I can still feel the lingering knots in my muscles from my interaction with Kane. I tried so hard to push him out of my head during the drive back, but it didn't work. How dare he speak to me—and how fucking dare he speak to me about Grayson of all topics!

My jaw clenches, and I do my best to calm down because I don't want Kane souring my Sunday with Grayson.

"Gray?" I call out when I hit my staircase. There's no response as I travel upward toward my bedroom. "Are you reading my Kindle again?" I tease, a smile already on my lips as my aggravation begins to leave my body.

When I enter my room, there's no sign of Gray, but my window is wide open with a slight breeze moving my curtain.

I decide to climb through the opening and onto my back porch to see if he's on the beach. When I peer over the banister, I gasp as butterflies instantly take flight in my stomach.

"Hey, Red," Gray says, holding a bouquet of flowers and standing next to a large, woven blanket splayed out over the sand.

"What is all of this?"

"Why don't you come down here and find out?"

Grinning, I hop down the stairs becoming lighter with each step I take. Stopping at the landing, I take off my shoes and let my feet brush over the warm sand. Gray meets me halfway, his free hand reaching for mine and walking me over to everything he has set up.

"Once upon a time, a drunk girl told me what she thought was romantic, so I figured it was time I delivered," he states.

My eyes automatically water as I take in the whole setup. He made me a picnic with candles and books on the edges of the blanket.

"I know gardens were on the list. Obviously, I couldn't pull that off, but I did my best bringing a garden to you." Gray holds out the bouquet, and I take it from him, admiring the pastel colors. "I asked Miles if he knew of any florists, and he hooked me up with some lady, but she kept asking me what kind of flowers you liked, and I didn't know the scent of your candles."

"Wisteria."

"Wisteria," he mutters to himself as if he's memorizing it. "Well, I don't know if any of these are that flower, but I told her your favorite color is rose gold, so she picked these."

"They're perfect." I sniffle, holding in happy tears.

Gray moves onto the blanket, where a traditional-looking picnic basket sits. He opens it up, taking food out as he speaks. "Now, I know this food isn't romantic, but I know it's your favorite." He showcases a McDonald's bag along with two large sodas, causing me to laugh.

Joining him, I rest the flowers next to the arrangement of new candles he must've recently bought. Kneeling across from him, my champagne-colored dress with pink roses detail on it hits right above my knees.

My heart flutters fast, little fireworks flying out of me the longer I stare into Gray's enticing eyes. The ocean tenderly rolls up to the shoreline creating a peaceful melody.

"I can't really do anything about kissing you in the rain." He glances up at the cloudless sky, squinting. "But I'll make it happen one day."

"I'll settle for kissing you under the hot sun," I say before leaning forward and planting my lips on his.

My fingers weave their way through his thick hair, and my body crawls closer to his. I devour each subtle breath he takes, positioning myself on his lap as my need for him strengthens.

"Wait—" He abruptly pulls away. "One more thing." Extending his arm, he reaches across the blanket toward some books. I recognize the one on top, his brown leather notebook. "They're not romantic letters by any means, but I can read you some of my prose."

My breath hitches. "You...you want to read your writing to me?"

He nods.

"I don't want you to feel like you have to share it, Grayson. It was wrong of me to snoop. I know how personal your writing is."

Without responding, he scoots me to sit in between

his legs and opens his notebook. Quietly, he skims the pages. His eyes roam the words until he lands on what he's looking for.

"To have her know my mind and embrace it is a different form of intimacy. One I never knew I needed," Gray recites, plucking the words from the middle of a handwritten poem. Before I can respond or ask for more, he closes the notebook. He stares at it for a beat then says, "I've never been one for talking, Emma. Being around you is the most comfortable I've ever been with speaking, and even so, I still sometimes suck at expressing my thoughts." Lifting his chin up to look at me, I get another round of butterflies. "Let me read some of my writing to you. I want you to get to know me this way."

A glistening of joy coats my eyes. "I'd love nothing more." Arching up, I lean over and give his temple a peck.

For the rest of the afternoon, we settled into each other's embrace. We eat in between talking and sharing tidbits of our lives.

Gray picks out a few poems to read to me, each one more heartbreaking than the last. I notice how careful he is when selecting what to expose to me. He doesn't relay any thoughts about either of his sisters, skipping right over his memories with the both of them.

Once my belly is full, I lay my head on his lap admiring the calm waves in front of us. Grayson idly runs his fingers through my hair, coaxing me into a deeper relaxation.

"Keep reading," I say.

"I feel like I should change it up a little, the shit I write is depressing." Gray chuckles. "I also brought

Pride and Prejudice out here." He points to the small stack of books. "And your Kindle's here, too. You know, just in case you felt like reenacting any smutty beach scenes."

I snort. "That's definitely on my list of things to do during the week, but for right now I'd much rather listen to your poems."

His hand trails down my neck and skims over the strap of my dress. Even in the hot weather, goose bumps prickle on my arm as he slips a finger under the strap, coyly playing with the idea of pulling it down.

"What else is on your list for this week?" he asks with a rich huskiness in his voice.

"Lots of sex." I turn and glance up at him. "Oh, and I want to hang out with Rae and Miles. Maybe the four of us can have a beach day or something."

"I'm going to choose to fixate on the first part of that list." His wandering hand travels down the length of my body until he hits the hem of my dress. Eagerly, he slips under the thin fabric and lightly massages my thigh.

I gaze up at him, my pulse excitedly beating the longer I await his magic touch. Brushing a strand of hair off my forehead, he looks down at me with the simplest, yet sweetest, smile. It's such a genuine expression of joy that I want him to remember it. Remember that this feeling is possible for him and that he doesn't always need to be tortured by the past.

"This is the most incredibly thoughtful gesture anyone has ever done for me," I tell him.

"I'm glad you like it," Gray says. "I wish I could've done more."

I shake my head against his lap. "This is beyond perfect."

"At the very least, I wish I had something more romantic to read to you." His face twists as if he's unsure he should say his next thought. "Actually, I do have a little something. But I wasn't sure if I should share it."

My heart flutters. "You can read me your grocery list, and I'd still love it."

Picking up his leather-bound notebook once more, he chuckles as he flips right to the spot he was thinking of. Clearing his throat, he begins.

"She's bearing the weight of other's sins,
the pressure doubling down, snapping each bone.
With clean hands she crumbles from their crimes.
Crushed and turned to dust.
Yet, she rises.
And if she is the phoenix, ascending from it all,
red flames igniting her spirit,
then I am the ashes,
delicate flecks of gray smoke worshipping her at her feet.
Neither of us afraid of the fire."

I shoot up, wide-eyed in disbelief. My body buzzing as if I touched a live wire drenched in saltwater. My heart hammers so quickly, my breaths can't keep up.

"You wrote that about me?" I whisper, unable to wrap my head around how those beautiful words were inspired by *me*.

Gray nods, closing his book.

"That's how you truly see me? That strong?"

He cups my face, his thumb grazing over my cheekbone as our gazes stay locked on one another. "I see how strong you are. You might not believe it, but there's a fire inside you, Emma. And I'm drawn to your flames. They're the only light in my life."

Heat spirals out of the center of my chest, emanating a tingly sensation throughout my insides. For a third time since our picnic started, tears well up, only this time I don't hold them back.

Droplets of adoration roll down, hitting Gray's hand. He doesn't wipe them or tell me there's no need to cry. Instead, he stays with me silently in this moment, absorbing the tears as they fall.

"For someone who doesn't like talking, you sure knew the perfect thing to say." I smile.

His lips land on mine, and our bodies instantly melt into one another's.

If I could bottle up this moment and keep it forever, I would.

CHAPTER THIRTY-SEVEN

Emma

I LUG the last of Dad's bags in front of the door as he scarfs down the omelet I made him.

"You're all set," I state, with possibly too much pep in my voice.

"Thank you, sweetheart," he says, walking out of the kitchen and into the foyer where I'm anxiously waiting for him to leave.

"I pressed your charcoal suit this morning in case you wanted to wear it during your sermon tonight," I say, pointing to the garment bag.

"What about my black one?"

"It's also in there."

Dad inspects the bag as if I'd be lying about something so absurd. Meanwhile, I watch him with a quizzical look tugging on my features. It's always been so bizarre how within sixty seconds, he can go from thanking me and calling me his sweetheart to distrusting me.

The more I stare at him, the more I realize that all this man truly cares about is himself. When he states his appreciation, it's not genuine. It's so that *I* can trust him, getting me to follow his rules. Just like his congregation blindly follows him. He's built his image on false compliments and lies. And somehow it worked.

But not for me.

"I assume you remember what's expected of you this week," he states, standing taller once he's done checking his suits.

I nod, adjusting my stature as well.

"No visitors, and no going out with young men. You should be spending your time cleaning and checking up on Kingdom Church."

"Yes, Dad."

He scoops up his belongings and turns to face me once more. "Be good." The tone of his voice makes me shiver.

I respond the same way I normally would, "I always am."

Before leaving, he gives me a peck on the top of my head. It's not out of the ordinary, but I'm learning that it's not a sign of fatherly affection. It's more of a mark, saying that I'm a good, doting daughter, and we both know it.

"See you Sunday."

"Have a safe trip."

Dad gives me a small smile before exiting. I watch as he carries his baggage down the steps and into his car. It feels like years, but he finally backs out of our driveway.

As I watch him travel down the road, making sure he doesn't turn back around, I hear soft footsteps creaking on the stairs behind me.

"He's gone?" Gray asks, making his way to me as I linger by the window.

"Yep." I glance over my shoulder, a devilish grin dances on my lips as I look up at Grayson. "Let's break some rules."

CHAPTER THIRTY-EIGHT

NEVER IN MY wildest dreams did I think that when Emma said she wanted to break some rules, that she would want to come *here*.

"Wow," she whispers.

"Yep."

I watch as she nervously blinks at the wall in front of her, taking it all in. I tried warning her the whole ride to Sindarella's that she might be a bit overwhelmed walking into a sex shop for the first time. But she didn't care, so that's why we're here staring at a giant display of dildos.

"That thing is supposed to fit inside someone's body?!" Emma points, her cheeks turning pink.

Chuckling, I respond, "I guess so."

Her head tilts to the side, examining all the different types of toys and lotions. "What should we get?" She's quiet as we tiptoe around the store which smells like latex and fruity perfume.

My hand is linked to her lower back, not wanting to

leave her side. "How about this?" I tease, grabbing a leather whip.

Emma starts giggling, taking it right out of my grip and spins around, spanking me with it.

"Oh, I'm gonna get you back for that." I laugh along with her. "You better get ready for tonight."

One of her eyebrows arches. "You better keep that promise."

Sometimes I forget how easy it can be to have fun with Emma. We've both bogged down by the seriousness of our lives that it's become second nature for us to neglect the enjoyment of being young.

There's no one else I'd rather flirt and laugh with in a sex shop. And there's no one in the world who would get away with spanking me.

"What about these?" She discards the whip and picks up yellow star pasties. "They would look really good on you," she jokes, placing them over my nipples.

"I'm not sure if yellow is my color."

Emma's mouth scrunches to one side as if she's actually giving this some deep thought. "You're right. You look much better in cool tones."

She twirls around and scours for more items to poke fun at me with.

I love seeing her this playful and carefree. My face begins to hurt from smiling so much as I watch her bubbly self float around the store.

Her eyes fall out of her head when she passes a blow-up doll. "I think I was a little in over my head committing to this," she admits, holding back laughter.

"We can go, we don't need to hang out here."

"No, I want to get something." I watch as her gaze lands on the skimpy outfits hanging up on the wall across from us. My cock twitches, envisioning her wearing one of those.

I adjust my pants. "Do you know what you want?"

She shakes her head, and I notice a blush creeping up her neck.

Leaning in, I place my hand on the dip of her back once more. "Think about the books you've read. Anything in those you might want to try in real life?" I whisper in her ear.

Her mouth parts, and she wets her lips. There are words on the tip of her tongue, but she doesn't speak them.

I know she has a few fantasies in mind, and if she doesn't remember her annotations, I sure as fuck do.

"Why don't you hang out in the car, and I'll pick us out a little something," I suggest.

Her eyes light up as a sense of relief loosens her shoulders. "You and your surprises."

I shrug. "What can I say, it's my habit when it comes to you."

She gives me a soft kiss on my lips and heads toward the parking lot.

I take my time browsing through the selection, trying my best not to get too fixated on an image of Emma doing the various dirty things that I come across.

When I finally settle on what I want to get her, I pay for the two items, and the cashier slips them into a black bag.

"Have fun." She winks.

There's no use in holding back my smile from this stranger, so I wear it proudly all the way back to my car.

"What'd you get?" Emma practically pounces on me when I go to sit in the driver's seat.

"You'll find out later, Red."

"How much later?"

"I'll give you one of the things tonight."

She lets out a tiny gasp. "How many things did you buy?"

"Just two, don't get too excited."

"I should split the cost with you," she says, unzipping her purse to take out money.

"Not a chance."

Besides, the cash I used to pay for it wasn't technically mine. I stole money from two drug dealers, and since I barely used to go anywhere before coming to Golden Bay, the wad of cash has been sitting in my wallet patiently waiting for me to spend it on something useful.

Obviously, I'm not going to tell Emma that part. She doesn't need to know that I used to take my aggression out on other people and occasionally ransack their pockets when they were too limp to move.

That was my past. And Emma's my future.

Our day moves on, filled with little things that probably don't mean as much to the average person, but neither of us has led average lives, so for us, the small things, such as hanging out in her living room, have a big impact on us.

By the end of the night, I think I've tortured us enough by putting off the gifts I bought at the sex shop. We're lounging in her bedroom when I decide to take one of the items out of the bag.

"Can I finally see what you got me?" Emma asks, excitedly kneeling on her mattress.

Red lace slides through my fingers as I delicately place a see-through bodysuit on her bed. "I guessed your size," I state. Not that I would care if I bought the piece of lingerie too small. If anything, it would further enhance her curves, making them pop out even more.

Her jaw drops. "You bought me lingerie?"

"I told you I would buy you anything you feel sexy in," I rasp, blood already rushing to my lower half. "Why don't you try this on and see if it does the trick."

With a large grin, her hand drifts over the fabric. "It's red."

"The most sexy and wild color there is."

My gaze dances over the waves of her hair, and I take note of the blossoming pink tinge that forms on her cheeks. The subtle color makes my body heat up even more.

Emma stands up holding the skimpy outfit and makes her way to her bathroom. "Give me two minutes."

"Take your time."

As she closes the door behind her, I decide to explore her house a little more.

We're in desperate need of a change in scenery.

CHAPTER THIRTY-NINE

Emma

I CAN'T STOP STARING at myself in the mirror.

I look hot as hell.

I twist and turn, admiring my reflection in my bathroom. The red, lacy number is a leotard of sorts—only, the sides are cut out leaving a strip of lace down my center and there's also a cut-out at the very bottom for easy access.

Aside from the underwire which creates ample cleavage that's spilling over, the outfit is completely see-through, my nipples piercing through the sheer fabric. Thin red straps wrap around my shoulders, holding the whole thing up.

I twirl a few more times, fluffing my hair to give it a more tousled look. My fingertips skim over the outfit, anticipating what it's going to feel like when they are replaced with Gray's.

"Emma," Gray's voice calls out over my intercom, and I freeze.

A striking panic hits my bones in a momentary

lapse of memory, forgetting that Dad's not here, and he's not the one talking.

Hearing someone other than Dad speaking on the intercom is foreign. It's only ever been me and him.

"Emma?" Grayson calls again, and this time I'm brought back into the present.

Traipsing out of my bathroom, when I get to the white box that's mounted onto my wall, I press my finger against the button and speak. "Yes...?"

"Can I see you in your dad's office, please?"

Worry and confusion cause my stomach to dip. Reaching for my robe, I wrap it around me as I dash out of my room and eventually down the staircase. I hastily make my way to Dad's office.

My feet freeze in the doorway when I spot Grayson standing over Dad's desk. His fingers are perched on the expensive oak as a look of hunger builds behind his eyes.

Gray's gaze floats down my body as my arms fall to my side, the robe opening as if it has a mind of its own. A flushed sensation warms my insides as I watch him admire the red lace that's conformed to my skin.

My breathing turns ragged, and not because I just ran from one end of the house to the other. But from the way he's drinking me in, every curve and every inch.

"What's going on?" I ask, still unsure why he's standing in this room.

Grayson's tongue gradually grazes his bottom lip as he leisurely brings his attention back up to meet my eyes.

"I'm going to fuck you on your father's desk."

Utter shock rips through my chest. I stare wordlessly across at Grayson, my heart heavily thudding.

This would be bad—like, *too* bad.

The ultimate fuck you.

And yet, desire sizzles in my core. Heat building between my thighs as a deep ache to be touched by Gray takes over.

Sliding my robe down one shoulder and then the other, it drops to the floor until I'm standing in front of him wearing nothing but the lingerie he picked out. Wild and sexy—my new adjectives that I'm about to claim.

The way his eyes rake over me once more causes my pulse to surge with passion.

The wicked smirk that only pops up when he's ready to fulfill my sexual desires appears on his face, making my insides melt. "That's my bad girl." The raspy words fall from his kissable lips.

Everything else in the room disappears, and my focus zeros in on Grayson. With each slow stride I take, my body burns as if I'm leisurely walking over hot coals, relishing in the flames as I make my way to him.

I reach the opposite side of the desk, the tension between us rippling waves of anticipation through my veins.

"Crawl up here for me, Red." He pats the desk.

Even though I'm weak in the knees, I manage to do as he says, hopping up onto the desk until I'm kneeling directly in front of him.

His intoxicating scent makes my heart hum a song of desperate hunger. His gaze drops down, noticing the heavy rise and fall of my breasts. Inching forward, his mouth hovers over mine. But he doesn't kiss me.

Instead, he lets his lips ghost over me.

My jaw, ear, neck.

His warm breath floats over my flesh, and I shudder at how good it feels even though he hasn't even touched me. His energy alone is enough to lull me into a high.

My fingers curl on top of my knees as I savor how he teases me.

Finally, he drags his hand over one of the straps and follows the hemline down to my cleavage.

"You look gorgeous in this." The deep pitch of his voice causes the tiny hairs on my arm to rise. "Do you feel sexy?"

I nod, trying to tame my quickening pulse.

"Show me how sexy you feel."

Without giving it a second thought, I reposition myself, sliding my legs out from under me and spreading myself wide.

A flickering of pleasure and pride ignites beneath the cloudy blues in his eyes. His attention goes straight to the opening in the fabric, and he smiles. "I didn't realize it had this when I bought it." His finger runs down my slit, my head immediately rolling back at the sensation.

Reaching for my left hand, he brings it over my body, placing it on my wetness.

"Touch yourself for me."

With him standing over me, watching my every move, I begin circling my clit. He bites down on his lip, becoming mesmerized by my actions and small whimpers.

"You like what you see?" I taunt.

His eyes shoot up to lock on mine, an expression of surprise crossing his features as if he didn't expect me to start speaking.

"Fuck, yeah I do," he says. "But I'd like this even more."

Taking my hand away for a brief second, he takes hold of my middle and ring finger pushing them inside me. I gasp when I feel just how wet I am. Moving my wrist, he helps me move my fingers in and out until my legs start trembling.

When he notices that I'm getting closer to the edge, he pulls my hand away. Taking my two fingers, he sucks them clean. Suddenly, his tongue is replaced by his teeth, and I feel them scraping over my skin.

Carefully, he pulls his mouth away with my purity ring between his teeth.

The sight of him literally releasing me from my confinement has my nerve ending electrified with pleasure. My head dizzies from the overwhelming flood of tingles throughout my body.

The stammering breaths coming from my mouth increase as I watch Grayson toss the ring on the far side of the desk. "Much better." He smirks as he lowers himself down to sit on Dad's leather office chair.

Silently, his calloused fingertips encircle my ankle, and he bends my knee, placing my foot down on the desk. He does the same with my other leg so that my pussy is at the perfect angle for him to devour me.

My racing pulse skitters under my skin as I lean back on my forearms. Another side of me comes to life when he gazes at me like he's about to own every millisecond of my pleasure. A goddess awakens inside, wanting to completely surrender to him.

Grayson leans forward, his tongue meeting my warmth. The gentle rhythm causes me to quiver instantaneously.

He starts off tender and slow. His arm reaches out to push down on my stomach, getting me to relax my back against the solid oak. Shutting my eyes, I completely lose touch with where I am—but I know for certain Gray is the one who's bringing me closer to a rush of ecstasy.

His hands move to my thighs, spreading me wider with a slight burn in my leg muscles. Thrusting his tongue inside me, I grip onto his dark hair and cry out his name. My hips buck up to meet each lust-driven lash he gives me.

Pulling away only slightly, he speaks with ragged breaths hitting my clit. "Fuck my face, Red."

Looping his hands around my thighs, he slams me against his mouth. Gone is the sensual touch, and it's immediately replaced with something much more savage as he consumes me.

"Holy shit!" I scream.

My fingers bury into his hair, yanking at the roots. I keep his mouth exactly where I want it as I grind my pussy against him. He's letting me use him to get off. He's letting me have control as my hips move faster.

Moan after moan, the both of us become more unhinged, every inhibition thrown to the wayside. He tugs me closer and closer as if he can't get enough of my taste, his fingers pressing down on my legs in a beautiful, bruising hold.

My back arches, and I writhe across the desk. Legs shaking, heat bursting through my veins, lungs heaving—the whirlwind of pleasure overtakes my body.

Soaring higher and higher, waves of euphoria cascade throughout my insides.

"Grayson!" I cry out as I shatter under his hungry touch.

A billion stars exploding under my skin as I reach my climax. Screaming, twisting and turning and continuing to nearly rip the hair out of his head.

He keeps licking me as I come down causing me to quiver and gasp, the aftershocks becoming too much to endure.

Turning limp against the desk, my back relaxes, and a lazy smile pulls on my lips.

Gray matches my sentiment, his mouth glistening with my arousal. Then he begins giving me kisses across the length of my body. Making a path, he continues to mark me with small pecks over the lace.

When he reaches my nipple, his tongue darts out, and he flicks it in a satisfyingly fast motion. My arms wrap around him, and I grip his shirt, and he chuckles, knowing that he's getting me going again.

He draws the fabric and my nipple between his lips and starts sucking. I'm hit with an immediate craving, pushing into him wanting more as I shamelessly moan.

Dragging his mouth over my chest, he does the same incredible torture to my other nipple.

"Fuck me," I say, still out of breath.

Grayson's hooded eyes darken with desire. "As you wish."

Straightening his spine, he unzips his pants, freeing himself. Beads of precum already drip down his cock and the burning between my legs intensifies.

As if I'm putty in his hands, he swiftly moves me. My feet fall back down on the ground, and I'm spun around so that my stomach now rests on Dad's desk.

Grayson's hand slides up my back. "This is the most

perfect view," he rasps as he carefully draws his fingers downward, lingering on my bare skin.

Suddenly, his hand comes crashing down as he spanks me.

I yelp in surprise, the corners of my mouth lifting upward.

"Told you I'd get you back for playing with me in the sex shop."

"I think you need to get me back again." I back up into him.

"Such a bad fucking girl letting me do this to you here." His hand comes down once more, only this time much harder.

I gasp at how good it feels and how unaware I was that this would turn me on. "Again," I whine. Bracing myself, I'm met with another harsh spank which lights me up.

"Hold on to the desk," Gray says, his deep voice straining.

Doing as he says, I stretch out my arms, curling my fingers around the edge of the oak. Lining himself up with my entrance, inch by inch he dips himself in and out of me.

My grip on the desk strengthens as I wait for him to fully consume me. He keeps moving in a teasing manner, wearing my patience thin.

Suddenly, he thrusts inside me, causing me to yelp as I jolt forward. His hands lock on my hips, and he picks up his pace.

My knuckles turn white, and my tendons flex against my skin as I tightly grasp onto the oak. The deep, guttural moans that are coming from both of us are loud enough to fill my entire house.

"Oh my god." I gasp for air.

Each harsh thrust ignites a flame in my bloodstream until my insides start turning into a full-blown, raging fire. My stomach and chest rub up against the desk, the lace chafing my nipples in the most deliciously painful way.

"More," I demand, overtaken by passion.

Being this bad has never felt this good.

"You love how my cock makes you feel, Red?" Gray says the word through sharp breaths.

I nod, too busy shrieking to actually speak.

"You like me bending you over and fucking you into your father's desk?"

Both of our grips get tighter, his on my hips and mine on the desk, as I nod once more.

Never in a thousand lifetimes would I have thought I'd be doing this. But here I am, abandoning my old self and enjoying every minute of it.

Grayson changes his pace, slow and rough striking my insides each time. My legs quiver and toes curl as I bask in the sensations. With my eyes screwed shut, passion explodes down my spine.

Every fiber of my body tenses as I inch toward my second orgasm of the night. I search for air, panting.

And with one final thrust, I'm gone.

Crying out in glorious pleasure and clawing my nails into the desk, my climax peaks as sparks fly off every which way. Tears prickle behind my eyes from the immense amount of bliss swimming in my veins.

"Fuck, Emma," Grayson moans.

My pussy spasms around him as he struggles to keep up his rhythm until the both of us are finished.

His body finally stills. Pulling himself out of me, his cum leaks out, dripping down my thighs.

Gray leans forward, folding over my body so that his front is on top of my back. His breath hits my shoulder, and he leaves tiny kisses on my skin. My cheek pressed into the desk, I grin each time I feel his lips brush over me.

He reaches up for my hands and threads his fingers in between mine and even though we just had sex, something about that small gesture brings a buzz of joy to my racing heart.

As we catch our breath, he brings his mouth to the shell of my ear and whispers, "I'm definitely a fan of this outfit."

"Me too," I say, panting.

"Just wait until you find out what your second gift is."

"I'm getting it now?"

"Nope. Another day, Red."

With that, he slides off my body, and I slowly start to rise. Turning around to face him, he wears the most satisfied expression when his eyes drift over me. I'm sure my hair is a mess, and my makeup is smudged. And when I glance down, I can see that my chest is flushed, and my hands are still regaining their color.

Giving me a tender peck on my forehead, he pulls away and says, "You're breathtaking."

CHAPTER FORTY

Grayson

EMMA'S WEEK of freedom has also become mine.

I haven't fixated on any parasitic memories, haven't shut down or isolated and haven't felt the urge to fight. I also haven't seen my sister aside from running to her condo to pick up my duffel. Not that I particularly minded not seeing her, but Emma thinks it's a big deal so she invited Rae and Miles to hang out tonight.

"Keep stirring," Emma instructs as she peeks over my shoulder.

"I'm gonna fuck this up," I state as I continuously circle the wooden spoon around the pot. The fresh, savory smell of the sauce whipping beneath my nostrils and making my stomach growl.

"It's impossible, all you have to do is stir so it doesn't burn."

"Oh, believe me, I've ruined much simpler meals."

She chuckles as she continues to grate the mozzarella cheese. When I suggested pizza, I meant ordering a pie from some place on the boardwalk—not make them from scratch. But Emma thought it would be fun if everyone made their own personal pizzas with the ingredients, so she somehow wrangled me into cooking.

The past few days we've spent glued to each other's side. From hand-holding along the beach to fucking her raw into the living room floor, we've been inseparable.

She even wants to spend our time together teaching me how to cook, so here I am trying to learn the basics of making a grilled pizza.

"Does Rae like roasted vegetables?"

"I don't know."

"What about olives?"

I shrug, focusing on the sauce. A sense of embarrassment crawls over me for not being able to answer simple questions about Rae.

"Some people like to drizzle ranch on top. Do you think she'd like that?"

"You sure you don't want to have another night with just the two of us? I think that would be a lot more fun than having to spend time with Rae and Miles," I say, knowing that if I stop talking, then I might get stuck in my head, and I don't want that. I don't want that ever, but especially during this time with Emma.

There's a muted sound of her gently placing the knife on the cutting board. "Oh," she whispers as if things are clicking in her head. Glancing over, her amber eyes look at me softly. "Is this not going to be enjoyable for you? Do you want me to call it off?"

"No. No, it's fine. It's just..." I trail off figuring out the best way to describe how I'm feeling. "It'll be awkward. Rae and I don't spend time together. We haven't at all yet this summer even though that's the reason behind me staying in Golden Bay. My parents want us to rebuild our relationship or some shit. She's the only sister I have left—" I cut myself off, clearing my throat.

I train my attention back to the sauce as it starts to bubble.

A long stretch of silence hangs over the kitchen. I can spot Emma out of the corner of my eye, shifting her weight from foot to foot as if debating how to respond.

"But I'm sure tonight will be fine," I break the quiet. I need to.

"I know about Cara," Emma whispers.

I freeze for a split second, hearing her state my sister's name. My focus jumps back to Emma, and I swallow around the lump that's forming in my throat. "You do?"

She nods. "Yes."

"From Rae?"

"Yes," she repeats, nibbling on her bottom lip with concern.

"Did she tell you how Cara died?" I have high doubts that my sister actually told someone about the event that fucked us up forever.

"A school shooting." The words are quiet but they land on my ears like a missile.

Emma's eyes well up, her nose turning rosy as she fights back tears.

Tears for me.

And Rae.

And Cara.

"I'm sorry, I shouldn't have brought it up—I just didn't want you to think that you had to dance around it or hide your pain from me." Emma's voice cracks.

Salt is poured onto my never-healing wound as it reopens for the millionth time. And as my agony simmers, making my eyes sting, I'm also struck with something else. A feeling that is utterly confusing to me at this moment.

"I don't want to talk about it," I begin.

"I'm sor—"

"But, I'm glad you know."

Her shoulders drop at the same time mine do, and her head tilts to the side. "You are?"

"Yeah," I state as relief is spread throughout my chest. "I don't have to eventually tell you. I don't have to relive anything."

"Oh. That makes sense."

"I don't know if you can tell, but I'm not great with expressing myself," I try to make light.

She gives me a small smile. "I get it. Loss is complex."

"How do you deal with yours?" I ask, and I'm not sure it's because I selfishly want to know how to handle all of this. It's been a decade, and I'm still struggling.

Emma shrugs. "I don't mind talking about my mom. Of course, no one ever asks about her because no one dares to bring up the dead mom topic—which I understand. But talking about her makes me feel closer to her."

I lean against the countertop. "Talk to me about her. I'll jump headfirst into a dead mom conversation if that's what makes you feel better."

Her head falls back in laughter.

"I'm serious! What's her name?"

"Allison. She was apparently very set on naming me Emma, so at least I know she chose that for me."

"What else?"

"I don't know much about her aside from the fact that she was very charitable and liked to donate to causes that were important to her." There's a twinkle in Emma's eye, and I can tell that's something she'd like to replicate. Even if her mom didn't do that, I can still see Emma donating as much as she can to others. "Oh, and we have the same hair," she adds.

I grin, admiring her long auburn locks. "Do you have any pictures of your mom?"

"Yes! I'll be right back." She starts moving out of the kitchen but spins around. "Keep stirring!"

"Oh shit." Immediately going back to the sauce, I begin stirring, not sure if there should be browning along the edges of the pot. "I told you I'd fuck this up!" I call out to her as she trails away.

Within seconds she's scurrying back, holding a photo frame in her hand. Her face is lit up, excited that she gets to share this with me. My heart melts a little bit more getting to have this moment with her.

Emma twirls the frame around. "Here she is!"

Carefully taking it in my hands, my chest swells with emotion. "You look just like her." My gaze takes in the way the red waves of her hair border her face. Then over to a sparkling smile that's sweet enough to enchant an entire room. And noticing a dusting of freckles over her button nose. "She's beautiful," I say as if I'm looking at the future version of Emma.

"She's perfect."

I glance up at Emma, who's admiring her mom with me, her eyes glistening. "I always think about what it would be like if she were still here. How different my story might've been."

Those words twist a knife around in my heart, and I feel a prickle at the corner of my eyes. "Yeah," I respond, blowing out a puff of air. "I can relate to that."

One of her arms comes around me, and I do the same to her. I'm not really sure which one of us needs the comfort, but I think we're both in need of this embrace.

Kissing her hair, I ask, "Do you have any more pictures?"

Emma shakes her head. "My dad doesn't keep pictures of her around, this is the only one. It sits on a shelf in his office."

My face drops. "I feel like I need to apologize to her after what went down in that room the other day."

Emma bursts into laughter, breaking the tender moment. "But not my dad?"

"No, fuck him. But, I might've chosen a different spot if I knew her photo was there."

Still chuckling, she takes the frame from me. "Relax, it's just a picture. It's not like I feel her presence when I'm in that office of his."

"Do you feel it in other places?"

"Of course."

"You do?"

A tendril of despair weaves its way through my bones. I've never felt Cara nearby.

"Not specific places," Emma continues. "But when certain things happen, I get this feeling around me—I can't explain it, but I know it's her."

I blink, staring at her, wishing I could grasp what she's saying. I understand the grief on some level, but I don't get this part.

"I should probably put this back." She changes the

subject, gesturing to the frame in her hand. "If anything happens to it, I'm toast."

I watch her walk away, but before I can process my thoughts, I get a whiff of something burning. "Fuck—the sauce!"

Spinning around, I turn the stove off and keep stirring, doing my best to salvage the red paste.

"They're pulling up!" Emma shouts from the hallway. "Are you sure you're okay they're coming?" she asks, dashing into the kitchen. Her cheeks are raised high as she beams, and there's no way in hell I'm going to take that joy away from her.

"It's all good, Red." I wink.

The doorbell chimes, and Emma claps her hands, bouncing on her toes. "I'm so excited!"

Heading out of the kitchen and toward the foyer, I hear them greet each other and spot Emma hugging Rae and Miles. I wouldn't expect anything less of a welcome from Emma and seeing the way she lights up from being able to have them over makes my insides turn to mush.

"Thanks for inviting us over," Rae says, her gaze traveling all over Emma's gigantic home, from the crystal chandelier, over to the large living room and back to the double staircase.

"We brought some sodas." Miles lifts up a shopping bag. "Not as festive as the drinks you guys had on the boardwalk, but at least it's something," he teases.

"You didn't have to do that," Emma says, guiding them farther inside.

"Hey, Grayson," Miles says.

"Hey."

Rae crinkles her nose. "Is something burning?"

"I left the sauce on the stove a little too long, but it's fine," I snap.

"*You're* cooking?"

"Yep!" Emma interjects. "I've been teaching him. We made the sauce together. I figured we could make some pizzas for dinner." She takes Rae's hand. "Come on in, let me show you both around!"

After the grand tour and grilling our pizzas, we decided to chill on the beach. Me and Miles dragged out Emma's old outdoor lounge chairs that were kept in storage under her wraparound porch.

I'm slowly finding myself settling into being around everyone. It's uncomfortable, but it's not the worst thing. Plus, Emma is really good at diverting conversation or filling up any awkward silences.

The sun sets before us, the gold beams glowing half in the sky and half in the ocean. Orange, red, and pink are blurred into the light blue, and the scenery begins to relax me, creating ease.

"You guys wanna go for a swim?" Emma asks.

"I'm down," Miles states.

"Yeah, whatever," Rae responds.

Emma glances over to me, waiting for an answer. "Uh, sure."

With that, we all hurriedly change into our swimsuits. By the time I walk back outside, Emma and Miles are talking, while Rae eventually trails behind me.

I try not to stare too long at Emma in her white bikini. The way it accentuates her figure causes me to get distracted. I've seen her in various states of dress and bare-ass naked, but something about the way the strings wrap around her skin makes me want to unravel them, and her, in an instant.

"All set?" she asks me, tearing my attention away from her body.

"Yep."

The four of us stand at the shoreline, entranced by the rolling waves and the partially hidden sun beaming across from us.

"On your mark—" Miles starts talking.

"We're racing?" I ask, my brows drawn in.

"Get set—"

"Guess so," I mutter.

"Go!"

The four of us take off, running straight into the ocean. There's a pull at my lips as I begin to smile when the warm water splashes my legs. The girls squeal with excitement as we keep rushing forward.

Wind pushes through my hair, my smile getting wider.

Exhilaration bubbles in my chest as I tear through the ocean.

Glancing over at the three of them, I chuckle watching them having the same burst of enjoyment as I am as they swim into the water.

I'm too caught up in the current of freedom crashing through me to give any attention to the thought of how stupid it is that something so minute can act like a stitch on my wounds.

A large wave moves closer, and I dive straight for it, holding my breath as I become saturated in salt water.

When I'm on the other side, and the wave has crashed into the sand, I pop my head up, shaking my hair out of my face. Emma's directly in front of me, glimmers of delight sparking all over her freckled face. Her hair is soaked, turning it into a reddish-brown color.

I spot Rae and Miles off to the side, laughing and swimming—and suddenly, I'm struck with an idea.

Reaching out for Emma's waist, I say, "Hop on my shoulders."

"What?"

"Get on."

As I tread water, I lower myself so Emma can climb onto my shoulders. Once her legs are hooked over me, I take hold of them to steady her while also noticing how silky they feel under my fingertips. She plants her hands on my head and lets out a little shriek as I move us toward the other two.

Miles sees us and instantly knows what's going on. "You think you can beat us in a chicken fight?" he instigates.

"Oh, god." Rae playfully rolls her eyes but gets on Miles's shoulders anyway.

"I don't think I can beat Rae," Emma says to me as I move us closer.

"You got this."

"She's gonna knock me down in like, one second." She laughs to herself.

"I won't let her." I give her legs a little squeeze.

We meet the two of them, all of us wearing similar grins.

Immediately, we're in a round of chicken where the objective is for Emma to make Rae fall in the water.

The two of them link hands, pushing and pulling all the while giggling.

My calves ache from keeping us afloat as Emma sways back and forth. Tightly holding onto her legs, I keep her sturdy.

Water splashes up into Miles's and my faces as the girls inadvertently kick their feet. Droplets scatter across my lashes, making it difficult to see clearly, but I can make out the laughter coming from all of them.

And that's when I realize that I'm laughing right along with them.

I can't stop.

My cheeks hurt from smiling even though endless amounts of saltwater sprays into my mouth and eyes, and I'm struggling to balance Emma.

An abrupt screech comes from my sister. Glancing upward, I watch her tumble into the ocean.

"I'm so sorry, Rae!" Emma shouts through her giggles.

"We won!" I shout, and Emma kisses the top of my head.

Rae bobs up, spitting out a mouthful of water. "Best two out of three."

"Let's fucking go!" Miles amps us up, hoisting Rae back on his shoulders.

After several high-stakes games of chicken fight, we called it a draw.

The night is finally winding down with the four of us enjoying a bonfire on the beach. We dug a hole in the sand, found a massive amount of driftwood, and used Rae's lighter to start a small flame.

"Do you have stuff to make s'mores?" Miles asks Emma.

"Hmm. I'm not sure."

"I want to get a drink anyway, I'll check when I'm inside." I rise, dusting off my shorts.

"I'll come with you." Emma jumps to her feet.

Together we walk inside, but I can tell there's something off, judging by the way she's playing with her fingernails and bouncing with nervous energy in her steps.

"Everything all right?" I ask when we get into the kitchen. I grab myself a soda then start scouring her pantry for the ingredients to make s'mores.

"There are no marshmallows!" she blurts out.

Her eyes are wide as if she'd just been caught in a sticky lie and is about to get in trouble. Suddenly, Miles appears with his car keys in his hands.

My eyes narrow as I assess both of them. "What's going on?"

"Miles and I thought this could be a nice environment for you and Rae to talk and maybe, I don't know..." Emma fidgets while she speaks. "Maybe start to repair things."

My attention shoots over to Miles for confirmation.

"She thought of the idea. I thought of the execution." He put his hand on his stomach. "I could really go for some s'mores."

I shake my head. "It's been a nice change of pace getting to relax and hang out today—but no. I'm not talking to her about any of the heavy shit."

"You don't have to," Emma explains. She glances

over her shoulder at Miles, then back to me. Taking a few steps closer to me, she whispers, "You don't have to do anything you don't want. I just wanted to give you an opportunity to make a nice memory alone with your sister."

I don't think I have any nice memories of just me and Rae. All the nice ones include Cara, and after Cara, well, it was nothing short of devastation.

Emma's amber-infused eyes peer up at me. I don't even need to admire the soft expression she wears to know that this gesture was out of the pure goodness of her heart.

She never mentioned what she read in my notebook that had to do with Rae, but I'm beginning to wonder if it was more than just a passing complaint.

"Go get marshmallows," I tell her, and she smiles. "But I'm not making any promises that I'll walk back out there."

She nods. "Okay."

"We'll be back in a little bit," Miles adds.

Emma gives me a peck on the cheek, and before I can blink, the two of them are walking out of her front door.

A mixture of emotions skims across my chest as I pace the foyer. Slightly annoyed Emma and Miles pulled that, but also sort of...okay with it?

Sighing, I walk to the back of the house and glance out the glass door. The fire has gotten bigger, and Rae sits next to it in the sand, smoking a cigarette. She looks perfectly content being alone. Just like me.

I was absolutely fine with being a loner until Emma turned my whole world upside down and made me feel something other than despair and rage. She makes me experience an array of emotions, one of them currently encouragement as I stare outside at my sister.

"Whatever," I mumble to myself as I open the door before I can talk myself out of stepping back on the beach.

Rae checks over her shoulder and watches me plop down in the sand. "Where are the other two?" she asks.

"Went to get marshmallows."

"Both of them?"

"Yep. They left us to talk about shit."

She snorts. "Figures."

Silence.

Neither one of us knows what to say even if we wanted to.

Instead, we stare at the midnight-blue sky. Zillions of stars flickering through the darkness.

Rae clears her throat. "How are things with you and Emma?"

"Good." There's an awkward beat. "What about you and Miles?"

"Good."

Rae blows out a puff of smoke, and I reach for her pack, needing something extra to endure this conversation.

"You smoke?" she asks as I light the cigarette in between my lips.

"Not usually. But you used to leave them around the house, so I'd take some from time to time."

"What else did you use to take?"

"I never tried any of your drugs if that's what you're asking." I draw in a long breath and slowly exhale.

"It is." She nods. "And good."

The fire crackles next to us as we smoke, still focused ahead of us.

"Do you like Golden Bay?" Rae asks, cutting through the quiet.

"Yeah, it's cool. Nice scenery, too." I gesture out at the ocean.

She tilts her head up, taking in the vast sky above us. "There's an endless amount of stars," she states.

I do the same, glancing up at the glimmering spots. "Yeah."

"Miles thinks they're dead people."

"That's weird."

"It's comforting." Her voice gets soft, every defense that I've known her to embody evaporates with that one sentence.

Immediately, my face scrunches, and I glance over at my sister who's still admiring the sky above us. The corners of her eyes well up, and she presses her lips into a fine line as if that would be the way to hold back any tears that might be surfacing.

And it's in this exact moment that I realize she's changed. For the better.

Something about the comment, or the way she's looking at the sky, or the way she's sitting here with me and being vulnerable—something in all of this tells me she wants to reconnect with me.

"I've started feeling her around me," Rae whispers and chills run down my arms.

"Cara?"

She nods, still fixated on the stars. "Do you feel her nearby?"

My brows dip. There it is again, that notion of sensing someone. I thought that sentiment was only made up in books and movies—I didn't know people actually feel their loved ones around them.

"No," I quietly respond, the answer yanking at my heartstrings at the painful admittance.

If something like that were to exist, I don't know if I ever gave it the chance.

We're quiet once again, but this time it doesn't feel uncomfortable. There's a shift in the air between us. We've never spoken about the missing piece to our family. And although this isn't a deep talk about Cara, it's something.

A truce.

A way of letting the other know that maybe we don't hate them. And maybe a repair could be possible.

"We're back," Emma chimes from behind us.

I take one last drag and toss the cigarette into the fire.

"Got everything we need for s'mores," Miles states, placing graham crackers, chocolate bars, and of course, marshmallows next to the bonfire. He then wraps his arm around Rae and kisses the top of her head. "How are you and Grayson doing?" he asks while casually glancing over at me.

Rae draws her attention over to me. "We're good."

CHAPTER FORTY-ONE

Emma

"I PROMISE there's no way for you to mess this up," I assure Grayson as we whisk eggs in my kitchen.

"You'd be surprised," he states, cracking one more into the bowl. Some of the yolk gets on his fingers so he runs them under the sink.

It was my idea to cook breakfast together this morning. Teaching him how to cook has quickly become a new hobby of mine.

"Now we need to add milk, vanilla extract, and cinnamon," I instruct, rummaging through my kitchen to grab the ingredients.

"I thought French toast was just eggs and bread."

"Basic French toast is, but I like to make mine a little sweeter. And then I top it with butter and sugar." I place the milk gallon down on the counter. "Here, pour some in."

"How much?"

"Eyeball it."

Grayson's brows raise, looking at me as if I'm insane. "I'm supposed to wing it?"

"Yep. You watched me toss stuff into our pizza sauce last night. I didn't measure anything out. I just did a little at a time until it looked good."

Last night was a blast. If I could have them over every week I would. If anything, the four of us hanging out and having fun without any time constraint or fear of Dad coming home has made me even more eager to leave this place. I can't wait until I have my own apartment and get to have guests over whenever I want.

Milk splashes into the bowl. "Is that enough?" Grayson asks.

Leaning over to check, I nod. "Good, now add vanilla and cinnamon," I instruct.

I watch as he carefully drops a few dashes of both into the mix.

I didn't ask him what he and Rae spoke about last night, let alone if they spoke at all. Maybe I meddled a tad, but they're both so important to me and to each other–I can't idly sit by and watch their relationship dissolve.

"Now what?" Grayson wipes his hands on his shorts.

"We start cooking!" I heat up the skillet and saturate the bread in the mix he just made.

Within a few minutes, our stomachs are growling, the sweet scent of the breakfast dish filling up the room.

His face lights up when he takes the first bite, some powdered sugar getting on his lips. "This tastes incredible."

"Told you! Now you can add it to the list of things you can cook."

"I wouldn't go as far as saying I have a list. This and a cold-cut sandwich are about it."

"And grilled pizza."

He smirks. "Yeah. I guess that, too."

My focus goes back to my plate, enjoying the combination of melted butter and sugar over the egg-soaked bread. I get a little too wrapped up in eating. When I'm about to dig into the final piece, I glance up at Gray who's staring at me.

He's barely touched his meal despite saying he likes it. Instead, he's frozen with a starry-eyed expression and a relaxed smile on his face as he admires me.

"Everything okay?" Nervously, I wipe my face with my napkin in case I look like a mess.

Grayson rests his chin on his rounded fist that's clasping his fork. "Thanks for doing all of this for me."

"Teaching you how to cook?"

"All of it," he states.

There's a deeper meaning laced in those three words. I can tell by the way he's looking at me, the flicker of vulnerability around his irises. This is his way of acknowledging last night.

"Of course, Gray." I outstretch my arm, and he meets me halfway, holding my hand.

"You're something special, Emma." My stomach flutters. "I want to give you whatever you want. You deserve that. What do you want?"

I smile. "Right now, I just want to continue having fun."

"I'll keep making that happen."

Loud, carnival-themed songs play as we walk up to the ticket booth of Adventureland. "We got too wasted to enjoy the amusement park last time. Let's go on some rides," Grayson says as we each get a wristband for unlimited rides.

"Do you want me to pay for mine?" I ask.

"Nope."

We both placed our small belongings into a locker, which he also paid for. Then he links his arm around my hip. "Come on, let's find something to go on."

"The Twister?" I point to the yellow rollercoaster across from us.

Grayson smiles in surprise. "You like big rides like that?"

"Oh, I enjoy lots of big things." I wink and immediately start laughing.

His other arm wraps around me as he chuckles, bringing me into an embrace. I latch onto him as he whispers into my ear. "I'll take you on a wild ride later on."

"Promise?" I grin into his shirt.

"Swear."

We give each other a squeeze, then break apart, heading to the rollercoaster.

As hours tick by, the sky gets darker as the both of us continue to go on every ride that doesn't have an absurdly long line. We can't stop grinning, our hair blown out

from being spun around and flipped upside down.

Flashing colorful lights move around us as we keep hopping from one ride to the next. We get a whiff of popcorn and churros every so often as we pass the food stands. As the evening continues, the more the crowd grows with people around our age.

"I need a drink," I say, my throat raw from screaming and laughing.

"Want a water?" Grayson asks, motioning toward a nearby vending machine.

I nod, and we head to the locker to get our belongings so we can buy a drink. As Grayson's stuffing his things into his pockets, something on the boardwalk catches my attention. The memory is hazy, but I fixate on a far bench in front of a bar, and I'm pretty sure it's *the* bench. The memory brings a rush of heat between my thighs.

My gaze flickers into a bar where people are dancing.

Craning my neck to look at him, my lips curl. "I've got a better idea."

Threading my fingers through his, I pull him forward, whisking us toward the semi-familiar bar.

He chuckles when he realizes where I'm taking us. "Should I tell Rae and Miles to get ready for our antics?"

"We're not going to get wasted—we'll have a drink or two. But we *are* going to dance!"

"In that case, I'll need more than two drinks."

When we reach the bar and maneuver our way around the people dancing, we order a round of shots. Before the alcohol hits us, I drag Grayson near the speakers, in between sweaty bodies and begin spinning around him.

He barely moves his feet.

"I've seen you dance before," I shout over the loud music.

"That was in an empty parking lot."

"So, pretend it's just you and me in here."

I wrap my arms around the back of his neck and wiggle my hips against him. His hands fly to my waist.

"If you keep moving like that, you're going to cause trouble, Red," Gray says, bringing his lips to the shell of my ear.

I kiss his neck. "I'm up for some trouble."

His chest shakes in laughter against me. "Did that shot already hit you?"

"Nope, I'm completely sober." I grind into his shorts, and he gives me a warning squeeze. "We had fun at the amusement park, now I want to let loose and have some more fun."

Spinning around, my ass lines up to his growing hardness. I keep moving to the beat of the song, and he finally starts to sway with me.

"Can I tell you a secret?" he asks, and I nod, my heart jolting with anxiety from the question. "I brought the second gift with me."

Instantly, I stop dancing and spin back to face him. "You mean the gift from the..." I glance around to make sure no one can hear me. "Sex shop?" I whisper.

That devilish smirk appears, and he nods.

My face pinches in confusion, unable to think of what it would be.

He brings his cheek next to mine. "Go to the bathroom. I'll be right behind you."

My heart strums faster, not a single beat of hesitancy building within me. Drifting away from him, I check over my shoulder to make sure he's following and that no one else is catching on to what's going on.

Stepping into the single-stall bathroom, anticipation

buzzes in my bloodstream. An impatient grin tugs at the ends of my lips, and when the door creaks open, I suck in a big breath of excitement.

Grayson shoves himself into the bathroom, immediately locking the door behind him.

"What are we doing?" I can't contain my eagerness as my cheeks continue to push upward.

"You wanted to have some more fun, yes?" His voice drops.

"Yes."

"And you wanted to be wilder, yes?"

He stands dangerously close to me. My back hits up against the porcelain sink as he invades my space, the flames of desire sparking off in his hooded eyes.

"Yes." I wet my lips.

My pulse zips through me, racing faster and faster as I watch him dig into his pocket and pull out a little black box. Opening it up, there's a similar U-shaped vibrator to the one that he initially bought me, only this one is smaller and purple.

Silently, he takes my hand and places the toy in my palm.

"It's synced up," he says, taking his phone out of his other pocket.

"What—"

Before I can finish my question, a burst of vibrations hits my hand. I look over at Grayson, who's pressing something on his phone with a cocky smirk plastered on his face.

Heat coils between my legs. "Oh my god."

Taking the toy out of my hand, he hikes up my dress and trails it along the seam of my panties. "You're going to let me fill your pussy with this vibrator." He moves the fabric aside. "Then you're going to sit down at the bar." He runs the toy over my slit, and I can already sense how wet I'm getting. "And let me get you off in public all night long, like the bad girl you are."

Instantly pushing the vibrator into me, I gasp. My hands fly to either side of me as they grip onto the sink for support. He lines the outer part up with my clit, causing me to shudder.

He dips down slightly, pressing his lips to my neck. "Does that sound like a good plan, Red?" His words are husky, scraping the back of his throat.

My head quickly bobs up and down, agreeing to this insane, yet extremely hot, plan of his.

"Good." He rips himself away from me. "You go out first, and I'll be out soon."

He clicks his phone, stopping the vibrator. I stand up straight, wiggling a few times to adjust myself. The smaller part of the U is hitting exactly on my clit while the bigger end hitting a glorious spot inside me. I can already feel my panties becoming wet.

"See you out there." I blow him a kiss and whisk myself out of the bathroom.

When I reenter the bar, I adjust my dress tugging at my hem. It feels as if all eyes are on me, knowing my little secret, but in reality, no one knows.

Rolling my shoulder back, confidence strikes my core, and an overwhelming sensation coaxed with sexiness rolls through my body.

I sway my hips and follow Grayson's instructions, sitting down on a stool at the bar.

Surveying the space, people are still dancing while more trickle in from the boardwalk. Multiple bartenders are helping out people at either end while I wait here patiently. My gaze flickers to the bathroom and then around the room, seeing if I can spot Grayson, but there's no sign of him.

Seconds turn into minutes, and anxiety starts to swell in my chest. I begin fidgeting, crossing my legs one way, then the other.

Taking my phone out, I send him a message.

Me
where are you?

An abrupt buzz shoots off in my panties, and I squeak. A few heads turn to glance my way, and I give them a tight-lipped smile.

Adjusting my posture and bracing myself for the incoming waves, my phone goes off.

Gray
enjoying the show

My legs squeeze together as he intensifies the setting on the vibrator. My eyes dart around until they land on Grayson's sexy smolder across the room.

Me
are you going to come over here and join me?

Gray
I will. I just want to make you sweat it out first

My heart pounds, lust pulsing through me at the same fast rate as the toy buzzing against my clit.

Keeping my attention on Gray, he plays it off cool

ordering a drink as if he's not about to make me come in front of everyone. I'm at the mercy of his fingertips tapping against his phone. Just the sheer thought revs me up even more, my breath wavering.

When I shift on the stool, I can feel the increasing amount of wetness in my panties. My body temperature rises while I continue to stare across the crowded bar.

Grayson locks his attention on me, his drink in one hand and his phone in the other.

> **Gray**
> you don't nearly look flustered enough

I quirk my eyebrow at him, daring him to up the intensity. And he does.

Stronger waves hit me. I brush my hair to one shoulder, getting even hotter.

"Hey." A guy who looks around my age sidles up next to me sporting a sweet smile.

"H-Hi." I try not to look like my insides are wringing tight with passion.

"I've never seen you around here before, are you visiting?"

"Oh, no, I'm from Golden Bay. I just normally don't go out."

"Well, I'm glad you're out tonight." He leans his body weight against the bar.

My phone goes off in my hand, and I angle it away from this stranger.

> **Gray**
> he thinks you're hot

Me
no he doesn't

"I'm Carlos," he says.

"Emma."

I twitch as Grayson increases the speed. A flushed feeling spreads down my neck as my chest rapidly rises and falls.

Gray
I wonder what he'd think if he knew I was fucking you from across the room

I squirm, pressing my forearms into the bar as my lower half goes insane.

"Are you in college?" Carlos inquires, casually getting closer to me.

I nod, biting on my lower lip. My pulse zooms through my body. I can't keep up with my own heart rate.

"What year are you going into?"

"My s-senior."

"Nice." He smiles with dazzling white teeth. "Me, too. What are you studying?"

"Um." My muscles tense, heat burrowing into my core. The toy doesn't give up, and neither does Grayson. "Business and marketing." A shaky sigh escapes me. "Y-You?"

"Sports medicine."

"Cool."

"Can I buy you a drink?"

"Water," I blurt in a panic.

"You sure I can't get you anything else?"

Gray
look at you letting me make you come
in front of a complete stranger

Gray
bad fucking girl

The tension between my thighs quadruples, and even though the vibrator is working away, I need more friction. With my eyes glued across the way on Grayson's alluring eyes, I press my legs together even tighter and rock my hips back and forth in a slow, nonchalant motion. But internally, the movement ripples desire out of my veins.

I push stray hairs out of my face as sweat forms at my hairline, my cheeks getting hot. Grayson's smug smirk only ignites my fire further. He looks incredibly sexy—almost as if he's about to get off from watching my interaction. I watch his thumb run over the screen of his phone, and the faster speed has me seconds away from screaming his name out.

The growing pleasure in his expression lets me know that he's loving this as much as I am.

"Emma?" Carlos says, tearing my attention away from Grayson.

"Yeah?" I pant.

"Are you sure you only want water?"

I nod so quickly my head might pop off. "Water—I need water."

Tingles pour down my spine as Carlos orders my drink from the bartender. My legs begin to shake as every part of my body pulls in tight.

I steeple my hands and press my forehead against

them in a poor attempt to grasp onto a thread of composure.

"You all right?" Carlos's voice softens next to the side of my face as he inches nearer.

Suddenly, there's a hand on my lower back, and I straighten in surprise. "I'll take over from here," Grayson says, moving his hand around my waist in a side hold.

Just hearing the deep timbre of his words makes me shudder, on the brink of tumbling over the edge.

"Uh—" Carlos starts to ward off Grayson, but then Grayson places a kiss on my head. The bartender puts the glass of water in front of us, and Carlos glances at it and then back at me and Grayson, things clicking in his head. "Got it." He tilts his chin in understanding. "Nice meeting you, Emma," he politely says.

"You too." I'm barely able to speak.

In the blink of an eye, I'm spinning around to face Grayson.

"You really think I'd give him the privilege of being with you when you came?" His voice is gruff as he speaks lowly.

"You never know with you." I chuckle.

Grayson leans in, whispering in my ear. "Your orgasms are mine, Red."

I cling to his shirt as his fingers move over his phone. My eyes roll back as I get wrapped up in his arms, letting the vibrations fully take over me.

I try to subtly move my hips. My body rattles against his, and his embrace gets stronger, holding me up.

"Gray," I whisper-moan. My nails dig into his torso so hard I might've pierced through the fabric.

"Get that pussy nice and wet for me because I'm going to devour it when we get back to your house."

Nestling my head into his shoulder, I heave, struggling to get a full breath. I writhe in the middle of the bar, fully on display to anyone who might be watching. And just the sheer thought of that has me reaching my climax.

I gasp into his shirt, and he squeezes me. "Come for me, Red."

In a millisecond, I'm shattering. Flames blazing through my bloodstream as ecstasy coils down my body. My wetness soaks the toy and my panties as I muffle my sounds, trembling and shaking in Grayson's embrace.

Passion pounds through my heart as my insides get electrified. A rush of heat washes over me, melting me into Gray's hold.

I go completely limp, panting.

Gray shifts his hand, and suddenly the vibrator stops.

Dazed and dizzy, I peel my forehead off of him in order to glance upward. He eyes me cautiously, unsure of how I enjoyed that experience.

And instead of telling him, I yank him forward for a kiss. My lips claim him in a needy connection. Excitement instantly nips at my fingertips, looking forward to what the rest of the night has in store.

CHAPTER FORTY-TWO

Grayson

MY FINGERS WRITE *their own form of poetry over her body,*

composing stories across the constellation of freckles that adorn the silk that she's wrapped in,

giving new life to a hidden masterpiece.

"Are you asleep already? You've been awfully quiet." Emma's voice carries from her en suite as she does her nightly routine.

"No, I was just..." My words trail off as I stare at the prose in my notebook while I sit on her bed.

The words on these pages have changed quite a bit over the past several weeks. I'm not really sure what to make of that except for the fact that my life has been exponentially better since Emma entered it.

"...getting stuck in your head?" Emma continues my thought.

"Yeah." I close the book, getting off of her bed and going to where she is. Leaning against the doorframe of her bathroom, I watch as she washes her face with a special face scrub.

It's our last night before her dad comes back, and I'd be lying if I said I didn't feel a weight drop on my chest, saddened we won't be spending the majority of our days together.

When Emma realizes I'm gazing at her, she turns in my direction. "Do you want to talk about what's going on in your head—I know you usually don't want to, but—"

"You," I cut her off.

She pauses, a look of concern appearing in her eyes. "In a bad way?"

"Not at all." I push off the doorframe and hop up on her large, marble vanity with my feet hitting the cabinet doors. "I'm bummed your dad is coming back tomorrow." There's a lot more that's dancing around my brain regarding Emma, but my mouth is only allowing me to get out that one sentence.

"Me too." Emma goes back to scrubbing her chin once she realizes there's nothing to worry about.

Glancing near her sink, I look at the different bottles and jars of cleanser stuff. "What is all this shit?" I ask, mindlessly picking up a lotion.

"What you're holding is moisturizer." She freezes for a beat, studying me. "You know, you're a little sunburnt. You could definitely use some."

I chuckle. "Yeah, and I'm sure I need some of your..." I pick up another tube and glance at the name. "Exfoliant."

She gasps, and I watch as the idea gets planted in her mind. Immediately, I know what she's thinking, and I shake my head.

"No way."

"Please!" Emma whines.

"I'm not letting you give me a facial."

"Come on, Gray, it'll be so much fun!" She exaggerates batting her lashes, making me laugh. "What's the worst that will happen—you get glowing skin?"

Dipping my finger into her open jar of grainy scrub, I swipe a blob onto her nose. She scrunches her face in the cutest way imaginable, giggling, and I know that in a few minutes I'll have the same gritty crap on my face.

"Fine." I playfully glare at her. "But my skin better be fucking radiant after this."

"Oh, it will be."

Abandoning her own routine, Emma shifts gears, giving me a clean washcloth to wet my face with before she applies it with overly expensive goop.

She stands in between my legs, the both of us smiling as she goes through all the steps. My skin goes from feeling wet to cool to stiff as she paints some type of mask on me. Thankfully my back is to the mirror so I can't see how ridiculous I look. I can only feel how nice it is to hug her hips with my knees as her sweet laugh tickles my ears.

"Moments like this are what I live for," she states, still focusing on the task at hand.

"Giving me a facemask is the highlight of your summer?" I tease.

She chuckles, her velvety fingertips smoothing over the space between my brows. "No. The simplicity is what brings me joy. That's all I've ever wanted." Her voice becomes quieter as she continues to speak, "My one true goal is to have a comforting home where my children can grow up feeling safe. A simple life."

The reminder that life exists outside of this bath

room creates a hollowness in my chest. "Seems simple, but it's probably the most cumbersome task."

"What is?"

"Making sure your loved ones are safe."

Emma's hand hovers over me as she pauses. Her expressive eyes focus on mine, realizing the gravity of my comment. I can tell an apology is on the tip of her tongue, but I don't want her to say it, nor do I need her to because I'm not the only one in the room who it applies to. She's suffered, too.

"Remember when you told me you sometimes feel your mom's presence?"

"Yes."

"What..." My voice wavers, emotion clogging my throat. "What does it feel like?"

She drops her hand, her features pinching together as she takes in my question. "Have you ever been in a crowded room and felt so incredibly lonely?"

I nod.

"It's the opposite of that." A sense of hope glimmers through her. "It's being absolutely alone, sitting in the quiet and knowing that there's someone looking out for you, despite everything." She takes a long inhale before continuing. "It's like when you're isolated on the beach at night, and everything calms, and you're alone with nature. It's that sense of knowing that everything's working together—your breath flowing in and out of your lungs, the methodic crashing of the waves, the chirping of the crickets. We're never truly alone."

My eyes burn, and I fight with myself to not expose those emotions, blinking several times. I never experienced any of what Emma described. Not even close.

I never even viewed nature as something therapeutic or spiritual.

In my mind, it just exists. Like me. No real purpose...it's just there.

"And there are other times where I pray to my mom and know she's listening," Emma adds.

Never experienced that either. If I tried praying to Cara, it would probably end up more like a one-sided conversation, and I'd overthink the whole thing and get pissed that I even attempted.

"You still pray?"

Emma slants her head to the side, looking at me quizzically. "Of course I do."

I remember she briefly made a comment about praying the night we were drunk, but I assumed it was an alcohol-induced ramble.

"I thought maybe after everything that happened to you, you wouldn't. Or maybe you viewed things differently." I clear my throat as a prickling sensation tries to settle between my vocal cords.

"I do view things differently," she clarifies. "I don't follow the same laws my dad proclaims. Someone's faith should be used as a means of connection, not a manipulation tactic to control others. So, I found my faith in other places."

"Where?" I ask, struggling not to sound desperate for an answer.

An innocent smile pulls the corners of her mouth upward. "The sand. Laughter. Late-night talks. Thunderstorms. S'mores." We both softly chuckle, and I catch a twinkle in her eyes as she adds, "You."

Tingles spark inside me, spiraling out of my heart and skittering down my limbs. And even though it feels beyond incredible to have her say that, I know it's wrong.

I don't see the world like she does. Nothing about me would give anyone a semblance of faith. I probably have the opposite effect.

Shaking my head, I start to open my mouth to object, but Emma starts before I can.

"But even though I have faith, I understand why someone wouldn't. And I respect that."

Our gazes lock. Even though she's speaking universally, we both know she means me.

My pulse quickens as she gently places her hand over mine.

Emma sees me for who I am. And accepts me.

There's a clamoring against my ribcage the longer we sit in this stillness, peeling away each layer of my hardened shell until I'm left feeling open. I hate it and love it and need it all at once.

Brushing her hair away from her face, I cup her cheek. Emma leans into my touch with a soft smile.

"I'm not a man of faith by any means. But if I was, I'd find it in you."

Her lashes flutter as she blinks, the amber color of her eyes becoming glassy. Leaning forward, she presses her lips to mine, and yet again she brings a new wave of aliveness through my veins.

And we spend the last night before her dad comes back, basking in simplicity.

CHAPTER FORTY-THREE

Grayson

THE STRAP to my duffel weighs on my shoulder as I open the door to Rae's condo. She's perched on a stool at her kitchen island, focusing on several documents in front of her. Lifting her eyes to me, she smirks as I make my way into her home.

"How was the rest of your staycation at Emma's?" she asks, her attention back on the paper in front of her as she signs something.

"Wish it was longer." Dropping my bag next to her couch, I realize how that sentence might've sounded. "No offense."

"None taken. I'd rather hang out with Emma than me, too."

This is the first time I've seen her since the night the four of us hung out at Emma's. The ice is definitely thawing between us, but we're both unsure how to approach this new territory.

Miles emerges from Rae's bedroom. "Hey, Grayson." He goes to put on his sneakers. "Wanna come for a run with me?"

"A run?"

"Yeah. I ate a bunch of leftover marshmallows and need to burn them off." He gives me a grin, and my face twists.

Is this some type of code I'm supposed to pick up on?

Rae shuffles her papers together, tapping them on the granite before flipping them over so no one can read them. "You can always come to NA with me," she says, hopping down from the stool.

"I think I might be the odd one out if I went," I joke.

"This time slot isn't a closed meeting."

I stare at her for a beat, not sure if she's being serious or not. Surely, she wouldn't actually be inviting me to join her. We barely had a conversation about Cara the other night, there's no way we're jumping straight into Rae's addiction.

"Shit, I'm late," she mutters, checking the time. "See you guys later." She comes up to Miles, and they give each other a quick kiss. "I love you."

"I love you, too," he says, watching her walk out the door with his eyes glued to her. When the door closes, he swings his attention to me. "Let's go for a run."

"Who the fuck runs in the summer heat?" I pant, my lungs burning as I pull in short bursts of air.

"It's just a quick jog," Miles says as we pace around the boardwalk.

Sweat drips down my body, soaking my shirt.

When we finally slow down by a nearby bench, I lift the bottom of my shirt to wipe my hairline.

"Couldn't we have gone to the gym like fucking normal people?"

Miles shrugs. "I like being outside."

"Well, I like being inside. There's no sun and fewer people."

He chuckles. "You and Rae are more similar than the both of you realize."

My heart rate begins to steady as I take longer breaths. "Is that why you dragged me out here? To talk about Rae? We could've done that in her condo while she's at her meeting."

"Yeah, but I needed to get my run in, so I figured two birds with one stone." He gives me an obnoxious grin, and I mutter curses. Tossing his head back, he laughs once again.

Sighing, I sit down as Miles plants himself on the other end of the bench. "Might as well get to the point. What did you want to talk about?"

"How was it when Emma and I left to get marshmallows?"

"Fine, I guess?" Immediately, I sense my guard going up, and I shake my head. "I'm not doing some heart-to-heart bullshit with you."

"I'm not either. I wanted to let you know that Rae seemed really happy that you two spoke. She didn't tell me what you guys talked about, that's your business, but I know that things shifted for her."

"Shifted how?"

"She's been talking about you going to an NA meeting with her."

"So, she *was* being serious when she asked me before?"

"Yep."

I gaze out at the busy beach. It's crammed with umbrellas, chairs, and coolers.

"Why?" I ask him with my attention still in front of me.

The bench wiggles as he rests his back against it and stretches out his legs. "She wants to make amends, Grayson. It's time for the both of you to turn the next page."

"Did you and Emma come up with another plan for me to go to Rae's meeting?"

He chuckles. "No. This is just coming from me, as your maybe-future brother."

My head snaps to look at him as my eyes explode out of my skull. "You want to marry Rae?"

"If she believed in marriage, yes. But your sister doesn't like to do things the conventional way, so I'm trying to figure out my next best option. She wants to take things slow, so I've got plenty of time to think it over."

I blink, unable to wrap my mind around this. "You like her that much?"

"No. I *love* Rae that much."

My stomach does somersaults as my pulse gets louder in my ears. I know they said their I love yous when she left, but I didn't know how serious that was.

How does he know he loves her? How does anyone truly know they love another person?

I break out in a sweat, but this time it's not from the sun. Anxiety clenches around my ribcage, and I can't for the life of me figure out why I'm having this reaction. I'm happy for the two of them. But the word "love" is terrifying to me.

"When—" I clear my throat. "How did you realize that you loved her?"

"It's not something that can be explained. It's just something that you know and feel deep within your soul."

My teeth grind together as I become frustrated with people telling me about these intangible, life-affirming feelings.

I don't know what it's like to feel Cara's presence.

I don't know what it's like to feel in love.

Can someone just give me some fucking clue on how to grasp these things?

"Anyway." Miles's hands clap down on his lap. "I wanted you to know that Rae might be asking you to join her again. Something for you to think about if you're ready."

"Yeah," I mutter. "I'll think about it."

CHAPTER FORTY-FOUR

Emma

I'M quick to fall back into the routine that was my life before Gray stepped into it. With Dad home, I make the meals, help him with whatever loose ends are left at his church, and work at SeaScape. Of course, Gray still climbs through my window and spends the nights with me, but I long for the next chapter in my life where I can have my own apartment and don't have to hide him.

My eyes glance down at my phone in my hand, checking my bank account. I've watched it fluctuate over time, but I'm finally at a point where it seems to be growing at a faster rate. I just need an extra little cushion, and who knows? Maybe I'll be out of Dad's house by the holidays.

"Excuse me, are you the artist?" An elderly woman approaches me, and I instantly put my phone away.

"Oh, no, that would be my friend, Rae." I gesture to Rae who's hanging up a new painting in her art studio. I wanted to have some time with her before I go to work, so I stopped by so we could spend the hour together.

"Thank you, dear," the woman says and heads over to Rae, telling her how beautiful her beach mosaic is.

I can't help but grin as I watch their interaction.

Rae uncomfortably soaks in the compliments from this woman before she buys her artwork and leaves. I head to the register where Rae's standing.

"I don't think I'll ever get used to people telling me how much they like my shit," she says to me.

"Well, you better start! I bet after that documentary comes out, this place is going to be pretty popular."

Her face scrunches. "You think?"

I nod. "People are going to know who you are and your story. They're going to want to come in here."

"I didn't think that far ahead and realize people might want to come in here to talk to me about...everything. I don't know if I can handle that." She blows out a puff of air, moving a blond strand of hair out of her face as she takes some documents out of her canvas tote bag. "But I filled out the forms for the documentary, so what's done is done. The guy, Jake from IntraFilms, sent me this consent form to have the viewing here." She showcases the papers.

"Are you still going to do it?"

"It still feels like I should. I'm just nervous about it."

I give her a soft smile. "I'm here for you, no matter what you decide."

"I didn't tell Grayson about it," Rae states.

"About the viewing?"

"About any of it. He doesn't know I did the documentary to begin with, and honestly, I don't know how he'll feel about it." She chews the inside of her cheek, looking at me for some guidance.

"Um..." I clear my throat, knowing that we're both

assuming he's not going to be a fan of the whole idea. "I can talk to him if you'd like."

"Thank you, but no, I should." Rae sighs, putting the papers aside. "So, spare me the disgusting details, but are things still good between you two?" she asks, shifting the conversation.

"They're amazing." I mindlessly coil the ends of my hair around my finger.

"That look on your face tells me more than I want to know."

I chuckle. "It's more than just that. He's incredibly thoughtful and romantic."

"I can't picture my brother as romantic, but if you say so," she teases.

"He put together the sweetest picnic on the beach and read to me."

Rae grins. "I'm glad you're happy, Emma. You deserve nothing but the best—whether that's Grayson or not."

"Trust me, it's Grayson."

CHAPTER FORTY-FIVE

ONCE EMMA'S dad came home, our schedule instantly went back to the way it was. Which is why I was shocked to receive a text from her Saturday afternoon asking me to come over.

Me
isn't your dad home?

Red
he had to make a house call

Me
when will he be back?

Red:
'm not sure but we can make it quick

My brows rise as a smile tickles my lips.

Me
holy shit, are you asking me for an afternoon delight?

Red
I'm asking for a little something to hold me over before you inevitably crawl into my bed tonight

Before I even finish reading the text, I'm off of Rae's couch and heading to my car. Emma's appetite has transformed into something fierce—not that I'm complaining in the slightest. I get to live out every fantasy with the most perfect girl in the world, all the while she keeps begging for more.

Before long, I'm parked at the dead end, dashing through the sand, and climbing through her window.

Emma laughs as I stumble into her room. "You could've used the front door. He's not here."

"I'm not exactly thinking clearly," I say, a little bit out of breath.

"Allow me to make things crystal clear for you."

Instantly, her arms wrap around me as her lips crash against mine. Heat courses through my veins as yet another latch on Emma's restraints breaks open as she embraces her own needs and desires through the use of me.

As I bunch up her sundress, she drops her hands lower and searches for my belt.

My cock immediately hardens as she struggles with the buckle. Our heady breaths flow in and out of each other as our kisses get sloppy.

Dragging my lips down her jaw, to her neck, she quivers under the harsh nip of her skin. Yanking on my zipper, her hands plunge into my boxers setting my dick free.

Her small hand works me at the same time she pushes her hips toward me in urgency.

"Damn, Red, what's got you so fucking needy?" I taunt, my mouth running over her.

"I was reading one of my romances and kept picturing you," she pants the words without any hesitation.

Our chests rise and fall at an erratic pace against one another. My heart pounds so loud, I can hear it in my ears.

As I slide my hand into her panties, I moan when I feel how wet she is.

"Tell me what was happening in your book," I demand, pushing my fingers into her.

Emma lets out a loud sigh. "He—" She tries to grind her clit against my palm while jerking me off at the same time, her movements stuttering. "He ripped her thong with his knife and fucked her against the wall."

My legs tense with lust from hearing her speak. My mind flashes to the small scene she described, picturing if I did the same—and if she'd let me.

I don't have a knife, but there are plenty of walls. Without another passing second, I'm walking forward, pressing her into one. A grin appears on her swollen lips as we break apart for a beat. Her sensual gaze drifts over my entire face, dropping down to my body. A flame of hunger ignites in her eyes when she sees how ready I am for her.

My hands fly to her hips, spinning her around. She gasps as I yank her ass closer to me, running my length between her thighs.

Her arms dig into the wall as she pants with heavy

anticipation. I dip forward, planting a gentle kiss on her shoulder.

"I'm going to fuck you better than any of your book boyfriends could."

I immediately slam into her soaked pussy, and she shrieks with pleasure. My fingers press into the delicate skin wrapped around her hip bones, knowing that my mark will be left with colorful bruises—an artwork of our rough desire for each other.

Harder and harder, I move in and out of her. Her warmth coats my cock, making me feel euphoric. Sinking my teeth into my bottom lip, I focus on the way our bodies work together. It's the sexiest fucking thing to watch.

My heart rate accelerates, buzzing throughout my bloodstream. Sweat rolls down my back the same time my spine is struck with a bolt of pleasure.

The uneven rhythm of her ribcage moving up and down spurs me on almost as much as the sweet symphony of ecstasy that's leaving her mouth.

However, the beautiful sounds are immediately halted when we hear muffled chattering come from downstairs as the front door closes.

Panic seizes Emma's body as she becomes rigid. "Oh my god!" she whispers. "My dad's home—and he brought people with him!"

There's laughter and more talking coming from the far end of the house. They don't have a clue what's going on upstairs.

"It's okay," I say in a hushed tone. "I'll keep you safe."

My oath relaxes her. She arches her back once

again, and I can't help but smile, knowing that I'm the one she trusts to protect her.

I keep pounding into her. This time at a slow, deep pace.

Emma sucks in a breath as quietly as possible, pushing up into me.

"There you go, Red. Keep getting off on my cock while everyone's downstairs," I whisper, my breath brushing against her hair.

Tension builds in my legs as it becomes increasingly difficult to ward off the massive wave of pleasure that's about to rip through me.

"Emma?" Her dad's voice comes through the intercom.

She gasps in fear—but not enough fear because she doesn't stop writhing against me.

"Answer him," I command, not letting up.

I never liked the guy, but now that I have all the pieces to the corrupt puzzle—I have zero respect for him. So, yeah, I'm gonna fuck his daughter while she talks to him.

Emma's trembling hand reaches toward the intercom as I continue to thrust into her. She tries to steady the short spurts of air coming from her lips.

"Yeah, Dad?" she says as evenly as possible while pushing down the button.

"You'll have to set two extra plates for lunch. Mr. and Mrs. Gardiner are visiting," he states.

My grip around her inadvertently tightens. "He invited that asshole's parents into your home!?"

"It occasionally happens," she explains as if it's nothing, then reaches for the button again. "Okay, Dad."

Once she lifts her fingers off the button, I snap, "Is he serious—!"

"Fuck me, Gray," Emma lets out a sultry demand. "I don't want to think about them or anyone else. Just you." Glancing over her shoulder, her hair falls to the other side as our eyes lock. Heat spirals out of my core at the sight of her wetting her lips and hearing her whine, "Please."

Even though my anger is threatening to take me out of this moment, seething at the surface—I made a goddamn promise to her. And I'm going to keep it, fucking her better than anyone real or fictional ever will.

One hand stays on her hip, and my other extends forward, clutching her throat.

"I'm going to make you come so fucking hard, and when you go downstairs to deal with those horrible people, you'll have my cum dripping out of you to remind you of what a bad girl you are."

"Fuck, Gray." Her soft moans float to my ears as an approval of my statement.

Delivering my promise, I pound into her.

In a raw act of possession, I move even faster, my desire for her overriding every other thought. Each thrust becoming rougher, the both of us struggling to stifle our noises.

Snaking my hand around her waist, I dip my fingers into her panties, circling her clit in a hurried fervor. She begins to tremor, her knees buckling with every harsh movement.

Tingles coil around the base of my spine, basking in how incredible it feels to slide through her wetness.

Unable to control myself any longer, a lustful blaze

scorches my insides. My heart nearly explodes from the strength of my orgasm as I endlessly pump into Emma. Her pussy spasms, completely emptying me as she shakes and squirms.

"Grayson," she cries into the wall.

Still circling her clit, I reach my other hand up to cover her mouth as she struggles to stay quiet. Heaving and shuddering, her body goes tense, and then she loses all restraint, rattling in my arms as she hits her climax.

Gasping into my palm, she finally goes limp, each muscle easing into my hold. Her back falls against my chest as both of us begin to even our breaths.

Releasing my grip from her mouth, I wrap my arms around her torso to help hold her steady. Kissing along her shoulder and neck, she shudders once more.

"I'm definitely a fan of quickies," Emma whispers, regaining some energy.

Smirking, I gently spin her around and right her dress, flattening out the wrinkles, then fix my pants. Her chin tilts up as she studies me, the expression of utmost trust and admiration swirls around the intoxicating color of her irises, causing my belly to flip-flop.

"We'd like lunch in a half hour." Her dad's voice breaks our moment, causing both of us to cringe at the sound of his voice.

Emma shifts toward the intercom. "I'll be right there."

Instantly, my anger is back, encasing my bones. "Why the fuck did he bring them here?"

"So he can remain on good terms with them and keep them as donors."

"If Kane is downstairs, I'm going to—"

Emma puts her hand up to my riotous heart.

"You're like a ticking time bomb." She chuckles. "I promise Kane's not here. I just need to go downstairs and smile through a bullshit lunch, and then it'll be over."

I shake my head, the intensity in me building. "Fuck that, Emma. It shouldn't be like this—you shouldn't have to go down there and oblige to everything your dad says. Just fucking leave now—I'll take care of you."

"Shhh." She smiles. "As much as I appreciate that, your plan is to go back home after summer, remember?"

My heart shatters, the jagged pieces crashing into my stomach, slicing up my insides on the way down.

I don't have a plan. I never had a plan until Emma entered my life. *She's* the only light guiding me toward some type of future.

"I'm not going back home after the summer," I announce to the both of us for the first time.

Emma's face brightens, hope lighting up around her as if all the planets aligned the moment I said that. "Really?" Her quiet voice fills the room with optimism.

"Really."

Flinging herself on me, she jumps in my arms with excitement, kissing me nonstop.

I have nothing figured out, but I know I'm never giving up this feeling with Emma.

Planting her feet on the floor, she hurries to the door. "I have to go downstairs, but come back tonight."

"I'll be back for round two and three." I wink.

"And four."

My tongue peeks out, wetting my lips. "Such a bad girl."

She adjusts her dress, and I start to become hard

again thinking about her sitting at her kitchen table with my cum running down her thighs.

She blows me a kiss before leaving me to stand alone in her room.

I crack the door open, listening to the faraway voices and when I finally hear the chatter coming from the kitchen and the sound of silverware clanking against plates, I sneak out. With the promise of sneaking back in later tonight.

CHAPTER FORTY-SIX

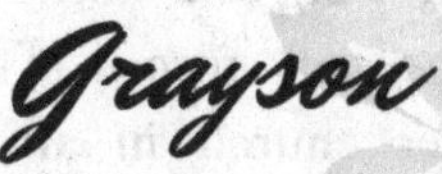

WHEN SUNDAY ROLLS AROUND, I find myself in the last place I want to be: Kingdom Church.

Sitting in the last pew, I keep an eye on everything and everyone. Emma glanced back earlier and seemed surprised to see me here again. Although we didn't discuss me showing up to her dad's church for a second time, I don't know why she's shocked I'm here. I plan on making this pew my notorious spot every Sunday until she no longer has to attend.

As her dad, Pastor William, drones on about repenting for our sins, my gaze drifts over to the organ player. His attention is fixed on the pastor, nodding along like he's taking to heart every hypocritical word that pours out of the man's mouth.

My teeth grind together as I watch the two deceitful men act as if they have any authority to be stationed up on a pulpit.

The more I stare at Kane Gardiner as he plays the part of a holy parishioner, the more the fibers around my muscles weave with wrath.

I've had a lot of downtime now that Emma's dad is back home, and we're not stapled to each other's side. I did some digging and within a matter of minutes I found out about the whole Gardiner family. Already coming from old money, his father hit it big as a stockbroker and tripled their income. The only record of donations was years ago to another church in an affluent neighborhood. I assume they get more accolades and attention from Pastor William and his followers since there's less financial competition, which is why they've made Kingdom Church their second home.

"Let's all join hands in prayer," Emma's dad says after I zoned out during his entire sermon.

We all rise, and I give fake-ass smiles to those around me as I take their clammy hands. Bringing my attention to the front of the church, I look at Emma as she pretends to fix her hair so she can move her head around and steal a glance.

Giving her a subtle wink, her cheeks turn rosy, and she turns her focus back on her dad.

Feeling the heat of someone's stare, my eyes jump over to someone glaring at me.

Kane Fucking Gardiner.

Jealousy and rage spark out of his dark eyes. He must've caught my wink at Emma and is piecing it together that, no, I'm not here because of Pastor William's meaningful speeches.

"Let us bow our heads, asking for forgiveness," the pastor says.

Everyone's head drops.

But not mine.

And not Kane's.

As Emma's dad continues to pray, we have a stare-off. Each millisecond that passes, Kane's glower hardens into something that should make my skin crawl. But in reality, the evil dancing across his face makes my lips tug upward.

I can't stop smirking. If he wants to pretend that he's not the villain, that's fine by me. I'll pretend that I didn't find his address, know what car he drives, which country club he plays golf at, and that I don't have a history of taking my aggression out on people's faces.

"Amen," says Emma's dad.

Everyone repeats him, and while I glare at Kane, I mutter, "Amen."

Kane goes back to his organ, playing a joyful tune as the choir sings. Pastor William, followed by Emma, walks down the aisle giving smiles to everyone. Amber-colored eyes drift over in my direction, and my stomach flutters when our gazes connect—instantly defusing the bomb that was about to be set off.

Perhaps I'm inserting myself too much by being here and wanting to make Kane pay for what he did. But I can't sit and do nothing. Even if I don't get the opportunity to hurt him, at the very least I keep a close watch to make sure he doesn't go near Emma again.

While Emma and her dad shake hands, I loiter around making small talk with some others who hang back. Kane remains with the musicians but keeps tabs on me, casually looking my way every so often. A chuckle comes from behind my closed lips the more agitated he appears with my presence.

When the line by the front door finally dies down, Emma separates herself, pretending to look for something in a nearby pew.

"Excuse me." I meander over to her, and her head pops up. "Emma, right?"

"Yes. And you're, Greg?"

"Grayson."

Emma snaps her fingers. "That's right–Grayson. I'm sorry. I meet so many people."

A few people glance our way as we speak, but they're all waiting to talk with her dad, and as soon as he makes his way toward them, their interest in us is dropped.

"Will you be here every week?" she whispers through a smile.

"Does it bother you that I am?" I respond lowly, with a similar expression on my face as if we're chatting about the weather.

"No."

"Good, because I wasn't planning on stopping."

She beams. "Really?"

I nod. "You're never going to be in a room with that asshole without me."

"You can't curse in a church."

"I think God is more worried about the rapist and the man who covered for him, than the word asshole."

Her gaze darts over my shoulder in fear that someone might've heard my hushed comment. When she realizes no one did, her shoulders relax. "You've got a point."

"You better get used to seeing me here, Emma."

"I look forward to it," she says a bit louder, ending our private conversation. "It was nice speaking with you, Grayson, but I'm heading home now."

"Safe drive."

We part ways, knowing that we'll be seeing each

other again momentarily, and as my gaze lifts up, I spot Kane staring right at me. Daggers shoot out of his eyes, attempting to threaten me, but I'm not phased.

I give him a wave with a condescending smile and leave this unhallowed church.

CHAPTER FORTY-SEVEN

Emma

AS I'M GRACEFULLY swiping mascara over my lashes, getting ready for a Monday morning shift at SeaScape, Dad's voice summons me through the intercom.

"Emma. I need to see you in my office immediately."

My stomach nose-dives onto the floor at the sound of his commanding tone.

Without even answering him, I'm racing out of my room and toward his office. My mind floods with horror, hoping me and Grayson didn't leave any incriminating evidence that he just so happened to find a week later.

As my feet race against the hardwood, I do a mental recap of when Grayson bent me over the desk. We cleaned up afterward. No clothes were discarded. I moved Mom's picture later on in the day, but I put it back perfectly in its spot.

When I stand in the doorway, I aim to keep my breath steady as I do a quick sweep around his office, noting that everything is in place. My shoulders relax when I realize that he's not calling me in here to discuss me defiling his desk.

Noting me standing under the doorframe, Dad's head snaps up from his computer, and his glare lands on me.

"We need to discuss the boy from church." His voice is cold, but it doesn't freeze me up the way it once would.

Tilting my head to the side, my forehead wrinkles as I play dumb. "The boy from church?"

Dad rips off his glasses, tossing them on the oak desk that I recently braced myself on.

Suddenly, something inside me clicks into place as if my neurons are coming together to gift me courage and authority.

Grayson literally fucked me right where I'm staring, and Dad has no idea. He has no idea about any of it. My masterplan to leave him and his church, sneaking in and out of the house, this new fuse that's been lit since the start of the summer—Dad doesn't know how I've been playing the part he designed for me just so I can break out of it when all the pieces finally meld together.

"I just got off the phone with Kane. He tried speaking to me yesterday, but the other parishioners had taken up most of my day," Dad states. "If I had known how pressing this matter was, I would've told everyone that they have to wait while I dealt with the information Kane brought to my attention."

My jaw tenses, causing my teeth to smash into each other with a painful pressure. "I'm not sure I understand what you're talking about, nor do I understand why Kane is speaking about me," I snap.

Dad's brows shoot up in pure shock at my response.

His shoulders inch up his neck as his anger toward me grows. "Sit down," he commands, pointing to the leather chair across from his desk.

"No."

He rises to his feet in an attempt to overpower me. "Have you been talking to that boy?"

"I spoke to him yesterday at church when he told me how much he enjoyed your sermon. Aside from that, Kane must be making up stories like he usually does. But we all know how likely you are to take his word over mine."

My chest pinches as my eyes bulge with surprise that those words just flew out of my mouth.

I swear Dad grows double in size, towering over me. My bones knock with fear, knowing I shouldn't have said what I just did. Glancing over his shoulder, I quickly look at the picture of Mom resting on his bookshelf. As crazy as if might seem, her smile seemed to get wider. And despite the hysteria pumping out of my heart, I lift my chin with pride.

"I'm leaving for work," I state, pivoting into the hallway.

As I run to my room to get my belongings, Dad stomps out of his office, shouting after me. "You do not speak to me that way, young lady! Have you no respect for your father?" Grabbing my keys and phone, I race back downstairs as he continues to have a tantrum. "I raised you better than this—"

Stopping at the front door, I put my mask back in place. I can't let everything fall apart when I'm this close to the finish line. I'll give him a pseudo-heartfelt apology as long as he continues to give me a roof over my head.

"You're right," I exhale, taming my frustration. "I'm sorry I snapped. I didn't sleep well last night, and it must be catching up with me. I won't speak to the boy at church if you don't want me to, but I was just being hospitable like you've always taught me to be—especially in your place of worship."

My sudden twist in emotions has him thrown off. His features pull in tight as he opens and closes his mouth. "Yes, well,"—he clears his throat—"I'd like you to keep your distance from him."

I nod. "Understood. I'll see you this evening."

We say our goodbyes, and I'm out the door. As I drive to the south side of Golden Bay, my heart clamors with an array of opposing emotions pouring out of me.

I can't process everything I'm feeling—both positive and negative. But I know that I need to keep my charade up for the time being. My head starts to pound with a dull ache. Every move with Dad has been a game of strategy. I can't risk losing my plan.

Pulling into the parking lot, I draw in a long breath hoping it will alleviate the whirling thoughts in my mind.

At the very least, seeing Grayson during my shift will brighten my day.

CHAPTER FORTY-EIGHT

Grayson

THE BRIGHT SUNLIGHT pours into Rae's living room, and if my phone ringing wasn't waking me up right now, the blinding light sure would.

When I see Mom's name popping up on the screen, I clear my throat to sound more awake before answering. "Hey, Mom."

"Hi, honey. I just wanted to check up on you to see how you're doing." The kind familiarity of her voice brings an ease to my chest.

"I'm doing well. How are you and Dad?" I ask before yawning.

As she goes on to tell me about their past several weeks, I sit up and stretch from side to side, gently lengthening the muscles in my back.

"Have you been shadowing Miles?" she asks.

"Uh...a little bit."

"I hope you're learning some new skills. Your dad wanted me to find out which trade school you'd like to enroll in. It'll be starting soon."

Her comment wakes me up even more, realizing

how fast the summer has been flying by. "About that," I start and already can hear the change in her breathing as she prepares for disappointment. "I think I want to stay here past the summer."

"Oh," Mom chirps with pleasant surprise. "That sounds like a lovely idea. Will you be going to trade school there? Is Rae okay with you extending your stay? Maybe you could work with her if you didn't want to go to school—"

"I haven't figured all that out. I just know I don't want to leave yet."

"What does your sister think about it?"

"I haven't crossed that bridge yet."

"Oh, okay." Mom's pause creates a slight twinge of nervousness in my gut. I haven't brought the idea up to Rae, but I don't necessarily think she'd be against it considering my conversation with Miles from the other day. "Well, if you happen to speak with her about it before Friday and need us to bring some more belongings, let me know."

"You're coming to visit?" My stomach growls, and I make my way into the kitchen to eat some cereal.

"Of course. We'll be there for the viewing."

"Viewing of what?"

"The documentary."

Taking a bite of sweet cereal drenched in milk, I crunch into the phone. "I don't know what you're talking about."

"Rae didn't tell you?" Her voice morphs into somberness, and I immediately drop my spoon into the bowl.

"No..."

Anxiety rolls through me, crashing into my heart

over and over again the longer Mom takes to respond. Seconds tick by, and I'm not sure if I should be petrified or enraged, but I know both emotions are bubbling inside me, and my brain will soon cling to one.

Mom lets out a long sigh. "This past spring was ten years since we lost Cara—"

"I'm aware."

"Rae, along with Miles and a few other survivors, was approached to do a documentary about the s—"

"She did a fucking documentary about Cara?"

Rage. My brain chooses rage.

An angry flare heats up my neck, my jaw set tight.

The start of making amends with Rae vanishes instantly.

Rae has left me out to dry, borderline forgetting my existence for *years*. And up until recently, she barely blinked in my direction. My life has been a living hell as I was left in the aftermath of her addiction—begging her to get clean, crying to her, tossing her stash, spying on who she was hanging out with, reporting to my parents, finding her fucking overdosed in her bedroom. And for what? For her to tell me that I'm dead to her? For her to fucking hate me?

She might be trying to make up for it now, but at this point it's too goddamn late.

We were supposed to grieve for our sister together.

Not Rae, alone, making a motherfucking televised production about it.

I lost my sister, too. Not just Rae.

And it could've been a lot less torturous of a process if we leaned on each other, like siblings should.

"Grayson?" Mom grows worried. "Grayson, talk to me."

"I'll talk to you later," I mumble, hanging up.

The thunderous pounding of my pulse makes it difficult to think straight, my anger clouding my judgment. Before I know it, I'm getting my shoes on and heading to the elevator to hunt down Rae.

I'm confronting her as soon as I possibly can, seeing that she didn't have the courtesy to let me know—not that she didn't have ample opportunities over the course of the past several weeks that I've been crashing on her couch.

Stepping out of the elevator, I make a beeline for SeaScape's exit.

"Hey." A sweet voice ricochets off the nautical-themed walls of the lobby.

Immediately whipping around, I spin on my heels and spot Emma at the front desk.

In my sudden burst of madness, I forgot that she'd be working today. Regaining some clarity, I focus on my beautiful girlfriend.

Only, there's something off about her.

There's tension building in her arms and creases in her forehead as she gives me a weak smile.

"What's wrong?" I hurry over to her.

"Nothing, my dad was annoying this morning. That's all." She rolls her eyes.

My spine straightens as alarms go off in my head. "What'd he say?" I try to conceal my angry tone, but I don't think it worked.

Emma studies me as she debates giving more information. Finally, her shoulders drop. "It was stupid. He got pissed that I was talking to you."

"He knows you're seeing me?"

"God, no! Apparently, Kane saw us talking in

church yesterday and decided to tattle on me, like the grown man he is."

Another dose of wrath hits my bloodstream, only this time it's worse.

Biting into my bottom lip, holding in any explosive thoughts, I keep quiet.

Emma and I are opposites when we get overwhelmed. Where I shut down, she can't stop talking. And as her mouth impulsively divulges more context, my anger escalates.

"I'm forbidden to go near you." She mindlessly rearranges her office supplies but in a harsh manner. A stapler comes crashing down next to her computer as she continues, "My dad hates you even though hatred doesn't belong in a place of worship. But what do I know, I'm just his idiotic daughter." Her paperclip container falls out of her hand, and rose gold paperclips fly everywhere. An aggravated sound comes from the back of her throat, but before she has the chance to get too frustrated, I'm scooping them up. "And get this—Kane tried *warning* me about you!"

I freeze.

"What?" The one syllable grates against my vocal cords as I fight to keep it together.

"Yeah—out of all the people to open their mouths on that topic, *he* felt like he had the place to say something!"

"When did he speak to you?"

"Not yesterday. The first time you went to church." Emma takes the paper clips from me and puts them back in the container. "He said something about you being trouble—I don't remember. All I know is that I need to get the hell away from these people."

Yes. She absolutely does. And I need to figure out how.

Pinching the bridge of my nose, I force myself to calmly inhale and exhale. I'm struggling to think straight, but I need to at least pretend I'm not about to lose my shit in front of Emma.

"Gray?"

I peel my hand away from my face and see a concerned look in Emma's eyes. "We'll figure out how to get you away from them," I promise her.

"I have it all mapped out. I just need to suck it up and deal with it until I graduate."

I shake my head.

No, I'm not letting her deal with them for that long.

Her brows draw in as she takes a beat to assess me. "You're getting lost in your thoughts," she states as fact. I open my mouth to tell her no, but then close it back up. It's pointless to lie to her. "Maybe this was a bad time for me to unload on you. I'm sorry."

"No." I clasp her hands in mine. "I want to hear everything you have to say, even if it takes me a while to process it."

"Okay." The corners of her lips tip up slightly.

Before we can get lost in each other's gazes for too long, the elevator dings and someone steps off. We slowly break our connection, and Emma shifts back into work-mode.

"I'll be back in a little bit," I state before stepping into the sun.

The combination of the heat, hearing about Kane attempting to rat us out, and the news of Rae's documentary has my blood boiling.

The bustling boardwalk makes it difficult to weave

in and out of obnoxious tourists, and my annoyance increases with every person who tries to cut me off.

My molars grind against one another as tension hikes up my shoulder blades.

Darting my way in and out of the crowds, I finally reach Rae's art studio. Swinging the door open, the blast of cool air does nothing to thaw the scorching blaze shooting through my bloodstream.

Rae's perched at her long counter, painting on a canvas. Her gaze drifts upward, and when she spots me at the opposite end of the room, she gives me a knowing look.

"Mom called me," she says, wiping orange acrylic paint off her fingertips.

"You made a fucking documentary?" I snap, but then do a quick survey of the space to make sure we're alone.

"I was *interviewed* as a part of a documentary."

"Why?"

She looks at me with genuine confusion tugging at her features. Her usual icy, unapproachable eyes soften the more she stares at me.

Even though my heart punches into my ribs, and my joints are still clogged with tension, I walk closer to her.

Sitting up straighter as I approach her, she responds, "Because it's important, Grayson."

I remain quiet, not sure on how to answer, so she continues.

"We lost Cara ten years ago, and this shit is still happening. Look at what it did to me, look at what it did to us, look at what it did to our family." Rae tosses her canvas to the side. "We're all supposed to go on and live a normal life—but none of this is fucking normal."

A weight drops in my gut because I know she's right, and I hate it.

"I want things to change, and the only way I know how to advocate is through art," Rae states. "Whether it's my art or supporting someone else's. Whether it's my gruesome paintings, a filmmaker's documentary, or some random story you've written in your notebook—"

"What?" My head does an immediate spin. "You've read my notebook?"

"No, of course not, but I know you used to write stories, and I'm assuming you still do."

"No," I grit, pissed that my creativity has shriveled up and pissed that she needed to remind me of it.

"Well, whatever—this is the way I'm grieving Cara. You don't have to like it or understand it." She crosses her arms in front of her chest, getting increasingly irritated with me. "And you probably won't like the fact that I'm doing an early preview of the documentary here, either, but that's what's happening on Friday."

"Yeah, you're right, I don't want to sit in here and watch a recap of one of the worst days of my fucking life."

One of her hands reaches up to her neck, fidgeting with her choker. "It's not a recap. It's a film to increase awareness not only about the shooting but also how we were all left hanging in the aftermath. I thought if you were here to watch it, it could be a way for you and me to..." She shifts awkwardly on her feet. "I don't know, start healing together or some shit. We're both victims in this—"

"I am *not* a victim."

"Yes, you are, Grayson."

"No, I'm not."

The term victim seeps into my pores, burrowing deep under my skin where it itches and irritates to no end.

"You've endured a terrible loss when you shouldn't have had to, just like me," Rae insists.

A gust of anxiety pumps through me.

"And it's not just us, millions of people have been dealt a shitty hand because bad people keep doing all sorts of god-awful things," she continues, her face turning red the more invested she becomes.

All of this is too much for me to digest at one time. Too much to process for my overcomplicated brain. My thoughts tangle together as Rae unfolds her true feelings in front of me, things we've never spoken about or felt comfortable bringing up to one another. Key words stick out in my head—grieving, victim, bad people. I hate those words, but they swim into my veins, making me shudder with anger.

Unable to focus on one thought at a time, I bounce from Cara to Rae to Emma to me being a motherfucking victim.

My emotions rise to the surface, choking me as they swell in my throat.

"Don't you want things to change?" Rae keeps going. "Aren't you tired of shitty people ruining people's lives?"

Yes. I'm tired of all of it.

I'm exasperated by the fact that the fictional villains who once lived on the paper of my stories are now in my daily life. Even those who act as if they're decent, moral humans and devout followers of a religion can be nothing but deceitful, heinous people.

Even though Rae's talking about us and Cara, my mind can't help but fixate on Emma.

I can't change my sisters' fates, but I refuse to let the villain of Emma's story get away with what he did.

I can't fix anything that's happened, but at the very least I can start making Kane pay for his sins.

My blood boils over, steam pouring out of my ears. Waves of rage-fueled heat blast over my body every few seconds.

Rae goes to open her mouth, but if I hear another word, I might combust.

"See you later." I pivot toward the door.

"Wait, where are you going?" she calls after me. "We're in the middle of a convers—"

The door slams shut as I step onto the boardwalk. Every cell in my body fills with anger that I know I'm not going to be able to shake off.

My eyes dart around, checking each passerby as I walk to my car.

My fists ball up, my forearms tense with anger.

Becoming blinded by my emotions, I know writing out my feelings isn't going to fucking cut it this time. Any progress that I might've made since coming here has evaporated into thin air, my anger causing it to dissipate.

I need to get some of my aggression out.

CHAPTER FORTY-NINE

Grayson

MY HAND WRINGS my steering wheel, knuckles turning white. I try to cling to a thread of rationality, but each time I do my anger comes back fiercer.

As my foot presses down on the gas pedal, the whizzing sound of my pulse makes it difficult to hear my GPS, but I know I'm getting close to where I want to be.

Is it slightly insane to drive forty minutes out of the area just to use someone as a punching bag? Possibly. But not as insane as Kane is for thinking his actions wouldn't catch up with him.

It's a crapshoot as to whether he'll even be at the country club he belongs to, but I'd rather beat the shit out of him than a random person at a bar like last time—even though that asshole deserved it, too.

My cheeks heat with rage once again.

There are so many assholes walking these streets, ripping innocent people's lives to shreds just because they think they're entitled to. Most of them don't get caught. Most of them get away with it and continue doing whatever atrocious crime makes them feel powerful.

Fuck that.

I pull into a vast parking lot, a white sign with gold lettering with the words East Hollow Country Club sits in a small garden in front of an old school mansion with columns and several high peaks in the roof.

Getting out of my car, I compose myself even though internally a tornado of vengeance is swirling around me.

I glance around, noting a huge golf course which disappears into the green scenery and a few smaller houses off to the side. Checking the cars as I approach the front door, I spot a white Rolls-Royce in the VIP parking.

The corners of my mouth stretch into a sly smirk. My heart pounds faster.

Stepping into the lobby of the country club, there are stairs on either side and a restaurant dead ahead where the scent of orange juice and champagne lingers. My gaze flows around the room for a familiar face, and when I don't spot him, I decide to move further into the space.

"Excuse me!" A pretentious-sounding voice stops me.

Looking over my shoulder, I spot a brunette with a high ponytail standing off to the side. She's wearing a white button-up with a name tag that I don't bother reading. "Yeah?" I ask, the annoyance obvious in my tone.

"There's a dress code."

My gaze drops down, realizing I'm in gym shorts

and slides. My nostrils flare as I take a stabilizing inhale. "I was just stopping by to see a friend."

She shakes her head. "I can't let you in wearing that. However, there's a shop downstairs next to the cigar lounge. I know they sell polos, but I'm not sure about shoes." She grimaces when she looks at my footwear.

My jaw wiggles back and forth as I contemplate what to do. There's a moment of hesitancy as I consider turning around to leave. But then Emma's freckled face and wavy red hair flashes into my mind.

"Thanks," I say, and make my way to the lower staircase that's labeled as the cigar lounge.

Guess I'll have to sneak my way around in order to find Kane.

Bypassing the shop, I overhear people speaking about golf clubs and other bullshit I have no interest in. As I slink around, searching for a way to get back upstairs without running into that bitchy staff member, the aroma of aged liquor and sweet tobacco wafts under my nose.

Sneaking past the cigar lounge, I catch the end of a conversation with men speaking about starting a game of golf.

Tiptoeing down the hall, I freeze when I hear one of the men speak. "Will you be at Sunday's tournament, Kane?"

An explosion of adrenaline bursts into every fiber of my being the second I hear his name.

"I'll be spending the day at Kingdom Church," Kane states.

Any anger that might've been suppressed as I

entered the country club has been reignited at the sound of his voice.

"Oh, that's right," the other man says. "Well, I'm about to head over to the driving range to get some practice in. Care to join?"

"I'll use the bathroom quickly and meet you over there."

A sinister feeling bellows in my gut. My focus latches onto the restroom sign at the far end of the hall.

Moving as fast as I can, sparks of fury fly inside my body. A pinching pain hits my chest the faster my heart races.

Getting to the bathroom, there's a small vestibule area before a row of stalls, urinals, and sinks.

Beads of moisture surround my hairline.

Pulse thrashing with wrath.

My mind spins.

Emma keeps popping up in my head, but it's not just her. It's her and him.

I blink, trying to force the image away.

Bile creeps up my throat thinking of all the horrible things Kane did to her.

And how he's traipsing around looking fucking virtuous.

I'm sick of the villains always winning. I'm so fucking sick of it, I'm a millisecond away from snapping—

"Whoa!" Kane sputters as I push him up against the bathroom wall.

I force my attention to him. I'm so wrapped up in my rage, I don't even remember him walking in.

My fists shake with anger as they ball up his shirt, holding him in place.

Kane's dark eyes are wide with shock, and when he realizes who's staring back at him, they transform into something vicious. "I knew telling Emma you were nothing but trouble was the right thing to do," his voice gets raspy as he takes shallow breaths.

Hatred violently rushes through me, my veins pushing up against my skin nearly popping out of my body.

"If you ever want to speak to my girlfriend again, you're going to have to go through me."

I drive my fist into his cheek, blood splattering across the freshly painted walls. Kane shouts in pain, but as soon as he lifts his head back up, he starts swinging.

I duck, dodging each blow.

Excitement zooms up and down my spine, and a smirk dances on my face.

It's been a while since I've gotten into a fight–I've forgotten how fucking satisfying it is.

The old me from just a few weeks ago continues to take over. Landing another punch to his face, my emotions flood down my arms, circling my fists with pent-up aggression. "I know what you did to her, you sick bastard," I grit between clenched teeth.

His fist comes flying at me, and I don't dodge it quick enough, getting sucker-punched in the side of the head. Panic strikes me as I lose my balance, my ears ringing from the strength of the blow.

On impulse, eclipsed by white-hot rage, I grip onto his shirt and fling him across the vestibule.

Kane smashes into a full-length mirror, shards of glass erupting across the room. Tiny slivers finding their way under the skin of my feet and calves.

With blood running down Kane's face, his left eye already swelling, he sneers. "You'll pay for this."

"No." I swipe the sweat away from my forehead, catching my breath. "You're gonna pay for what you did. This was just the beginning."

Kane starts to rise, open cuts all over him, chunks of glass clinking together when he moves, and I know that I'm on borrowed time.

Before he can regain his strength and fully come to his feet, I hightail it out of here.

CHAPTER FIFTY

Grayson

WINCING, cold water hits my open wounds on my knuckles as I wash my hand off in Rae's condo. Wrapping some ice in a paper towel, I cover my knuckles, hoping the swelling goes down before I see Emma.

Luckily, she was busy with a resident when I came back, so we didn't have time to talk, and she didn't catch a glimpse at my hand as I hurried to the elevator.

The sound of keys jingling in the lock has me turning my attention to the front door, my mind trying to figure out how I'm going to explain this to Rae.

Relief flows through me when I see Miles entering. "How's it going?" he says as he makes himself at home.

"All right," I mutter, adjusting the ice on my hand.

"Whoa, what happened?"

"Nothing."

"Let me rephrase my question: who'd you get into a fight with?" Miles leans on the kitchen island awaiting my response. When he's met with only a glare, he shrugs. "Truth's gonna come out eventually, you might as well say it now."

Dropping my line of sight to my hand, when I spot the open gashes on my fingers a sense of pride swims through me. "Some asshole named Kane."

"Who is he?"

"He's from Emma's past." My gaze darts up at Miles. "But you can't say anything to her."

"You think you're going to be able to hide that hand from her?"

"I know I'll have to tell her, I'm just figuring out what to say." I take in a sharp breath as I begin to wiggle my sore fingers. "That is, if her dad doesn't speak with her first."

"Why would he?"

"Kane's connected to him."

"Oh."

"Yeah. I might've overcomplicated things a bit."

Miles pushes himself to stand straight. "Did Kane deserve it?"

"Fuck yes. And worse."

"I would've done the same for your sister."

There's a beat of silence as we have an unspoken conversation, where we can both relate to one another on this matter.

Then the moment is gone, and Miles goes to the fridge while I figure out how the fuck to handle this when Kane inevitably blabs to Emma's dad.

Sitting on Emma's bed, I anxiously pick at my cuticles, causing a dot of blood to rise to the surface. The tiny little mark is nothing in comparison to the rest of my wounded hand. My belly knots with worry, knowing that I potentially made Emma's situation worse. Thoughts bounce around my brain with the possibilities of how this can unfold, and each scenario is worse than the last.

Emma gasps when she enters her bedroom, hand slamming on her heart. "Jeez, you scared me," she whispers.

"I told you I'd see you back at your house," I tell her quietly as she closes the door. I was able to catch her at the tail end of her shift and thought I made it clear I'd be here when she'd come home.

"I thought you meant tonight, not now when my dad's awake." As she speaks, she slips out of her work clothes and into comfortable loungewear.

"I didn't want you to be alone, so I chanced sneaking in."

"Why didn't you want me to be alone?"

I pause, realizing word hasn't traveled to her dad yet. Covering my bruised hand with the other, I shrug.

"Okay, well, I have to make dinner, so I won't be up here for a while."

"That's okay. I'll keep myself occupied." And I'll keep an ear out in case her dad happens to get the news in the middle of their meal.

Frankly, I'm surprised Kane hasn't ratted me out yet, considering he was bothered by me breathing the same air as him in Kingdom Church.

Emma puts her clothes into the hamper, straightens up her desk and starts lighting her candles. Within moments, the soothing scent, which I now know is wisteria, is wrapping around me.

"What are you doing?" I ask.

"Making it nice for you so you can relax while you wait." Emma smiles at me, and in this moment, it's enough for all of my unease to wash away. "Be back in a bit," she says before brushing her lips to mine and scooting out of her room.

The entire time she's downstairs I attentively listen, expecting there to be explosives going off. But to my surprise, I hear nothing.

My stomach twists and turns, anxiously anticipating needing to race down there and intervene. Pacing around Emma's room, I attempt to occupy my worried thoughts by finding things in her room to look at, but even browsing her extensive bookshelf doesn't calm my frayed nerves.

"Hey," a gentle whisper comes from behind me, and as I spin away from the books, I spot Emma tiptoeing back into her room. "I snuck some dinner up for you." She showcases a Tupperware container of some type of pasta and a can of Pepsi.

"Thanks," I say, smiling.

I've been too nervous to think about food, but I know I'll need to eat eventually.

"We'll still have to keep it down until he's asleep," she states, placing the container on her desk. Hopping onto her mattress, she sits cross-legged as I still meander around the room, hiding my bruised hand from her. "Why'd you come here so early? Not that I mind, I'm just curious."

"I wanted to make sure everything's okay."

"Of course it is, why wouldn't it be?"

My feet stop directly in front of her, a knot forming in my gut. "Remember when you did something you thought might make me mad, but you did it anyway?"

"You mean reading your notebook?"

"Yeah, that." I slowly peel back the hand that's covering my other, and when Emma sees how fucked-up it is, her face drops. "I did something kinda similar. Only worse."

Emma's eyes harden, her jaw set tight. It's the first time I've ever seen her visibly angry, and to my surprise, it doesn't upset me. It makes me glad that she's expressing herself with me.

"Who did you fight, Grayson?" Emma asks through clenched teeth.

"I think we both know the answer to that."

Her fingers go to the side of her face, rubbing her temples as if she had just been struck with a terrible headache.

"I know I fucked up," I admit.

"Yeah, you did, and I don't even know how badly," she snaps as she rises to pace around like I was doing mere minutes ago.

"I'm sorry, I—"

"I have a plan, Grayson." Emma sharply turns to face me, and even though her voice is quiet, there's anger powering through it. "I have had a plan for years. I didn't need someone to come in and rescue me."

My chest squeezes in pain when I hear her say that.

"My dad already suspects something is up between us. If Kane tells my dad that you beat him up because we're together and I told you my story, my dad will kick me out!" She continues. "I'll have to drop out of college, find an apartment, blow through my savings, and find a higher paying job than SeaScape all in the matter of a day! Or who knows, my dad's response could be worse than kicking me out." She roughly pulls her hair out of her face and goes back to pacing with anxiety brewing in every step.

"I know—I know, I'm sorry, Emma." I place my hand on her shoulder to get her to remain still. "I didn't think about how this would impact you in the future, I only thought of your past, and I thought about it so much that I exploded."

She lets out a huff of air, her gaze narrowing in on mine. "I'm pissed at you," she states.

"I understand."

"But..." She nibbles on the inside of her cheek, debating to say the next part. "I'm also sort of appreciative of you."

The corners of my lips twitch, and I notice how Emma's holding back a small smile. The muscles in her arms ease up, as does the look of contempt that was pouring out her eyes.

"I came here early in case Kane told your dad, and he flipped out on you," I tell her. "But honestly, if Kane hasn't snitched about me yet, then he might not at all. I might've scared the shit out of him."

She wobbles her head back and forth, considering what I'm saying. "How badly did you beat him up?"

"Wasn't the worst I've ever done, but I had limited time so I made sure to get my point across."

"So that time you injured your hand and told me you dropped something on it—"

"I lied. I punched someone."

"Why'd you lie?"

My eyes float off her, and I create some space between us. "Because I didn't think a girl like you would want a guy who tends to get into fights because he doesn't know how to deal with his fucking baggage."

My admission makes my breath stutter with panic.

There's a drawn-out silence as we stand on opposite ends of the room.

My heart pounds, waiting for Emma to tell me to leave but wanting her to tell me to stay.

Cautiously glancing at her, she studies me without an ounce of judgment reaching her features. Instead, her face softens.

"Okay," she whispers.

Immediately, I let out a sigh of relief. I'm not sure where to go from here, but the fact that she's not pissed enough to cut me out of her life sends immense relief through my veins.

"I'm sorry," I repeat myself from earlier, my voice dropping even lower.

Her body relaxes as she makes her way back to her bed. "You don't need to be, Gray."

CHAPTER FIFTY-ONE

Emma

THERE'S a definite shift in tonight's energy between me and Grayson. He seems extra restrained around me, and even though I'm still peeved, I'm also grateful for his actions. We've been dealing with the thick tension between us until well into the night. Knowing that Dad's been passed out for a while, we relax a little more.

Gray finally let me tend to his wounds and similar to last time, he's sitting on my bed with me standing in between his legs.

"This better be the last time I'm doing this," I say, applying ointment to the cuts across his knuckles.

He flinches as I touch him. "I'll try my best."

"You're lucky I like you, otherwise I wouldn't let the answer slide," I respond, giving him a playful glare.

"I'll have to thank my charismatic personality for winning you over."

I smirk, holding back a chuckle as I press a Band-Aid onto his skin.

"What's so funny?" he calls me out. "You're not in

awe of how charming I am? I can win an entire room over the second I enter it," he jokes, lightening up the mood.

"Ah, yes, I forgot about how much you enjoy being the center of attention. My mistake," I tease back.

"I don't think that was a sincere response." With a smile, he hooks his fingers around mine. "It must've been the earth-shattering orgasms that made you like me so much then."

I laugh. "Yeah, those definitely help."

Cautiously, his injured hand travels up my body until it's cupping the side of my face. My breath is uneven as a recognizable haze of lust clouds his eyes.

"Would you be less angry with me if I took care of you and gave you some now?" His voice drops, heat flooding between my thighs.

"I'm not angry," I softly say. "But I'm not going to turn down your offer."

He adjusts his hand, placing it at the base of my neck right before drawing me in for a possessive kiss. I melt at the contact, enjoying the strength of his hold.

His mouth claims me with more fervor than usual. He nips at my bottom lip, tugging it gently, and I squeeze my legs together, relishing in the sting.

I clasp my palms around his cheeks, pulling him even closer, instantly desperate to have him mark more than just my mouth.

Tingles spiral around my veins, realizing that there's a major part of me that thinks it's so fucking hot that he defended my honor against my assaulter.

Yanking him closer, his feet hit the floor, and he stands over me. Breaking contact, his labored breaths fall onto my skin while he continues to stare at me like he's about to apologize to me in the best way possible.

"Take everything off," he rasps.

Getting seduced by just the sound of his voice, my clothes are on the floor in seconds.

His gaze washes over me, every part of my body lighting up at the heat of his stare.

"Get on the rug."

Stepping toward my rug, I coyly loop strands of my hair around my ear as I follow his instruction. Sinking onto the soft, pink fabric, I kneel before him.

He swallows at the sight of me, and I can see the growing hardness in his shorts. Taking off his shirt, his abdomen glistens in the flickering candles that I lit hours ago.

I'm mesmerized by the way the dim light dances across his corded muscles.

It's beautiful to watch.

"Can I..." Anxiety stirs in my chest as my brain creates a vivid, sensual scene behind my eyes. "Can I try something?"

Gray smirks. "You can try anything you'd like."

Reaching for him, I have him join me on the smooth rug. He lies down, propped up on his elbows, and I hover over him as I slide his shorts and boxers off. My attention falls on his cock, eagerly awaiting my touch.

"I want to try something a little different," I attempt to mask the nervousness building between my vocal cords.

"I'm down for whatever my bad girl wants."

Slinking over to my nightstand, I grab one of my glimmering candles and place it next to him. "Do you think it would be fun if we tried using wax?"

Gray's eyes flame with passion. His hand tracing over my kneeling legs, sneaking its way in between my thighs. "I've been burning for you since the day I met you. I want all of your flames, Red."

I nervously clutch the candle, hesitating, concerned that maybe this will be too much and actually hurt him. He senses my delay and brings his hand over mine.

Together, we pour a small droplet of wax down his chest, and he sucks in a breath.

"Painful?" I ask.

He shakes his head. "Amazing."

Letting go of my hand and leaving me in control, his stormy eyes fixate on me as I slightly tip the jar and let a little more spill onto him.

This time he moans as the wax trickles down his contracting stomach. I watch as the liquid hardens over his skin, leaving beautiful streaks of color.

"More," he chokes out. The sound of his plea makes me drip with desire.

I do as he asks, drizzling wax from the top of his chest and down over his torso, letting it puddle below his belly button. His legs stiffen and release at the feel of the heat flowing over him. The tip of his cock begins to leak as we work together to create the perfect build-up.

He groans behind closed lips as I keep going, repeating similar motions. Our ragged breaths make the singular flame waver.

Sneaking his hand between my legs once more, he says, "I want to see how turned on you get when you control my pleasure like this." With that, two fingers connect with my wetness, and he smirks. "What a bad, bad girl."

As I continue, so does he, swirling around my clit. I start shaking, the wax covering him in erratic lines.

It becomes more difficult to focus on what I'm doing the more he works me, wringing my insides tight with lust. Trembling, some wax splashes onto my knee, the burst of heat making me gasp. I stop, studying how it clings to me.

My breath races as my body temperature rises.

"You want a turn?" Gray asks, noticing how entranced I became from the one little stream of wax.

I nod, and before I know it, the comforting touch of my pink rug is protecting my back as Grayson kneels over me.

He massages my legs, splaying them open. "If it's too much, tell me to stop."

"Okay," I whisper, my muscles tensing as I brace myself.

My heart pounds as I watch him cautiously lean the candle over, drawing a horizontal line over my thigh.

Air gets trapped in my chest at the sensation of the hot liquid. But as it quickly cools, so do I, relaxing into the feeling.

"Keep going?" Grayson's gaze is locked with mine.

"Please," I whine.

Holding back a full-blown grin, he crisscrosses the stream of liquid over one thigh and then the other.

I become flushed, moaning at the sudden warmth and then coolness.

Settling between my legs, Gray travels the wax upward, just inches away from where I want it to be. My fingers dig into the fibers of the rug as he continues to give me the most blissful torture.

"Fuck me," I plead, yearning for a release.

He chuckles. "Not yet."

Hovering over my body, he rains wax along my pelvis, having it pool in the little divots created by my hip bones.

I writhe under him, my back scraping up against the rug as my heels press into the floor.

Taking his time, he leisurely creates hot lines over my stomach. My muscles strain at the immediate flood of warmth, then ease up as it solidifies on my skin.

Working his way up my body, I can feel the warmth from the flickering flame by my chin. I draw in a sharp breath when the wax goes just under my wildly beating heart.

"You okay?" Gray checks in.

I nod, urging him for more. Carefully, two droplets mark my breast, sliding over my peaked nipple. "Oh my god," I moan, my eyes clamping shut to savor the sensations.

He gives my other breast the same attention, showering it in wax.

I'm careful not to move too quickly with the flame nearing my face, so I slowly wrap my legs around his slick body. His cock brushes up against me and his arousal mixes with the candle wax on my skin.

"I don't think I can wait any longer," I whisper.

"Just one more." The sound of his rich voice has me opening my eyes. "Don't move too much," he breathes out.

The heat from the orange glow in front of me gets hotter on my neck. My pulse jumps under my delicate flesh as wax weaves over my collarbones in a seductive caress.

Gray's trembling breath fans over my body as it aches for him to do more.

"You look fucking gorgeous," he says, his gaze wandering over the dried wax.

Placing the candle on the floor, he roams his hands over me, his fingers slipping through the slick texture.

Adjusting himself to be at the perfect angle, his lips find mine as he lines up his length to my wetness. We both moan into each other's mouths the moment he enters me.

My insides burn brighter than any flame ever could the more he thrusts me into the rug. The silky residue on our bodies makes us effortlessly glide together.

His hips drive into me at a rapid pace as my insides coil with passion.

"I'm never gonna get over how incredible your pussy feels," Gray's voice strains.

He slips his hand under the arch of my back, shoving me closer to him. My clit grinds up against his body causing me to quiver in ecstasy.

We pant as we work in harmony to get each other off.

The flicker from the candle illuminates his dark hair and side of his face, lighting him up in an ambient blaze. The more I study him attempting to fight off his orgasm, the more my heart spills over.

Gray suddenly changes rhythm, his pace moving quick and hard. I gasp each time his cock slams into me.

My muscles seize with each thrust.

Our grip on each other tightens.

My legs shake.

Eyes screwed shut.

And with one final movement, I'm exploding.

Waves and waves of overwhelming pleasure wash over me. Gray covers my mouth as I scream behind his palm, squirming.

My pussy spasms around him, and I can hear the sounds of his own heavenly desire bursting through him as he moans behind clamped lips.

We keep moving until we can't anymore.

Our bodies go lax, him lying on top of me in a sweet embrace. The wax sticks to us while our arms wrap around each other. Our labored breaths match, hearts pounding into one another's chest.

Gray tenderly brushes his lips on my forehead, making me smile.

And for the rest of the night we enjoy each other. And the candle.

CHAPTER FIFTY-TWO

Emma

AS THE DAYS GO BY, I wait for the shoe to drop, anticipating Dad calling me into his office once Kane lets him in on Grayson's assault.

But all has been quiet. Kane hasn't run to Dad as a way to retaliate against both me and Gray. And I'm beginning to believe that maybe he truly is spooked after getting his ass kicked.

After settling into the thought that Kane is going to keep his mouth closed about this, I start to breathe easier. And now I'm able to focus on other things, such as getting ready for the documentary viewing at Rae's studio.

"Emma, you're putting way too much effort into this," Rae teases as I carry bags of goodies into her condo.

"Nonsense. This is a lovely event, it should be treated as such."

"Try telling my brother that," she says under her breath while helping me unload the bags.

I glance over to the balcony where Grayson is

sitting, writing in his notebook. Apparently, he and Rae have spoken less than usual after he found out about the documentary. I can understand him not being pleased with Rae for doing it and wanting to grieve in private, but I really wish he'd come around and see what's actually living on the other side of his anger.

"How much cheese did you buy?" Rae laughs, pulling out blocks of assorted cheeses.

"I want to make sure we have a wide variety. I also bought different kinds of crackers. As well as sparkling water and juice."

"You covered all the bases."

"I also got these cute fairy lights to put around." I take out a multitude of tiny strands of lights.

"Have you ever thought of being an event planner?"

"Oh definitely. That or a manager of some place that allows me to design everything to my aesthetic."

"Once you get that business degree, I'm sure you'll have no trouble finding the perfect job."

"I need that reassurance more than you know. My senior year starts soon, and then I'll be taking a massive leap."

"You'll be fine."

As we continue to unpack the rest of the things for tomorrow's viewing, I begin to reminisce about my summer. Even though it's still a zillion degrees outside, there's a definite change in the air with tourists coming for one last hurrah before school begins, and people beginning to talk about autumn activities that they're looking forward to.

"What's Grayson's deal once you're back in school?" Rae asks.

"Um..." I look back over to him; the glass door is

closed so he can't hear us. But I can tell he's lost in his own little world, so I don't know if he'd hear what we were saying even if we were standing two feet away from him. "I'm not really sure," I answer.

He had said he wanted to stay here, but I don't know if that still stands now that he's irritated with Rae.

Rae nods her head, expecting my response. "I'm assuming that even though he doesn't know what the fuck he's going to do with his life, that you'll still be in the equation regardless?"

"Yeah." I smile. "We're stuck with each other."

Gazing over to Gray once more, my heart leaps forward wanting to capture him in my arms and know everything that's going on inside his head. We've learned a lot about each other and ourselves this past summer, and even though it's been riddled around heartache, I'm glad that he's the one I've been lucky enough to explore this new chapter with.

CHAPTER FIFTY-THREE

Grayson

THERE'S a huge weight sitting on my chest, knowing that tonight is the viewing of the documentary. I have yet to make up my mind on if I'll be going, but I know Emma is headed there soon to help Rae and Miles set up. My parents are already on their way, and both of them have been continuously asking me if I'm attending.

After showering and getting dressed, I step into Rae's living room to find her putting a canvas in her tote bag. I can't see what it is, but I catch glimpses of midnight blue and dashes of orange.

"Hey," she says when she sees me.

I lift my chin, giving her some type of acknowledgment as I make my way to my notebook.

"I know you're probably not coming tonight, but would you mind helping me out with something beforehand?" Rae asks.

Normally I'd shut her down, but considering my girlfriend is committed to offering her time, I'd feel like a dick if I said no.

"What do you need help with?" I ask, mumbling the question as my focus goes to the leather book in my hand.

"I need help getting extra chairs from the community center where I go to NA." She clears her throat. "Supposedly there are going to be more people in attendance than what we initially planned, so we're in need of more chairs, and Sam said we can use the ones from meetings."

"Who's Sam?"

"He's the owner of Sam's Dinette. He also runs some NA and AA meetings."

My mind flips to when I first got here, and I'm pretty sure Miles took me there to get lunch. I remember a nosy old man. I forgot his name, but I'm guessing that's who Sam is.

I nod.

"So...can you grab some chairs later or no?"

My attention doesn't lift off of the clean page I open to. "Yeah."

We go back to doing our own thing, not paying mind to each other. My pen drifts over the paper as chopped-up phrases bounce out of my mind and onto the page.

The room is filled with silence that suddenly gets sliced by Rae's aggravated sigh. My hand freezes at the sound for half a second, but then I go back to writing.

Until I hear it again.

Followed by her snapping at me. "Can you not fucking act like this right now, Grayson?"

My gaze darts up to look at her getting ready to leave, keys in hand and a tote bag by the door.

Pinching my eyebrows together, I ask, "Act like what?"

"Apathetic. Some form of support today from my brother would be nice."

"I'm getting the chairs."

She lets out a bitter laugh, one that stiffens my corded muscles as they become tense. "Yeah, that's exactly what I meant," she sarcastically bites out. "Are you *that* pissed at me that you're not going to come tonight?"

My gaze ices over, and I choose not to reply as I stare at her.

"What are you mad at me for? Doing the documentary, having the viewing, or calling you a victim? Or is it a combo of all three?" Rae's antagonism lights a match, anger clawing its way up my throat making my insides bleed with its sharp, unforgiving nails scraping up against me. "Hello?" She obnoxiously waves a hand as if to wake me up from a daydream. "Are you gonna answer me or just sit there?"

"Can you shut the fuck up?" I raise my voice at her at the same time I stand, my irritation immediately catapulting to an extreme level.

"Sorry, guess I'm just used to speaking for two," Rae snaps back, scowling at me.

"You know what?" I throw my arms up. "Let's just have it out—right here, right now. A decade of pent-up anger toward each other. You tell me how terrible I am, and I'll do the same to you—but I can fucking guarantee I'm still gonna come out being the better person in the end."

"What the hell is that supposed to mean?"

"You know exactly what it means. Your history is way more sordid than mine, Rae."

"Are you insinuating that I'm a shitty person because I'm a drug addict?" Her arms fold over her chest.

"No. But you are a shitty person for telling me that I'm dead to you because I was trying to stop you from using." The awful memory pops right out of my brain and into the room.

For the first time, I'm able to speak about it.

A cocktail of blistering emotions forcefully rushes through my bloodstream, my insides whirring.

"I wasn't thinking clearly."

"Is that your version of an apology?" My body heats up as my voice gets louder. "You fucking *overdosed*, Rae!" Images I wish to bury away for the rest of eternity come to the forefront of my mind. "I was the one who found you." I dig my fingers into my chest hard enough to create a hole. "I was the one who saw you lifeless on Cara's bed." I stalk toward Rae and watch her shrink into herself. "I was the one who found you covered in vomit. I was the one who found your skin turned blue. I was the one who called for help." My chest heaves as the traumatic event comes to life behind my eyes. My mouth spills with words I've kept in since the winter—and fuck, does it feel good to get them free, even if they hurt Rae as they land.

"I was the one who got the Narcan," I continue. "I was the one who pulled the needle out of your arm. I was the one talking to the EMTs and police officers when Mom and Dad went to the hospital with you."

Rae's eyes turn glassy as her chin quivers. She struggles to keep it together, and I know I am, too, as my eyes begin to burn.

"Miles might've saved you in high school, but I fucking saved your life, too!"

The comment flies out of me, detonating the condo. Rae's hand flies to her mouth to cover her cries as her shoulders shake.

Instead, I keep unleashing my thoughts because now that I've started, I can't seem to stop.

"For ten goddamn years, I needed someone—I needed my sister. You cut me out of your life, but I would've done anything to help you, Rae." I run my slightly bruised hand through my hair, yanking at the roots. "Hell, I even went as far as stalking your dealer and beating the shit out of him!"

Rae gasps, her eyes popping out of her head.

"If I didn't find you, your last words to me would've been that I was dead to you. That fucks with my head, Rae. All of it does." I start pacing. "So forgive me if I don't want to sit through a documentary about how I lost my one sister and started losing my second."

Rae begins to tremble, taking in short bursts of air. It looks like she's on the verge of a panic attack.

Worry weaves its way around the wrath that's settled in my bones, and I'm not sure what to do or how to handle her or myself. My anger has taken over to the point of not doing anything while I watch my sister struggle to keep it together.

Before I can process anything else, she's managed to walk out the door.

And I'm left alone, crashing.

Crashing from the high of liberating the excruciating memories that lived in the closed tomb in my soul.

Crashing from saying all of it out loud.

Crashing from ten years of pain flowing through me.

And I suddenly don't know how to deal with the amount of reality that I just acknowledged.

CHAPTER FIFTY-FOUR

Grayson

I'VE WALKED UP and down the boardwalk so many times, my feet are stinging and sweat is rolling down in between my shoulder blades. I've been battling my emotions and my wounds. I'm so caught in my head, all of my insides have become tangled in knots.

Clouds shade the sky, darkening the daylight to match my mood.

"Hear there's a nasty storm rolling through tonight," someone on the boardwalk says to the person next to them.

I glance up, noticing how gray the sky is becoming signaling that a bleak outcome is in the near future.

"Motherfucker," I mutter to myself.

As unsure as I am about being anywhere near Rae right now, I'm not gonna make her lug chairs in the rain. And I sure as hell am not gonna make Emma do it either.

I haven't reached out to Emma since spilling my guts out to Rae. The cut is too fresh, and I need some time to wrap my mind around everything before trying to unpack it with her.

A quick Google search, and I'm headed toward the community center, which is off the boardwalk.

When I get there, I spot a sign which reads "NA/AA Meetings" and an arrow pointing downstairs. As I walk down the steps, the building becomes a bit dreary.

The fluorescent lights flicker overhead as the humidity coats my skin.

When I approach the basement, the door is ajar, and I see people sitting in a circle of chairs. Hesitant as to what I should do, I pause.

Rae told me to grab some chairs here, but she never told me when, and they're clearly in the middle of a meeting right now. I decide to leave, turning and placing one foot on the stairs in front of me.

"Hi, I'm Rae, and I'm an addict." The sound of her voice makes me freeze.

All the members reply back as I slowly twist my head around to look over my shoulder. When I see her standing, I can tell she's been crying judging by the way her dark makeup is smeared under her eyes. Strands of her white-blond hair fall out of her messy bun and scatter across her face.

"As you guys know, my brother has been staying with me this summer."

Pressure hits my ribcage, my stomach seizing up.

I know I need to move the rest of my body, but I can't seem to will myself to do so.

Rae clears her throat, taking a moment to compose herself as she stares at her shoes. "I have a tremendous amount of guilt over how everything played out between us. My addiction ruined the opportunity for us ever getting close." She sniffles. "I know I fucked up in the past, and it was me who kept pushing him away. And as much as I would love to have a tight-knit sibling bond with him, I don't know how to have one."

The seams in my heart pop open, one by one, in a slow and excruciating way.

Rae lifts her head, her attention floating over the circle of people. As she looks at them, her gaze gets pulled over their heads and lands directly on me.

My stomach constricts, waiting for her to get mad that I've been listening in. Anticipating her snapping or an icy twist in her features, I become stunned when her expression changes into utter sadness.

"I don't know how to fix this," she whispers. My eyes immediately burn, and I'm tempted to run up the stairs so I don't have to live in this feeling for a second longer. But I'm still frozen. "I don't know how to be a good sister because that was Cara's job." Rae brings her focus back to the other people but occasionally glances my way. "I really wish my brother knew how sorry I am for having him be the one to find me when I overdosed. He never should have gone through that."

A range of emotions spiral throughout my body, the stinging in my eyes becoming fiercer, and I know if I don't get out of here soon the tears will spill over.

Running up the stairs and out of the community center, I gasp for air the moment I'm outside. The vise around my chest squeezes tighter and tighter.

Running a shaky hand through my hair, I continue to walk around, forcing the flood of memories and feelings to race up and down my limbs.

This is all too much for me.

CHAPTER FIFTY-FIVE

Grayson

Red
where are you?

I STARE at the notifications on my phone: the one from Mom letting me know that her and Dad are here, the one from Rae informing with the same info, and last the one from Emma.

The wind has picked up. The once gentle sea breeze is now shoving its salty air across my body as I sit on one of the benches on the boardwalk with my fingers pausing over my phone.

It's getting late, the sky turning darker than usual at this time of night due to the hovering clouds. The viewing of the documentary will start soon. And I'm still not sure if I can bring myself to go or not.

I've been aimlessly wandering around for hours, the thoughts in my head spinning a harrowing web throughout the nooks and crannies of my brain. And at the end of it all, nothing has been made clearer. If anything, all of my emotions are even more chaotic.

An annoyed sigh falls from my lips, my chest deflating as I shove my phone into my pocket instead of responding to Emma.

Pushing myself up, I begin to stroll down the boardwalk in the direction of Rae's art studio.

With each step I take, a buzz of anxiety shoots out of my core.

Way down, I can spot a ton of people standing outside of her studio, some with umbrellas in hand to prepare for whatever storm is looming overhead. They're too far away to see any faces or hear what they're chattering about, but I know in my gut they're all there to see the documentary.

As I get closer, a zing of panic dances up my spine.

Instead of moving ahead, I blindly dart into the closest establishment. A bell chimes overhead as I open the door, and the smell of burgers has my stomach instantly growling. Putting my hand over my abdomen, I blink, realizing I entered the diner Miles took me to a while ago.

An older man with gray hair and wrinkled skin, who I'm pretty sure is Sam, lifts his attention toward me as he stands behind a long counter. Rae said he runs some of her NA meetings, but I don't think he was at the one I overheard earlier.

"Wanna sit?" He gestures at the empty, backless stools lined up in front of him.

I nod, walking over. There's not a single soul in here, just me and him. As I go to sit down, he quietly places a menu in front of me then whistles as he wipes down the far end of the counter.

As I glance over the options, the words start to blur.

The letters get muddled together as my anxiety takes over my vision.

"You're Grayson, Rae's brother, correct?" the man asks, snapping my focus over to him.

"Yeah. You're Sam?"

He nods, smiling. "That's me." He goes back to whistling, only this time there's an odd undertone to the song, as if he half-expected me to show up here out of the blue. When he notices I've been watching him, he stops and looks over at me. "Ready to order?"

Without bothering to check over the menu, I order. "Burger and a Pepsi, please."

While Sam disappears in the back, my leg bounces up and down as my nerves continue to build. My fingers jitter, tapping on the counter. The urge to write comes over me as I stare at a lone pen, abandoned at the far end of the counter.

As I start to stretch, reaching for it, I get distracted by my phone buzzing in my pocket. I'm quick to grab the pen, switching it out with my phone.

My insides wring tight, knowing it's someone inquiring if I'll be at Rae's soon.

Red
are you okay?

I know I need to respond so she doesn't continue to worry.

Me
yeah, sorry I didn't answer earlier. I'm at the diner

"Here you are," Sam says, placing down my food and drink.

"Thanks. That was quick."

"It's an easy order."

I place my phone to the side and dive in, realizing I haven't had anything to eat for the majority of the day.

As I'm focused on filling up my belly, Sam starts talking to me. "Are you attending the event at your sister's studio?"

I pause, the half-eaten burger frozen right in front of my face. His question irks me, my eyes narrowing at him. "Are you?"

"Yep. I'm closing early to go. A lot of people from town are planning to show their support."

Ignoring him, I go back to my food so he doesn't keep trying to speak to me.

As I'm chewing, I hear the bell chime overhead as someone enters.

"Hey," a soft voice travels over to me, unfurling the tension that's been sewn into my muscles.

Looking over my shoulder, my heart skips a beat as I watch Emma make her way next to me. She's radiant in a pastel purple dress and her hair pulled back, showing off more of her beautifully freckled face. Making her way over, she plants a sweet kiss on my cheek and sits on the stool beside me.

"Are you all right?" she asks, her mascaraed lashes fluttering as concern swirls around her amber eyes.

"Yeah." I conjure up a smile. "Just getting a bite to eat then heading over." I gesture to my barely there burger, then take a sip of my drink.

"You don't have to come tonight, Grayson. It's okay."

The strings in my heart yank from either direction, feeling conflicted.

"Why don't you hang out at Rae's and write, then we'll all meet up afterward," Emma suggests. "Or you don't have to meet up with any of us. Or you can just meet up with me—"

The sound of her phone going off pulls her focus away from me. Her face turns white as she swallows, glancing down at the screen.

When I see her dad's name flashing, my jaw clenches. I watch as she sends it to voicemail and types a text that she's working.

Dad: We need to talk immediately

He calls her again, and she declines it once more.

"Shit," she says, pinching the bridge of her nose.

Her phone rings again.

"You think he knows what I did to Kane?" I ask, the hammering of my pulse quickening.

"Yeah." Her phone rings once more. "That's the only reason he'd be calling me like mad." Emma sucks in a short breath, clicking her do not disturb button on her phone. "Whatever." She slams it face down on the counter. "If he's that pissed, he'll have to come down here and find me. I'm not missing your sister's viewing tonight."

All of my hairs stand on end. "Do you think he'd come looking for you?"

She shakes her head. "He'd threaten to. But he knows he'll see me when I get home tonight, so there's really no point in him traveling down to the 'sinful mayhem' of southern Golden Bay."

"There's no way in fuck I'm letting you go home alone tonight."

Emma lets out a small smile. "Let's focus on one event at a time. I don't want him or Kane to impede on this night, and I certainly don't want it to take away from Rae." She takes a few drawn-out inhales and exhales to collect herself. "We'll deal with him, and everything that's going to come along with it, later."

I blink, watching her neatly pack away the one thing that gives her the most anxiety, saving her moment of crisis for later.

She said she was good at compartmentalizing.

I noticed how she did it at church, but that's been years of practice.

But this, right now, watching her in real time place all her worries on the back burner so she can show up for other people, pains me to witness. And it's because she's never been given the space to release what she's actually feeling.

I'm now realizing what a gift it was to have her be mad at me in her bedroom right after she found out about Kane, even if it was only for a few minutes. I allowed that space for her then, and she took it.

"Emma." I place my hand over hers. "Let's deal with this now. Let's figure it out."

"No." She shakes her head so fast it might fly off.

"Emma, it's okay that we need to make this a priority, Rae will understand—"

"I've always made my dad a priority. I'm not letting that happen tonight." Her voice softens. "I *want* to be there for your family. And for you, if you're going."

My chest swells from her kindness, knowing that she's going to win this battle. "I'll be there," I make a promise to her and only her. I'm not sure how long I'll stay for, but at the very least Emma will see me make an appearance.

Her energy shifts as she plucks a fry off of my plate and noshes on it. "I have to go back and help Rae, but if you decide not to come, it's okay. And if you do, I'll see you soon!"

She hops down the floor, pressing her lips against my cheek once more and turns to leave.

The sound of the bells ringing lets me know she's gone, and her absence brings an immediate sour feeling over my body.

"Wow," Sam says from across the way.

My head swings in his direction. "What?"

"I've never seen someone light up and then deflate so quickly." He chuckles to himself. "I imagine I looked the same way when I first fell in love with my wife."

My heart stops.

Everything freezes as time stands still.

In love?

As my brain catches up with the words, everything around me suddenly moves at a rapid pace. A whirlwind, throwing me off guard as the room spins, and my heart gallops.

No. No, I can't be in love.

Panic sets in, the nervousness coating my skin.

I know I'm attached to Emma, but I can't love her.

Because I know what happens when you love someone.

It's followed by insurmountable pain.

Pain that I can't bear to feel.

The thumping against my ribcage has me rubbing the center of my chest as I wince from the intensity of the beating rhythm.

Jumping to my feet, I back away, staggering. "Um." I fish for my wallet.

"It's on the house," Sam says.

I nod, struggling to catch my breath, then dart out of the diner.

As I rush outside, the moisture in the air is thick, the winds growing angrier. Squinting through the blustering air, I make my way to Rae's studio.

There are still people hanging outside the door, talking on the boardwalk. I push my way through them, navigating my way inside where it's even more packed.

Every single chair—which I fucked up and didn't get the extras because I was too lost in my head—is taken. A projector screen is in front of the back wall where Rae painted her mural. She stands off to the side with our parents, who are speaking to Emma and Miles.

Emma effortlessly fits in. I can tell Mom is enamored by her from the way her face lights up as Emma talks.

Cara might be the missing piece to our family, but Emma is the glue that sticks the remainder of us together.

Hysteria builds inside me, knowing that Sam was right.

The more I stare at Emma, the more I realize just how in love I am with her.

Immense fear strikes my body like a forceful lightning bolt, wreaking havoc.

"Welcome!" a man with glasses steps in front of the screen, and people begin to lower their voices. "I'm Jake from IntraFilms. If everyone from outside could make their way in, we'll be starting the documentary momentarily."

People shuffle around, finding a place to stand, some opting to sit on the floor. Emma doesn't see me yet, but she and my family start stepping out of the way, and the moment they do, my stomach falls to the ocean floor.

There's a large collage display of various families, but mine is dead center. My parents, Rae, Cara, and me. It's from a lifetime ago, when we would vacation at Golden Bay. We're posing on the beach, me and my sisters making a sandcastle while Mom and Dad are caught laughing. The pier from Adventureland is in the distance, only a couple of rides are recognizable.

We all look so carefree and joyful, the five of us with wide smiles on our faces.

I can't even glance at the image of Cara standing next to me for more than a second. My eyes prickle as my body starts to shake.

The room gets hot—too hot. As if I'm being suffocated from the heat of all the people in the room. People who are anxiously waiting to hear the story about how my sister was murdered.

Knots twist around in my gut.

A growing lump forms in my throat.

My shoulders heave, trying to fucking breathe—trying to compartmentalize, trying not to be consumed by my emotions.

Feeling as if I'm stuck at sea and the water is starting to rise, I panic.

Abruptly spinning around, I shove my way toward the door. Once outside, I fight to breathe, gasping for air.

My head spins, vision getting spotty with colorful lights from the amusement park.

I walk, needing space from this.

It's too much.

All of it.

I'm drowning in emotions and thoughts.

My pulse whirls through my veins, painfully pushing up against my skin. Overcome with intensity, my mind bounces from past to present, from joy to despair, from love to loss.

Nausea takes hold of me, bile rising to the surface as I'm unable to process everything.

This entire summer strong-arming me into tackling everything I didn't want to—even bringing the colossal fear of loving another person.

My body temperature continues to rise, unable to make peace with all of my demons in one night.

A light mist fills the air, causing the crowd on the boardwalk to dissipate. A neon light at a nearby bar catches my attention, and I gravitate toward it, needing something to drink to cool myself down.

When I walk in, there are a decent number of others hanging out, and I make my way to the bartender, desperately needing water.

Sitting down, I place my order and close my eyes, trying to focus on steadying my breathing.

The air flowing in and out of my lungs starts to calm. My water magically appears when I peel my eyelids open, and when I take a sip, the icy liquid placates the smothering warmth that was overtaking my insides.

Staring down at a damp napkin, my hand twitches, needing to write. I grab the pen from the diner out of my pocket and begin to unload my thoughts.

The epicenter of all my suffering rests in the arms of love.

If I'd never loved, it would've never hurt to lose

I've lost by way of person, future, hope.

Because all that ever comes with love is never-ending grief.

Beginning to write the next line, I pause, sensing someone staring at me. My spine stiffens as I lift my gaze across the room where I'm met with dark, glaring eyes.

A shockwave of rage hits my core as I stare back at Kane.

My heart rate revs back up.

His mouth moves as he says something, but I can't make it out. Suddenly, two other guys appear by his side, all of them glowering at me.

There's an immediate gut reaction, telling me that this isn't going to be like my usual means to get my emotions out.

This time it's going to be three against one.

I need to get the fuck out of here.

CHAPTER FIFTY-SIX

Grayson

MY PULSE SPIKES as I dart down the boardwalk. Checking over my shoulder, I spot three people making their way out of the bar, their gazes fixed directly on me.

Fuck.

Moving faster through the misty air, my feet move rapidly as I hear the sound of shoes pattering against the pavement.

Squinting, my eyes start to water as I move against the angry winds. I pick up the pace, hoping to disappear into the darkness.

My lungs burn, my breathing getting heavier.

On impulse, I flee from the boardwalk, running down the stairs to the beach. Hurriedly dashing along the sand, I turn in all directions in an attempt to find another staircase that will lead me back to Rae's studio and keep the three assholes looking the wrong way.

The strong gusts kick up the sand, blowing it straight into my eyes. But I keep moving forward, my heart sputtering the faster I go.

Even though it's difficult to see, the flashing lights from Adventureland lead me closer to where I want to be.

Sweat rolls off of me, short pants of air flowing from my lips.

My leg muscles ache from the resistance of the sand. But I keep going.

The sound of my pulse screaming in my ears is battling with the roaring waves, the two noises creating the perfect ominous symphony as I continue running.

Nearing the giant pier that juts out into the sea, housing Adventureland above it, I hide behind one of its massive wooden legs.

My hands fall to my knees as I hunch over, catching my breath. Each time I inhale, it stings my insides, my chest clenching tight.

Cautiously, I glance around the pier leg to see if I've been followed. My shoulders rise and drop quickly as I try to calm myself down. My gaze darts around the gloomy beach. My stomach settles back into place when I don't spot any silhouettes lingering in the fogginess.

I swipe my hand over the beads of moisture on my face and as I turn back around, there's a flash of someone's fist. I'm met with an immediate blow to the face.

Losing my footing, I stumble.

My mouth fills with copper.

The spark of pain stuns me, but as soon as I hear a low cackle, I'm standing up straight.

"Told you I'd make you pay." Kane's dark voice hovers in the thick air, as he and two shadowy figures stand opposite me, ready to attack.

I spit out a mouthful of blood. "That's not fucking happening."

I start swinging.

My fist driving into his nose, cracking against my knuckles.

His two minions are on me in a heartbeat, colliding with my face.

My ears ring.

My skin stings as it's ripped open.

Blood trickles down my face, dripping onto my neck.

Adrenaline seizes my body, firing through my bloodstream.

Pure wrath ignites from the very depths of my soul. Hating Kane. Hating them. Hating every single evil person that's ever been born.

My bones rattle from the ireful storm that has been unearthed from me.

Suddenly, I'm not just fighting them. I'm fighting all the villains I wished only lived in my stories.

Every punch I throw, I'm met with more. But I fucking *refuse* to let another bad person win.

My nose fills with blood.

I find more strength to fight.

My eyelids swell.

I elbow someone in the throat.

My cheek breaks open.

More anger floods me.

Someone grabs my shirt, yanking me to the ground. Sand smothers me, the gritty grains piercing my open flesh.

Multiple cackles hover above me as I wince. I heave as I plant my hand into the sand, trying to push myself up, but my muscles tremble.

"Ready to give up?" Kane taunts, wiping blood from under his nose.

As he stands over my weakened body, the hairs on the nape of my neck lift. A chill sweeps over me. Nausea churns in my stomach, twisting and snaking.

Hating that this was the vision Emma had to see.

Hating that Kane, along with so many others, present as decent people, but behind closed doors, they're despicable.

Hating that I can't fucking change any of it.

"I'm just getting started," I sputter out blood as I speak. My legs wobble as I rise, standing face-to-face with Kane.

"All your talk isn't going to make you come out of this a winner. Might as well call it quits before things get worse."

The menacing threat looms in the air.

"All your prayers won't wipe away your sins. And all your money won't exempt the fact that you're a rapist."

I watch in slow motion as something in him snaps. As if hearing the truthful word aloud summons the complete villain to the forefront, engrossing his essence in totality.

Paranoia stabs my center, the same exact time thunder booms over the ocean.

The mist gets denser.

It gets more difficult to breathe.

"What did you just say to me?" he seethes.

The two men who are with Kane step next to him, their figures casting a dark shadow over me.

I'd call this my karma for beating up strangers in the

past, but if people truly got what they deserved, my life and all the players in it would've lived peaceful lives.

And Kane wouldn't still be walking the streets, regarded as a noble man.

They take a step forward, and I take one back, immediately feeling the wooden splinters from the leg of the pier.

Shit. I'm cornered.

My heart leaps to my throat, and I try my best to swallow it back down.

Even though my arms shake, my muscles exhausted, I still ball my fists, ready to keep fighting. So, I answer his question.

"I spoke the truth."

Jabbing my fist into his stomach, he's caught off guard. I attempt to get out another swing, but I'm sucker-punched in the jaw by the man on my right.

My vision goes dark.

Head spinning.

I'm hit again.

I fall.

Sand flies into my mouth, and I cough in a panic.

My eyes won't stay open.

I can't see.

A foot strikes my gut.

Immense pain radiates throughout my body.

My arms wrap around me, and I wheeze.

More blows and kicks. Every part of me aching.

If I could scream, I would.

But no one would hear me.

My sounds would be muted by the amusement park, violent waves, and thunderous clouds.

My muscles give out, surrendering. And I can feel

every part of my heart break, knowing that I couldn't defeat evil.

Someone slams their fist into my temple.

I go limp.

I feel the assault, yet don't. My awareness is fading.

Help.

The word says in my head.

Someone help me.

My mind focuses on my silent plea.

Please. Anyone.

I let out a defeated breath, crashing more and more into the sand.

My body gives out, my mind floating away.

There's a sudden, faint whisper that I cling to. "Grayson."

Then everything goes black.

CHAPTER FIFTY-SEVEN

Emma

THERE ISN'T a dry eye in the studio once the documentary finishes. Everyone is hugging, arms wrapping tight among others. The room is filled with countering emotions, but through all the despair, it's glowing with love.

There is a sea of people, and everyone is grieving, supporting, and caring for each other. Tears trickle down my cheek as I try and process everything I just witnessed. Seeing Rae and Miles holding each other as they wipe their faces has my heartstrings yanking.

Listening to their awful trauma and how it affected the past decade of their lives has my soul yearning to do more with my life path. The only reason the both of them agreed to do the documentary was to bring about change, and I feel called to be a part of that change—no matter how small.

Rae's parents join her in a big embrace, all of them crying together. Rae's mom lifts her gaze to me.

"Come in here, Emma," she says, waving me over.

Without any hesitation, I rush over to the group as

they open their arms to me. The second I'm in their hold, I get an overwhelming sense of family, as if I always belonged with them. I just wish Grayson decided to come so we could've all been together for this moment.

My heart swells, and I choke back tears. "Thank you for letting me in the group hug." I sniffle.

They all smile at me, but Rae is the one to speak. "Thank you for being here tonight."

Rae's mom rubs my back, comforting me as I cry with them, even though it feels wrong to cry when I'm literally hugging the people who went through what was described in the viewing.

Others begin to form a line next to us, waiting to speak to Rae.

We break apart and compose ourselves to the best of our ability as an elderly woman, who has popped in here before, approaches Rae.

"I'd like to make a donation to your studio." She hands Rae a check.

Rae stands frozen, caught off guard by the gesture. "I can't accept this."

"All right then." The woman takes the check from her and hands it to me. "Accept this check on your friend's behalf and make sure it goes to her studio." She gives a knowing wink and turns away.

"O-Okay," I stutter, not sure how to respond.

Before Rae and I can speak, she's getting multiple people coming up to her offering all types of gifts. Miles sturdily stands by her side, anchoring her through it.

Moving toward my purse, I slip the check in then take out my phone. Going through the notifications, my stomach clenches when I see all the missed calls from

Dad. I skip right over his texts, not wanting to read them.

I scroll through, looking for a text from Grayson, but there's nothing.

I deflate, hoping that he would've shown up. But even though I would've liked him to be here, I still respect that he chose what was right for him.

> **Me**
> The viewing is over, do you want to come by?

Several minutes go by, people not wanting to leave as they continue to hang out and talk. Glancing down at my phone, disappointment comes over me when I notice Gray hasn't texted me yet.

> **Me**
> you don't have to stop by. Are you at Rae's condo?

I chat with some familiar faces from town, each of us not sure how to fully digest the movie we just watched.

When there's still no text from Gray, a sense of nervousness rumbles around my gut.

> **Me**
> it's totally cool if you want to me alone, just let me know you're okay

My gaze flickers over the crowd, searching for him. Maybe he did show up, and I missed him. I peer over people's heads, looking for those stormy-blue eyes that make me melt.

But still nothing.

I decide to call him, hoping that my texts aren't going through. But when I'm met with his voicemail, panic prickles under my skin.

Something's not right.

I know it's not.

In a hurry, I scoot around everyone, getting to the door as fast as humanly possible. When I step outside, a hazy mist makes it tough to see clearly.

"Grayson?" I call out.

Moving quickly down the boardwalk, my pulse begins to whirl.

I glance into the bars and restaurants as I speed walk. None of the faces are familiar, so I keep going, hoping to stumble upon him soon.

"Grayson?"

Nothing. There's no one out on the boardwalk that I can see.

Holding up my phone, I try calling him again. And when he doesn't answer for the second time, anxiety wrings my veins tight.

My legs move faster, running in the direction of SeaScape. My hair whips around in the abrasive wind, and I have to squint to see through the fog.

As I race forward, the reflection of the amusement park lights bounce off the stormy sea. Through the thickness of the air, I'm able to make out a figure limping out from under the pier.

The person gravitates toward the ocean, the size of the waves making the person look minuscule.

Getting closer, I still can't clearly make out who it is, but the bells going off in my head tell me that it's Grayson.

So, I run off the boardwalk and onto the beach.

CHAPTER FIFTY-EIGHT

I'VE ALWAYS WONDERED what happens right before death.

In that nanosecond before the final heartbeat, does the mind go blank or violently cling to life until it's too late?

I've been wondering that since I was ten.

Did every thought imaginable come crashing into Cara's head right before she was murdered point blank? Did Rae's thoughts start to quiet themselves as she lulled herself into an overdose as she injected her veins with poison?

The last breath, is it a gasp or a sigh of relief?

Will there be a vision of white light? Someone waiting on the other side?

My questions only increased, becoming more complex over time.

And as my eyelids sluggishly pry open, the darkness of the night surrounding me, I'm met with even more questions.

And still no answers.

Even though I lie here with a copper taste coating my tongue, and my lungs squeezing tight every time I breathe, my mind can only focus on one thing.

I heard her.

I swear I heard her.

The soft voice whispering my name.

An excruciating pain shoots out of my spine, pouring over my entire body. Sucking in a sharp breath, I move to sit, every inch of my body bellowing in agony as I work against the sand.

My head dizzies as I glance around me to make sure I'm alone.

When there's no sight of anyone, my shoulders ease.

I don't know how long I've been passed out under the pier, or how long they continued beating me—all I know is that everything fucking hurts.

They might as well have left me for dead. I'm sure that was their end goal.

My tongue grazes over the split in my lip as I reach for one of the pier legs, gripping into the wood, pulling myself up. A stabbing pain jabs my insides as I rise, my body turns flimsy with my wearied muscles.

Hobbling out from under the pier, my head pounds as I struggle to see through my swollen eyes and the murky air.

I should go in the direction of the boardwalk, find someone and get help. That's what a normal person would do.

But nothing about the thoughts that eat me alive are normal.

And as if the ocean were calling my name, I head in that direction. The stormy sea is beckoning me.

A loud clap of thunder reverberates across the beach, making my insides vibrate.

Even in the dark of the night, I witness the intensity of the ocean. The waves are mammoth, crashing down ferociously onto the shore. Over and over again in a violent motion as the sound roars across the land.

I'm hypnotized by the endless release of emotions.

Never in my life did I think I would find something in common with nature, but here I am drawn to the furious ocean. It lets out its pain with every harsh wake breaking into the sand. Growing with fury, the waves become larger as the wind gets wilder.

In a trance, I limp closer to the water.

As I slowly approach the shoreline, the misty salt air burns my skin.

Everything burns.

Everything hurts.

Everything becomes too much to bear.

I lift my chin, watching another massive wave form. It's so close to me, if I took a few more steps, I'd be under.

In just a couple of movements, I could let the sea take me away.

My heart races at the inviting thought.

There would be no more living in agony. I wouldn't have to undergo the loss of another loved one. I would know all the answers to my questions.

I'd be with Cara.

The voice I swear I heard.

"Grayson!"

Goose bumps rise, hearing my name being called out once again. Only this time, it's coming from behind me.

"Grayson!"

My head screws back on as a rush of reality blasts through me. Turning around, my chest surges seeing Emma running in my direction.

She races up to me, the glowing lights of the amusement park behind her forming a colorful halo around her figure as she moves effortlessly through the sand. Her hair whips from the fierce winds, pushing it to one side.

"Grayson, what are you doing?" she pants, getting closer. When she reaches me, she gasps, holding her hand to her mouth. "What happened!"

Getting nearer, I can see the welling of tears behind her eyes. The look on her face pinches my heart tight. My chest collapses in as I expel a ragged breath.

"Are you okay?" Emma's arms wrap around me in an attempt to hold me together. I nod, drawing in air. "Who did this to you—where did you go—why are you down by the water?" she asks in a hurried panic.

"I just needed to be alone with my thoughts."

"No," Emma snaps and my gaze swings back to look at her. "You've spent too much time alone in your head. I'm here, Grayson. You've got *me*."

My eyes prickle, tears threatening to spill over.

"Tell me what's going on," she pleads. "Tell me everything that's going on in your mind."

The quivering of my chin exposes my true emotions. "I don't know if I can get the words out."

"Try," she whispers.

The one word skitters up and down my limbs as I turn my focus back to the ocean. I pry my jaw open, it snaps at the joint as I attempt to let my thoughts flow freely from my brain to my mouth.

My pulse swirls in my ears, almost drowning out the sound of the waves.

"I—"

Nausea hits my stomach. Bile creeps up my throat, burning me. My hands shake, terrified of letting her know the thoughts that are tearing me to shreds.

She brushes her fingertips over my forearm, soothing me.

The stinging in my eyes intensifies.

"I'm so tired of living in this world," I admit, a singular tear rolling down my cheek, hurting my cuts. "I'm so tired of the bad guys always winning."

Cara's murderer.

Rae's dealer.

Emma's rapist.

Defeat shrouds me, draping me in sorrow. There's nothing I can do about any of it except live with it.

"The world broke me, Emma." My voice cracks as I fixate on her, empathy pours from her being. "It shattered me."

"Then give me all your pieces, and let me help you put yourself back together."

A bolt of hope springs from my heart as it flutters fast. The both of us entrenched in our own little bubble, forgetting about the raging sea and the looming storm.

God, how I have longed for someone to say those exact words to me.

But it's fucking petrifying to hear them.

"I'm so scared to let people into my life, Emma."

"Why?"

"Because bad things happen all the time. I can't handle any more terrible things happening to the people that I care about."

"But good things happen, too." Her hold on my arm gets a little stronger, as if concerned I'm a flight risk. "Life isn't just black and white. It's gray."

I hold my breath, trying to keep in the rest of my tears. Attempting to choke them back, as I come to terms with my true feelings for Emma. "This wasn't supposed to happen," I say, sniffling.

"What wasn't?"

"You."

Her face drops, appearing devastated by what I just said. The look in her eyes twists a knife in my gut.

She's speechless, so I continue unraveling my thoughts, knowing nothing eloquent or poetic will come out as I release my hidden truth.

"This is going to come to an end eventually—one of us moves, we break up, or death—at some point in our story, the book is going to close." Every single one of my defenses drops as I stand in utter vulnerability in front of her. "I can't deal with that—if I can't bear the thought of someone hurting you in the past, how am I going to bear losing you one day?"

Emma lets out a trembling breath, her shoulders shaking as she begins to cry.

"I'm terrified of loving you, Emma, because love *hurts*."

The thunderous storm that brews behind my eyes finally sets free, raining tears of agony. My ribcage is split open, pouring my fear all over as I continue to sob.

More of me breaks, the fragments of my soul getting whisked away by the powerful winds.

The stream of tears soaks my wounds in salt, making them hurt that much more. But not as much as my heart ever will.

Emma wraps her arms around me as I shove my head into the crook of her neck, doubling over in emotional warfare.

Her hands cautiously rub my back, and her stuttered panting hits the ends of my hair.

The more I release into her, the more I never want to let go, feeling at home in her embrace.

"Love also heals," she whispers in the shell of my ear.

My heart is yanked in opposite directions as her comment floods me with a tingling sensation.

"We wanted to be young and free this summer," she continues. "Not letting fear stop you is a part of that. Don't let your fear rob you of enjoying your life, Grayson."

I cry even more, although this time it's because of how damn good it feels to have someone know me.

My life froze in time, somewhere between Cara getting carried away in a casket and Rae shooting up in the bathroom. But when I'm with Emma, it's as if she hit the play button so I can carry on with my story again. I want to chase the feeling I get when I'm with her. I want a chance to be alive, as scary as that might be.

I've mourned my life, yet all the while, I've still been breathing.

But Emma is the one who revived me.

"You are the light to my darkness," I whisper against her.

She shakes her head. "I'm just as broken."

"Then I'll put you back together," I promise like she did with me.

"I don't want my old pieces back. I want to find new ones with you."

A flash of lightning strikes as thunder roars. The sky rips open, warm rain instantly pouring from the dark clouds.

We pull away from each other slightly, my lips tingling with the urge to kiss her. Her eyes are wide with expectation as she gazes at me.

"Your kiss in the rain deserves to be better than this," I shout over the storm.

"No. I deserve to be kissed in the rain by the man I love and have him love me back."

Without a second thought, my lips are on hers.

My heart soars, my aching body miraculously feeling lighter.

As I cup her cheeks, rain slips in between us, mixing with the tears and blood. We both embrace the beauty amid the chaos, swept away by exposing our souls to one another.

The locks and chains around my heart burst open as I free myself from my distress and bask in this moment with Emma.

CHAPTER FIFTY-NINE

Emma

OUR WET CLOTHES cling to our bodies, the both of us sopping from the downpour. My arms wrap around Gray's torso as he leans into me, ambling out of the elevator and toward Rae's condo.

I've been ignoring the sickening feeling tumbling around my stomach every time I glance at him, but he looks awful. Both of his eyes are swollen, flecks of dried blood are under his nose and chin, his bottom lip is split open, and there are black and blue bruises forming all over his exposed skin.

I have a million questions on the tip of my tongue, but I want to focus on getting him inside so he can sit.

Of course, my heart is still reeling from his love confession. In true Gray form, it was swathed around so much emotion, but I wouldn't have had it any other way.

I'm yearning to relish in our joy, screaming from the rooftop how much I love him—but all of that is paused until he's taken care of first.

"Holy shit!" Miles exclaims as we come through the

door. He's quick to lend me a hand and help Grayson walk to the couch.

Rae comes out of her bedroom, and when she spots us she sprints over. "What the fuck happened? Are you okay?"

"I'm fine," Gray says.

"Like hell you are," Miles chimes in.

"Who did this to you?" Rae looks over at me to see if I know the answer, panic building behind her eyes.

My gut churns because I have a feeling I know who did this. I just need confirmation.

When neither of us responds, Rae and Miles rush to take care of us instead of demanding answers. Rae gets us towels, then hands us dry clothes to change into, and Miles gets Grayson aspirin and a glass of water.

Once we're settled, both of us in warm clothes, we all sit in the living room together.

"You should go to the hospital," Rae says. "Mom and Dad are staying in a nearby hotel because they didn't want to drive in the storm. I'll tell them what's going on, and they can go with us."

Grayson shakes his head. "There's no way I'm letting them see me like this."

"They're gonna find out eventually. They're expecting to get breakfast with us."

"If they see me in this condition, they'll assume I'm doing worse and drag my ass back home. There's no way they'll let me stay past the summer."

Rae perks up. "You want to stay here longer?"

"Yeah. I was gonna ask you earlier, but then all that shit happened between us." He waves it off, and she nods.

"Well, you can if you still want to."

"Thanks." A small smile appears on his face as he glances at me. When he shifts his attention back to Rae, a remorseful expression takes over his quick spurt of joy. "I'm sorry I wasn't there tonight," he says to Rae.

"It's all good."

"No, I should've been there. I want to make it up to you."

"You can make it up to me by telling me who beat up my little brother," she quips.

When all Grayson does is playfully glare, Miles interjects, "Did the guy from the other day retaliate?"

My eyes are glued to Gray's face, waiting for his face to tell the answer. There's a slight quirk in his right eyebrow acting as confirmation.

"Was it him?" I demand, my voice becoming stern.

Grayson sighs, his focus moving off me as he nods.

"Who's the guy?" Rae jumps to her feet.

"Someone my father adores."

Her eyes widen, realizing that this just got a whole lot messier.

I haven't even checked my phone, but I can only guess that Dad is still trying to get through to me. I smirk, realizing I'm giving him a little taste of his own medicine since I spent my entire existence trying to get through to him and am still met with hollowed replies.

But after I speak with him tonight, I'll make sure to get my point across perfectly clear.

My heart bangs against my bones as the weight of what happened sets in. My fingers cramp around my steering wheel as I drive back to my house. The windshield wiper moves at a frantic pace, trying to combat the torrential downpour that's falling from the stars.

Abhorrence bellows in my nauseous stomach, beyond livid at Kane for what he did to Gray *and* at Dad for not kicking Kane out of our lives years ago.

I have no idea what's awaiting me on the other side of my front door, but Dad doesn't know what he's in for either.

I slipped out of Rae's once Grayson fell asleep. She and Miles know I'm here even though they tried to talk me out of it. But I know I have to get this over with eventually. Dad has been calling me nonstop.

As I open the door to my house, my hair dripping wet even though I only ran from the car to here, I half expect him to be angrily standing in the foyer, awaiting my arrival.

But the moment I hear his harsh voice traveling throughout the house, I know exactly where he is.

And the moment I notice another male voice speaking, an explosion goes off inside me.

My face burns with rage, fists balling at my side as I storm down the hallway. Each stomp I take vibrates throughout me, overfilled with disgust.

My nostrils flare as I reach Dad's office, my teeth grinding together at the sight of him and Kane conspiring.

"Emma!" Dad springs to his feet, his skin scarlet with anger.

Bypassing him, the lasers shooting out of my eyes go straight to Kane. "You."

He stares at me blankly with several bruises on his face, both recent and healing from the last time Gray punched him. He looks like shit, but nowhere near as injured as Grayson.

"Where have you been!" Dad snaps, rounding his desk to get closer. "We were about to call the police to find you and get you away from the young man who assaulted Kane!"

"Assaulted *Kane*!?" My arms shake, eyes catapulting out of my skull. "What about when *Kane* assaulted *me*!" I scream at the top of my lungs, my throat burning. "Why weren't you banging down the doors of the police station then?"

"Come on, Emma, we all know the truth," Kane interjects, insinuating that I'm lying.

Insinuating that I seduced him and that what happened is my responsibility.

"Fuck you!" I bite out, standing dead center in the room, the two of them on either side of me.

"Emma!" Dad shouts, his wrath making him taller. "I did not raise you to use profanity—is that boy influencing your immoral behavior?"

"Oh, you mean the boy that Kane jumped and left in the middle of the beach to bleed out?"

"It was self-defense—he attacked me!" Kane says.

"If Kane's two friends weren't with him to fend off that young man, God knows what would've happened," Dad adds.

"You weren't even there!" I push my hair out of my face, trying to cool down my body temperature. "God, why do you believe everything that comes out of this horrible person's mouth? Is his family's money so important to you that you turn a blind eye every chance you get?"

"Do not speak to me that way!"

"Why not? I'm only saying what the three of us already know. Your only priority in life is to gain more power, whether it be manipulating me to live here, schmoozing with the wealthiest family in the congregation, or sitting at the pulpit every Sunday pretending you're better than everyone else," the thoughts race out of my mouth. "You know nothing of family values or charity or morals. You're a fucking hypocrite! And for someone who preaches love and reverence, you're the least godly person there is!"

Dad's hand rears up to strike, and as I flinch, jumping back, there's a voice booming behind me.

"Don't you dare lay a finger on her." Gray's deep timbre echoes in Dad's office. "Either of you," he states, glaring at Kane.

"Gray!" I rush over to him. "What are you doing—"

"How did you get into my house?" Hysteria raised in Dad's voice.

"The same way I did all summer," Gray responds with a smart-ass remark.

I blink to make sure he's really here. He looks just as battered as when I left him, now with droplets of rainwater rolling down the sides of his face.

"You've been letting him come into my house the entire summer?" Dad screams his question at me. His features draw in tight, the wrinkles in his skin becoming more prominent as he scowls.

"Yep," Gray cockily interjects, then points to Dad's desk. "I even fucked her right there."

My heart stops, a sharp breath getting stuck between my ribs.

Dad's furious gaze lands on me, hatred pouring out of his eyes. "You are an abomination to this family!"

Turning around, he yanks the photo of Mom off of his shelf, then points it toward me. "What would your mother think of the woman you turned out to be? You're a disgrace!"

"My mother never would've stayed in business with my rapist for her own selfish gain!"

I lunge forward, trying to grab the picture frame from him. He pulls it back, but I snap my hand out once again, my fingertips touching the edge, making it tumble out of Dad's hands.

We watch as it collapses, crashing onto his desk, shattering.

Dozens of shards of glass scatter across the floor.

Dad tries to reach for her picture beside my feet, but I'm quicker, swooping down to grab it. As soon as I make contact with Mom's image, I can feel a piece of paper hidden behind it.

The entire room falls silent, the energy changing with all eyes cautiously watching me. My heartbeat flutters at the ends of my fingers as I unfold the paper.

Scanning the words, my brain can't process what I'm holding in the palms of my hands.

Slowly prying my gaze away from the paper, I drag my attention up to Dad. He's as white as a ghost, gulping down guilt.

"This is a bank document," I state. "With my name on it."

Dad remains mute as Gray approaches me, looking over my shoulder to read the paper. "What!" he yells when he sees what's written.

I skim over the page, but it's all there. Chase Bank informing me, Emma Carnell, that I am the trustee to my mother's, Allison Carnell, trust.

And five hundred thousand dollars is able to be accessed once I turn eighteen.

Tears build behind my eyes, and I look at Dad, a complete stranger in my life. "You hid this from me," I whisper, not able to fathom I've been sitting on half a million dollars for years without any knowledge. "Mom left this for me." My voice grows stronger. "*Me.* You had no right to keep this secret."

Chills run down my arms.

Mom knew. She knew exactly who she married and left this for me as security.

She made sure I'd be free.

Gripping the paper and her picture, I still stare at Dad, who remains mute. Confusion tugs at me, wanting answers—needing them. "Why?"

I was hoping—*praying*, that deep down he owned a shred of decency. But he never has and never will. It's all about power with him, obtaining it any way he can, even if it means keeping my money from me so it's more difficult for me to have a way out. For all I know, he could be scheming on ways to keep me here even after I receive my degree. He'd keep me here for as long as he could, having me wait on him all day and make appearances at church so he seems like the perfect family man.

I loved him like he was my father.

But he loved me like I was an object he could control.

Before he can respond, there are several hard knocks at the front door, causing all of us to lose focus.

"Police," a man's voice booms.

Both Dad and Kane's faces drop.

"What are they doing here?" Kane asks, panic simmering in his tone.

"I called them," Grayson states, then glances down at me. "Figured I'd try a different means of stopping the bad guys from winning."

Twisting to gaze at him, the look floating across his bruised features let me know that no matter what, he'll keep me safe.

Feeling Mom's protection encasing me, I dart out of the office. With the key to my freedom in my hands, I come up with a new plan for myself. A plan that I never wanted to act on before because I believed it would be pointless, and I felt guilty if other people's lives turned into shambles.

Gray is right behind me, the strumming of my heart moving faster than my feet.

"I'm going to tell them everything, then we're going upstairs to pack my stuff, and I'm leaving," I say to Gray over my shoulder.

"Emma—" Dad chases after me.

Swinging my front door open, thunder shakes the entire house, and a flash of lightning illuminates the two men in uniform. "I need to talk to you," I say to the officers.

And in the blink of an eye, everything changes.

This castle on the sand crumbles.

We all talk to the police officers, arguing with each other about who gets to speak to them first.

By the end of the night, Dad's reputation is tarnished, and Kane is taken into custody.

Adrenaline still courses through us even though it's way beyond bedtime. It's finally quiet in my house, Kane was taken away in cuffs, and Dad was taken in for questioning.

Even though no one is here, Gray and I swiftly

shove as many of my belongings into my old suitcases as we can, wanting to leave as soon as possible.

"Did Rae and Miles wake you up to tell you I was going to my home?" I ask, speedily tossing books from my shelves into my luggage.

"No, I was in too much pain to be in a deep sleep. When I flipped over and opened up my eyes and saw you weren't in Rae's condo, I knew exactly what was going on." He balls up my clothes, squeezing them into the sides of an already overflowing suitcase.

I pause despite wanting to rush out of here. "Thank you, Gray."

Reaching over to grab the last item on my bookshelf, he places the captain's hat on my head. "I'll always do what I can to protect the woman I love."

He brings his lips to mine, and I finally feel completely free.

CHAPTER SIXTY

Grayson

THE STORM HAS PASSED, although there's still a lot to take care of. Mostly legal shit on Emma's end, but I'll be by her side through it all. It's only been a couple of days since everything came to a head, changing the course of our lives.

Not only did Emma find out that she has a massive sum of money and can afford to move into her own space, but she also found her fire and set her whole fucked-up world ablaze.

I couldn't be more proud.

Squeezing her into my chest as she sits on my lap while we lounge on Rae's balcony, the both of us admire the sunset. I'm still sore, and it's taking a lot longer than I'd like to heal from getting the shit kicked out of me, but I still take every opportunity I can to hold Emma, even if it aches when she leans herself against my collarbone.

"I'm still so hurt that my dad withheld my trust fund from me," she says, looking out at the peaceful sky.

"Sometimes we never know why people do fucked-up things. I've been wondering about it for a decade."

"We'll never have all the answers."

"No," I whisper. "We won't."

We settle into each other's embrace, knowing that for the rest of our lives, we'll be pondering this, never being able to wrap our minds around the evilness of someone else's actions.

But at the very least, we'll be dealing with this reality of life together.

"We're back!" Rae calls from inside.

Emma slowly moves off of me and helps me walk into the condo. I probably should've gone to the doctor to get some x-rays, but I'll be fine eventually. A couple of fractured bones is nothing compared to what I've endured.

Miles takes out the Chinese food containers that he and Rae picked up for dinner. The four of us grab what we ordered and sit down in the living room. Someone puts on an episode of *Friends,* and we all relax into the evening, hanging out with each other.

It's as if the events from the other night needed to happen in order for us to come together like this. We're all closer, a bond forming, knowing that in different ways, we have each other's backs.

"I finally finished a painting I've been working on," Rae announces as I take my last bite of lo mein. "I've been debating whether or not to show you guys, but here it goes." She stands up and goes toward her tote bag.

Pulling out a canvas, she flips it around so we can see.

It's an image of the four of us sitting on the beach at

night. There's a bonfire in the center, hypnotizing orange and red flames melding into a midnight-blue sky where hundreds of stars are scattered above. There's one star that's twinkling gold, but the rest are in shiny silver.

"That's beautiful," Emma whispers in awe.

"It really is, Rae," I say, shocking her. "I love it."

After a beat of processing my compliment, she smiles. "Thanks, Grayson."

I'm not sure if I truly heard Cara's voice the other night, but as I sit here with the three of them, Rae's grinning at me, and it feels as if the universe pulled some strings to get all of us together. Being here with them is starting to give me a sense of belonging as if coming to Golden Bay was the start of a new chapter.

And for the first time in my entire life, I'm not scared to see how the rest of the story unfolds.

"You should think about teaching classes at your studio," Emma says and Rae comes back to join us, canvas still in hand.

"I'd probably suck at teaching people, but I have thought of maybe doing an art night for trauma survivors." She shrugs. "I don't know. It's probably a stupid idea."

"No, it's not," I chime in. "Think about all the people in the world who have endured different types of trauma. If you brought them together where they could create a piece of art—no matter what kind, while also supporting each other, it would be really meaningful."

Everyone stops and stares at me, surprised I opened up that much to Rae.

"We've actually been tossing the idea around of

opening up a bigger place to do things like that," Miles breaks the silence. "Rae got *a lot* of donations, and I can only assume she'll get more once the documentary is officially released."

I glance at my sister, my lips tugging upward. "Cara would be really proud of you."

Her eyes instantly water, and she whispers, "She'd be proud of you, too."

I snort. "I haven't done much with my life."

"I have a feeling you will soon." Rae's gaze drifts in Emma's direction.

I have to admit, loving Emma and being loved by her makes me believe that Rae's right. I'll be starting the next phase of my life soon, even though I have no clue what that is.

As the night moves on, Emma and I are left alone on the couch while Rae and Miles hang out on the balcony. Emma's been staying at a hotel but has already started looking for places to officially move into.

She lets out a long sigh. "As thankful as I am for getting this trust, I have no sort of plan of what I'm going to do next. Where do I live? Do I save this money and go with my original financial plan? Do I buy a house? Go on an exotic vacation?"

"You're stressing yourself out," I say, chuckling.

"You should be one to talk," she playfully takes a jab at me.

I draw Emma into me, holding her into my chest. Her head rests on top of my beating heart which moves at a rapid pace for her, and only her.

"Maybe we don't need a plan right now," I say. "Maybe we just need to be young and free."

Epilogue

THE NEXT SPRING

The shards of my soul were scattered.
But she carefully picked me up, piece by piece.
Each fragment of me in her delicate hands.
Gluing me back together differently,
with some of her pieces where the cracks once were
And mine finding their new home in the empty spaces within her once-broken heart.
A new masterpiece created fusing both of our shattered parts together.
It is the purest form of our love.

I SIP on my dark roast coffee, staring at the poem I jotted down on a napkin. A lot has changed over the course of the seasons, including my writing. With Emma's graduation tomorrow, I wanted to compose the most perfect prose outlining the depth of my love for her, but I'm beginning to think that's not possible. There aren't enough words in the world to express how much I love that woman.

Red
Ready!

Smiling at my phone, I pull my attention away from the poem, stuffing it in my pocket, then wave down Sam. "I'll take the check when you have a chance," I say to him as he walks over to my table.

"It's on the house." Sam grins, the lines around his mouth deepening. "It's a thank you for helping me out with the dishwasher yesterday. If you didn't fix it, my whole diner would've been flooded."

"You already paid me for yesterday," I state.

Once I decided to stay in Golden Bay Beach, I also chose not to go to trade school but instead work with Miles as his assistant. It definitely isn't my calling in life, but it pays well, and Miles and I have fun on the jobs.

"Well, consider this another payment," Sam insists. "I'll see you later tonight."

I nod. "See you tonight. Thank you."

Stepping out of Sam's Dinette and onto the boardwalk, the warm sea breeze floating around me reminds me that summer is within reach. Another summer with Emma.

Of course, I'd take any time of year with her. I love

that she forced me to go pumpkin picking, decorate her Christmas tree, go ice skating, and stroll through some lavish garden she found on Instagram. And I can't wait to do all those things again, over and over until I can't anymore.

She purchased a small bungalow several blocks off the boardwalk in the fall, and I moved in shortly after. She refused to take rent from me, so we agreed on me paying the utilities and groceries. I plan on giving her more one day, and even though I'm still not sure where I'm headed in terms of a career, I'm certain more doors will open soon.

"Hey!" Emma swings open the door to Rae's art studio as I approach. "I can't wait for you to see what I did for tonight's event!" Excitement pours out of her as my lips curl up, watching her beam with pride.

"I bet it's incredible." I place a gentle kiss on her forehead before she takes my hand, leading me inside.

When we enter, my gaze bounces around the space, taking in all of Emma's event-planning skills. There are cocktail tables adorned with shiny, inky blue cloths, large easels displaying my sister's artwork, twinkling lights hanging up around the entire room, and chairs set up for all the people who will be joining. It's a tad reminiscent of the early viewing of the documentary, only tonight will be less stressful. In fact, dare I say, I'm looking forward to the event.

"I was right," I say, placing my arm around Emma's waist. "You did a fantastic job."

"Do you think Rae will like it?"

"I think she'll love it."

Rae received an influx of donations since the documentary release, so much so that she didn't feel right keeping it all. So, the four of us put our brains together and came up with an idea to create a wellness center in Golden Bay. It'll specifically be a place to help those who've experienced trauma and need extra support. Rae and Miles are the founders and decided to name their soon-to-be new space Cara's Haven, while Emma will be the office manager and unofficial interior designer once the place is up and running.

They're planning on having all sorts of groups and meetings, as well as having a space to do various types of art. Tonight's event is to raise money to hire full-time specialists. It'll be live-streamed, and Jake from Intra-Films is creating a mini-series about the whole thing in hopes that it'll generate more traction.

"I tried not to go too over the top for Rae," Emma says. "But I obviously wanted to make everything look cute."

"You succeeded." I stare at her, becoming starry-eyed. The way she lights up a room makes me melt every single time. I wish I had a better present to give her for her graduation, but before I can start to think of more ideas, she begins speaking.

"No running off this time. If you don't want to be here, that's fine, but go straight home, and text me when you're safely back."

I squeeze her into my embrace. "I'm going to be here tonight. I want to be."

Pressing up on her tippy-toes, she brushes her lips right under my left eye where I have a small scar from the night everything went up in flames, yet somehow worked in our favor.

Emma had to go through ongoing legal nonsense, but Kane is finally locked up and will be for twenty years. And even though this scar on my face serves as a memento from the time I got my ass beat, it's also a reminder that the bad guy didn't win in the end. In this little corner of the world, in this individual story, justice has finally been served.

Drawing her mouth a bit lower, her lips caress mine. We quickly become wrapped in each other's embrace when we realize we're alone in the space. My body becomes hotter, my fingers playing with the bottom of her dress. Her hands snake down my torso, hitting the zipper of my shorts.

"You guys literally live together—can't you do this gross shit in the comfort of your own home and not my place of business?" Rae teases as she enters.

Me and Emma break apart, and she wipes the bottom of her lip. "You were supposed to let me know when you were on your way so I could make a whole spectacle out of my setup!"

"Oh, shit, sorry." Rae slams her hand over her eyes to block herself from seeing anything else.

Together, me and Emma guide her into the center of the space so she can fully take in Emma's arrangement. When we tell Rae to open her eyes, there is an immediate glassiness that follows as she looks around the room.

"This is perfect, Emma," Rae says.

"Oh wait, one more thing." Emma goes to one of the tables to retrieve her purse. Taking out an envelope, she hands it to Rae.

"What's this?"

"Open it."

I hover over Rae, wanting to know what the last piece to Emma's puzzle is. When she pulls out a check made out to Cara's Haven with several zeros at the end, both me and Rae are frozen in shock, staring at Emma.

"I-I can't accept—" Rae starts to protest, but Emma interjects.

"Cara's Haven is a way for you to honor your sister. Donating to the wellness center is a way of honoring my mom," Emma states, empathy cascading out of her being. "Please, let me do this for you. All of you."

I draw in a long inhale while Rae twists her choker necklace. My heart nearly explodes with Emma's kindness. Warmth spreads across my chest as I watch her beam with compassion.

"You've got one amazing girlfriend," Rae says to me.

"I sure do."

Rae impulsively hugs Emma, the both of them becoming teary but doing their best to hold it together. I bite down on my bottom lip to keep myself in check and not let my emotions overflow.

When they finally step back, they wipe their eyes and smile at each other.

"Okay, I'm going to go back to my condo and start getting ready," Rae says, heading toward the door. "Try not to be too gross in here."

"I'll see what I can do," Emma says, shocking the both of us.

Rae leaves, chuckling, and I turn my attention back to Emma.

"I bet your mom would be extremely proud of the woman you are," I say to her, threading my fingers through hers.

"I sure hope so." She takes a step in, leaning her head on my chest.

Our focus floats around the room, landing on the

large mural in the back, mesmerized by the sun and stars.

"Tonight's going to be a lovely night," Emma says.

And it was.

More people than we could count came to the event, including Jake and his film crew and my parents.

It was an evening of love and community. And for the first time ever, it felt like we were making a difference. I know Cara's Haven won't save the world, but I truly believe that it has the ability to change people. And quite possibly heal them.

The excitement from last night's fundraiser carries into today.

Emma's red hair stands out in a sea of silver graduation gowns.

"Where is she?" Rae asks, sitting next to me in this stuffy auditorium.

"Right there." I point to the row of graduates walking toward the platform.

"I got my phone ready," Miles says. "Don't worry about taking a video, I got it. You just cheer for your girl."

My cheeks raise higher and higher the closer Emma gets to the stage.

"You take a video, too," Mom says to Dad while they sit on the other side of me.

Emma might not have her family here, her father refuses to speak to her, but she has all of us. Her new family.

"Emma Carnell." Her name gets spoken into the microphone, and electric bolts filled with pride strike my body.

We all go wild. My eyes glass over as I watch Emma hold her head up high, receiving her degree.

With a wide smile on her face, she glances upward, looking for us, applauding her. Our gazes finally lock when she gets to her seat, and she blows me a kiss.

"I'm so fucking proud of her," I say to everyone.

And I've never been more excited to see what comes next in our story.

"What did you end up getting her for a gift?" Rae asks.

Rubbing the back of my neck, I answer, "Not much."

"Grayson!"

"I couldn't think of anything good enough. I wrote her a poem, but that was a stupid idea because she reads my shit all the time."

I've let her have free rein of my notebooks. It serves as a great communicator if I'm struggling to express myself.

Rae smirks. "Nah, she'll love that crap."

I chuckle. "Thanks."

We impatiently wait for the rest of the graduates to get their degrees, the hours dragging. Mom, Dad, and Miles chat about random stuff while Rae grabs my focus away from them.

"I've been wanting to ask you something, but I wasn't sure if you'd go for it," she says, biting her nail beds.

"Okay...what is it?"

"Once Cara's Haven opens, would you be interested in leading writing workshops? I want to get all types of art in there, and writing seems to help you, so I figured I'd ask."

"Oh." My heart strums with a sense of motivation that I don't think I've ever felt before. A beating that ignites a new passion inside me, signaling that this might be the new door I need to walk through. "Yeah." I clear my throat. "Yeah, I could do that."

"Cool."

Smiling, I focus back on Emma who's holding her phone in her hand. Within seconds, mine starts buzzing.

Red
I have a surprise for you later

Me
You're the graduate, I'm supposed to be the one surprising you

A poem. That's the lamest fucking surprise I have for her. That and some flowers, which I left back at the bungalow like an idiot.

Red
you've given me more than a fair share of surprises. This time I wanted to give you one as a thank you for supporting me this year.

I've done nothing spectacular for her, just assisted with studying, edited her papers, and helped her with her thesis. I wish I could've done more to support her.

Me
did you take another trip to Sinderella's?

I send off the playful text and watch when she reads it, laughing to herself.

Red
Not quite. You'll see later.

Later seems like an eternity, and after we get lunch with the family, and they shower Emma with admiration, I'm finally alone with her.

"You're supposed to do this once we're married, not when I graduate," Emma says, laughing as I scoop her up in my arms before we cross over the threshold and into the small, inviting home we created.

All right, technically, *she* designed the whole thing, but I had some input. Like choosing where in the bedroom her bookshelves would look best and which photo of us to hang in the living room.

"I'm practicing," I say, placing her down on the kitchen table.

I'm careful not to mess up her decorative candle centerpiece as I take the graduation robe that she's been holding in her hands and toss it on one of the upcycled chairs.

Spreading her legs to wrap around my hips, her pink dress hikes up, exposing more of her gorgeous thighs.

"My present to you is shit, but I'll make it up to you in other ways," I say right before sucking on her neck.

Emma jolts, nails already digging into me at the feel

of my mouth. "You didn't need to get me anything," she sighs.

"I didn't." I nip at her skin, then run my tongue over where I just harshly marked her. "I wrote you something instead."

She immediately pulls back, the amber in her eyes gleaming with joy as if she hasn't read any of my work before. "You did?"

I nod, glancing at the bouquet of flowers next to the kitchen sink that I forgot to give her. "And some flowers," I add. "But like I said, I fully intend on making up for the shitty gifts."

Attempting to lean back into her embrace, she puts a hand out to pause me. "They're not shitty in the slightest. You know how much I adore your poetry and how much it means to me."

"Yeah, I guess."

Emma studies me for a beat, my heart picking up speed the longer she gazes at me. "I think it's time I give you your surprise." She hops off the table.

"I already told you I don't need a surprise," I say as she drifts into our bedroom. "But I'm not going to turn down slutty lingerie."

Emma pops back into the room, laughing. "We'll have to raincheck the slutty lingerie." Extending her arm toward me, she holds a silver gift bag with various shades of red tissue paper sticking out of the top. "For now, this is the only gift I have for you."

My brow arches as I suspiciously take the bag from her. Confusion pulses through me as I riffle through the fancy tissue paper. Pulling out a black book, my chest instantly swells as I admire the title engraved in a shimmery gray.

"Fragments of Gray," I state, my eyes automatically prickling. "What is this?"

"It's a collection of your poetry," Emma says, her cheeks getting rosy. "I went through the notebooks you let me read, and I picked out a bunch of different ones. And I named it Fragments of Gray because what's on those pages are pieces of you—your love, anger, grief, fear, heroism." Tears threaten to spill over as she continues speaking, "I wanted to publish your art. Not to make you sell the book or anything—it's only for you to own." She fidgets with her hands. "I mean, you could sell the book if you wanted, but I only made the one copy because I wasn't sure, and I wanted to do something for you—"

My lips are on hers, instantly needing to thank her in any way possible. Gratitude bursts out of my core, flooding my body. My hands shake as one of them holds on to Emma and the other on the book... my book.

Breaking apart for a split second, I ask, "Why?"

"Because of everything you did for me." A soft breath escapes her and lands gently on my lips as she talks quietly. "You changed my whole life around, and I can't thank you enough."

I shake my head, glancing down at my published work. My chest swells as a tear drips down onto my thumb.

"You were never the one who needed saving, Emma. I was."

She places her hand over mine, the both of us holding the book. "We were the hero in each other's story."

I nod. "And I'm going to make damn sure the rest of our lives will be lived as a happily ever after."

I whisk Emma up in my arms while she wraps hers around me. We kiss unceasingly, our open hearts pouring out to one another in a never-ending gesture of love.

Grasping her as tightly as I can, more tears of joy run down my face.

Emma is the one who illuminated the darkness of my hardened soul.

Emma is the one who lifted the fog, letting me see clearly.

Emma is the one who took all of our fragments and created something new from them.

And though once broken, together we are whole.

Resources

Victims of Sexual Assault: www.rainn.org

Substance Abuse and Mental Health Support: www.samhsa.gov

Advocating for Gun Safety: www.everytown.org

A Look At

RIGHT WHERE YOU LEFT ME

2004 was the year of MySpace, digital cameras, and pop punk—and the year Ivy met her brother's best friend, Paxton.

What started as innocent teenage longing turned into years of near-misses, lingering glances, and what-ifs. One night, a kiss tipped everything over the edge, leading to a passionate lapse of judgment and a fallout that ended in heartache and silence.

Now in their thirties, Ivy and Paxton find themselves reunited in the most unexpected way: standing side by side in her brother's wedding party.

For Paxton, life has taken a turn. Early retirement from the NHL and a devastating family health crisis have left him searching for solid ground. Seeing Ivy again sparks something familiar—comfort, longing, and the one thing he thought he lost: hope.

But Ivy isn't the girl he left behind. Fiercely independent and guarded, she's not ready to hand over her heart to the man who once broke it.

Can they rewrite their story and find healing in the wreckage of the past? Or are some second chances meant to stay in the rearview?

AVAILABLE FEBRUARY 2026

Acknowledgments

If you've made it this far—thank you.

Rae and Miles came to me in a dream in 2022. The scene was the two of them in the supply closet. I woke up the next morning knowing I had to tell their story, but I wanted to explore what they were like as adults. I have so much more left to say on the topics that were touched upon, but I don't want to ramble for another couple hundred pages. So, if you'd like to continue this conversation with me, send me a message! There's nothing I love more than hearing from my readers.

Which brings me to the first person I need to thank: you!

Without you reading and supporting my work, my creations would stay locked away on my computer. Your support helps me become more comfortable with sharing my art with the world. In a way, you are the Miles to my Rae.

Second, to my wonderful alpha, beta, and sensitivity readers—you're all amazing! Thank you for taking the time out to read my book in its messy stages and helping me bring it to life.

Thank you to Ellie, Kayla, and the whole Love N. Books Press team for believing in my work! It's so surreal having Rae & Miles's story be my first traditionally published book. I am beyond grateful.

Last, thank you to my husband. I couldn't do any of

this without you. (For someone who has written multiple romance books, I sure do suck at summing up how much you mean to me.)

My final parting words to anyone who is still reading: you're the artist of your own life, enjoy the beauty and the mess.

Until the next book,

Holly

Want to connect?

Follow me on Instagram @hollycaste_author

Holly is a new adult & contemporary romance author. Lover of all things steamy and angsty— you're sure to get your fill of these in her books! She also likes to have an underlying message in all of her stories, bringing awareness to bigger issues that are close to her heart.

When she's not reading or writing, you can find her eating an unhealthy amount of bread and cheese, rocking out to emo music, or cherishing wife/mom life

www.hollycasteauthor.com

More Trigger Info

Hi!

If you're back here, then you either finished the book (thank you, I hope you enjoyed the journey), or you're checking out more details of the death scene before you commit to reading the story. I'd love for people to try to piece things together as they read, however I'm aware that the topic is very sensitive, so I'd like to be mindful of different readers. The death scene depicted is a school shooting, including gunshots and blood. Please note, by knowing this information, you might lose the element of trying to draw your own conclusions as the story progresses.

If you're still planning on reading, I hope you fall for Rae & Miles. And I promise they get a happily ever after!

www.ingramcontent.com/pod-product-compliance
Lightning Source LLC
LaVergne TN
LVHW041935110826
845146LV00008B/1275

* 9 7 9 8 8 9 5 6 7 7 0 9 4 *